It do...
you come...
u...

Marrying Stone

Pamela Morsi

J
JOVE BOOKS, NEW YORK

MARRYING STONE

A Jove Book / published by arrangement with
the author

PRINTING HISTORY
Jove edition / August 1994

ISBN: 0-515-11431-6

A JOVE BOOK®
Jove Books are published by The Berkley Publishing Group,
200 Madison Avenue, New York, New York 10016.
JOVE and the "J" design are trademarks
belonging to Jove Publications, Inc.

PRINTED IN THE UNITED STATES OF AMERICA

10 9 8 7 6 5 4 3 2 1

With grateful acknowledgment for the work of
Vance Randolph,
John A. Lomax, Alan Lomax, Carl Sandburg,
and the hundreds of other folk song hunters
past and present
who have done what they could, where they could,
to preserve our musical heritage.

And with special thanks to my favorite Ozarker
Mitch Jayne
for making it all real to me.

"Two roads diverged in a yellow wood, and I, I took
the one least used by cows."

M.J.

FROM THE JOURNAL OF
J. MONROE FARLEY

April 12, 1902
McBee's Landing, Arkansas

Arrived this noon on the steamboat packet Jesse Lazear. *The trip was noisy, crowded, unclean, and uncomfortable. The local accommodations are no better. My portmanteau was wetted in the unloading, and I fear my wardrobe may not be the freshest. The Ediphone, however, survived the treacherous White River crossing intact and for that I am properly grateful.*

These Ozarks are an unkind, primitive wilderness, near hellish in isolation and solitude. As I watched the shoreline we passed, I was awed by its never-ending silence. It is eerie and unnatural. Were it not for the importance of my work and my strong desire to prove my thesis, I believe that I might, with great haste, return to the relative civilization of lower Missouri and the Mississippi river valleys.

Heard the word fornent *today uttered by a raggedy, unlettered farmer who had come riding to the packet with his crop. I was so startled, I fear that I must have stared at the man aghast. To hear such a beautiful old Elizabethan word on the lips of a backwoods man was concurrently joyous and profane. But surely it leads me to hope.*

The pilot, Captain Dochelin, assures me that these local inhabitants are far removed from the primitive people farther back in the woods. On the morrow I begin a mule trek back into the darkest depths of the Ozark Mountains. And, one could say, back into history itself. My heart beats wildly with anticipation and wonderment. What songs and stories and long-forgotten words may I discover there?

CHAPTER ONE

"SOO-EEEE!" MEGGIE BEST hollered the standard hog call. The half-dozen lazy pigs continued lounging in the morning sun around the small mountain clearing that she and her father and brother called home.

"Soo-eee pig! Come on, now, I ain't got the blame day to idle."

Though her words sounded harsh, she was humming softly to herself and her heart was unusually light. She'd been mostly lost in a pleasant daydream all morning long. A daydream about a handsome prince who rescued a virtuous maiden from a life of boredom and drudgery in the lonely mountains. It was a wonderful dream. Her favorite. Even the lazing pigs couldn't mar her mood. She sighed aloud. The sweet romantic words of a fine old tune came to her lips.

> "Well met, well met, my own true love,
> Well met, well met, said he.
> I have just returned from a journey long
> And 'twas all for the love of thee."

Suddenly, as if nature itself had heard the longings of her heart, a strange thrill of expectation swept through her. Gooseflesh skittered across her skin. She stopped singing, stunned to silence, and looked across the clearing. A stranger, a man she'd never seen, a man she didn't know, stood beside the rail fence at the far side of the unpainted barn. Meggie's breath caught in her throat and tiny stars began to sparkle around her. She thought she might faint.

He, the stranger, was speaking to her brother Jesse. The sun was at his back and it shone around him like a golden halo. Even from the distance she could see that he was handsome in a curious way. He was finely dressed and worthily shod. Real pince-nez spectacles of circular glass were perched upon his nose. And his trim form and deignful expression gave him a princely air.

Meggie's eyes widened. Her heart beat faster and the blood sped through her veins.

A prince. Her prince.

"Hey, Meggie!" Jesse called out. "Come and meet Roe. He's my frien'."

Unable to move, Meggie merely stared as the two young men walked toward her.

"He's lost his mule," Jesse continued. "I ne'er had a frien' afore, Meggie. Can we keep him?"

Jesse's question momentarily surprised Meggie out of her trance. Her brother was speaking of the prince as if he were an orphaned coon or whistle-pig pup.

"No, we can't *keep* him, Jesse. He's no critter, he's a gentleman. Have you never seen one before?"

Jesse glanced over at the fellow on his left and shrugged. "Don't reckon I have, Meggie."

The prince offered a tiny smile to Meggie's brother and her heart expanded. She sighed loudly.

He took one step toward her and bowed formally from the waist. "A good day to you, Miss Best. Your kind brother has told me much about you."

His voice was low and cultured. To Meggie it sounded like a cross between the roar of distant thunder and the harmony of a church hymn.

The prince was tall, nearly as tall as Jesse, but there the similarity ended. While Jesse was as blond and fair as cornfields in October, the stranger was as dark as winter-green syrup and nearly as slick. She watched the long elegant movements of his hands as he reached for a snowy white handkerchief and patted the perspiration that had accumulated upon his brow.

He was not so terribly old, Meggie decided. He simply carried himself with a casual confidence unusual for a man still in his twenties. His smile, faint as it had been, revealed a small dimple in his right cheek and straight white teeth that gleamed in the sunlight. He was dressed in city duds so fine they would have outshone the Sunday best of the entire congregation of Marrying Stone Church. His skin, totally free of marks or scars, would be the envy of the local hill girls who religiously washed their complexions in soured buttermilk.

Meggie felt a strange wonderful expansion in the area of her heart . . . which took up beating at a faster pace. She felt a strangely queer notion of welcoming home. She'd been waiting for this handsome stranger all her life, and he'd finally arrived. It was magic.

As she stood there, staring mutely, the prince, his dark brown eyes curious, gazed at Meggie. She trembled. Beyond that, she couldn't move.

The prince apparently recognized her predicament. In a movement as graceful as a lady at a dance, he swept his hand-plaited straw panama from his head and bowed deeply.

"J. Monroe Farley, miss, of the city of Cambridge in Massachusetts, the Bay State, at your service."

Meggie fluttered slightly and tried to copy his elegant manners.

"Margaret May Best, sir, of Arkansas." Her words were so breathy they came out almost as a sigh. She held her hand out to him.

When he grasped her fingers gently in his own and bent over her hand formally, she gasped aloud.

He looked up at her curiously. His brown eyes seemed puzzled behind his spectacles.

Meggie glanced toward Jesse for help, but her brother seemed unaware of her befuddlement. Meggie cleared her throat.

"I lament you find me in poor habiliment, sir," she said in her gentlest and most refined tone. "I had not foreseen wayfarers this morn."

The young man's eyes widened and he chuckled.

Meggie's brow furrowed. Certainly she didn't look her best, but she'd just apologized. Still it was clear that the fancy young man was amused. Her cheeks reddened. "I am working, I—I suppose I do look rather a sight."

The prince's expression sobered immediately. "Indeed not, Miss Best. I am delighted to make your acquaintance and deeply regret that my appearance was untimely."

From the tips of her bare toes to the top of her untidy hair, Meggie was dirty and tattered. But the elegant young man standing before her spoke in a way that sounded as if he were addressing a great lady. He was a foreign prince for sure, but he sounded nice. She liked his voice, she decided. She liked it very much. She gave the stranger a long, slow smile of approval.

"I invited him to take dinner with us." Her brother Jesse abruptly shattered the strange flowery haze that had settled around Meggie's heart and temporarily clouded her thinking and judgment.

"What?" Meggie glanced at the city man. He nodded in agreement. She wanted to scream in frustration. "Dinner?"

Her brother nodded.

Meggie couldn't believe her bad luck. The most handsome man that she had ever seen in her life, the prince of her dreams, had finally come to rescue her from her lonely tower, and she was about to drive him off before they were properly acquainted.

The gentleman must have sensed her dismay. "I wouldn't wish to intrude," he said politely. "Perhaps your brother's invitation was given out of turn?"

Meggie raised her chin. She was caught. Jesse had invited the man. There was nothing to do for it. He wouldn't have a chance to know *her* before he knew her cooking. But, so be it. Maybe—oh, please heaven! she pleaded—maybe today, for once, her meal would turn out fine.

"Mr. Farley, don't give it a thought," she said loftily. "My brother's word is as good as any man's on the mountain."

"But I wouldn't wish to be a burden."

"Nonsense, it's our Christian *duty* to feed the homeless and hungry at our door."

Young Farley raised an eyebrow. "I'm not exactly homeless, Miss Best. But I do admit to being hungry."

His expression was neither charming nor coaxing, but actually quite matter-of-fact. Still, though she fought against it, Meggie felt herself slipping into the flowery trance once more.

The stranger reached into the depths of his gray tweed trouser pocket and pulled out a fancy Moroccan leather boodle book. "I can pay, of course," he said easily. "Whatever you think a meal might be worth."

Meggie stared at the fat, city-man wallet that he held so casually. Not only handsome and refined, her prince was rich!

"Your money is not needed here, sir," she told him. "It's our pleasure to make you welcome."

Farley nodded graciously. "You might want to reconsider, it's all genuine U.S. currency, not a wooden nickel in sight."

"The Best family does not take charity or need money to feed a hungry stranger." She wanted to assure him of the high principles of her family. "If you wish to take dinner with us"—she considered for a long minute—"then you can help Jesse split cordwood."

The prince was momentarily taken aback, then nodded. "It would be my pleasure, Miss Best." His smile was polite and friendly. "Especially if it means a meal prepared by your own hand."

Jesse snorted. "You better not hope for much. Meggie ain't the best for cookin'."

Meggie held her temper though she was tempted to reach over and box her brother's ears.

Farley only smiled diplomatically. "It takes a man far from home to be able to appreciate home cooking," he said.

Meggie sighed.

With a romantic tune on her lips, stars in her eyes, and the memory of his warm, citified voice still in her ears, she hurried to the house, pigs forgotten.

Once inside, she had only a minute for a lovelorn sigh before she noticed a distinctly unpleasant smell, like old shoes left too near the hearth.

"Dad-burn and blast!" she snapped. Hurrying to the fireplace she yanked the crane, pulling the pot of limas away from the fire. The beans were scorched a half an inch deep. She glared at the half-burned mess in dismay. Now, what was she going to serve the stranger for dinner?

Glancing outside, she saw him in the cutting yard with Jesse. He was holding the ax as if it were a yard rake and was ineffectually jarring the sharpened blade against a big tough piece of half-dried spruce. Jesse's rhythmic chopping was interspersed with the stranger's thumps.

Meggie eyed him curiously. He was obviously not used to hard work.

"A *gentleman* prince," she whispered to herself with awe.

Quickly she looked about her for some substitute victuals. All she had was day-old light bread, and some dried venison for gravy, and sixteen quarts of piccalilli she'd put up the night before from some early tomatoes that were caught by the late freeze. The city stranger wanted a meal. Well, she'd fix him a meal that would go straight from his stomach to his heart. Right then and there, Meggie Best silently declared herself in love with J. Monroe Farley. And she'd do everything within her power to win him.

FROM THE JOURNAL OF
J. MONROE FARLEY

April 15, 1902
Marrying Stone Mountain, Arkansas

Became separated from my mule. Portmanteau and my belongings lost. The Ediphone is safe. Became ill. Have taken shelter with a local farming family.

CHAPTER
TWO

AN INNOCENT-LOOKING, GLEAMING blue quart jar had started the trouble between Meggie and her prince.

"Is this a local delicacy?" Roe Farley had asked, gesturing to the open jar.

After a morning of cutting cordwood, his shoulders were achy and several nasty blisters had formed on his right palm. He had no idea that so much effort—and skill—was involved in chopping wood or he would never have volunteered. The noon break had not come a moment too soon and Jesse had sent him ahead to the house to have his hand tended.

The young woman beside him shrugged slightly as she gently rubbed sticky yellow salve that smelled of goldenseal and tallow along his palm. "It's just piccalilli. Folks around here eats it."

The young local female, to Roe Farley's thinking, was a rather nice-looking woman. Not pretty, of course, in the way that fine genteel ladies appeared, but neat and scrubbed free of dirt she had a certain earthy appeal. She was tall. At least taller than a woman ought to be, he thought. But she wasn't excessively thin. Her bosom was quite generous and her backside typically rounded for a descendant of Scotch-Irish peasant stock. Her hair was not as cornsilk-blond as her brother's, but it was a silky honey color that hung down her back in a thick plaited rope. No, she was not a beauty in the fashionably accepted sense of the term, but he could well imagine one of the local Ozark backwoodsmen finding her desirable. And, of course, there were her feet. Long, feminine naked feet. As she padded across the dirt floor, her bare feet held some strange fascination for him. The ladies of his acquaintance would have died of embarrassment to have shown him so much as an ankle. The young woman walked with such confidence and unconcern, one would have thought she wore the most elegant of dancing slippers. Roe smiled. He liked her bare feet, he decided. And he liked her. Her touch as she tended his hand was sure yet gentle. It had been a long time since he'd felt a woman's touch and it was welcome.

He was still quite new to these sparsely populated Ozark Hills, attempting to prove his theoretical premise that, through their isolation, these mountain people had managed to preserve, in culture and song, traditions common to the British Isles more than two hundred years before.

He'd convinced the Harvard fellowship committee to allow him to spend the summer rooting out Irish and English ballads from the mouths of the poor, ignorant, isolated folks who lived in the mountainous regions of Missouri and Arkansas. As a scholar of Medieval and Renaissance musicology, he had done many sojourns in the wilds of the Scottish Highlands, politically explosive Ireland, and the rocky barren coasts of the Hebrides. It was only recently that he sought to prove that the keys to Celtic musical heritage might lie closer to home. Accepting a fellowship, J. Monroe Farley was to be the first to seek the origins of Goidelic song among the Celtic descendants in the primitive wilderness known as the Ozarks.

He'd expected the task to be easy. He imagined that the locals would be so in awe of his curious recording machine—and so grateful for an opportunity to contribute—that he'd have all the stories and songs he could record before the first fall of leaves. Of course, he'd had a setback losing his mule. Who would have imagined that the lazy, slow-moving animal would suddenly jump and run at the sound of a prerecorded cylinder on the Ediphone?

And now he was here. Wherever that was. He gazed around him. The hand-hewn logs that formed the walls and the plain pine shutters that were opened to the breeze bore no relation to his living quarters near the Cambridge campus. He couldn't immediately recall the name of the specific hamlet, but he of course remembered the name of his hosts. The fellow he'd met in the forest, the girl's brother, was Jesse Best.

"Do you need help?" the voice had called out to Roe from the thick woods.

Roe had stopped, breathless, his legs shaky, and glanced around in surprise. He had not seen another soul on the narrow wooded path. But someone had called to him, and he looked around eagerly.

Actually, he was grateful for the excuse to pause for a moment. He considered himself to be in excellent physical condition, sparring regularly at Flanagan's Boxing Salon. But the climb, straight up the mountain, had been taxing. And he'd started out hungry. Now, he was not only sore and breathless, he was famished. After he'd given up on recapturing his mule he had begun to follow this narrow track in hopes that it led to some sort of civilization. He carried the small wooden trunk containing the Ediphone Recording Machine on his own back. Now halfway up an unnamed mountain toward a community he hoped existed, he found that such exertion was not particularly advisable for a hot spring morning.

"Where are you?" he called, squinting between the thick trunks of trees on either side of the narrow, clean-cut trail.

"Up here."

Adjusting his spectacles more securely upon his nose,

Roe glanced to the high first limb of a sturdy hickory above him. A handsome, young male face smiled back at him.

"Hello."

With one graceful movement, the man dropped to the ground beside him. He was tall. A good three inches taller than Roe, and he was muscular. His broad physique evidence of hard outdoor work. Roe became wary. The blond giant just stood there, grinning. He truly had no idea how welcome he might be in these mountains. He'd been told that Ozarkers were an open, friendly people and he'd expected them to be dazzled with his knowledge and intrigued with his work. But the Ozarks themselves were a strange and dangerous place. It was quite possible that the locals might prove to be standoffish or even downright belligerent.

Now he'd come across this one, about his own age but much bigger and taller, and ominous-looking. And the giant just stood mutely before him with an expression that bordered on stupidity. His eyes were as wide and guileless as a child's. Roe shook his head. These were a strange and unfathomable people. There was nothing to do but take charge of the situation.

"Good morning, sir," Roe said with a mild bow of polite deference. "I am J. Monroe Farley of Cambridge, Massachusetts, the Bay State. I'm visiting your majestic mountain for the purpose of writing and recording for posterity the traditional ballads and folk songs of your people."

The young man continued to just stare at him. Apparently, he was unfamiliar with the manners of society. Farley extended his hand to the big fellow and offered less formally, "You may call me Roe, if you like, there is no reason to stand on formality."

The young fellow looked at the hand with momentary confusion. Then with a rush of understanding he grasped it forcefully and pumped it up and down with excitement. "I'm Jesse Best of just right here," he said proudly.

There was a strangeness to his speech. Farley suspected it was not merely his accent and not quite an impediment, just something different.

"You can call me Simple Jess," he told Roe. "Everybody does."

"*Simple* Jess?"

The young man nodded enthusiastically. "That's me," the blond fellow said proudly.

Roe stared at the young man for a moment. Obviously, Jess was unaware of the negative connotations of his nickname.

Roe sighed loudly and then muttered aloud. "My luck is certainly running true today. If I were ever to find a friend in these lonely mountains, it would undoubtedly be someone with a name like *Simple* Jess."

The big fellow's eyes widened and he gazed at Roe in near awe. "You wanna be my frien'?" he asked quietly.

Momentarily startled, Roe looked at the young man curiously. He felt a strange sense of compassion for the simpleminded man so near his own age.

"Do you know anything about music?" he asked.

Jesse grinned and nodded enthusiastically. "Yep. I play 'n' sing up a storm. Near ever' Literary."

"Literary?"

Jesse's chin bobbed up and down affirmatively, but he made no attempt to explain. "Are you gonna be my frien'?"

Roe watched the young man swallow convulsively and could see the eagerness in Jesse's blue eyes. "I ain't ne'er had a frien' afore," he said. "I got me a sister and a pa, but never no frien'."

The young man's emotions, so honest and so close to the surface, touched something in Roe. He, himself, had dozens of friends, well not friends perhaps but colleagues, and he'd never given a one of them a moment's thought or consideration. He felt a twinge of guilt at his sarcastic comment about friendship. With the bad luck of losing the mule and his belongings, he could certainly use a friend, of any type.

"Certainly," Roe said, "I'll be your friend, Jesse." He offered his hand once more.

The delight that shone on the young man's face was almost tangible. Roe felt an uncomfortable sense of responsibility at being able to please him so easily. Well, maybe the simple fellow *could* be a friend to him. He certainly needed help climbing up this mountain, and with no other friend or even foe around, the fellow seemed to be in possession of a strong back.

"That's right, Jesse. We are friends," he said, slapping him companionably on the shoulder. "And friends generally help each other."

Jesse had helped. Up the steep mountain trail where the trees had been cut at ground level, but the stumps left to be bounced and tripped over, Jesse had carried the Ediphone, with its carton of individual fitted containers. Following behind with only his journal to carry, Roe smiled for the first time in several days.

"What do you call this place?" he asked his newfound guide.

"We don't call it nothing," the fellow answered.

"You don't call it anything?"

Jesse looked thoughtful. "Well, this here hill is called Marrying Stone Mountain; that big one there that kind of shades us in the afternoon, it's called Squaw's Trunk; the one in the distance is Uncle Wilkie."

Roe raised an eyebrow at the strange names but made no comment.

"The little crick that runs along here into the river is called Itchy Creek, 'cause the poison oak grows along it real bad. You got to be careful where you go into it. Our place is pretty near right on the creek bank. That's real good, 'cause I don't have to go far to fetch up the water."

Roe nodded vaguely. "What's the name of the nearest town?"

The big blond fellow shrugged. "There ain't no nearest town. There ain't no town at all."

Roe looked at him curiously. "There's no church, no school, no store?"

"The church and school's on the far side of the mountain. They got a store over there, too. They call that Marrying Stone."

Roe nodded. "Just like the mountain."

"No," the young man replied, "it's named for the Marrying Stone at the church." As if that explained everything.

Roe shook his head. This was definitely the Ozarks with its strange names and its truly simple folks.

"I cain't wait for you to meet Meggie," Jesse said.

"Meggie?"

"My sister. She's just going to love you."

Roe grinned. "Oh, really?" he said casually. He looked at Simple Jess as he walked ahead, his tall, straight back balancing the heavy weight of the Ediphone on his shoulder as if it were nothing. He tried to imagine a female version of Simple Jess. No doubt she'd be an Amazon.

"Is your sister like you?" he asked.

Jesse stopped in midstride and turned to him, his eyes wide with shock. "Oh, no! Ain't none of my family like me. I'm plumb unusual."

Roe was struck at the fervency of his declaration.

"Meggie," Jesse continued, "why she's about as smart as a person can be. She wins the spelling bee purt-near ever' time. And she was the only gal in the school that ever made it clear through that yellow fifth-grade reader. Meggie ain't nothing like me." His smile was one of sheer brotherly pride. "She knows near everything! But she don't put on much like she's better or nothing. She just likes me for myself. I suspect she'll take to you right off. You being my frien' and all."

Taking to him right off had proved to be a little more interesting than Roe had expected.

Sitting at the scarred, worn table in the tiny cabin, he had glanced over at barefooted Meggie Best and smiled. His long-ingrained sense of propriety and manners dictated that he make polite luncheon conversation while they waited for her father and brother.

"And did you make this piccalilli yourself?" His tone was intimate, barely above a whisper. "Because if you did, I will certainly want to taste it."

The young woman blushed prettily and lay a hand against her heart as if to still the butterflies that fluttered there. Curious at her reaction, he looked deeply into her eyes. They were not the dark, vivid blue of her brother's, but rather a clement sky color of blue and gray, as welcoming as a summer morning.

"I did stir this batch up, after the freeze," she admitted with shy modesty. "Though folks say I'm not much of a cook."

He raised an eyebrow. "These *folks* must be wrong," he assured her. "I am certain that your accomplishments are legend."

Meggie's eyes widened.

He watched her fingers tremble as she wound the clean cotton bandage around his hand.

He smiled. Her nervousness actually warmed him. He was reserved by nature and usually felt slightly uncomfortable in polite social situations with strangers. He had studied fashionable manners because they were necessary in his work. But he couldn't like august soirees and witty at-homes. The young woman here in the isolated cabin appeared as shy and sheltered as the most cosseted debutante. Instinctively, he felt a kinship with her.

"Please won't you allow me a small taste of your wonderful creation now, I don't believe I can wait for your brother to appear?" he asked in an exaggerated tone.

She raised her head and gazed at him, her expression curious. Roe was unsure of what it meant.

"The piccalilli," he said. "I'd love to sneak a little taste."

"Oh, the piccalilli."

The young woman grabbed a carved-out bone dipper and dished a huge portion of the relish in the old tin plate set on the table before him.

Roe sat staring at it for a long moment. He looked up to find her staring at him expectantly. He smiled. "I need an eating utensil," he said.

"You don't carry your own?" she asked, surprised.

"Why no, I don't."

"Here." She picked up a hollowed-out wooden dipper from her pocket. "You can use mine."

He stared at the primitive spoon, her spoon. It was old and the edge that touched the mouth was worn smooth with use, but it had a pretty little leaf design cut into the handle. Somehow it seemed so intimate to eat from it, but he had no other. He reached out with his freshly bandaged hand and gently took it from her.

"Thank you very much." Dipping into the soggy mass he brought the first taste of piccalilli to his lips.

He smiled at her. She swallowed nervously and jumped to her feet. "I'll fetch you a hunk of bread."

She hurried to the cupboard. He watched her, assessingly, curiously, and she went to the rough-finished safe on the far corner from the fireplace. Yes, he was right about her: healthy Scotch-Irish peasant stock, long, sturdy legs and buttocks ample to the point of generous. He allowed his gaze to linger there a bit longer than was necessary. Derrieres were the focus of all the fashion rage in the East. Women tied wire and horsehair contraptions on their backsides until they stood out with such prominence that it was said that a girl could rest a tea tray upon a fashionable bustle.

Gazing at the young Ozark woman's rounded behind in the thin homespun skirt, Roe doubted that horsehair or wire would ever be necessary for Meggie Best.

As she hurried back to the table, Roe allowed himself to

consider the rest of her figure. Her bosom was not voluptuous, but the soft curves were certainly in evidence. She was high-breasted and even without the enhancements of a corset she appeared firm and round, as if she carried two lush, ripe peaches in her front shirt pockets.

She stopped in midstride. Roe realized that she had caught him staring. Guiltily, he dropped his eyes.

"The bread is a day old," she said brightly as she smeared it lavishly with a pale white cream in a jar. "If you sop it in the juice from the piccalilli, you won't be able to tell."

She was smiling warmly, welcoming now as she lay what appeared to be a half loaf of coarse brown bread on the blue tin dinner plate before him.

Roe glanced up at her and then took a bite of the bread. "Oh, Miss Best, the bread doesn't need sopping in the juice. It's quite good on its own."

She sighed with obvious pleasure.

"And this butter," Roe continued. "It's quite unusual, but I believe it to be the finest tasting that I have ever eaten."

"Oh, it's not butter," Meggie told him. "We don't have a cow. It's just bear grease, but it is pretty good fare."

"Bear grease?" Roe cleared his throat a little nervously. He casually set the bread down next to his plate and concentrated on the piccalilli.

Companionably, Meggie sat down in her place and dished herself some of the relish.

"How will you eat if I'm using your spoon?" he asked.

With a nervous little giggle she shrugged. "I can ladle it up with a piece of bread," she assured him.

The two smiled at each other uncomfortably across the table. Her color was prettily pink. Roe found his eyes were drawn to the sight. The barefoot young woman was actually quite comely. She seemed to be waiting for him to speak. The silence lingered.

"Do you like it?" she asked finally.

Realizing he had not complimented the cook, Roe

scooped up a huge amount of the relish and shoveled it into his mouth. With deliberate charm he dramatically closed his eyes as if in ecstasy.

"Mmmmmmmm. Mmmmmmmmm."

Meggie giggled.

Opening his eyes slightly, Roe shoveled in another large mouthful.

"I guess that means you like it?" Meggie asked anxiously.

Roe was feeling well disposed and friendly. He ignored the strange, sour aftertaste of the green tomato concoction and forced himself to take another bite.

"It tastes wonderful, marvelous, heavenly," he said extravagantly. "I don't believe I've ever eaten anything so palatable before."

His words were no more than standard dining-room compliments, but Meggie sighed with delight and laughed again. He really enjoyed hearing that sound.

They were grinning at each other now, strangely companionable. And it truly seemed quite natural when she got up and moved her ladderback chair around the corner of the table and closer to his own. For one fleeting moment a niggling feeling of concern pulled at him, but he ignored it. She was perhaps hard of hearing, he thought. Or maybe she was nearsighted like himself and found it necessary to be closer to converse. He didn't draw away.

Graciously he downed another bite of piccalilli. He'd barely had time to swallow before he felt the tentative touch of her hand on his own. A warm tingle traveled up his arm. He swallowed and turned to stare at her over the top of his spectacles.

"I'm so sorry you hurt your hand chopping wood," she said.

There was something about her backwoods accent that was charming, beguiling. The hairs stood up on the back of Roe's neck. He began feeling distinctly uncomfortable and yet enticed. Nervously, he glanced toward the door wondering what in the world was keeping Jesse.

"We all must use our hands to work," he answered her evenly. "Why even putting up this piccalilli involved using your own."

"Oh, Mr. Farley." Her words were a breathy whisper. The stars in her eyes shone as brightly as jewels. Pushing an errant strand of burnished blond hair away from her face, she nervously tucked it behind her ear.

Her reaction was curious. It was as if he had said something intimate, personal. He tried to remove his hand from her grasp, but she didn't easily relinquish it. The space between them crackled.

Roe pulled back and cleared his throat. Obviously making conversation in the Ozarks was different from the dining tables of the Bay State. He was unfamiliar with the strange air of warmth that surrounded him. It was friendliness on a level that was both seductive and a little bit menacing.

He smiled with excessive politeness at the young woman, hoping to dispel the unexpected closeness of the little cabin. He took another big bite of the piccalilli relish and savored it for a long moment before nodding.

"Very nice," he said.

She was gazing deeply into his eyes as if entranced.

"Oh, yes, it is very nice," she whispered.

Suddenly alert, Roe looked at Meggie curiously. Her comment was extremely strange. But nothing could have prepared him for the moment when she raised his knuckles to her lips and graced them with the gentlest of kisses.

J. Monroe Farley sat frozen in shock as the tremors resulting from the unexpected intimate touch coursed through him. He was not unfamiliar with the attentions of the female gender. But he was not prepared for the reaction the young hill girl had provoked.

"I was right," she said. Her blue-gray eyes were open

wide, but glazed with visions that were inside her head. "I knew this morning when I saw you standing with the sun behind you that you were my prince come at last."

"What?"

Meggie Best let out her breath quickly as if she'd been holding it a long time. She picked up the carved wood spoon that he'd left carelessly in his plate. "See the spring buds and first flower," she said with quiet reverence. "It's a token of affection, Mr. Farley. And you accepted it from me." Her smile was dreamily serene. "And this, well, it's just piccalilli. But I'm hoping it'll be nostrum to make our love forever true."

She had moved up closer, her face only inches from his own. J. Monroe Farley choked. "Miss Best, I—"

"Oh, Mr. Farley, something really fine, some wonderful token, would be the taste of your sweet lips."

She leaned forward, her mouth very close.

He stared at those lush pink lips in disbelief.

"My dear Miss Best," he cautioned uneasily.

"It's all right, Mr. Farley, it's just the two of us here."

Again, he made a choking sound. It wasn't permission, but she took it as such. Parting her lips and turning her head with unpracticed expertise, her mouth was on his for only a second, one tiny, warm, thrilling second. It was as if a spark of lightning ran through them.

"Oh, Mr. Farley!" she exclaimed, her lips still close to his. "I knew when I saw you that you were the one."

"Uh." Roe made the startled sound. He hardly had time to make sense of her words before she threw her arms around his neck and plopped herself down in his lap.

The young Ozark woman squeezed him tightly to her ample chest and parted her lips. She was kissing him with such enthusiasm even a stone would have responded.

Monroe Farley was no stone. His life had not been one of beau around town, nor was he a slave to his passions. But he'd held women in his arms often enough to relish the pleasure. And the feel of the eager young arms that embraced him now was pleasure indeed.

With a sigh of satisfaction, he gave himself up to the kiss, tasting and exploring the sweet lips that were offered. He allowed his hands to clasp her waist, unbound by restrictive stays and soft beneath her thin covering of homespun cotton. He wanted her. Desire surged through him, hot and keen.

"Meggie," he managed to choke out as she pressed herself more tightly against him and sighed. Her firm round bosom was flattened against his chest and her hands fluttered up and down his back.

"Miss Best, I don't—" he tried again.

Her lips were everywhere, his mouth, his cheeks, the soft skin of his earlobe, and the ticklish length of his throat.

Desire, sizzling and ardent, overrode his better judgment and he kissed her back with passion. He allowed his own hands to roam the long length of her back and along the sides of her breasts. Pulling her even closer, he thrust his tongue into her mouth and was rewarded by her tiny cry of response. The sound enflamed him. One hand held her waist while the other was seeking the hem on the homespun skirt.

They broke apart momentarily to catch their breath. He felt her heart pounding against his chest.

"Oh, Mr. Farley, I knew, I knew," she whispered. "The minute I saw you, I knew. All the fellows on the mountain have been giving me the eye for years, but I knew someday you'd come for me and you have."

"What?" Roe's thoughts were befuddled.

"From the time I was a little girl, I read all the fairy tales, Mr. Farley. And I knew, there was a gentleman prince out there somewhere and that someday he would come to this mountain and love me and marry me and make me happy for all my life to come."

The words *love* and *marry* seeped into Roe's passion-addled brain and splashed a bucket of cold water upon his desire.

"What?" Immediately he removed her hands from his person. She grabbed his hands in her own and placed them once more around her waist.

"I waited and waited. At night I dreamed about you 'til I was near crazy with wanting. I thought I might grow old waiting. But you have come at last, Mr. Farley. Just like I always knew that you would. And now I will love you forever. Do you want me to let down my hair?"

"What?"

"Do you want me to let down my hair? Like Rapunzel," she added almost shyly. "Oh, Mr. Farley, this mountain is my tower and now you've come for me." She released her hold on him only for a moment to pull at the pins in her hair. They scattered about her as thick waves of dark honey-blond hair fell to her shoulders.

"Miss Best, I—"

"Oh, Mr. Farley, I do love you, already," she told him, hugging him close once more. "And the fact that you like my cookin', well it couldn't be anything but fate."

"I don't know I—"

"Mr. Farley, I'm going to make you the finest wife that any man on this mountain ever had."

"Wife?" The word felt like a chicken bone stuck in his throat.

He came to his feet with such haste that he knocked over the chair they'd been sitting on and dropped the young woman in his arms to the floor.

Meggie Best stared up at him in dismay. "Dad-burn and blast! You dropped me right on my tailbone."

Roe was gazing at her in horror. He glanced toward the doorway and held his arm out as if to ward her off.

"Miss Best, I believe you have the wrong idea here."

"Wrong idea?" For a moment she seemed genuinely

puzzled. "Why, you were kissing me," she said. "How could I get the wrong idea?"

"It wasn't—well, I didn't mean. Well, you were kissing me!"

"We were kissing each other," she said.

"Yes, well, I didn't mean for that to happen," he said.

Her eyes narrowed. "You didn't?" Her voice was suddenly wary. "What are you about, Mr. J. Monroe Farley?"

"I'm not *about* anything, Miss Best. I was simply eating a bit of luncheon and you threw yourself upon me. I realize these mountains are isolated. But I assumed there would be sufficient males in the area that a woman would not need to accost strangers." He was overstating the case a bit, but he hoped this woman would understand his point.

She gazed up at him from the sweep-polished dirt floor. Her hair was wild about her face and her skirt was up around her knees, revealing two very naked female legs and a pair of bare feet.

"Accost strangers!"

"Miss Best, I—" he began, but couldn't quite think of what words to speak next. Slowly, he began to back up toward the door.

"Where are you going?"

"I think perhaps I should be getting along. It's nearly afternoon already and I do have . . ." he began. As she continued to stare at him warily he held out a hand. "Miss Best, I certainly never meant—"

"Never meant what?"

"Well, I never meant . . ." He looked down at her, disheveled and dangerous on the floor. "I never meant more than to carry on a simple dining-table conversation. That fellow, that prince that you are waiting for, well I'm sure we can both safely assume that I am not him."

Her face was pale as she stared silently at him.

"I'm really not the type of man you'd want for a husband. You'd really require someone more—more like yourself.

I'm from a completely different world, a world of civilization and scholarship. Where I intend to return at the earliest opportunity."

She stared at him in apparent disbelief for a long moment, then fury took over. "Why you—"

"Believe me, Miss Meggie, I never intended any disrespect or—"

"You lowlife, lowland, city-rounder." She came to her knees, her voice getting higher and shrill. "You worthless excuse for a two-toed varmint."

"I beg your pardon?"

"You sweet-talked me into a kiss and now you're thinking to throw me out like I was a churn of oversoured skimmings."

Roe glanced toward the doorway. Her voice had grown louder and angrier with every word. He was more than anxious to take his leave. He began inching toward the exit.

"Do you think you can come in here in my own house on my own mountain and sweet-talk me out of my virtue over a jar of piccalilli?"

"Miss Best, please, I wouldn't—"

"You wouldn't, would you? Jesse!" Her voice was as loud as hog calling in a thunderstorm and wild with fury. "Jesse Best, get in here this minute."

Farley was still easing toward the door. What if her simple brother were to misconstrue his actions? Despite his later protestations he had kissed the young woman quite of his own free will. And he had touched her in a manner not consistent with polite conversation. He had no idea what the customs of these mountain people might be. But he was fairly certain that he had overstepped the bounds of propriety.

"Miss Best, Meggie, please."

"What's it, Meggie?" Simple Jess, huge and blank-faced, asked curiously as he stood blocking the doorway. When he saw Roe he grinned amiably. "You having a set-to with my new frien'?"

Her eyes were wild with anger as she hurried to her feet. She was clearly outraged. "Your new *friend* is making unwanted advances to me."

Simple Jess, three inches taller and twice as muscled as Roe, looked at him with surprise.

Roe swallowed nervously. After spending an hour watching the youth split wood, Roe was sure the big mountain man could easily break every bone in his body without even working up a sweat.

"Jesse, I can explain," he began. His voice was calm and rational. "Your sister has misconstrued . . . well perhaps not misconstrued, but . . ."

"He tried to take advantage of me, Jesse!" she snapped. "You're my brother. Beat the tar out of him."

"Miss Best, really. It was only a kiss."

"It was a kiss all right," she snarled angrily as she hurried to her feet. "And it turned you right into a frog! Beat him up, Jesse."

Shaking his head, her brother clearly didn't like the prospect. "He's my frien', Meggie," Jesse protested. "I don't want to fight him."

"There is no need to fight," Roe assured him quickly. "I merely wish to make a humble apology and express to you, Miss Best, my deepest remorse over any distress my presence here might have caused you."

"The only apology that you can make to me, Mister J. Monroe Farley, is to get your worthless hide out of my sight and never venture in these woods again," Meggie stated adamantly.

"I deeply regret any . . . any—"

Roe stopped speaking and brought a hand to his stomach. A strange pained sound emerged from his lips and he bent over as if stricken with a cramp.

Jesse eyed him curiously. "You know yer face is lookin' kind of downright green," he said.

Roe didn't wait to try to make his explanations. In a rush of panic, J. Monroe Farley put his hand over his mouth and raced past Jesse out the door.

A sharp, stabbing pain seemed to rip through Roe's gut as sweat broke across his brow. He ran away from the smoky-smelling cabin, away from the taste of green tomato relish that now burned in his throat. He ran to the cool shade of the Ozarks woods, his head spinning and his stomach in cramps.

Weakly he staggered and dropped to his knees next to the shallow stream that skittered along shiny, slick rocks. He labored to catch his breath. A swirl of green flies buzzed around his head. Ripping open the tight, starched collar, he fought the dark weakness that crept up on him. He cupped a handful of the icy, Itchy Creek water and splashed it liberally upon his face. He trembled from the combination of freezing water and nausea.

"Roe! Roe!" He heard Jesse calling but couldn't waste his strength to answer. He felt faint and the reality of that weakness embarrassed him. He lay down against the cool spring grass hoping to garner strength, but slumped to the ground and blackness swirled around him.

"He's here, Pa!"

Vaguely, he heard a voice calling out behind him. It seemed unearthly and far away but it revived him nonetheless.

"He's here by the crick."

Help was on the way. Help was almost here. The thought bolstered him somewhat. He rolled to his back and felt the warm spring breeze upon his sweat-drenched skin as he gazed at the slate-blue sky overhead. Thickly leafed branches of sassafras trees stretched out into the cloudless sky, but still a gray darkness cast shadows before him. He was sick, green sick, as Jesse had said, and miserable.

He moaned loudly.

The two men rushed up beside him. The one whose face he did not know was gray-bearded and held a hand-whittled hickory staff to aid his unsteady gait. The older man awkwardly knelt down in the grass beside Roe, his pale green eyes concerned.

"Mr. Farley?" he asked. "Mr. Farley, are you all right?"

Jesse stood back, nervously fidgeting. His blank look of bewilderment and guilt was heart-wrenching.

"Are ye sick, Mr. Farley? Mr. Farley, can ye hear me?" The gray-beard spoke louder than was necessary.

"Poison." The word came out a stiff and croaky sound.

"What?"

"Poison," he said again. "She poisoned me."

"Who?"

"Your daughter."

"Meggie?"

"I don't know why, but—" His voice faded as his eyes rolled back in his head and he fainted dead away.

Shocked, the older man turned to the younger standing close by. "What the devil is going on here, Jesse?"

The boy shrugged. "I tole him not to eat none of Meggie's piccalilli."

CHAPTER

THREE

"I JUST DON'T understand why we had to bring him here!" Meggie Best complained as her father and brother laid the sick, moaning man in the small rope-sprung one-poster bed built into the far corner of the little mountain cabin.

"It's the least we can offer a sick stranger," her father said. "Good God, Meggie, you nearly killed the man!"

"Maybe he deserved to die!" she exclaimed, before her father silenced her with a look.

"I don't know what happened between you two, but we'd sure to heaven better keep him alive if they's need of him declaring for you."

"Declaring for me! I wouldn't have that no-account if he come with a pink ribbon around his throat."

Her father gave her a long look. Meggie's harsh words shamed her. She was humiliated.

"Nothing happened between us. And besides, he's no-where near dead. A little touch of bad food isn't likely to kill a sharp-talking wily fellow like Mr. J. Monroe Farley."

She spoke the name in such a disparaging way, her father could only shake his head.

"For that we can be grateful," Best replied. "It's a good thing you didn't know that before you fed him the picca-lilli."

"Pa!" Meggie gave a little cry of indignation. "You talk like I did it on purpose."

"We know you didn't mean it," her brother Jesse said quietly. His handsome young face was innocent and without guile. "It ain't your fault, Meggie. Your cooking just makes folks sick. It happens every picnic."

"Not every picnic!" Her expression was stricken.

"Often enough that you ought to give up trying to feed the unwary," her father said.

Meggie raised her chin bravely, made a dramatic huff, and turned to leave the cabin.

"Where are you going?" her father called out.

"You don't expect me to actually stay in here with a man who tried to sweet-talk me."

Her father shrugged. "No, I suspect not. Tho' why in heaven would this city fellow take a notion toward you is a mystery."

"Pa!"

"I'd not meant it that way, Meggie," he said. "It's just that you've always been so standoffish when it comes to wife-lookers."

"And she cain't cook neither," Jesse added.

"I'm going to the cellar," she snapped.

"What for?"

"I might as well throw out the rest of that batch of piccalilli."

Meggie couldn't quite hear her father's chuckle behind her, but she knew it was there. She had never been so humiliated in her life. She'd been so overwhelmed by the stranger she'd lost her good sense. To think she'd allowed that fast-talking city man to kiss her and hug her and all that cooing and spooning, and he'd not been thinking about marrying her at all.

There was a loud choking sound from the bed and Meggie heard her father call out, "Hand me the basin, Jesse." She hurried out the back door, unwilling to listen to any more. Maybe he wouldn't survive. At least then she wouldn't have to see his face again. What had she been thinking?

On the far side of the porch, she opened the trapdoor to the root cellar. The ladder was narrow and steep but Meggie negotiated it easily. She lit the small tallow candle in the lantern that hung from the ceiling. In its yellow glow, the brightness of unshed tears shone in her blue eyes.

"Dad-burn and blast!" she exclaimed quietly to herself. She knew exactly what she'd been thinking. She'd been thinking the same silly, foolish thoughts that had been flitting in and out of her mind since she was old enough to know the difference between little boys and little girls.

It was that reader that she'd found in Mama's trunk. At the schoolhouse they had *McGuffey,* good lessons about good boys and girls. But Meggie had found the worn, faded book of fairy tales. They had been much more interesting than the stern admonitions of *McGuffey.* And her imagination had taken flight. Fanciful, that's what her father had called it. And when she'd read about Rapunzel, she'd decided that none of the local boys would ever do. A real prince was coming up the mountain for Meggie Best someday. She was sure of it. Unfortunately, this morning she'd thought that he'd arrived.

Meggie shook her head and gritted her teeth against the pain of embarrassment that welled up inside her. It wasn't bad enough that she had blurted out her secret thoughts and thrown herself at the fellow. She had been rather rudely thrown back, and now she'd gone and made him gut-sick. Pa would see that he stayed 'til he was on his feet.

How would she stand it? To look into those dark, handsome eyes and remember that she'd gone after him like a bear to a honey pot. What a fool she had made of herself. Meggie moaned aloud and covered her face with her hands.

Making her way to the back shelf, she found her piccalilli on the top right side. Lined up in perfect order and looking downright beautiful were sixteen quarts of the relish. Shaking her head, she sighed. She couldn't figure it out. She was twice as smart as most of the women that she knew. And yet even the silliest women on the mountain could stir up a light, airy batch of biscuits or a mess of cooked greens with both eyes closed. Meggie did everything that they did. But somehow, in Meggie's kitchen, the results could never be guaranteed. Cooking was definitely one of her failings. A fanciful nature was the other. And, dad-burn and blast, the city stranger had discovered both of them in one day.

With a sigh of disappointment she began loading the piccalilli jars into an empty bushel basket.

"With my luck, it'll make the hogs sick, too," she said.

Her thoughts drifted back once more to the handsome young man now lying ill in her brother's bed: J. Monroe Farley.

"Who ever heard of such a name," she whispered indignantly.

She certainly hadn't heard anything like it, not before that very morning.

Roe Farley's eyes fluttered open. It was late, the last light of evening pierced through the window at a sharp angle. The room had stopped spinning, but the memory of his sickness lingered. For a long moment he didn't remember where he was. His mouth tasted bitterly sour and his stomach felt empty and hollow from his breastbone to his spine. Then the memory came. A gleaming blue quart jar of piccalilli and Meggie Best.

He glanced over toward the fireplace that glowed brightly orange in the dim light of the cabin. She favored her brother some, he thought. But her hair was a darker blond and her eyes were not as blue. And of course, he was simple. And she was deranged.

He heard the soft sounds of her bare feet padding across the floor. He remembered those feet. He'd heard jokes about barefooted Ozark women, but somehow he hadn't expected to encounter it in one so young. The feet that had captured his attention were neither dainty nor prettily pink. They were long, narrow feet with high arches and skinny little toes. Those very sturdy, very ordinary, very feminine feet had captured his imagination. In all his years of being enticed and attracted by the opposite sex, never before had the woman's feet ever played a part.

Enticed and attracted! He quickly pushed the thought away. Even now with his stomach still quaking and his head still spinning a bit, he swore to himself that he was not in any way attracted to Meggie Best. Still, the thought of those bare female feet brought a smile to his face even through his sickness.

He was alone in the cabin, except for her. Deliberately he remained quiet so that she wouldn't know he was awake. If she threw herself upon him when he sat in a chair, there was no telling what she might do to a man in bed. And he was too sick and weak to even attempt to fight her off. Fight her off? Mentally he reprimanded himself. He had been as much to blame for their moment of indiscretion as she. More so, since he was a learned gentleman with some experience and she was . . . she was . . . well, he wasn't sure quite what she was.

He settled more snugly into the soft clover ticking that covered the rope-sprung bed. The cabin was one big room of hand-hewn logs with a big river rock fireplace on the south wall. It was a primitive cabin, but there was a softness to it, too. The softness no doubt stemmed, at least in part, from the multitude of homespun throws, covers, and curtains that appeared to be draped and tucked into every conceivable location.

The upper loft made the ceiling low in the half of the room where the bed was built into the corner. The half near the fireplace was open to the rafters, from which hung skeins of onions and peppers, bunches of drying herbs and long strips of jerked venison. Near the fireplace an old dried sycamore trunk was set up on legs as a meat block. In the center, near the hearth, was the small square table covered with a carefully pressed homespun tablecloth. It was the place where he'd sampled Miss Meggie's special near-deadly piccalilli.

Just the thought made Roe groan. It must have been audible because the young woman glanced in his direction. He tensed.

"Jesse," she called out through the door. "He's waking up." Without another glance in his direction, she untied her faded apron, hung it on a nail by the doorway, and hurried outside.

A moment later a familiar blond head peeped into the open door. With concern in his bright blue eyes the simple young man made his way to Roe's bedside. "You better, frien'?"

Roe smiled bravely. "Hello, Jesse," he said. "Yes, I believe I'm much improved over earlier in the afternoon."

Jesse nodded solemnly. "Pa said you'd probably wake up hungry." He gestured to a pot left warming over the fire. "Got some bear broth to make you strong again. It should gentle your belly some."

Roe looked toward the kettle warily.

"Don't worry," Jesse assured him. "Meggie ain't laid a hand on this soup. Pa and I put this up ourselves last winter. I shot the bear myself."

Roe swung his feet to the side of the bed and waited for the room to stop spinning. He was famished, he couldn't deny that, but he wasn't very interested in trying any more unusual Ozark food. Still, he supposed if the two big, brawny Best men could tolerate the stuff, he'd probably live to tell about this meal.

"If you'll hand me my shirt," he said to the anxious young man at his bedside, "I'd be pleased to take some soup at your table."

A few minutes later, and still somewhat weak, Roe was assisted into the cane-bottom chair.

Meggie and her father came inside and she immediately began stoking up the fire in the grate. Pinching biscuits into the bake oven that she set in the hot ashes at the edge of the fire, she did not even glance at him.

"Good to see you up and around," Best told him, slapping Roe smartly on the shoulder. "You eat up good, that bear broth is better than mustard plaster for what's ailing you, boy."

Roe smiled amiably. The carved wood spoon, *her* spoon, lay beside Roe's plate. He hesitated momentarily before touching it and then mentally scoffed at his own foolishness. It was simply a spoon and would work as well as any other. He dipped out a bit of food and tasted it. The strongly flavored broth almost burned his tongue.

Roe's glance settled on the young woman who had fed him the nauseating piccalilli. Though her form partially obscured the hearth, he could see the fire which seemed stoked a bit hotter than necessary. One of the pans hanging on the crane was smoking ominously. The young lady, herself, was cleaned up and better dressed than earlier in the day. Her dove gray dress was neat, and she held herself with the prideful carriage of a society belle. But her long, brown feet were just as bare as they had been that morning.

"You'll be back to your old self in no time a'tal." Jesse's father remarked, taking the empty chair at the head of the table. "Meggie, your brother and I are ready to give your cooking another chance. We cain't live forever on bear broth."

Roe smiled at his host. He remembered that rugged face leaning over him, the long gray beard untrimmed, cooling his brow with a damp rag, and holding his head over a chipped metal basin. He was not used to people taking care of him. It had always been necessary for him to take care of himself.

"Mr. Best, I cannot thank you enough for coming to my aid this afternoon."

"Don't think a thing about it, boy. Why I couldn't let Meggie's cooking kill ye dead."

The old man chuckled at his daughter's expense and all three men glanced in her direction.

"Although I did hear that you tried stealing a kiss, so maybe you paid your due."

Roe flushed slightly and cleared his throat.

"And don't give that another thought neither. If more fellers had tried kissing my Meggie, maybe she'd be cooking for some other man today and her brother and I would be spared the misery."

Jesse laughed heartily at his father's joke. Roe managed a wan smile. Meggie, however, was not amused. She set the now heavily smoking black kettle on the hearth with a loud and disgusted bang and then turned her back on them.

The old man winked playfully at Roe.

"And don't you be callin' me Mr. Best like I'm some shoe peddler from St. Louis," he continued. "Just call me Onery like everyone else what knows me."

"Onery?" Roe had never heard such a name.

The old man chuckled again. "Yep, that's what they calls me. My name's Henry. Henry Best. But my mama was kindy Frenchy-fied and the way she said Henry sounded kindy like Onery. And since I *was* o'nery from the day I's borned, folks just took to calling me that."

"Onery," Roe said, smiling with genuine good humor. "Please just call me Roe, like Jesse does. It is truly a pleasure to make your acquaintance, sir." He offered his hand in a gesture of polished politeness.

A disapproving huff could be heard coming from the far side of the room.

Best took his hand. "Even if you had to be nearly poisoned to do it?"

Meggie's huff turned to a cry of fury as she turned to face

the men at the table, the long wooden serving spoon held in front of her threateningly like a weapon.

"Now Meggie-gal," Onery said, smiling. "Don't you be a-getting riled now. It's not good to show off your temper to your new beau."

"My new beau! I wouldn't have that mangy, two-toed varmint a-calling on me!" she snapped.

Roe was more amused than insulted by Meggie's words, but didn't like the inference that he might be calling upon her. He quickly sought to change the subject.

"I would like to apologize, Onery, for my dreadful manners," he said to the old man.

"What dreadful manners is that?" her father asked.

"Why, why upsetting your daughter and becoming ill in your house when I've hardly made your acquaintance."

Onery just chuckled.

"It weren't your fault, Roe," Jesse piped in eagerly. "It was Meggie. She gets upset with me a lot, too. And she ain't much for cooking. Her piccalilli would give an ox a bellyache."

"Jesse!" The word was spoken shrilly. Jesse held up his hands as if fearing his sister was going to use that spoon on him.

Roe didn't say another word. He just kept his eyes on his broth and hoped for a change of subject. Inexplicably, he allowed his gaze to drop to the floor beneath Meggie to spy the long bare feet that he remembered. Despite everything he'd been through Roe found the sight strangely alluring.

Mr. Best chuckled loudly. "Now, children, don't you get in a spat over this." He smiled at Roe. "Got to have a sense of fun about ye, boy, if ye live in the Ozarks. Mother Nature is having a joke on us folks near about all the time. And don't mind these younguns of mine," Onery continued. "Jesse just says whatever comes to his fool head and Meggie's a dreamy sort and a bit sensitive about her cooking."

"Pa!" Meggie protested.

"Meggie, show some manners with our guest. And get some victuals on the table 'fore I faint to the floor with hunger. Jesse, take your seat there by your new friend."

Onery chuckled at Meggie's dismay and smiled companionably at Roe. "We're always glad to have company down our way. And my Meggie ain't had a gentleman caller in a month of Sundays."

Meggie slammed the cornbread skillet on the table with a loud thump. "He's not *calling* on me."

Roe found himself amused with the exasperation in her voice. The joke was a good one, but he wanted to make sure the old man didn't get to thinking that perhaps there was some truth to it. "Did Jesse or Meggie tell you about my mission?"

"Mission? Nope, neither of these children said one word. You a preachin' man, Roe?"

"It's not that kind of mission," Meggie snapped. She slapped a huge hunk of cornbread on the table in front of the men's plates. Roe reached for his and flinched when his blistered hand tore a piece off the hot loaf.

"What's ailing you?" Onery reached over and grasped the young man's hand. Pulling off the bandage, he gazed with worry at the raw, red blisters he found on the palm.

"Lord, boy, you sure got your hands in a mess. What'd you do, slip a rope?"

Roe looked down at his hands. The pain in his stomach had temporarily made him forget their sting.

"It's nothing," he answered.

"Meggie made him split cordwood for his meal," Jesse said.

"What?" Best's eyes widened in disbelief.

"Tattletale!" Meggie snapped, glaring at her brother, a hot flush of color rising in her cheekbones. "And I didn't make him. He said he would."

Best glared at his daughter. "Mr. Farley, I don't know

what to say. This is not the way that mountain folk treat visitors."

"Remember, my name's Roe, and please, don't give these blisters another thought," Roe insisted. "It's as your daughter says, I wanted to do something to help. Unfortunately, I'm not accustomed to chopping wood. I'm sure they'll be healed very soon. And Miss Best has already put some salve on them."

"That's what they was doing when Roe kissed her," Jesse volunteered with some pride in his understanding of the situation.

"I swear, Mr. Best, I wasn't trying—"

"Onery, boy, call me Onery." Best continued to eye his daughter with disappointment as she set the rest of the food on the table and took her place across from Roe.

"You're a city man, a one-eyed dog could see that a mile away," he said. "You'll toughen up a bit in time and your hands'll be all the better for the blisters on 'em now."

Turning to Meggie, the old man shook his head. "Now you, little gal, you shouldn't put your new beau to work. It'll turn a feller off you quicker than milk'll sour."

"He's not my—" she began uselessly. Her father loved to tease.

"I'm proud Meggie's done put salve on your blisters, Roe," Onery continued. "She's right good at nursing and that's a fact."

Meggie flushed slightly at the unexpected praise.

"Still," the old man continued. "This family owes you an apology and I'll be giving it to you now."

Roe shrugged and glanced down at this hands with unconcern. "Apology accepted. Believe me there is no harm done."

"There certainly is harm done and this family is obliged to make it up to you."

Onery was looking directly and sternly at Meggie,

implying that it was she who ought to be doing the *making up*.

Less than enthusiastically, Meggie reached across the table and took Roe's hand in her own.

Roe felt her tremble slightly at the touch. A strange fluttery feeling expanded in his abdomen. He tried to attribute it to the bad piccalilli, but it was the taste of her lips that he recalled.

"The salve's purt-near healed him up already," she said. "It ain't our fault that the man ain't accustomed to working."

"It's 'cause he's a *scholar*, Meggie," Jesse explained proudly with emphasis on the new word he'd learned. "Just like I tole you. He's come from a college named Hazard."

Onery Best looked at his guest keenly. "Kentucky? My wife's folks got family in Hazard County, Kentucky."

"No, not Hazard, Harvard," Roe correctly quietly. "It's in Massachusetts, the Bay State."

"The Bay State? Woo-eee, Lordy, you've come one fer piece. Your people from there?"

"My people?"

"Your family."

"Oh, actually I don't have much family anymore. Just some cousins on the maternal side. They live in Philadelphia. I have a fellowship from Harvard."

"What's fellowship?" Jesse asked.

"It sounds like some kindy religious fal-de-ral," Onery said.

"No, not at all. The college supports my efforts to collect and catalogue folk songs of Celtic origin. I believe I will find some here in the Ozarks."

"What's folk songs?"

"Why it's just music," he said. "The music of the people. The kind of music you play, Jesse. Do you play music, too, Mr. Best?"

Jesse grinned proudly and spoke up before his father

could. "It was Pa what taught me to play fiddle. I'm the best around these parts now. Even better than Pa and he used to play *itinerant* for a living."

Roe's eyes widened with interest. "I'd be very interested to hear both of you. It's my conjecture, and I hope on this mission to prove it, that many of the ballads and play-party songs that are popular here can be traced directly to songs in the highlands of Britain and Ireland. These songs and their history are already lost in their native lands, through wars and assimilation. But since the Ozarks are so remote, the songs may still be sung. If they are to be saved at all, they must be saved by those of us in the current generation. Folkways are passing quickly and we must document all that we can."

Onery's brow furrowed. "And you think me and Jesse and the folks 'round here can help you *document* these old songs?"

"Yes, sir, I do."

"Well, it seems to me—"

"There is no playing nor singing when food's on the table," Meggie interrupted sternly. "That's just plain bad manners." She was as intrigued as her father and brother, but deliberately managed to break the spell that Roe's words cast.

Onery Best nodded in agreement. "That's true. The table's no place for music," he said. "But when Roe here's got some soup in his belly and the rest of us have eaten our fill, they'll be time for visiting and singing and the like."

Roe smiled. "I'd appreciate that, Onery. It would be a great help to me."

"A help you say?" Onery grinned big and broad. "Well, it's just like I tole you, this family owes you some making up. If just playing some good music and singing some songs be helping you, it seems like a right smart idea to me."

Jesse, Roe, and Onery were all smiling.

Meggie was not. Helping J. Monroe Farley *document* his

folk songs would mean his continued presence at the cabin. And Meggie wanted the man as far away from her and her family as earthly possible. Farley was a music man like her father and brother. She knew all about men like that. Playing a couple of tunes could turn into a day-long concert. Once the music was started and the men were playing, it was hard to get them back to the plow.

Meggie was not musical. She loved music and would catch herself singing a tune now and again. But it would never be for her the excuse for wasting a day's work that it was for them.

Clearly Roe Farley was to stay for a good long while. Meggie didn't want that. She'd embarrassed herself and felt humiliated. But worse, she still felt drawn to the dark-haired city man. It was only force of will that kept her at her distance now. And she didn't know how long her will could hold out.

"Jesse, say grace if you will," Meggie ordered.

The three men looked at her startled. They were already halfway finished with their meal and now she was calling for them to pray over it.

Onery cleared his throat and lay his cornbread back on the table. "Guess we did forget that."

Roe bowed his head politely, but his heart was pounding. He couldn't think of the prayer or the food or his still aching stomach. After all these months of hope and planning, he'd finally stumbled onto this unlikely family of authentic Ozark musicians. And they seemed to welcome him.

He glanced across the table at Meggie Best. Well, her father and brother had welcomed him. Her head was bowed and slightly turned in her brother's direction. Her blue-gray eyes were bright with love and pride as she gazed at Jesse. The sight was almost startling. Earlier that afternoon he'd thought her pretty. But with that gentle, caring tenderness upon her face, she was beautiful. Roe moved slightly, making her glance at him. Unfortunately, when those eyes did look his way they were wary and disapproving.

Onery and Jesse might be eager to help him prove his premise, but Meggie was only eager to see him gone from this place. She'd sure changed her tune since she'd dropped into his lap that afternoon. Then she'd been as sweet as sugar candy. And soft and warm as a feather bed. Now, it was almost easy to believe that she'd tried to poison him.

"Dear Lord in heaven," Jesse said beside him. "We thank you for food to eat and all the world and life so sweet. We thank you for the stars above and your eternal grace and love."

The words came out by rote in a singsong fashion. Then the young man hesitated. "And thank you, God, fer my frien' Roe. I like him."

CHAPTER

FOUR

THE BEAR BROTH was not the best soup that Roe had ever tasted. But then, it *had* seemed to ease his stomach. And he didn't think he'd been poisoned, so he supposed that could be considered success. The cornbread was more than half palatable and Roe found himself eating more heartily than he expected.

"So tell me about your people." Onery Best interrupted his thoughts.

"About them?"

"Where they come from, what they do. That sorta thing."

"Oh." Roe nodded, understanding. Apparently things were not so different in the hills than in fine houses on the Eastern Seaboard. All his life he'd been J. Monroe Farley, a scholar with few relevant family connections. It was like a mark he wore upon his forehead or a millstone he wore around his neck.

From the earliest days of his memory he'd been alone. When both his parents were still living, he was sent away to schools. His mother was in frail health and his father, an ambitious businessman, disliked having a child underfoot. By the time he was truly alone in the world, he was almost accustomed to it. His mother's cousins in Philadelphia had shown some inclination of taking him in. But by then, Roe was more inclined to simply lead his own life.

Presently, he was young and healthy and without attachments. He saw absolutely no reason to throw that away anytime soon. Music and history were his family and his life as well as a worthy pursuit. Worthy enough to be a life within itself for a man without family.

But even here, now on the top of this God-only-knows mountain, taking dinner with a gray-bearded Ozarker, his simpleminded son, and his barefoot daughter, here, too, his antecedents deserved consideration.

"My family is of English extraction from the states of Pennsylvania and New York," he said evenly. "The Farleys were here prior to the Revolutionary War. My own father read law in his own legal firm on Wall Street in New York City," he said. "He was a Harvard graduate, as was my grandfather."

"Lawyers?" Onery asked.

"Yes, Harvard lawyers, for generations."

That fact alone was usually enough to reassure the most persnickety society matron.

Roe smiled warmly, assuming his host was dutifully impressed. But when he looked at Onery, he saw that the older man's forehead was furrowed thoughtfully and his bright blue eyes, shaded by thick silver-tinged eyebrows, turned their gaze to Meggie, his expression thoughtful.

Roe cleared his throat nervously. "My mother's side of the family are old Philadelphia. Came over with William Penn and all that sort of thing. They are very severe Yankee blue bloods, of course."

"Yankees?"

"Yes, of course."

Onery shook his head. "It's best not say another word about this, boy," he whispered. "Folks around here still don't take the War of Secession very easylike."

Roe's eyes widened. He thought Onery was making a little joke. But he appeared totally serious.

"I don't hold nothing like that agin a fellow," Onery

continued with grave sincerity. "A fellow cain't be blamed for the family what birthed him. But around here, folks has got peculiar ideas about both lawyers and Yankees."

Shaking his head again, the old man made eye contact with his daughter as if making a pact.

"We won't say nothing about that, son. Claiming to be a Yankee lawyer ain't going to gain you too many friends."

Strangely, Roe felt stung by the criticism. "I wasn't actually looking for friendships," he replied.

"Well, if you're looking to get folks to sing and play songs for you, you'd best be looking for friends. Ain't nobody else going to leastwise."

"That's right!" Jesse said as he slapped his hand loudly on the table. "That's it edzactly." He turned his smiling face to Roe. "You're my frien', folks'll like ye 'cause they like me. Why, this is a lucky day for both of us. I was cheered to get a frien' of mine own. Now, I'm cheered to be a frien' to you 'cause you need one."

"Jesse's talking practically like he's got good sense," Onery agreed. "We'll take you along with us to the church and the Literaries and such. If you're a friend of ours, you'll be welcome. Afore you know it, you'll have ever' song in the hills for your own."

Roe was thoughtful for a moment. They were right, if he intended to make headway here he needed this family. Nervously he glanced in Meggie's direction. It wasn't the best situation here after the fiasco with the young woman, but Roe believed he could win her over. If Jesse and Onery Best were the local musicians, he needed to be with them. "That's wonderful of you, Onery," he said. "I am eager to get started."

Onery chuckled and gave Roe a teasing wink. "Aw, it's the least we can do for the feller what's calling on Meggie."

"He's not calling on me," Meggie ground out through clenched teeth.

Onery roared with laughter.

Roe pulled nervously once more on his collar. The joke about being Meggie's beau was wearing a little thin. "Is there a rooming house somewhere near here?"

"What do you need a rooming house for?" Onery asked.

"I'll need a place to stay."

"Why, you can stay here," Onery told him. "You can sleep up in the loft with Jesse."

"Oh, I couldn't impose."

"They's room in the loft," the older man said. "I sleep in that bed there in the corner and Meggie fixes herself a pallet on the floor. There ain't no impose about it. And there ain't no rooming house neither. In Marrying Stone you got to stay *with* somebody and we're inviting you to stay with us."

"Please stay!" Jesse begged. "We can be frien's all summer long." His bright blue eyes were wide with excitement.

Roe's glance strayed over to Meggie. Her expression was cold, and her blue-gray eyes so chilling that he could almost feel the stab of icicles at two paces. Clearly, she was far from delighted by this turn of events.

"I don't want to make a nuisance of myself," he said somewhat uneasily.

"You can help around to earn your keep," Onery declared. "Lord knows we need another hand around this place."

"I know nothing about farming."

"Ye can learn cain't ye?" the older man asked.

"Well certainly I could, but perhaps . . ." Meggie was glaring at him so frostily he couldn't finish his sentence. Once more Roe pulled his boodle bag out of his trousers. "I can pay."

Onery snorted. "We don't need yer money, boy. We need yer back."

Roe cleared his throat nervously. "I don't believe that I—"

"Don't ye worry. We'll start you out easy and we'll have those city-boy hands toughened up before the summer's half over."

The old man's tone seemed to settle the matter. Roe glanced over at the young man who claimed him as a friend. Jesse would be disappointed if he didn't stay. Onery might well be insulted. He needed them both.

Unwillingly he turned to the remaining person. "Miss Best, I—" he began.

"Oh, don't mind Meggie none," Onery said. "She'll be grateful for the help and I promise you, her cooking is something that you kindy get accustomed to after a while. She don't poison us ever' day." The old man howled with laughter and slapped his thigh.

Meggie's face was pale, her jaw set tight. The deed was done. Her father had invited the man and the only thing to do was to make the best of it.

"You'd need to stay right here," Onery continued. "Why, how else are you two gonna make up your little spat if you ain't around to sweet-talk her some more?"

Meggie thought that Granny Piggott had said it best. "Sweet-talking menfolk is a bit like razorback hogs. A *smart* woman knows to leave 'em alone."

As Meggie picked up the last of the dinner dishes from the table and emptied the scraps into the feed bucket, she remembered those words. She'd been mistaken. J. Monroe Farley, not a prince at all but some kind of professional man from that Harvard College place, was setting up his Ediphone on the far side of the room. He was the sweetest-talking man that she'd ever seen. And he'd had an openmouthed kiss, a good laugh—and a bad bellyache at her expense. She was determined to leave him alone. She had to, for the sake of her good sense and her heart.

"The Edison phonograph," he was explaining to Jesse, as if her brother could actually understand, "is one of Thomas Edison's inventions. You do know Thomas Edison?"

Jesse's face was completely blank.

"He's not from around here," her father stated.

"No, sir," Roe agreed. He appeared a little nonplussed.

Jesse was seated on the floor next to the machine. He picked up his long-stemmed clay pipe from the tobacco saucer on the hearth and tapped it thoughtfully.

"Don't you dare light that thing in this house!" Meggie's voice was startling and shrill even to herself.

"I'm just holding it, Meggie," her brother insisted. "I ain't done nothing to be scolded about."

Roe and her father were both looking at her curiously. She usually was so even tempered.

"Women, they get their humors in a snit when they's a gentleman in the house," Onery told him.

Meggie turned back to her dirty dishes, determined not to pay attention to any of them. *Humors in a snit!* Indeed. It was as if her father was trying to bait her.

"Mr. Edison designed a way to capture sound on wax cylinders," Roe began again. He held up one of the objects for the men to examine.

"Looks like a corncob weaving spool," Onery said. "It's made of wax you say?"

"Yes, sir," Farley answered. "It's just regular wax like candles or sealant. But it can catch whatever you say or sing and keep it until you want to hear it again."

"Why would you want to hear yourself again?" Best asked.

Roe didn't have an answer for that. "Why, posterity," he said finally.

Meggie turned back to look at them. Her brother and father were staring at him blankly waiting for him to explain. Instead he began setting up the machine.

"I want to demonstrate how it works for you," he told them. "Once you see how this new machine can accurately represent your own voice, and play it back to you, you'll be very enthusiastic to participate."

"We've already said we are gonna sing fer you," Onery told him. "And we've promised to introduce you around the mountain so folks won't think you're a stranger. I don't know why you'd be needin' us to be enthusiastic about it."

Roe didn't answer, but he did smile and then glanced over toward Meggie.

She blushed furiously. She'd be dad-burned and blasted before she'd show one more iota of interest whatsoever in this sweet-smelling, fancy-dressed city man, his strange machine, or his silly songs. She looked away. Saving their sounds for posterity! That was the biggest pile of foolishness she'd ever heard. Every song on the mountain was known to every soul that lived there. They sang them when they were happy or blue or grieving. They taught them to their children and those children taught them to theirs.

Writing them down! As if folks was likely to forget. It would be like writing down how to wash dishes or slaughter a hog. Everybody already knew how to do it, nobody'd ever want to read about how.

Still, the machine was curious and Roe Farley the finest looking man she'd ever seen. Meggie couldn't quite keep her mind and her attention on her dish basin and her dirty tins.

"This is the horn," Roe said as he attached a large metal piece to the top of the machine.

To Meggie it looked like a tin trumpet only it was black and shiny.

"You sing or play into the horn and the sound is recorded onto the wax cylinders."

"It must be kindy hard to get into that horn to sing." Jesse appeared confused.

"I 'magine it's even tougher to play a fiddle in there," Onery added with a laugh.

"It's not a perfect machine," Roe said, smiling. "But if you put your mouth or your fiddle as close to the horn as possible, and you sing or play loudly, the machine picks up the sound."

Both men appeared curious, but unconvinced. Roe cranked up the Edison phonograph.

"Come on, Jesse, say something into the horn."

The blond young man hesitated. "Ain't got nothing to say to it."

"Just tell it your name, like you did to me this afternoon."

His face screwed up with displeasure at the handsome city man. Meggie knew that look well: her brother was sure to refuse. But Jesse, appearing as if he were about to take a dose of summer tonic, leaned forward toward the big black trumpet.

"My name's Jesse Best. But folks call me Simple Jess," he said.

"Wonderful!" Roe was clearly delighted. "Now wait just a minute."

The entire Best family watched as Roe deftly unscrewed the sharp tip that cut into the wax and replaced it with a rounder, curved piece.

"That round thing won't cut the wax like the other knife did," Onery said.

"It's not really a knife," Roe answered. "It's called a stylus. It's made of sapphire. The sharp tip is used to cut when we're recording. Now we're just going to play it back."

Roe cranked up the machine again and gently set the round-tipped stylus against the turning wax spindle. For a moment there was complete silence in the room. Then the machine gave forth a croaky, gravelly sound.

"My name's Jesse Best. But folks call me Simple Jess."

Meggie gave a little cry of shock and dropped her wet dishrag on her bare foot.

Onery slapped his thigh. "Well, I'll be switched!"

Jesse jumped up and moved away so quickly he knocked his chair to the floor. He was pointing to the machine with disbelief.

"That thing is named Jesse Best, too?" His question was incredulous.

"No, no," Roc calmed him. "The machine is just saying back to you what *you* said."

"That's some kind of contraption you got there," Onery told him with genuine admiration.

"But it said, 'My name is Jesse Best.'" The young man still looked confused and agitated.

"It said that because that's what you said," Roe told him gently. "It's not named Jesse Best, you are."

Jesse wasn't quite mollified. "Well, what *is* its name then?"

"It's called an Ediphone."

"Ediphone?" Jess had never heard of such a thing. "What kind of name is that?"

"Well," Roe said thoughtfully. "It's a derivation, I suppose, a name made up of two names."

Jesse sat back down in his chair, but he still watched the Ediphone warily.

"You see the machine is a type of *phono*graph made by Mr. *Edi*son. Phono means sound in Greek. So, he called it an *Ediphone*. I guess it's kind of a nickname." Roe caught Meggie's eye and smiled. "It's like your sister's name is Margaret May and you call her Meggie. The Edison phonograph is called an Ediphone."

"It's a pretty strange name," Jesse said.

"It's a pretty strange machine," Onery Best put in.

Roe nodded. "With the Ediphone, I can make faithful reproductions of the actual performance of the folk songs. Performance is a major portion of what makes the songs important. Just writing down the words and the composition is not enough. I want to have the most faithful rendering of these works possible."

"Well, it sounds kindy croaky," Onery said.

"But it listens, Pa," Jesse told him. "It listens to what we sing or say. I'm going to call it a Listening Box."

Onery smiled at Roe and then turned once more to his

son. "Jesse, get your fiddle and play a song for that there Listening Box."

The young man hesitated for only a minute. Then from up above the pie safe, he retrieved a fine old fiddle, varnished richly with red oil and polished to a bright sheen.

Meggie noticed Roe looked surprised. Clearly, he hadn't expected such a fine instrument in such a modest home. Jesse's fiddle was beautifully made with its small neck and a fine scroll. But more than that, the instrument had perfect tone. Even when played loudly, it held a purity that was rare in these mountains—as rare as her brother's talent at playing it.

Jesse'd been fiddling for most of his life. The instrument had belonged to Onery, handed down from his own father. Casually the young man now propped the chin piece on his collarbone and held it in place. He closed his eyes. Meggie watched her brother with pride; the smell of pine tar and rosin filled the room, spreading a warm, secure feeling over her. It was hope and home and beauty and love.

Grabbing up the redwood bow, Jesse drew it down slowly across the e-string. A sweet soulful sound filled the room as Jesse adjusted the fine tuner at the base of the bridge. His ear was excellent and his pitch was perfect, and since those were the only gifts heaven had seen fit to give him, the young man wanted for no others. As he continued to tune the other strings, he walked toward the strange, unsightly machine with the big tin trumpet poised upon it.

He looked over at Roe and then at his father. "What do you want me to play?"

"Whatever you want," was Roe's answer.

His father was more thoughtful. "Play 'Barby Ellen,'" he said. "You play that one mighty nice."

Moving up close to the horn of the Ediphone, Jesse drew the bow across the fiddle strings and began to play an up-tempo version of the sweet sadness of "unworthy Barbara Allen."

Delighted, Roe rifled through his portable desk for pen and paper as Onery began to sing.

> "In Scarlet Town where I was born
> There was a fair maid dwellin'
> Made ever' youth cry well away,
> Her name was Barbry Ellen."

Meggie watched as the stranger's fingers literally flew across the paper writing the words as her father sang them. She'd never seen a human move a pen so fast. In fact, she would hardly have thought it possible. Meggie could write. But her sparse, graceful penmanship took much time and effort. Roe's hands moved across the paper with the same quickness and surity with which Jesse's fingers worked the fiddle's fingerboard.

The dishes now completely forgotten, Meggie stood by the kitchen table, listening to the beauty of her brother's fiddling, the deep vibrancy of her father's tenor voice, and watching the most interesting man she had ever seen, the man she'd thought for a while to be her very own prince, writing quick as a minute in the bright yellow glow of the tallow candles as if he belonged there.

> "'Farewell,' she said, 'ye virgins all,
> And shun the fault I fell in;
> Henceforth take warning of the fall
> Of unworthy Barbry Ellen.'"

As the last strains of the fiddle died away, Roe sighed in appreciation. "Beautiful."

Onery and Jesse both chuckled. "It's a right pretty tune," Onery agreed. "And there ain't none on the mountain that can fiddle as well as my Jesse."

Roe was smiling and nodded. "He's right, you know,

Jesse. I've heard the fiddle played all over the world and I've never heard anyone better than you."

The young man blushed and shrugged. "It ain't nothing."

"Oh, but it is, Jesse," Meggie insisted as she came forward to lay a loving hand on her brother's shoulder. "You've a wonderful talent. You should be proud."

He shook away the compliment. "It ain't like I can read or cipher or something. I just hear the music in my head and it comes out my fingers."

"That's something that a lot of people who can read and cipher can never do," Roe told him.

Jesse was clearly embarrassed by this praise. "You just say that 'cause you're my frien'."

"I *am* your friend," Roe answered. "And friends always tell each other the truth."

"They do?"

Roe nodded.

Jesse's blue eyes widened and his face beamed with pleasure.

"Let's hear what it sounds like on the machine," Roe suggested.

Meggie didn't even feign disinterest as Farley changed the stylus again. Maybe the stranger was right about the Ediphone. Once the mountain folks had heard the wonderful new machine, maybe they would help him collect the music.

As the stylus moved along the grooves in the wax, the music flowed out of the horn. Her father's singing was almost too faint to hear, but the sweet strains of Jesse's violin sounded almost as good in the reproduction as it had when he'd played it.

"Is that how my fiddle sounds?" Jesse asked curiously.

"Well, you sound better than that," Roe told him. "But it's close."

Jesse shook his head in disbelief. "This machine is like the magic in one of Meggie's stories."

He turned to smile with pride at his sister.

"Meggie's stories?" Roe asked.

The young man nodded. "Meggie, she reads real good. And she don't just read the Bible, neither. She's got a book of them fairy tales they're called. Sometimes she reads them to me."

Her cheeks were bright red with the stain of embarrassment. Meggie began to move back from the men and toward the dirty dishes she'd left behind.

"They's magic in them fairy tales," Jesse continued. "Things can happen that a feller wouldn't believe could never happen."

"So I understand," Roe agreed.

"And this machine of yours, it's like that. A feller wouldn't never believe that it can listen and then talk and play near as good as me."

"No, Jesse," Roe assured him. "The machine isn't magic. The machine can't talk or play at all. It simply records you and plays what it's heard back. Magic is only in fairy tales."

FROM THE JOURNAL OF
J. MONROE FARLEY

April 17, 1902
Marrying Stone, Arkansas

The family who have given me shelter are an interesting yet peculiar trio. Their speech and ways are old and curious and I find myself observing them as if they were living fossils. They are a musical family and have agreed to help with my work and to introduce me to other people nearby. The farmer himself at one time made his living in these hills playing the fiddle. His son is simpleminded, but is a very accomplished fiddler and has in his repertoire a wide range of tunes that he has begun to share with me.

On Friday next we are set to attend what the Bests call "the Literary." This is apparently a local social gathering where music and cultural events take place. I am very anxious to attend, but find much here in this wilderness homestead to draw my interest. It is as if I have stepped back into time.

The typical day begins with breaking fast before dawn. The personal habits of the Best family are difficult for me to accustom myself to. On the first evening I asked of Jesse, the son, directions to the privy. The young man looked momentarily confused and then explained in his simple way that the homestead did not boast a privy.

Subsistence farming in this rough, unbroken stretch of mountain that the Best family calls home proves to be laborious, backbreaking work. Due to the farmer's age and bad leg, the toughest and the dirtiest jobs fall to the younger and stronger son. And, to my dismay, the young man eagerly shares these chores with me.

Although I find the backwoods life interesting in an intellectual context, I can't help but think wistfully of Cambridge and the bustle of eager students and the musty aged smell of the library. I am eager to return to the world that I know.

The family also has a daughter. Her name is Margaret.

CHAPTER

FIVE

ROE'S MUSCLES ACHED and the back of his neck was red and scorched from the sun. He carried the bucket of fresh eggs he had collected from the wily and cantankerous old hens into the cabin.

For three days he'd been living and working like an Ozark farmer. It wasn't a role he had taken up without a bit of protest. He had tried more than once to pay Onery Best for his room and board. Cash money was clearly in short supply. Still, the old farmer had insisted that work was what they needed. So with a willingness that was born of years of fitting in at schools and among strangers, Roe had "put his hand to the plow" both figuratively and literally.

He didn't expect thanks, and he certainly didn't get it from Meggie Best. It was a curious situation—one he'd never encountered before. First she'd jumped on him as if he were her long-lost lover and now she avoided speaking to him as if he were contagious.

"Good morning," he said evenly when he saw her. No matter how remote she appeared, civility was second nature to Roe Farley. He would treat his worst enemy with politeness. Meggie Best wasn't his worst enemy.

Her vague nod of acknowledgment irritated him. He could well remember the warmth of her smile as she gazed at her brother. Though she wasn't the musician her father and brother were, it was clear she was the brightest in her family. If only she would acknowledge him, he felt they could be friends of a sort.

"Thought I'd try to be of help to you." He set the egg bucket on the chopping stump and smiled.

She nodded wordlessly.

Her iciness irked him and prompted him to teasing. "I wanted to give you more time to burn the biscuits."

She glared at him but held her tongue as her father and brother walked in the door.

"Meggie-gal," Onery said as he made his way to the table. "It's mighty early in the morning to be having a lovers' spat." The old man chuckled at his own joke.

Roe had had quite enough of that nonsense himself and took his own seat at the table.

The three men sat together every morning in the gray light to plan the day's work. Roe had come to look forward to these moments. The camaraderie of working toward a common goal and the warmth of the two men beside him were new experiences for him. His hands were already callusing over and although he knew he was yet no farmer, he was working hard and he thought he might well be shouldering his share of the work. Meggie set his tin of cornmeal mush down on the table in front of him without a word. The finely carved wooden spoon, her spoon, was dipped in the mush.

Roe murmured his thanks but when he glanced in her direction she'd already turned her back on him.

"Meggie darlin'," Onery said loudly with a teasing wink toward Roe. "Feigning disinterest is right ladylike and all, but if you don't get out of this snit, the fellow's gonna plumb lose interest in ye."

Meggie shot her father a furious look that only made him laugh harder.

"She's really quite good-natured when you get to know her," Onery told Roe.

Roe smiled and cleared his throat a little uneasily. Still, as he watched Meggie bend over to hang the cookpot back on the fireplace crane, he once more regarded the young lady with favor. She was a fine-looking woman, he thought, and she probably should have married long ago. Roe fervently wished that she had.

Uncomfortably, he vividly remembered the sweet taste of her mouth and the pleasant roundness of her bottom against his lap.

The young woman stood up quickly and almost caught Roe admiring her. Determinedly, he turned his attention to his plate, raising his foot up to rest it on the first rung of the chair. This caused his knee to jut out from the edge of the table.

"You got a rip in your trousers," Jesse commented.

Roe glanced down and nodded. The three days of hard physical labor was more than the knees of his gray and brown striped worsted trousers had ever been expected to endure.

"Perhaps I can borrow a needle and thread," he said.

"You can sew?" Onery asked with surprise.

"No, not really," Roe admitted.

"Then let Meggie tend your tears," the old man said. "She's right handy with her needlework."

Meggie approached him, giving a studied glance to the ripped knee where the small expanse of pale flesh was exposed.

"Those trousers weren't made for working," she commented.

Roe agreed.

"I'll stitch 'em up for you, but I'd best be making you some butternuts."

"Butternuts?"

Jesse slapped his knee. "Butternuts like mine," he said.

Roe looked over at the trousers Jesse wore. The heavy dark yellow fabric was homespun and looked sturdy enough to withstand a stampede of wild boars. The homemade breeches were straight cut and wide enough in the leg to fit two men his size.

"If you're going to be working here," Onery agreed, "then you oughter have butternuts. Ain't no need for you to be ruining your good clothes."

Roe nodded, civility preventing him from mentioning that the trousers he wore were far from his best.

"I don't wish to put you to any extra effort on my part, Miss Best," he said.

Meggie raised her chin defiantly, seeing insult where none was intended. "My cloth is as good as any on the mountain," she said with some pride. "They're not city clothes, but they'll keep you from being threadbare. Jesse can cut you some galluses and show you how to attach them through the hitches with a peg and a horseshoe nail."

Roe stared in daunted wonder.

She continued. "I can sew up your good trousers and wash them clean for Sundays."

"That would be very nice, Miss Best," he said. "I thank you."

Meggie's lip stiffened to one thin line as if he'd said something indiscreet and Jesse giggled.

"You'll have to measure the feller, Meggie," Onery said. "He ain't neither my size nor Jesse's."

She blushed then. "I couldn't *measure* him," she answered in a scandalized whisper. "I'll just make them the same as Jesse's."

Roe nodded and turned to look at Jesse, who was quite a bit larger than himself and whose pants hung upon him like two sacks seamed together.

Onery began to chuckle.

"We praise her biscuits and her pies,
    Her doughnuts and her cakes.

But where's the man who sighs for pants
Like Mama used to make."

Jesse snickered at his father's joke.

Meggie's expression turned from embarrassment to anger. "I'll measure him all right!" she said. "I'll make his butternuts to fit slicker than skin if he wants."

Roe reached over and took Meggie's hand and her eyes widened. Since their first embarrassing encounter, she had held her distance from him and he likewise. The trousers were being offered as a token of friendship, he was sure. And he wasn't about to let her father's teasing undermine that first step toward a more amiable relationship.

"I really do need the trousers," he said. "I hate to put you to the bother of sewing for me, but I would be very grateful."

"It's no trouble," she answered quietly. "I'll measure you after breakfast."

"Thank you, Meggie," he said.

Her father and brother's laughter faded away and Meggie nodded solemnly as she turned back to the fire.

Roe turned his attention back to breakfast. Onery began a long-winded story about the winter he'd had to make his own clothes out of hides and nearly got shot by mistake for being a bear. Again and again, Roe found his eyes and his attention returning to Meggie as she padded around the room in her bare feet.

He felt a light tap on his shoulder and turned to Jesse beside him, who was grinning with glee. The young man pulled something long and skinny out of his shirt pocket. At first Roe thought it was a piece of rawhide, but when Jesse lay the thin brown item on the table it twisted and wiggled.

Roe watched as Jesse held a finger to his lips to shush him. Casting a cautious glance toward his sister, Jesse carefully covered the squiggly little worm with Meggie's coffee cup.

They only had to wait a minute before Meggie took her place at the end of the table. Jesse was concentrating on the mush in his tin and Roe decided to do the same. He couldn't quite keep himself from occasional glances toward Meggie, who was listlessly stirring her mush with a makeshift spoon she'd fashioned for herself. Roe was still using hers.

As Roe watched he realized that the expression on Meggie's young face had changed. Slowly the worry and anger had faded from her brow and her visage was pretty and serene. She was obviously a million miles away from the dark, crowded little cabin in the Ozarks. It was a dreamer's expression, far removed from the hard work of everyday mountain life. Roe felt a strange yearning to touch her. But it passed as she raised her eyes to catch him watching her. Immediately, they glanced away, turning their attention back to the food upon the table. There was a strange bond between them that was disconcerting for them both.

When Meggie finally reached for her coffee mug, the worm, released from its prison, squiggled across the oilcloth on the table.

Meggie gasped, spilled her coffee, and jumped from her chair. Beside Roe, Jesse began to giggle cheerfully. Onery joined the chorus with a low, hearty chuckle.

"I hate varmints!" she screamed vehemently.

Gathering her wits about her, Meggie grabbed the unwelcome creature and threw it into the fireplace where the popping and hissing distinctly announced its demise. Scaring Meggie with unexpected small creatures was apparently so common an occurrence that not even a word was said.

But her brother, being cautious, didn't give her the time to get her anger wound up. Jesse jumped from the table and slammed his hat.

"Got to get to them hogs," he said as he hurried out the door.

Onery was chuckling also, but there was no rush to his gait as he left the table.

"You get some butternuts made for this feller of yourn, Meggie-gal. Roe, just take yer time here and mosey on out to help us when yer a mind to."

Meggie was blushing. Roe felt more than a little bit uncomfortable himself. He glanced around the woodbeam room where he was left alone with the daughter of the house.

"Well, let's get it over with," she said hastily as she rose from the table.

"You haven't finished your breakfast," Roe told her.

She shrugged and gathered up her straw sewing basket. "There is no call for you to be lolling around the cabin all day. I'll get your measure and send you on your way."

It sounded like a sensible plan. "Where do you want me to stand?" he asked.

"Here is the light," she said, pointing to the big rectangle of sunshine that shone along the dirt floor in front of the doorway.

Meggie's measure was a long piece of rough cord. When she wrapped it around his waist, Roe raised his arms out of her way. She was very close and Roe closed his eyes to savor the moment. Her scent was sweet and it was woman. A combination that had been absent from Roe's life for what now seemed a very long time. The touch of her hands at his waist was gentle, but sure. And once more he recalled the hot wonder of their illicit kiss. He recalled it with great pleasure.

"Your waist is half a hand narrower than Jesse's," she commented as she marked the spot on the cord by tying a knot in it. "Guess they don't have much good cooking back in the Bay State."

Her attempt at levity was a brave one and Roe wanted to answer with an equally lighthearted statement about the quality of her own cooking, but the words were stuck in his throat. She was close, very close. And he was enjoying it far too much.

"I'm gonna measure your pants leg," she said calmly. She dropped to her knees on the floor in front of him. Her voice was businesslike, but a slight blush crept up her cheek.

Roe looked down at her kneeling at his feet. The top of her head came almost exactly to the top button of his trousers. The dark, honey-blond hair parted so perfectly in the middle and the long hank of braid fell down toward her waist. From this vantage point, his hands would have felt so natural resting upon her shoulders, coaxing and caressing.

"Hold this," she said, placing one end of the cord against his waist just above his hip bone.

Roe did as he was told and then held his breath as she smoothed the cord down the outside of his leg to his ankle. She marked the spot on the cord with her fingernail and then carefully tied the knot. She wasn't hesitant then as she looked up at him.

She rewound a portion of the length of cord. Her cheeks were flushed, but her expression was determined.

"I need to measure your inseam."

Was it his imagination, or could he feel the warmth of her breath against his wool worsteds?

She held up the cord to begin.

He stepped back away from her.

"I've got a better idea," he said.

She sat back on her haunches, waiting.

"I'll take off my trousers and you can measure the pants instead of the man. That will be better don't you think?"

Meggie wanted to tell him that the measuring was nearly over, but she suddenly didn't want to be any closer to him either. She nodded.

"But what will you wear while I measure?" she asked. "You just can't stand around here in your . . . in your . . . well, you have to wear something."

Roe glanced around at the profusion of throws and rugs and for a moment his glance lingered on the tablecloth.

"Maybe I could wait outside," he suggested.

"What if someone were to come by?"

With a shrug, Roe imagined the scene. A Marrying Stone matron coming to visit would find him standing outside half-naked. It wouldn't work.

They stood together for a long moment, considering the possibilities.

"Get into the bed," Meggie told him at last.

"What?"

"Get into Pa's bed, take your pants off under the covers and hand them to me."

Roe glanced toward the sturdy bed. It seemed like a reasonable solution, but he was hesitant.

"It's the only thing to do," Meggie told him. "The only place where it's decent not to have your pants on is in the bed."

Roe reluctantly agreed. He walked over to the bed. While seating himself on the edge to take off his shoes, he glanced up. Meggie was watching him closely as if expecting something. She turned her back at last, but it didn't make the situation seem any less uneasy.

He undid the buttons on his trousers, wiggled out of his worsteds, and climbed into the bed, decently covering himself.

Meggie stood with her back to him, thinking. She didn't know why he'd stepped away from her so quickly. She had kept her expression as stiff as a rock and was sure that she hadn't given away any of the fluttery feeling that she'd felt when she had been forced to touch him.

She hated the unease of having him in the house. Obviously, neither of them was going to be able to forget the kiss that they had shared. But, they couldn't go on living together in such cramped quarters without ever exchanging a word.

"Here they are." She heard his voice behind her.

She turned to find him safely covered in the bed, the red and blue patchwork covering him. He held his britches in his left hand and she hurried over to take them without comment.

The soft, dark wool was warm in her hands as she lay the trousers out upon the table. She smoothed down the trousers, marvelling. The machine-woven fabric was flawless, its colors fast dyed in the cloth, its stitching precise. She'd never seen such material before. She hoped her own homespun butternut would not show up poorly by comparison.

Her mouth tightened. She was doing it again, worrying about what he might think. She shouldn't care. He was a stranger come to the mountain and soon he'd be gone. It shouldn't matter what he thought about them, what he thought about her. But it did.

It took her only a minute to measure the trouser's inside seam. It was nearly the same as Jesse's. Roe Farley might not be as tall as her brother, but his legs were just as long. She glanced over at the one-poster where he watched her in silence. Right now those long legs were naked beneath the bedcovers. She felt the roses blooming in her cheeks once more.

"Let me go ahead and patch up the knee in these," she said.

Roe nodded.

"There is enough cloth in the hem for me to cut you out a good underpiece," she said.

"Thank you," he replied.

Meggie started to sit next to the table. But after only a moment of hesitation, she dragged her chair over near the bed.

Roe watched her carefully, as if she might spring like a tiger.

"You don't have to look so fearful," she told him. "I'm not coming over here to crawl in that bed with you."

"I never thought—"

"I think," she said as she sat down and pulled the sewing into her lap, "that it's time that the two of us had a talk."

Roe cleared his throat rather noisily. "I'm not sure this is the best time."

"I'm not likely to get a better one. You are here in my cabin, I can say whatever I please, and you're not likely to get up and leave or chase me around the room if you don't like what I have to say."

He could hardly argue with that. He watched her as she removed part of the hem and carefully set it into place against the ripped knee. "What is it that you want to say, Miss Best?"

"You can call me Meggie," she said, as she carefully began to surround the patch with tiny stitches that were quick and deft. "You've already done it a time or two, and it's hard to keep up this miss and mister thing when we are here in the same house."

"All right, Meggie. What is it that you want to say?"

Meggie's blue-gray eyes met his brown ones and for a long moment she was speechless. She looked down to the woolen worsted trousers in her lap and continued her stitching. Somehow the activity helped her to get the words out the way that she wanted to say them.

"We need to talk about what happened the other day," she said quietly.

"There is no need," Roe answered as he watched her bright metal sewing needle dart in and out of the fabric that she held.

"There *is* need," she said determinedly. "I can't continue to pretend that you're not here, and you can't keep acting like nothing has happened."

Roe took a deep breath, distinctly uncomfortable. "Miss

Best . . . Meggie, I can only say how much I regret any embarrassment that I might have caused you," he began.

Meggie laughed humorlessly. "And I can only regret any embarrassment that I might have caused myself," she said.

There was silence between them for a long moment. Meggie continued sewing.

"I've always been kind of dreamy," she confessed quietly. "All the folks on the mountain will tell you so. And I have to admit that it's true. I just read those fairy tales so many times, I guess I started to making up fairy tales of my own."

"There is nothing wrong with having imagination," Roe assured her.

She shrugged. "Maybe not. I never thought so anyhow. But when I let my fancies steal into my real life," she shook her head with self-derision, "it sure makes me look awfully foolish and it makes you kindy jittery."

Roe was certainly *jittery* at that moment. He was not the kind of man to allow his physical desires to control him, but he was not unaware of them either.

Meggie looked up at him then. She didn't understand the expression on his face, but it wasn't pity and she was grateful for that.

"I'm not sorry that I kissed you," she said, her chin defiantly high. "I liked it and we both know that already."

"I liked it, too," Roe said quietly.

Meggie blushed as a kind of pride stole in her heart. He'd liked it too. Somehow that made it not quite so bad.

"But I know that you aren't my prince come up the mountain," she said. "You're just a man that's come to listen to our music and document it on that Listening Box."

"Yes."

"So, I won't be throwing myself at you anymore, and I'm not going to be walking on pins around you neither."

"I'd like us to be friends, Meggie," he said.

"I don't know that we can be that," she said. "It seems that friendship and kissing don't mix too well together."

"Perhaps not."

"But, I'm glad that you are Jesse's friend. It seems like you really like him some, and I hope that that's true. Because he likes you and I wouldn't want him to get his feelings hurt."

"Neither would I," Roe answered.

"Good," Meggie said with finality.

There was silence between them then as Meggie continued her sewing. But it was a comfortable silence. The first they had ever shared.

"So," Meggie said. "You and I will just go along the best that we can. Not pretending that it didn't happen, but just making the best of the way things are."

Roe nodded understanding. "Do you do that a lot?"

She made a small sound of shock. "Kiss fellows? Of course I don't!"

"Not that," Roe assured her quickly. "Do you just make the best of the way things are?"

Meggie shrugged and gave a positive tilt to her head as she leaned forward slightly to bite off the thread just above the knot. "That's Ozark ways."

The next morning, clad in his brandnew, homespun butternuts, Roe followed Jesse to the barn where Jesse cut him strips of leather for crossed galluses, a kind of suspenders, for Roe's new trousers. The pants were bulky and unfashionable. But, strangely, Roe felt rather comfortable in the cloth made by Meggie Best's hand. It was smooth and soft. Perhaps much like herself. Dressed this way it was hard to distinguish Roe from any other Ozark farmer.

The morning was already warm and heavy as they started out. The thick green canopy of woods overhead was dripping heavy dew onto the forest duff. As the two men made their way across the clearing Roe could smell the fresh scent of mint and dogwood. Everything looked green and slightly hazy. After nearly losing his spectacles in the wood pile, Roe had carefully stowed them in their tooled nickel case and left them in his shirt pocket most of the time. This caused him to squint more than a little. He could certainly see Jesse perfectly well and of course he could hear him, too.

Today, he was talking rapidly about his favorite subject. Hunting dogs. It was the young man's modest ambition to own his own hound. And although Jesse had never managed to memorize his numbers from one to ten, he seemed very much an authority on redbones, blue ticks, walkers, and Plotts. As Roe knew exactly nothing about the animals, he half listened to Jesse as if the man were speaking a foreign language.

"We could get a dog together," Jesse said. "A tree dog is what we need, no derby or bird hunter for us no ways. I could train her myself. But you could hunt with me."

Roe chuckled. "I don't know anything about hunting."

Jesse gave him a wide-eyed look of disbelief. "You know *everything*," he insisted naively. "You probably just forgot about hunting. But you'll pick it up again when the weather gets cool in the autumn."

"I won't be here in the fall, Jesse. I have to go back to where I come from."

"Why would you want to do that?"

"Because that's where I belong."

The young man considered his words. "You could learn to belong here. Pa was not from here once, but now he is."

Roe smiled at the young man's encouraging welcome, but he shook his head. "No, Jesse, I'll be going back east. It's what I want to do."

Jesse shook his head, clearly puzzled. "What's there that ain't here?"

Culture and music and civilization, Roe thought, glancing at the young man at his side, wishing he knew a better way to explain. He searched his mind for a concept that Jesse could grasp. "Back east, Jesse," he said, "they have privies at every house."

Jesse's eyes widened with appreciation. "At ever' house?"

Roe nodded. "Rich and poor, there are privies in the Bay State enough for all."

Jesse whistled and shook his head in disbelief. "Frien', that is downright amazing."

Roe chuckled and then gazed around at the primitive wilderness that existed on the same continent as his Bay State home.

"Yes, Jesse, it is downright amazing."

The morning's work consisted of rounding up the hogs that lived and lounged at their leisure around the homestead and driving them to the small patch that Onery and Jesse planned to put into corn. There were two big sows, one already heavy with piglets, one big huffing, noisy boar, and three yearling hogs as pesky as puppies, but not nearly as appealing. The pigs were a lazy and uninterested group. But Roe found himself surprisingly deft at the task. Still Jesse was much better. With one small stick and some loud encouragement, he shortly had the squealing swine headed in the proper direction.

The cantankerous creatures attempted to escape more than once, especially during the noisy, splashing moments when they forced the uncooperative hogs across the cold, rushing stream.

"This is our cornfield," Jesse told him proudly as they reached the small plot of cleared land on the far side of the creek.

Roe looked up and down the stubby undergrown hillside. It was far from level land, but appeared to be the flattest piece of ground Roe had seen on the Best farm.

"If it's your cornfield, why are you letting the pigs in it?"

"To hog it down," Jesse answered, as if that explained everything.

Shortly, Roe got the idea as he watched the snorty swine rooting up the leftover corn and early weeds that plagued the field.

"It feeds them and it makes it easier to plow," Roe commented.

The pigs, however, didn't know a good thing when they had it. Off and on throughout the morning a hog would attempt to wander off. Jesse had no trouble handling that problem. With a loud call and a flick of his stick, the errant animal would be back where he belonged in no time.

At midday the two men took to the shade of a big chestnut tree up on the rise. The blaze of sun streamed down through the hugh branches in dappled patterns across the ground on which they rested. They couldn't see the hogs from this resting place, but they could still hear the noisy rooting and grunting from over the hill.

For Roe it was with a curious sense of well-being that he rested from the morning's hard work. Peace and good humor had settled upon him like a cloak. He didn't understand if it was this place or Jesse and his family that made Roe feel so comfortable. He had always struggled to fit in wherever he was doing his work. Strangely, here in these desolate mountains it didn't seem much of a struggle.

The men joked together as they searched their respective lunch buckets to see if there was anything that Meggie had packed that might be remotely edible. Jesse found a greasy, half-burnt pork chop. Roe's meat was a jaw of jerked venison.

Jesse laughed. "Don't be thinking she was trying to short you," he told Roe. "That venison will taste a dang sight better than this old cold pork chop."

"At least we've both got gravy," Roe said.

Jesse nodded. "Yep, but it's just poor-do."

Roe and Jesse shared. In Roe's bucket there was an ample

supply of Meggie's special corn pone, hard and crispy on the outside, still half-raw in the middle. Jesse had a whole jar of last year's pickled okra, but it was overcooked and rather slimy. Hunger, however, could overcome a finicky palate and the two ate heartily.

"If a feller had a good dog and a steady hand," Jesse said, "he can make a fair living in these hills."

"It would be a pretty hard living," Roe commented.

"How so?"

"Well, it must get very cold here in winter. And the crops surely don't grow well on these hillsides."

The young man shrugged. "Pa says life ain't meant to be easy," he answered. "If it just ain't miserable you've got a lot."

Roe grinned at Onery's homespun philosophy. "I suppose there is truth to that," he admitted.

The two ate quietly together for several minutes, then, his mouth half full and a gob of jelly hanging off the side of his lip, Jesse spoke up again. "Meggie likes you, you know."

Roe raised an eyebrow in surprise at the abrupt change of subject. The ease of tension between them had been abrupt and obvious. Of course Jesse would be expected to notice.

"Your sister is just being polite."

"Oh, I don't think when it comes to fellers, Meggie cares much about being polite. You two just got started off wrong."

The memory of Meggie's passionate kiss gave Roe momentary pause. *Wrong* wasn't exactly the word he was thinking of.

"Meggie, she don't live with the world all the time," Jesse explained with quiet seriousness.

Roe nodded, hoping Jesse would continue.

"She's kindy dreamy and such," Jesse continued. "Folks make too much of it sometime. But I just don't take no mind."

"I have no criticism of your sister, Jesse. And being dreamy is not something I see as a great fault."

"She just got riled at you 'cause you kissed her. She gets riled at me pretty frequent, too," Jesse said.

"It's not the same thing."

"Near enough. And what I do is just tease her out of it. She can get high up on her horse, but I just kid her down to a Missouri mule and she likes me fine for it. I bet she'd like you for it, too."

Roe smiled at the open, guileless young man. He wondered about Meggie Best.

By late afternoon Jesse pronounced the field sufficiently rooted for the plow. Roe, using his own stick, helped herd the now overfed hogs back across Itchy Creek to the homestead yard. Jesse was singing an old Ozark ballad in rhythm with his swings of the hickory switch.

> "Lord Lovel he stood at his castle gate,
>   A-combing his milk-white steed,
>   When along came Lady Nancy Bell,
>   A-wishing her lover Godspeed, speed, speed."

Roe listened with pleasure as the familiar but strangely new words and tune of the song once popular in the time of Charles II were sung from memory by a simpleminded Ozark farm boy. This is why he had come to this primitive place. This is the kind of music and history that was his mission to save. This was the music that would prove his premise was true.

Silently he cursed his lack of paper and pen, but he would get Jesse to sing the song to him later when he could record it on the Ediphone. Nearly every evening Onery and Jesse would sing and play for him. But he was anxious to begin collecting songs from the rest of the community. He could barely wait for next week's Literary where he hoped to interest enough of the local people that the volume of his collection would multiply rapidly.

When the hogs began to recognize the terrain, they took off.

"They can find their own way to the house from here," Jesse told Roe. "By evening they'll all be laying in their usual spots."

As the two men approached the cabin, Jesse began to chuckle, pointing to the lines of freshly washed homespun clothing that hung upon the lines behind the barn.

"It's Wednesday washday," Jesse said.

For the life of him, Roe couldn't see what was humorous about that.

Jesse turned and walked a short way back into the woods. He knelt down on the forest floor and began pawing through the duff. Roe followed and stopped to watch him curiously.

"What are you looking for?"

Chuckling, the young man shrugged. "Oh, just whatever curious, slimy critter I can find," he answered.

Roe eyed him.

An excited fluttering occurred in the leaves Jesse had disturbed. Roe startled slightly as a small creature scurried out. Jesse managed in several tries and quick jerky movements to catch the little frightened creature. When he finally caught it, only a long blue tail flicked wildly from the bottom of his clasped hands.

"What is it?" Roe asked.

"It's a baby skink," he answered. "You want to see?"

Roe dutifully looked at the wiggly little lizard, not more than three inches long, and shook his head.

"What in the world are you going to do with that?"

Jesse only grinned as he carefully stowed the creature in his shirt pocket and secured the button. "Just follow me, frien'. We're going to have the best laugh of the day."

Sensing immediately that the skink and the laugh would somehow involve Meggie, Roe tried to get out of it. His arguments were shushed, however, as Jesse put a finger to his lips to indicate silence. Quietly following, Roe heard Meggie Best before he saw her. She was singing. And to Roe's well-trained ear, she was not particularly good at it. He might do well to have Jesse sing into the Ediphone, but he decided then and there that Meggie Best's voice would likely melt the cylinders.

As the two approached the back of the work shed, Roe could hear splashing. Apparently she was still washing clothes. Roe tried once more to ask a question. But again, Jesse cautioned him to silence. Slipping off his work boots, the young blond man climbed upon the back of the low-roofed building and motioned Roe to follow behind him. It seemed useless to try to argue. Joylessly, Roe removed his own shoes and shimmied up the roof behind Jesse.

Near the point of the pitch, Jesse gently began to wiggle a loose cedar shake from the roof. His eyes sparkled with mischief and Roe found himself grinning, too. Obviously, the plan was to drop the squiggly skink onto his sister Meggie as she worked. It was a childish prank, very much beneath Roe's dignity. But Jesse took such pleasure in these antics, he wasn't about to put a shade on his sunlight.

When Jesse got the roof open, he only hesitated a moment to grin delightedly at Roe before dropping the skink down the hole.

Roe heard the tiny splash of water, followed by a scream that could have awakened the dead as far away as New Orleans.

"Varmint!"

Jesse howled with laughter and then waving Roe to follow him, he began scurrying down the roof to make his getaway. Inside the shed, splashing and screaming were still going on. Before Roe could leave, he simply couldn't resist one look at Meggie Best attempting to kill the skink in her washpail. Grinning, Roe scooted up to the loosened shake.

He retrieved his spectacles from his shirt pocket and perched them upon his nose before peering down into the shed below him. His eyes widened.

Meggie Best was not washing clothes, she was washing herself. Standing in the round wooden washtub, Roe watched as she bent over to scoop the soaked lizard out of her bathwater. As the skink darted for the safety and anonymity of the shed's shadows, Roe was frozen with disbelief, staring at the young woman's pale, naked backside.

"Jesse Best! I'm going to murder you once and for all," she hollered as she gazed above her in the direction in which the unwelcome critter had made its entrance. When her blue-gray eyes made contact with Roe's brown ones her moment of anger became as highly charged as summer lightning and the intensity of recognition between them was almost tangible.

They stared at each other in utter silence for the longest moment, then with a wordless plea of horror, Meggie covered her bosom with her arms and dropped down into the soapy water in the tub in such haste that half of the contents sloshed out over the side. Roe jerked himself away from his peephole so quickly that he lost his footing on the cedar shakes and rolled off the roof, landing with an audible huff in the tall grass at the back of the shed.

Nothing was said for the rest of the day about Jesse's little practical joke or Roe's part in it. Hobbling slightly, Roe had apologized and made a diplomatic retreat to the woods. By evening, Meggie was holding her chin so high a good rain might have drowned her. And every time Roe caught her eye, her color brightened considerably. Roe kept his own profile suitably low. Over and over the memory of her wet and naked plagued him. He felt guilty. He was a gentleman of good breeding and he had behaved badly.

Jesse kept whatever his thoughts might be to himself.

Only Onery appeared able to see the humor in the day's events.

"I believe, Meggie-gal, you've 'bout turned the corner in this courtin' business."

If her father had been a chicken, Meggie might have gladly wrung his neck. As it was, she simply held her peace with difficulty and kept her eyes focused on the beans in her plate.

"You two boys best lay out in the morning to get back on that roof and fix all those shakes you broke loose," Onery said.

Jesse nodded without enthusiasm.

"We'll get to work on it first thing," Roe told him.

Onery gave him a long, lazy smile. "That's right good, right good. 'Cause I know you wouldn't be keen on no other fellers seeing the make of your prospected gal without so much as her josie for coverage."

Jesse giggled with delight.

Roe choked on his coffee.

Meggie looked slightly ill.

And Onery simply howled with laughter.

CHAPTER

SIX

MEGGIE'S GARDEN ROWS were not exactly straight. But after the night she'd spent, it was a wonder that she'd managed to get them dug at all. Tossing and turning on her pallet until dawn had not made the events of yesterday any less clear in her mind. And her reaction to them was more confused than ever.

Across the barnyard, she could hear Jesse and Roe on the shed roof. Every loudly hammered blow delivered to the cedar shakes was a vivid reminder to her of Roe Farley staring down from the ceiling at her naked body. Why hadn't she screamed? Why hadn't she jumped? Why hadn't she done something besides stand mesmerized as Roe Farley looked at her?

Meggie was a modest person. Yesterday's lack of it was notable. She had stood naked before a man for a minute at least. And she knew, with all honesty, that it wasn't merely shock that had held her immobile. There had been desire. And there had been pride, too.

Blushing with dismay at her own conclusion, Meggie slammed the hoe more forcefully in the ground and drew a long steady trough in the soil.

Her body was young and strong and sufficiently feminine. Meggie had not contrived to allow Roe Farley to see her, but she was somehow pleased that he had.

Swallowing with tremulous confusion, Meggie's thoughts were spinning. She propped the hoe against the wooden washtub that, overturned, served as a sorting table for her seeds. And with shaking hands she began to wrap up the remainder of her seeds into squares of coarse sacking cloth.

She struggled to keep her mind upon her work. Cultivating the little plot of ground was difficult but important. The produce she grew here would provide the only variation from the family's diet of bread and meat. The garden itself was nearly a quarter acre, surrounded by a four-foot picket fence. The fence was no protection from birds, moles, and gophers, but it kept the hogs from routing it and was some deterrent to rabbits and squirrels. Every bit of food would be needed next winter. For that reason alone, Meggie saw fit to scold herself for her wandering thoughts.

Her life had always been this way: a battle between her dreamy nature and the burden of her responsibilities. Her father's occasional bouts with the pain in his bad leg and Jesse's simple mind dictated that, from childhood, Meggie Best take charge of her family's welfare. While her heart had been *playing* house with a cornshuck doll, her reality was *keeping* house for her father and brother. And getting food to grow in this little garden patch was essential to that.

Most of the earliest plants were already in the ground, but she always kept enough seeds for a second planting if this one washed out or died. Carefully she stowed them in a clean burlap pouch, hoping that she would never need them.

Now all that was left was to get the rest of the numerous rows of potatoes into the soil. Raising her chin with determination, Meggie vowed to get them planted today. She would not allow the unsettling events of yesterday or her dreamy nature to deter her.

Slapping her hands together was not merely a gesture to shake off the dust from the garden, but to free herself from the thoughts of Roe Farley. The man was a stranger. A stranger she didn't really even like. Certainly he was kind to

Jesse, and her father found him interesting. But, she had no cause to waste so much as one minute of her time thinking about him.

With that firmly in mind, she reached for the sack of seed potatoes. Unfortunately still distracted by the sound of hammering, Meggie picked it up from the wrong end. Big half-moldy tubers spilled all over the ground.

"Dad-burn and blast!" she swore with vexation. Once again her dreamy mind was elsewhere and she'd made a mess.

"Roe Farley!" she whispered under her breath. Then honesty compelled her to admit to herself that the scholar from the Bay State had not spilled the potatoes, she had.

With a sigh of resignation she began picking them up, grateful that it was tubers she'd spilled and not the seeds.

Once a semblance of order was restored, Meggie gave full attention to her task. She cut the potatoes into pieces, making sure that each piece had at least two or three eyes on it. When she had enough to fill her apron, she walked to the far end of the tilled row. She dropped the pieces a few inches apart into the little trough of dirt. As she moved slowly forward, she used her steps to cover each potato piece with soil as she walked.

She did manage to plant almost one complete row before her thoughts again strayed. And once more the direction they traveled was to the wash shed roof.

Meggie had thought much about love in her life, but little about sex. Even the word was somehow foreign to her. Her fairy tales were full of romance. And romance instilled her with passion. Her scant knowledge of the actual acts of passion had left her with the impression that what men and women do together was embarrassing at best, at worst distasteful.

Meggie had been so wrapped up in her images of princes and fairy tales, she had never felt the slightest twinge of sensual desire.

But she had felt it yesterday. Stopping abruptly in the potato row, Meggie laid one hand upon the butterflies that had formed in her stomach. She felt it today.

It was enticing to allow herself to slip into this new dimension. To dream not only of a prince to love her, but one who excited her and desired her. Once more she saw Roe's eyes widening behind the dark rims of his spectacles and she sighed aloud.

Determinedly, she pushed the feelings of desire away. Roe Farley was not her prince. That he had seen her and liked what he'd seen was unfortunate. It would be more unfortunate for Meggie if she allowed herself to mistake for even a minute that carnal need with the romantic love that she wanted.

She finished her row and began to cut up potatoes once more. Roe Farley was not her prince. He had not come to this mountain for her. And when he left she was not going to be leaving with him. Whether he desired her was not important. And if she desired him, well it would bode well if she put such thoughts away from him this very minute.

Resolutely, she admonished herself to keep her mind as pure as her deeds and her attention on the needs of her garden.

She might have been able to do that, for a few minutes at least, if that infernal hammering wasn't so distracting.

Because of the necessity of fixing the shed roof, Jesse and Roe got a late start for the cornfield the next day.

By the time they arrived, the sloe-eyed black mule didn't even twitch an ear with interest. Roe felt just as lazy.

It was a glorious day, the sky was as blue as midsummer and big puffs of cotton-white clouds lazed high above. In the clearing of the field the melancholy call of a meadowlark blended with the soft, sweet sound of the wood thrush. Roe stopped in place to appreciate the fine music of the birds and the whirring of grasshoppers in the tall grass. How could he have thought of this place as silent?

The warmth of the sunshine brought tiny beads of sweat to his brow. He liked working outside, he decided. The realization surprised him. Perhaps when he returned to Cambridge he'd try to find a small house with a little garden. He could use some of the knowledge he was acquiring here in the Ozarks.

A broad grin lightened his expression. If he was going to use some of his new knowledge, he more likely should keep hogs and chickens! That would certainly give the city matrons a cause for concern.

He shook his head with good humor. He did think he might try his hand at gardening. It was a shame for the seasons to come and go without touching nature occasionally.

"Can you plow a furrow?" Jesse asked him.

The question brought Roe back to the task of the moment. He shrugged. "How hard can it be?"

Jesse turned his head and gave the hillside a long, thoughtful look. "It can be purty hard."

With a smile and a comforting pat on the shoulder, Roe reassured him. "I may not be from around here, Jesse. I know I'm just a city fellow, but I'm getting toughened up a bit, I think. See my hands." Roe held them out for inspection and Jesse did solemnly take note of the tough hardwork callouses that had begun to form. "And I'm very smart," Roe assured him. "A smart man can outthink his labors and make them easier."

Jesse nodded hopefully, but his expression said that he didn't understand. "I know you're smarter than folks 'round here. I ain't smart a'tal. I figure we kindy even things out."

Roe grinned at him. "Maybe you're right." Roe slapped the young man companionably on the back. To his surprise, Jesse hugged him warmly for a long moment. The affectionate movement surprised Roe and made him uncomfortable. Hugging was not something that was a part of J. Monroe Farley's life. Gentlemen did not hug each other. Roe couldn't remember a time when someone had hugged him.

His back stiffened slightly at the contact. But he did not want to hurt the feelings of the gentle young man. Bravely, Roe stood the contact as if it were a traveling dentist chiseling out one of his teeth. He even managed a half-smile when he was released.

"I'm glad yore my frien', Roe," Jesse said.

His answer was a polite nod.

Carefully checking the mule harness and the plow blade, Jesse Best appeared not simple, but competent and knowledgeable. Roe felt a sense of inexplicable pride in his friend as he watched the meticulous preparations for the fieldwork. The unwanted hug Roe had momentarily endured suddenly seemed less a torture to overcome and more a token of brotherhood and friendship. This simpleminded backwoods cracker from the Ozarks *was* his friend. He could never have imagined this being true a week or two earlier.

"Let's get to plowing," Jesse said with genuine pleasure.

Roe nodded.

Gloved and shod, the two young men commenced their labors. The ground was uneven and peppered with more than a few hidden rocks. Jesse set Roe to inspecting the field. Systematically he walked every square foot of the ground awaiting the plow, carefully clearing it of any unhappy surprises that the plow blade might unearth. The sun beat down on his back and the day was progressing from mildly warm to downright hot, but he didn't even think to complain.

Whistling a tune that Roe vaguely recognized as "I'm a Good Ole Rebel," Jesse led the plow-harnessed mule to near the middle of the field.

"Why are you starting there?" Roe asked as he followed the young man curiously.

Confused, Jesse looked down at the ground and then at the mule before he shrugged. "This is where I always start," he said. "This is where Pa showed me to start."

Roe shook his head. "Well, that doesn't make sense, Jesse. You should start at the edge and go to the edge."

Jesse gazed at one edge of the field and then at the other. His brow furrowed in concentration. "That ain't right," he said.

"Of course it's right," Roe told him, smiling. "It makes perfect sense. Starting in the middle doesn't make any sense at all."

Jesse bit his lip nervously as again he surveyed the field. "We got to start right here, Roe. I know we do."

Roe sighed and shook his head. "Now, Jesse, you just told me yourself that I was smarter than folks around here. And I told you that a smart man can make light work of his labors. You do believe that, don't you?"

Jesse nodded solemnly.

"Then you've got to trust me when I tell you that the place to begin is at the beginning, not in the middle."

To Roe's horror, tears welled up in Jesse's bright blue eyes. "We got to start right here," he insisted. "This is where Pa taught me to start and it's the way I know."

Alarmed at the young man's emotion, Roe voluntarily touched his shoulder in an uncertain attempt to comfort him. "It's all right, Jesse. Don't cry," he said.

"I ain't crying," the young man insisted through his tears. "I'm too big to cry."

Roe nodded as he passed Jesse his handkerchief. "Forget I even brought it up," Roe told him. "We can start plowing right here."

"No, no," Jesse answered, sniffling. "You're lots smarter than me and if you think it should be a different way, then we'll do it that way."

"It doesn't matter, Jesse," Roe said. "I don't want to upset you."

Jesse swallowed and looked around the field. Roe could see him struggling with his thoughts, trying to put them in a coherent order. "It takes me a long time to learn things," he told Roe finally. "When I learn 'em, I try to hold on real tight. It's kindy scary for me to try to unlearn 'em."

Roe nodded. "But, don't you feel great when you learn something new?"

Jesse nodded a little hesitantly. He gazed at the field once more solemnly, then managed to smile at Roe. "Where do you want to start the plowing, my frien'?" he said finally.

Following Roe's directives, Jesse led the mule to the far left corner of the field and made ready to set the plow in the ground.

"You're facing the wrong way," Roe said.

"Huh?"

"You're facing the wrong way. It will be a lot easier to plow up and down on the hillside than crossways."

Jesse looked confused and slightly scared all over again. "We always plow crossways," he said. "Ever' farmer on the mountain plows crossways."

Roe waved away his concern. "Just because everyone on this mountain does it that way, doesn't make it right. Plowing crossways on a hill like this is much harder. You have to stand crooked all day long."

Jesse nodded. "That's why they call plowing work."

"But, if you plow up and down the hill, you can stand straight up and every other furrow, the down furrows, will be much easier with the help of gravity."

"Who's grab-ba-dee?"

"It's a force that . . . well, it's what makes it easier to run downhill than up."

Nodding as if he understood, he stared at the field once more with worry. "You sure this is the best way?"

"Absolutely."

With his friend's certainty in mind, Jesse turned the mule to face up the hill.

*   *   *

Meggie tossed the thread-wrapped shuttle hand-to-hand through the multitude of cotton and linen lines that made up the weaving harness. Forcefully she tromped the first treadle, lifting the threads across the warp. Passing the shuttle back once more, she tromped the second treadle which raised the second harness of threads that had laid low before. After another throw of the shuttle, she pulled the batten toward her with a firm jerk. In this methodical, rhythmic pattern she, Meggie Best, created the cloth that was worn by herself, her father, and her brother. And now by Roe Farley. She did it with the ease of familiarity, but her mind was not on weaving.

She hummed quietly to herself as in her imagination she spun and twirled across the dance floor in the arms of a handsome prince. She was beautiful, of course. Her dark blonde hair had magically turned the color of the palest cornsilk and was twirled on top of her head in a braided coronet entwined with blue ribbons. Her dress was blue also. Not the blue that she could make by soaking homespun cloth in cedar tops and wild flag petals. But a real, dyed blue, like the bolts of fabric in Phillips' Store. Soft, shiny blue that would never fade to gray even if it was washed a dozen Wednesdays. The dress had a wide skirt reaching clear to the floor and yards of material belled about her with circular hoops. The tiny stitches in the seams and facings were flat-felled in thread of pure gold, and the yoke was so heavily embroidered it looked like a dozen gold necklaces graced her bosom. On her feet were shoes, the like of which she'd never seen before. They looked, at first glance, to be doe-skin dancing slippers, but on closer observation they were made of real glass and felt as light and comfortable on her feet as if she wore no shoes at all.

Meggie sighed languidly as again she continued to pass the shuttle through the harnesses and tromp the treadles. Her quill of yarn was almost finished and she turned to the huge broomgrass basket at her side to fetch another.

Again and again the handsome prince spun her around the dance floor. When the movements called for a moment of closeness, he would whisper sweetness in her ear.

"You are beautiful, my sweet Meggie," he would say. His voice was low and rich, and his speech was that of the learned and cultured. "My lonely life has been one long, rainy day until you, like the sun, shined upon it."

Meggie sighed again and looked up into the handsome visage of her own sweet prince. He was tall and strong, but in a courtly way, not beefy and muscled as a man used to farm work. His eyes were warm acorn brown, his hair was black as birch bark, his broad, welcoming smile was as white and gleaming as blossoms in the clover. He was so handsome. He was so perfect. He was J. Monroe Farley.

"Dad-burn and blast!"

Meggie came to reality in a single flash. Both from the disconcertment of having Farley invade her daydream, and from the huge mess she had managed to snarl into the loom. Her inept gardening had taken the whole morning and now that she was finally free to work at the loom, the image of Roe Farley followed her here.

Slowly and painstakingly she pulled out the threads of the new woof which were miswoven and lumpy, as she silently cursed the city man. Why in heaven was it her bad luck that the most princely man to ever set foot in the Ozarks would have to show up at her family's cabin? She blushed vividly at the memory of his face above her peeking down through the roof of the shed.

"Why, I was jaybird naked, and he hadn't even the decency to look away!" she complained out loud.

Still, through her self-righteous indignation shimmered a certain immodest thrill at the sound of the words. He'd got an eyeful of her and had promptly fallen off the roof for it.

Was that what Granny Piggott spoke of when she talked

of knocking a man off his feet? A little satisfied smile curved Meggie's lips.

Then, fortunately, the practical side of her mind took a turn at ruminating. She reminded herself that J. Monroe Farley was no more interested in her than a snake in a stump. She'd shared talk with Eda and Polly and Mavis and other girls on the mountain. Just because a man wanted a woman, didn't mean he wanted to marry her. And Farley had made it more than clear that he liked kissing her, but he surely didn't want to marry Meggie.

Certainly she wasn't the first woman to make a fool of herself over a man. But, most women didn't have to be reminded of it on a daily basis.

What must he think of her boldness yesterday? Certainly he thought her reaction to be shock. But what if she slipped again? What if she let him see that he could make her heart flop over like a wormy hog with only the slightest word of kindness? It was the biggest humiliation of all to be rejected by a man and still want him.

Meggie finally managed to work out the errant threads in the loom. She ran her hand assessingly along the completed part of the pale linsey-woolsey. It was not truly linsey-woolsey, of course. There wasn't a sheep within miles of the Best place. Meggie blended her flax with cool, lighter cotton. Still folks called it linsey-woolsey. Linsey-cottony sounded foolish and besides it was hard to say. But looking at the length of it, she decided that despite her inattention and mistakes, it was going to be a good piece of cloth. She set the shuttle through again.

The narrow, dark weaving shed was warm in the afternoon sun. Even with the door open to the breeze, beads of perspiration gathered at her forehead and the fringed homespun collar of the work dress clung damply to her neck. Most women left weaving for the dark days of winter. But Meggie weaved year-round, whenever she had a spare moment.

She loved weaving. Its rhythmic routine movements allowed her to enjoy the solitude, giving her imagination free rein to explore whatever strange and frivolous paths it might choose to take. Once the loom was threaded, the rest was simple. Occasionally, of course, she made mistakes. But unlike in cooking, on the loom mistakes could always be fixed or lived with. And sometimes they gave a piece of cloth its character. The Best cabin was filled with covers and quilts, curtains and rugs. And there was always fabric for clothes. Unlike cooking, she never had to throw a length of fabric to the hogs.

As she reset the threads on the warp Meggie thought about herself and her dreamy nature. It was not a trait common to her family or, for that matter, anyone on the mountain. At times she thought that perhaps the same unsettled humor that left her brother dim-witted flowed in her mind also, just with less severity; although Granny Piggott insisted that Jesse's simplicity was not something carried in the blood, but was caused by having the cord wrapped around his neck when he was born.

"Came into the world near hanged," Granny had said.

Beulah Winsloe said that God had tried to strangle the child to rid the devils from his nature, born out of wedlock like he was.

Granny Piggott had disagreed. "It's 'cause his mama raised her hands above her head when she was carrying him. Everybody knows that each time you reach for something overhead, you twirl the cord around the baby's neck."

Meggie didn't know who was right, but whatever troubles had weakened her brother's mind, she suffered in some way with her own.

How else would she have been so eager to make a fool of herself about Roe Farley?

Not that Farley was bad. He was, Meggie believed, truly Jesse's friend. And although her brother was well loved by her father and herself, everybody needed a friend. Just the

thought of Jesse's childlike eagerness for acceptance made
Meggie worry. Jesse was so innocent, so sweet, even when
he was up to some no-good prank there wasn't a smidgen of
evil in him. He was always looking for the good in people
and finding it. That's probably why Monroe Farley looked
so good to her. Because Jesse just brought out the best in
him.

That was all it was, she assured herself. Farley was no
prince or hero. He was simply a fast-talking city man that
had the good fortune to meet up with her brother.

Meggie gave herself a slight nod of self-approval and a
mission of determination. She suspected he might want her
body, but he'd made it clear that he didn't want her. The
sooner she got that straight in her mind, the better. She
wasn't under any illusions. She was not some kind of silly
scatterbrain.

As she watched the shuttle speed through the threads, her
cheeks reddened. *Scatterbrain* was exactly the word that
Granny Piggott called her. And most of the women on the
mountain said the same, though most had the good sense to
say it behind her back.

She did have trouble keeping her mind to daily life. And,
truth to tell, the mundane routine of daily life was forgotten
completely when she'd kissed Roe Farley.

It wasn't her first kiss, of course. Abner McNees had
kissed her at a Sunday picnic when she was only fourteen.
Lots of other fellows had tried since then. All last winter
Paisley Winsloe had called on her, and he'd even declared
his intention for her in front of Pa. But she was not too
scatterbrained to know she wanted no part of Paisley
Winsloe.

No matter how firmly Meggie had told him she wasn't
interested, he'd trudged through the cold and snow to sit in
the cabin with them after supper nearly every night.

The last night he came, Jesse was sniffling with a cold
and had gone up in the loft early. After a quarter of an hour

of boring farm talk, Pa was snoring in his chair, so Paisley had made his move.

When he came toward her she ran away, but he followed. He grabbed her, pushed her against the wall, and held her there while he smeared his warm, damp lips all over her face. He said that he loved her. He said that he wanted to wed her. When he finally let go, she slapped him so hard the noise woke Pa up.

Paisley left that evening and hadn't darkened their door since. When she saw him at church or gatherings, he barely nodded. Good riddance was Meggie's reaction. Paisley Winsloe was nobody's prince.

But if Meggie had been angry at him, she was furious with Pa.

"How could you just go to sleep like that and leave me unprotected!"

Onery merely chuckled. "I walked my tail off yesterday hunting that rascally bear," he claimed. "Besides, it was time for that mangy Winsloe bull calf to make his move on ye or get out of the pasture."

"He forced me to kiss him!" Meggie scolded. "If you'd been doing your duty as a father that wouldn't have happened."

"Meggie-gal, I'm being the only father I know how to be. I'm trying to let you find your own way in the world, just like my father did for me."

"I am never going to find my own way if some crazed hornet like Paisley Winsloe drags me off into the bushes."

Pa had actually chuckled at that. "I don't expect that you'd be going easy."

Meggie was mad enough to spit, but her father's next words consoled her somewhat.

"You're like your mama, you know. You're gonna do exactly what you've a mind to and all the rules and reasons and papas in the world ain't gonna stop that. It'd be like telling the river not to run over the rocks."

Meggie had felt a fleeting moment of pride. Mama had been the most sensible, strong-minded woman Marrying Stone Mountain had ever seen. She'd died of the pneumony when Meggie was only six, but Meggie knew most of her mama's story, or the "scandal" as some called it.

Onery Best had come to town, a liquor loving itinerant fiddler, just passing through. Her mama, in blossom of her prettiness at seventeen, had taken to the good-looking fiddling man right off.

Meggie didn't know much about what had happened between them that summer, but she did know that by the next winter, after Fiddlin' Onery was long gone, Mama's belly had swelled up like a mule eating baneberries.

Her Uncle Jess threw her mama out of his house. He had a low toleration for sinning of any sort. Young, pregnant, Posie Piggott had lived in an old barn up on the mountain for several weeks before Granny Piggott had taken her in.

Just before the spring thaw she had given birth to Jesse. When Onery returned to take up where he left off, he found himself with a ready-made family. Surprisingly he had been more delighted than dismayed, but Meggie's mother would have nothing to do with him.

"I ain't going to be the sometime wife of a traveling man," was the way Pa told it. "My boy ain't right in the head," she said. "He's gonna need a man by his side all day long for the rest of his days. If you ain't a-fixin' to be that man, then you'd best move along so I can find another."

Pa had not been dissuaded so easily. Uncle Jess had sold him this plot of rocky upland for a pittance, and Onery had taken to working it. Although farming was something he was never really very good at, he did try and his efforts were eventually rewarded.

During the harvesttime Posie Piggott had finally agreed to marry up. And the two had pledged themselves at the large, white Marrying Stone as soon as the winter stores were in.

Plenty of folks on the mountain thought less of Mrs.

Onery Best for her past. But Meggie admired her tenacity and bravery, and she'd always considered comparisons with her mother to be wonderful. In the same situation, Meggie hoped that rather than crying and grieving and throwing herself in the big river to drown—which was the expected solution to unwed motherhood on the mountain—she would also be as brave and determined as her mother had been. But of course, she reminded herself she wouldn't go looking for that kind of trouble.

Up to now Meggie had spent her days "swimming close to the willows," never venturing even near to sinful wickedness or breaking the rules of society. Resisting Paisley Winsloe and the other randy fellows on the mountain had been as easy as chewing apple butter.

Immediately the memory of Roe Farley's soft, sweet lips, his warm open mouth, and the enticing masculine smell of his thick black hair overcame her. She'd finally met with temptation. She set the shuttle down and placed a trembling hand against her heart as if to hold it inside so it wouldn't fly away. Roe Farley's kisses were not the kind that a woman could forget easily. But forget them she would. That strange city man was not to be her handsome prince and if she forgot that for one minute, he'd likely leave her big-bellied and ruined at the end of summer.

And unlike Onery Best, it was quite clear that J. Monroe Farley would never return.

FROM THE JOURNAL OF
J. MONROE FARLEY

April 28, 1902
Marrying Stone, Arkansas

Plowed the Best family's cornfield today. I actually enjoyed myself and was glad to make it easier on young Jesse, by teaching him a new way to plow. Of course, I realize that my education and good fortune all put me in great stead, but I never realized that I would intuitively have the knowledge to make subsistence farming easier for these backwoodsmen.

Have heard several interesting songs of Celtic origin and hope to have an opportunity to record them onto the cylinders very soon. I have also decided to start listing in this journal interesting words that I have come across here that may be of Middle English origin, a logical expansion of my work here. Young Jesse used the verb villified *this afternoon in terms of speaking ill of the local farmers. The use of such an undisputable Middle English term adds much credence to my premise. This morning I helped repair a cedar shake roof.*

CHAPTER

SEVEN

THE DAY'S WORK finished, Roe had found a nice quiet spot under a shade tree to sit and write in his journal. He had not kept it up with his usual enthusiasm. Since his school days writing down his work, his thoughts, and his progress had been a daily habit. He enjoyed seeing a blank page of paper and filling it with the words and thoughts he had no one else to tell.

The Ozark journal was even more important, since after all it was the chronology of his work and ultimately a vital piece of evidence to be presented to the fellowship committee. The ancient songs needed not only to be recorded and their lyrics written down, but their origin, their local history, and his impression of them were important to establishing authenticity. But strangely, despite sufficient time, Roe had found himself less and less eager to rush to the quiet aloneness of his own written word. More and more he simply spoke what he thought or observed to Jesse or Onery or exchanged wisecracks with Meggie. And those things that he couldn't say to them, he found he could not write on paper either.

As he pondered this strange mood in himself, he was distracted by the sound of a heated quarrel coming from the cabin. Although etiquette dictated that a guest should ignore any disagreements among family members, Roe found himself hurrying to his feet and taking off at a dead run toward the little homestead that he had somehow become a part of.

He clearly heard Onery's angry yelling long before he even reached the house. It had been a long, hot, sweaty day and he knew the old farmer was unlikely to work up much of a fury when he was tired and worn down. Obviously there was something very wrong and somehow Roe had a premonition that it concerned him.

Perhaps it was the lingering uneasiness he'd felt over plowing. He'd discovered that by starting at the edge of the cornfield, you couldn't turn the mule without leaving the field and tearing up the trees and cover around it. Roe had begun to suspect that maybe there had been some sense to Jesse's early insistence that the plowing shouldn't start at the logical point of entry to the field. But he had quelled his concerns. He was right; he was sure he was right. Jesse did things by tradition and memory. Roe did things by science. Science was always superior, he was sure.

As Roe stepped through the cabin doorway, he clearly heard Onery's angry words for the first time.

"Damnit, Jesse! I learn you and learn you and you do a thing right for ten years. Then up one morning you get a wild hair and do things all wrong as if what little sense you had just left you completely!"

Jesse stood before his father, head bowed, eyes downcast as he blinked back tears of shame and humiliation and endured his father's scolding.

"Your mind don't work right and we all know that. But that ain't no excuse for such plain foolishness as this. I done taught you better and if you cain't pull your share and do your work on this farm, then you're just a burden on the rest of us and we'd do well to just get shed of you completely. A man who cain't carry his own weight in this world is like a mule gone lame, completely worthless and beneath contempt."

Roe was frozen into silence.

Noticing his presence, Jesse glanced up at him for one quick minute. It was only a glance, but it was enough to see those bright blue eyes were red-rimmed and swimming with tears.

"Plowing up and down hill!" Onery continued. "I never heared of anything so dad-blamed stupid in my whole life. That whole field'll have to be replowed tomorrow morning. And we'll be damned lucky if it don't rain tonight and wash what decent topsoil is left up there right down the mountainside."

"I'm sorry, Pa," Jesse whispered.

"Sorry! That you are," his father snarled back. "Lord Almighty, Jesse. It ain't like we got a fine piece of corn bottom that we can just toss some seed near it and wait for the stalks to pop up. This is rocky, poor-yielding hillside ground and if we don't coddle it and nurse it along like a helpless baby, it's going to starve us out for sure."

"Yes, Pa," Jesse whispered.

"You're my son and I love ye. But I cain't let you starve us with your ignorant foolishness," Onery declared. "We're going to the woodshed. There's a board in there that might knock some sense into you."

Roe stepped aside as the two men passed him and went out the doorway, neither meeting his eyes. He stood mutely horrified. A strange silence lingered after they had gone and Roe turned his attention to the only other occupant of the room.

"My God, what is your father so angry about?"

Meggie looked up from the blackberries she was cleaning. Her cheeks were tear-stained but her blue-gray eyes met his directly. "You heard enough to know. The field was plowed wrong."

Roe nodded. "Yes, I understand that. But why is Onery so

furious? Why did he say such awful things to Jesse? I know the poor fellow is simple, but there's no ill will in him. How can Onery talk like that to him, to talk of getting rid of him? He's going to beat Jesse?"

Meggie looked up at Roe. Her jaw was set tightly, but not so much in anger as frustration.

"Pa loves Jesse. He loves him more than you could ever understand. It's because he loves Jesse that he has to make him do right and be right."

Meggie's eyes filled again with tears and she stood and went to the hearth to stoke the fire, clearly unwilling to let him see her cry.

"Don't fret about it. Pa won't hurt him all that much and it has to be done."

"*It* has to be done!" Roe flung her words back to her in anger. "*What* has to be done? The boy is simpleminded and he made a mistake. I don't think that demands a beating."

"Well, what you think, Roe Farley, don't matter much now does it?" Meggie's reply was brisk. Then, like a balloon deflating, she sighed. "You just don't understand, Roe," she said, turning away from him again. "Pa and I won't always be here for Jesse." She stirred the ashes in the grate listlessly. "At least we can't be sure that we will. We've got to make sure *now* that Jesse can fend for himself and make himself useful among whatever folks is living on this mountain. He can't be allowed to make foolish mistakes. Foolish mistakes cost food and some winters there just isn't enough for everybody. If folks see Jesse eating, but not producing victuals, it'd be like he was a raccoon or an old bear that was getting into their stores. They'd run him off or kill him for it."

Roe stood silently, stunned. The concept behind her words was medieval, but he couldn't simply consider the idea as another fanciful academic curiosity. This world of the Ozarks was a primitive place where danger and death lurked around every corner. People here were forced to behave differently from those in the brick-paved streets of the Bay State.

But still, it was difficult to fathom that such vehemence and anger could be part of a father's love.

Roe thought of his own father and the times, now so far away, when he'd stood before his desk in the chestnut-paneled library. His father had never been angry. Never. He had looked dispassionately at Roe over the top of his spectacles and observed him as if he were a piece of property that he was thinking to buy. Roe had never felt his father's anger and had certainly never felt his father's hand. But, then again, perhaps he had never felt his father's love either.

Lost in his own thought, Roe was startled when Meggie suddenly touched his shirt to draw his attention. Her blue-gray eyes were grave with worry, but her tone was soft.

"Pa won't hurt him," she said.

"It was my idea." Roe felt a rush of guilt in his confession.

Meggie nodded. "I figured as much," she said. "Jesse didn't so much as lay a smidgen of blame at your feet, but I know he wouldn't have gotten such a fool notion as this on his own."

Roe looked at her.

"You're right, Meggie," he answered quietly. "For me to think I could advise Jesse about farming *was* a fool 'notion.'"

"Still, you mustn't blame yourself," she said. "Jesse just has to learn, and one of the things that he has to learn is that he must trust what he knows is right, even when somebody tells him different."

Roe nodded. "Yes, he needs to learn that. And I should learn to trust him when he knows more about something than I do."

Without another word, Roe stepped out of the cabin. His

steps were determined and resolute. He was still angry, but now he was angry with himself.

He had been puffed up with himself and boastful. He'd read, he'd studied, he'd researched. But when it came to the lessons of life, he really knew next to nothing. Practical tasks had always been left to lesser folks than himself. Lesser folks like Jesse Best.

A loud sound cracked through the evening stillness of the clearing. Roe's eyes widened in shock.

"My God," he whispered under his breath.

He made it to the woodshed quickly. But not quick enough to stop the second blow. The shed door was wide open and Roe could clearly see the tableau inside. Jesse, his eyes dry now and his expression stoic, was bent over and supporting his weight on the crossbar of an old sawbuck. Onery stood behind him, his face a mask of pain as he raised the long green hickory limb he held in his hand and prepared to deliver another blow.

"Stop!"

Both men turned to face Roe, disconcerted by the interruption of a clearly distasteful task.

"You'd best go back to the house, Roe," Onery said quietly. "This ain't no concern of yours."

"But it is," Roe insisted. "You don't know the truth about what happened today, Onery."

"I told him right," Jesse interrupted.

"You lied to him."

"I didn't."

"Jesse, I know you did. We are friends, remember. Friends don't lie to each other."

The young man swallowed hard and stared silently at the dirt floor at his feet. "I won't lie no more, Roe. But I cain't say nothing against you neither."

Roe felt a strange lightness in his chest. No one had ever sacrificed anything for him before. Roe turned to face Onery.

"Jesse wanted to plow the field the right way, sir," he said with deference. "I talked him into what we did. I thought I knew better than he. But it appears that I don't know anything at all."

Onery nodded solemnly. Roe saw a new aspect to the old man's gaze. He recognized it as respect. "I thought as much," he said. "Although my boy didn't so much as even mention your name."

"You should know he wouldn't," Roe answered. "He's an honorable man."

"Yes," Onery agreed. "I suspect he is."

"Then you can see that he shouldn't be punished."

At that Onery raised an eyebrow and then shook his head. "Jesse's got to learn to do things right. Even when there is temptation not to. Wanting to please a man he likes and respects can be as dangerous a temptation as that snake in the Garden of Eden."

"Mr. Best, please!" Roe said. "It was my fault. I admitted that. Don't hit Jesse anymore."

The gray-bearded man looked over at him but didn't comply. "I've got to keep my word," he said simply. "I promised him five and five he's going to get."

Onery turned away from Roe.

"Wait!"

Stopping once more, Onery gave Roe an exasperated glance.

"He's got three more to go," the old man insisted.

Roe nodded. "Then let me take them."

Both men looked at him in shock.

"You promised him five," Roe said firmly. "Five it should be, but rightly most of those should be mine."

"Roe, no—" Jesse began.

Looking at the tall, broad-shouldered young man in plain homespun clothes, Roe smiled. "You know I deserve it," he said to Jesse. "Friends tell each other the truth and the truth is those licks belong to me. I can't have my *friend* taking them for me."

Onery looked at Roe thoughtfully, then at his own son. "I don't go around whipping strangers and visitors to the mountain."

Roe nodded in agreement. "But I'm not like a stranger. You've promised to help me with my work and let me stay here like one of the family. If I'm not to be treated like one of the family, I can't accept your hospitality."

"You don't have to take my licks, Roe," Jesse said with big, imploring eyes. "I don't mind 'em so much."

"They aren't your licks, Jesse. They are mine and I don't want you to take them for me."

For a long moment Onery and Roe stared at each other assessingly. Finally the old man nodded.

"I suspect you are right about that. It ain't quite the thing to see another man punished when you are as guilty as him." Onery nodded brusquely to his son. "Move along now, Jesse. It's Roe's turn."

His eyes wide with disbelief and admiration, Jesse moved to stand in the doorway next to Roe. Clasping hands, the two young men exchanged one brief moment of camaraderie before Roe took his place.

"Bend over and grab the sawbuck," Onery directed.

Roe did as he was bid, feeling a strange mixture of elation at having won the battle of words and humiliation at the ignominious position he found himself in.

He heard the faint whistle of green hickory through the air only an instant before the switch landed with considerable force against the seat of his trousers.

"Yeow!" Roe straightened immediately and turned to the man behind him. "That hurts!" he told Onery.

From the doorway of the shed came a little giggle. Roe turned to see Jesse's big silly grin. "It's supposed to hurt," he told Roe. "But you're not supposed to yell."

As the sting on his backside lessened, Roe could almost

see the humor in the situation. "I'm not supposed to yell?"

Jesse shook his head. "No. It ain't manly. Ain't you never took a dose of hickory limb oil before?"

Roe shook his head. "This is my first time."

Jesse nodded gravely. "Well, think real hard about not yelling out or making any noise and it takes your mind off the pain some."

"You don't have to do this," Onery said quietly beside him.

Roe nodded firmly. "Yes, I do."

Bending once more over the sawbuck, Roe dug his fingernails into the soft pine and willed himself to take the next blow in what Jesse would consider a more manly fashion. He secretly hoped that the old man would stint on the delivery, but the second blow was laid across his backside with the same force as the first. Roe clenched his jaw and ground his teeth, but he managed not to yell out. The third blow came almost immediately, before Roe had even a chance to catch his breath and a slight moan escaped through his lips. But apparently it wasn't too noticeable because when he stood up, Jesse was beside him, smiling and eager with praise.

"You did real good," he told Roe generously. "The first time Pa switched me, why I cried for half a day for sure."

Jesse's smile was so warm and so full of admiration, Roe found he could almost ignore the sharply stinging stripes on his backside.

"We're going down to the crick," Jesse told his father.

Onery nodded. "Don't you fellers be too late. I'll have Meggie set some supper in the warming bin for you."

Roe followed Jesse outside and they headed down the wooded path to the creek. The young man was laughing excitedly and talking about their shared punishment. Walking behind him, Roe listened with amused interest.

Taking those licks was exactly the thing to do. He felt a strange sense of pride in his actions. Still, he couldn't help but wish that they had made less of an impression upon him. When they reached the wide flat place where they usually fetched water, Jesse turned upstream. Roe followed him up the narrow snaky creek bank for nearly a half a mile.

The scratchy cadence of crickets portended the lateness of the day. The riffling and babbling of the little mountain creek beside him was surprisingly loud in the gray light of the evening. The air was alive with flying and buzzing creatures. And Roe watched with pleasure as the lightning bugs glowed in mixed concert across the creek and in the woods.

A big brown river rock jutted out into a wide place in the stream. A couple of inches of cool, clear white water flowed rapidly across the rock. Jesse stopped and began undoing his overalls.

"What in the world are you doing?"

The young man smiled at him. "Ain't nothing like an ice-cold mountain stream to take the fire out of hickory."

A few minutes later both men were naked and lolling out on the river rock, laughing and talking and sharing the beauty of the clear summer night, their stripes cooling in the crisp, clear water.

The moon was high in the sky before the two returned to the cabin. Onery was snoring in his bed and Meggie lay silently in her pallet on the floor as Jesse and Roe retrieved their supper tins from the small square warming oven built above the firebox.

Tiptoeing, the two went back outside to eat on the porch. There was a quiet companionship between the two men who, in the last hours, had become equal partners for the first time. The cool waters that had eased their pain and forged their companionship now chilled them in the evening breeze and spurred their appetites. Meggie Best's plain beans with fat back had never tasted better.

"Jesse, are you all right?"

The words came from the doorway and both men turned

to see Meggie standing there. She was bundled up in a thin cotton wrapper over her josie, her long hair hung loose down her back, nearly to her waist. Her blue-grey eyes were drooping with sleepiness.

"I'm as right as rain," Jesse answered, his voice a whisper in concession to his snoring father. He looked over in pride at the man beside him. "Roe took three, I only got two."

Meggie stepped out onto the porch. "I know," she said. "Pa told me."

She looked over at Roe, her expression free of its usual wariness. "I thank you very much, Mr. Farley." Her voice was soft and sincere.

"Don't be too nice to me, Meggie. I ain't sick," Roe answered, mimicking Onery's heavily accented words and the little Ozark joke he often used.

Meggie giggled, delighted.

Roe felt a strange lightness in his head. In the silvery moonlight, Meggie Best looked like an angel. Her sweet-spoken words had a gentleness that was both innocent and enticing. And tonight, to Roe's eyes, she was beautiful. Her long hair glistened and fell in loose attractive waves down her back and across her bosom. Those shiny curls lured a man's hand to reach up and touch them. Her amply curved figure was finely displayed in the soft, oft-washed home-spun cotton. And Eve in the Garden of Eden couldn't have managed more womanly allure.

Roe felt a tightening in his groin and an expansion in his heart as he looked at her. Neither feeling was especially welcome. He hadn't completely forgotten his startling view of the naked Meggie Best. Or her overenthusiastic kissing. But he had no business thinking those kinds of thoughts about a woman he hardly knew and to whom he had no intentions at all.

"He's just fooling with ye, Meggie," Jesse said with a happy giggle that echoed across the barnyard in the stillness of the night. He scooted over, leaving a broad empty space between himself and Roe. "Sit down with us, Meggie. It's as pretty a night as you can see on the mountain and the lightning bugs are twinkling all over the place."

She waited a long moment, giving Roe a hesitant glance before seating herself on the worn wooden slats between the two men.

Roe attempted to ignore her. Resting his arms upon his knees and studying the ground before him, he determinedly sought to cool the sensual warmth of the sight of Meggie Best in the evening.

But focusing his attention on the chicken-scratched yard in front of the house, and the big brown chunk of sandstone that was used as the porch step, also brought Meggie Best's long, narrow bare feet, pale in the moonlight, into his line of sight.

The scent of her surrounded him also. It wasn't the heavy, seductive fragrance of women of questionable repute. Nor was it the smugly sweet scent of lavender or rose water favored by Bay State debutantes. It was the natural, clean odor of plain brown soap and the barest whiff of fresh baked bread, the blackberries she'd been cleaning, and wood smoke from the fire. She was close, desirably close, and the warmth of her nearness in the crisp darkness of the evening lulled Roe into an unexpected sigh of contentment.

Jesse smiled. "You like it here, don't ye?"

Catching his wandering thoughts before they ran further adrift, Roe nodded, pretending that it was only the beauty of the Ozark night that held him spellbound.

Still avoiding eye contact with Meggie, he gazed off into the distance to a hill beyond these he knew. It showed up as only the barest outline in the evening sky.

"Is your home in the Bay State like this?" Jesse asked.

Roe was momentarily startled by the question.

"Like this?" The raw, primitive country around him was not at all what he would call home.

"No, it's very different."

"But it's pretty, too?" Jesse asked.

Roe shrugged thoughtfully. "I suppose so. I never really gave much consideration to it. Yes, I suppose in its way it is just as pretty as here."

Jesse grinned and turned to Meggie. "And Roe says back east they is privies near everyone. You don't ever need to poot without one."

"Jesse! Your language." Meggie flushed with embarrassment and hid her face in her hands.

Roe cleared his throat uneasily.

Jesse's brow furrowed. "Meggie, you've heard me say that plenty of times."

Roe couldn't hold it back any longer. His body began to shake with the humor he could no longer suppress.

"Roe's laughing," Jesse announced. "Roe's laughing."

He did laugh then, loudly and from deep inside himself. Chokingly, he indicated an apology to Meggie. "The two of us will just have to watch what we say around Jesse, here. He seems compelled to repeat what we least want overheard."

Meggie smiled shyly. It was a friendly moment. The most friendly the two had ever shared.

"If back east is your home," Jesse continued, "then I'm sure I'd like it. I like anything my friend likes."

"Maybe sometime you can go there," Roe said.

Shaking his head, Jesse disagreed. "No I cain't never," he said. "I'm safe here where folks knows me. I cain't never wander to some strange place."

"It wouldn't be a strange place," Roe said. "It would be my home. And if I were with you, you would be with folks that know you."

Jesse grinned. "You're a good frien', Roe. But I ain't ne'er going nowheres 'til I go to heaven."

Roe opened his mouth to speak, to tell Jesse that he wasn't bound to this mountain, but free to see the world as he might choose. But then he remembered the wrongly plowed cornfield. The Bests had made life safe for Jesse on the mountain. Tempting him to travel to far-off places was wrong and possibly dangerous. Fortunately, Meggie changed the subject, allowing the introspective moment to pass.

"Well, tell us what it's like," she said. "Tell us about this Bay State."

Roe turned to Meggie to find she and Jesse both staring at him curiously. He was thoughtful for a long moment. He didn't really know the Bay State. He knew Cambridge. And Cambridge was merely Cambridge. The things he knew most about it were the college, the library, the homes of his family and friends, the parks he had occasionally roamed in, the schools he had attended, and the stores where he had spent his money. Home was simply where he'd lived, where people that he knew lived, and he'd hardly given it more than a thought before.

"Well," he said. "It's big. And there are lots of people."

The two blank faces on the porch beside him seemed unimpressed. "I mean that it is *very* big and a *tremendous* number of people live there. It's so big that those people can't get from one side of town to the other by walking. There are cable cars that run on tracks day and night and take all those people from one side of the city to another."

"Why are they going to the other side of the city?" Jesse asked.

Roe shrugged. "To visit friends or go to their jobs, or maybe just to see what's on the other side of the town."

Jesse nodded. "I did that once. I walked all the way down the mountain to Plum's Ford just to see what was down there."

Meggie looked surprised. "What is down there?"

"Nothing worth seeing," Jesse answered.

"There is plenty worth seeing in Cambridge," Roe continued. "There are houses as big as churches. And churches with pipe organs as big as your cabin."

Jesse and Meggie both giggled with delight.

"For true?" Jesse asked.

Roe nodded. "I've seen them myself."

Jesse shook his head in disbelief. "I bet you can hear a big pipe organ like that all over the mountain."

"There are no mountains," Roe said.

"No mountains?"

Roe shook his head. "There are a few little hills, some higher-up places, but no real mountains, nothing like these."

Jesse nodded solemnly. Meggie's expression was worried.

"Must be pretty flat if there's no mountains a'tal."

Roe nodded. "Yes, I guess that it is. There's a river, though, and it's not very far from Boston, where the harbor meets the Atlantic Ocean. The ocean is bigger than any river in the world."

"I heard the Mississippi River is a mile wide," Meggie said.

"That's true, it's a mile wide in places," Roe answered.

"How wide's a mile?" Jesse asked his sister.

Meggie thought for a long moment. "It's about from here to the Sumac Falls on the good trail."

Jesse whistled with appreciation. "A water that wide? Seems kindy impossible. And this ocean place is wider than that?"

"Much wider." Roe nodded. "It is hard to imagine if you've never seen it. But it's the truth."

A silence lingered among the three as they all contemplated the marvel of the big river.

"Do ye catch a lot of fish there?" Jesse asked.

Roe shrugged. "I guess people do."

"But *you* don't?" The question was Meggie's.

"I've never been fishing."

"You've never been fishing?" Jesse was clearly shocked.

"No, I can't say that I ever have."

A wide, joyous grin spread across Jesse's face. "I been

fishing lots of times, couple of days nearly ever' week when the crick's not froze. I'll take you fishing tomorrow."

"Not tomorrow," Meggie corrected him hastily.

"But, Meggie, he ain't never—"

"Oh, no you don't. If he hasn't been fishing for his whole life another couple of days aren't going to matter. You two have got to replow that cornfield tomorrow. And if you don't get it done early, Pa won't let us go to the Literary."

Jesse nodded gravely. "And you'll be fit to be tied if you don't get to go do some gossiping at the Literary."

"It has nothing to do with gossiping," Meggie insisted. "It's merely catching up with friends. Roe needs to go to the Literary. Pa said that's how he'll do his work."

"It's not work, Meggie," Jesse answered. "It's a *fellowship*. That means gathering up a passel of old songs."

Roe laughed. "That's exactly what I mean to do," he said. "And you're right, it isn't work. I'm not fond of work very much at all."

Jesse chuckled in agreement. "There ain't too many of us that is."

"And I want to hear you play the fiddle again, too," Roe said.

Jesse seemed to be looking at something in the dirt beside him. Then his expression turned guarded as if he were hiding something.

"Shoot, you can hear me play most anytime," Jesse said.

"There are lots of things to do and see at the Literary," Meggie explained. "They have debates and recitation and kangaroo courts. The womenfolk all bring victuals and we share dinner together."

Jesse laughed. "It's the only time Pa and I eat good all month."

Meggie cried with feigned fury and punched her brother solidly in the arm. Jesse moaned as if she'd truly injured him.

"It sounds like almost a party," Roe said.

"It is something like a party," Meggie agreed. "But it's more serious, I suppose."

Jesse nodded. "It's kind of like if you crossed a hoedown with a Sunday service, you'd get a Literary."

Roe laughed at Jesse's description. "I'm sure that I'll find plenty to like about it," he said.

"For a certainty," Jesse told him. "I like it all, pretty much. The thing I like most about the Literary is the gals."

"Gals?" Roe asked with surprise.

"Yep," Jesse insisted. "Lots of pretty gals come to the Literary."

"Is that so?" Roe asked with exaggerated interest as he shot Meggie a teasing glance.

"Yep, lots of pretty gals. And lots of not so pretty ones come, too, of course. But I don't mind that much. They all smell good. At least mostly."

Roe laughed out loud.

Meggie didn't share his humor.

"Jesse Best, that is just about enough of this kind of talk. Daylight comes mighty early in the morning." Her voice was stern.

"Don't come no earlier than usual" was Jesse's answer.

Meggie might have said something more, but Jesse leaned over toward her and dropped something in her direction. "Did you lose this?" he asked.

With horror Meggie stared at the slimy brown slug that landed on her bare foot.

"Varmint!" she screamed, jumping to her feet and hopping around frantically until the creature fell back to the ground.

"Jesse Best!"

Her brother was roaring with laughter. Roe couldn't help but join him.

"Don't you ever do that again!" she said. "Don't you ever."

"Stop yer yelling, Meggie, you'll wake Pa."

"Promise me, Jesse Best, promise me right now that you'll stop teasing me with these awful varmints."

"Meggie—" he whined.

"Promise."

Jesse sighed reluctantly. "All right I promise."

Roe cleared his throat, deliberately swallowing his own laughter and stifling his grin. "Well, I suppose that we'd better get ourselves to bed, Jesse. We do have quite a busy day planned for tomorrow. We're going to be plowing that cornfield nearly all day and then spending the evening seeing all those pretty gals."

"Oh!" Meggie rose to her feet in a huff and stormed back into the house to the privacy of her pallet.

Roe and Jesse grinned at each other in conspiracy.

CHAPTER

EIGHT

THE LITERARY ON Marrying Stone Mountain was held on the new moon Friday, spring thaw through to the first bad weather of autumn, at the schoolhouse. For the Best family it was a two-hour trek walking the ridges. No one, however, complained. Jesse hooked the mule up to the skid: a low, narrow wagon bed on runners. Onery, favoring his bad leg, was seated inside. His clean, much mended overalls were as neat as he could manage and a bright choke rag necktie was knotted hastily around his throat. He made room on the narrow skid for a big black pot of venison stew and Roe's Ediphone Listening Box.

They were to take turns riding the mule. But when Jesse gave his turn to Meggie, Roe felt obliged to do likewise.

Jesse was slicked up brighter than a new penny. His homespun cotton shirt was sun-bleached to milky white and Meggie had carefully pressed the wrinkles out with a heated fireplace stone. His prize fiddle was carefully wrapped in bunting and carried in a tow sack that he slung over his shoulder.

Meggie's dress was plain homespun blue. It was faded now from many washings but still retained enough of the faint original color to bring out the blueness of her eyes. The style was deceptively simple, form-fitting only in the bodice, but it emphasized the youthful uplifted curve of her bosom and the narrowness of her waist, without drawing attention to the ample roundness of her derriere.

"Meggie looks pretty, don't she," Jesse said quietly to Roe.

He nodded. She was pretty in a simple country way. He had always thought so. And after catching sight of her in her bath, he knew it was true. He pushed that vision from his mind. Meggie Best was a kind, hardworking young woman with a bright mind and a vivid imagination. She also had a kiss that was sweeter than wild honey and a passionate side to her nature that could cause him to tremble.

Realizing how inappropriate his reactions to her were, Roe did his *best* to put Meggie completely out of his mind. He was a guest of this family, and should do nothing to take advantage of their hospitality.

"I guess Meggie will be one of the pretty gals we will see tonight," Roe said finally.

Jesse nodded and laughed. "Yep, she's mighty pretty, but she's my sister so I don't never say that to her or nothing."

Roe grinned.

By the time they pulled up in the clearing, the place was already packed. Jesse had hardly tied the mule to a tree when a gaggle of young women came running up to hug Meggie and talk all at once.

They were all dressed in either homespun cotton or store-bought calico, but clearly each and every one of them had prettied up to the very best of her abilities. Crocheted collars and bright satin ribbons were in abundance. Yet most, like Meggie, wore no shoes.

"Althea McNees is getting married!" was the excited news the girls had to deliver.

Meggie screamed with delight. "Who? Who's she to wed?"

The girls looked at each other.

"Paisley Winsloe's declared for her," Eda Piggott said finally.

"I know he was calling on you last winter," Polly Trace said quietly. "But I never heard you say you cared for him."

"Because I don't," Meggie answered, smiling. "But I hope he and Althea are plenty happy together. She's sweet, kindy quiet, but I always liked her."

The young women accepted this statement with complete assurance of its accuracy and the entire group would have run off together to leave the unloading to the menfolks if Eda Piggott hadn't caught sight of Roe Farley.

The young woman's bright brown eyes widened in appreciation and she smiled. Without so much as a word to the other girls, Eda stepped away from the group and approached Jesse.

"Evening, Simple Jess," she said with a quiet warmth that was simultaneously innocent and alluring. "Who's this fellow you got with you?"

Her brown eyes made a quick assessment from Roe's head to his toes. Clearly she liked what she saw.

"Hello, Miss Eda. This here is Roe. He's my frien'," Jesse answered with boastful pride.

His reply disconcerted Eda. Her face fell and she looked more closely at Roe as if to spot an expected weakness in his mind.

"It's a pleasure to meet you, Miss Eda," Roe said, bowing formally over the young lady's hand. "I'm a visitor to this mountain. And, as Jesse said, I'm his friend."

"Are you—? You're not—?" Eda couldn't quite get her question out.

She was saved by the arrival of the entire gaggle. Meggie, her chin held haughtily high, did the introduction. "This is Mr. J. Monroe Farley who is visiting with us for the summer," she announced to the young ladies. "He's a scholar collecting songs and he has a machine that listens and repeats what you sing or say."

"For truth?" a redheaded girl asked. "I never heard of such a thing."

Surrounded by the group of mountain beauties, Roe explained, as best he could, the purpose and the performance of his work.

When the group, at Meggie's insistence, finally left to find Althea McNees and congratulate her, Roe chuckled. "No matter where you are or what are the circumstances, women are all the same."

Jesse nodded. "Yep. They all smell good."

"Yes, I guess that is so."

"That Eda Piggott she smells better than most, but she most times don't come close enough to speak to me."

Roe agreed. "Yes, I suspected she was rather shallow."

"Shallow?" Jesse asked. "Like in the river?"

Grinning, Roe nodded. "Yes, I guess so."

Jesse was thoughtful for a moment. "Oh, I see. A shallow woman is like a shallow place in the river. A man is not likely to find much of value there."

Roe clapped his friend on the back proudly.

The two men made their way up to the crowd gathered at a raised place on the hill between the poled pine schoolhouse cabin and the tiny native stone church at the summit.

The church had been built by the two families to first settle on the mountain of the Marrying Stone, the Piggotts and the McNeeses. The late-afternoon sun cast shadows over most of the ground, but the church itself shone with bright golden highlights that disguised the faded whitewash on the pointed clapboard steeple.

The innocent-looking steeple had caused a long-standing feud in the community. Twenty years earlier it was decided that a real church needed a real church bell. The Piggott family had agreed to build a bell tower. The McNees brothers were charged with going down the mountain to find a proper church bell. And they had.

Spending the church's entire cash savings, they'd bought

an enormous brass bell from a near-empty Catholic monastery near Calico Rock. Hauling the huge piece of molded metal up the mountain had been a monumental task. The proud young men had been expecting the congregation's grateful thanks. But it hadn't worked out that way.

The bell was clearly too large and heavy for the flimsy tower built by the Piggotts. The McNees family wanted a new steeple. The Piggotts wanted the giant bell carted back down the mountain and traded for one of more reasonable size. It was typical of the Marrying Stone congregation that now, nearly twenty years later, the tiny steeple still rose over the large stone church and the huge brass bell sat on a small rock platform near the church's front door.

As Roe circulated among the menfolk gathered on the rise, Onery introduced him to all sizes and asundry of men named Piggott and McNees as well as in-laws, cousins, and shirttail kin of all descriptions. Roe attempted to talk about his project and ask about the local songs, but Onery interrupted him so frequently and changed the subject with such precision, he finally realized that maybe bringing up the subject on the first day of his introduction was not the best idea.

Following Onery's direction, Roe met and shook hands and shared pleasantries with man after man.

Buell Phillips, the storekeeper, was the leader of the small community. Although clearly Buell was more certain about his position as leader than any of the men he tried to lead. He kept his gangly young adolescent son, Oather, beside him. The boy was generally ill at ease among the menfolk and he spoke with gravity and feigned maturity; Roe wished he could simply instruct the fellow to go find his friends and have some fun.

Phillips was part of the Piggott family as was the tobacco-spitting Pigg Broody. The old man's streaked gray beard hung down nearly to the middle of his chest. His eyes were rheumy and glazed, but Roe thought he had a pretty lucid vision of the people and politics of his little community. He also had a wry humor that Roe could appreciate. And his way of talking was punctuated by amazingly propelled spits of tobacco and flourished with some of the most raw curse words that Roe had ever heard uttered.

Pastor Jay, the very aged and bent old man who tended this mountain flock, appeared not to notice Pigg's raucous speech. But then, the old preacher may not have noticed anything at all. Three different times he asked Roe who he was. And still, before the old man wandered off he told Roe that he "recognized him as one of Gid Weston's boys" and to "tell Gid that the preacher had asked about him."

Tom McNees was the undisputed head of the McNees portion of the Marrying Stone community. A rangy bachelor of middle years, Tom was a deep thinker and a thoughtful speaker. Not so his brother-in-law, Orv Winsloe, who seemed to say out loud whatever foolish, ignorant thought passed across his brain. Apparently the only thing that Tom and Orv had in common was Beulah Winsloe, Tom's sister and Orv's wife. Without even meeting Mrs. Winsloe, Roe was quite certain who ruled the roost at the rugged little farm that the three shared.

After nearly three quarters of an hour of meeting the menfolk and listening to their problems (coons in the corn crib) and successes (shot that thieving panther that was holed up near the summit), Roe found himself relaxing with these men as if they were simply more underclassmen at school.

As they talked, the women set up the meal on the plain pine planks laid between the sawbucks on the near-level place at the far side of the school, until the planks were groaning from the weight of the supper fare. The menfolk were called to eat first. Roe followed Onery and made his way along the impressive spread of food as the ladies smiled at him and served him their cooking.

After his bad experience with Meggie's piccalilli, Roe

was a little hesitant to try anything that he didn't recognize, but the ladies eagerly piled his plate high with local delicacies. Discretion being the better part of valor, Roe moved away from the general crowd with the hope that he would be able to throw away some of the less promising items on his plate without insulting any of the local cooks.

He found a seat near the foot of a hickory tree. Almost immediately he was joined by a lighthearted and grinning Jesse.

"Where did you run off to?" Roe asked as his friend took a seat beside him. His plate was even fuller than Roe's and a huge chunk of light bread covered the whole of it.

"I don't like standing 'round talking with the menfolks," Jesse admitted. "I walked around smelling the gals while I had a chance."

Roe grinned. "You mean you won't have a chance later?"

Jesse pinched off a big piece of bread and scooped up a large bite of one of the offerings upon his plate. He held it up to Roe for him to look at. "These is fried ramps and new potatoes," he said. "Nearly the best eating on the mountain and I suspect the gals'll be eating it same as us."

"So?"

"So they ain't no other smell as pungent as ramps. By the end of supper, me and you and every other soul on this mountain gonna smell like wild onion."

Meggie was uneasy yet she couldn't put her finger on why. It certainly wasn't because Paisley Winsloe had decided to marry up. But she worried that if she seemed unhappy or concerned, everyone would think so. She was genuinely happy for Althea, although it was difficult to imagine the soft-spoken, quiet young girl with a blundering, loud bragger like Paisley Winsloe.

She suspected that the cause of her uneasiness more likely might be Roe Farley. She had hoped that her girlfriends would have the good sense to ignore the handsome stranger. Unfortunately, her hopes were not to be realized.

"Ain't he just the slickest-looking feller you ever seen?" Mavis Phillips asked, pretending to swoon. Her dramatic gesture was ruined by the pile of red corkscrew curls that fell into her eyes.

Polly Trace giggled. "I cain't believe he's been staying out at your place, Meggie, and you didn't have the decency to warn your friends to wear our good dresses."

"Oh, go on, Polly," Alba Pease chuckled. "These *are* our good dresses and you know it as well as the rest of us."

Polly laughed along with her and the two young women hugged each other companionably.

"Well, I would have let you know," Meggie told them. "But the way I heard it, Polly, if a fellow isn't Newt Weston he just isn't interesting at all."

Polly blushed a fiery red. The diminutive, flaxen-haired blonde had been wearing her heart on her sleeve for the younger Weston boy for over a year.

"Mercy sakes alive!" Mavis Phillips exclaimed. "That fine-looking Mr. Farley could make every man on the mountain look about as appealing as old Pigg Broody."

Alba feigned a gasp of shock. "And all this time we thought you were saving yourself with the hope of becoming Pigg's missus," she teased.

The girls laughed uproariously as Mavis raised her hand in a pretense of threatened violence.

"Well, you girls just get your minds right off that new fellow," Eda Piggott declared. "He's just not meant for the likes of you."

"Eda's right," Meggie agreed. "He's not just city-bred and scholarly, he's rich, too. He's got a boodle bag of money big enough to choke a horse."

"How do you know that?" Polly asked.

"He offered to pay me cash money for his meals."

"Someone was willing to *pay* to eat your cooking?"

Alba's tone was facetious in disbelief. "He must have been nearly starved to death!"

Meggie took the jibe good-naturedly. "I guess it's just more evidence of how ill-suited he'd be as a mountain husband."

"Meggie's absolutely right," Eda said. "If any of you are thinking sweet about him, you'd best just stop it right here and now."

Meggie nodded.

"Because the truth is," Eda continued, "I'm the only one among us who could even have a chance with the fellow and I intend to have him."

"Oh!" the young gaggle of girls cried in unison.

Meggie's mouth dropped open in shock and she stared at Eda in disbelief.

"What are you talking about?"

"I'm talking about staking my claim," Eda answered calmly. "I just want it understood here and now that I've got my eye on that Farley fellow and I don't want a one of you intruding on my quarry."

"That's the most foolish thing you've ever said in your life, Eda Piggott," Meggie declared.

Eda deliberately raised her chin and looked down her nose at Meggie. Her heart-shaped face and perfect complexion were only exceeded by her vanity. "I don't know why. You never get nothing in this world if you don't go after what you want. And I've decided that I want this fellow. I don't know why you're taking such a tone about it. I've spoke first," she said. "Unless you think you got a prior claim, Meggie."

A strange feeling welled up inside Meggie. It was almost as if the hairs on her back had raised like a mad cat and her fingernails had magically turned to claws. Involuntarily she recalled those first magic moments when she thought Roe to be the long-awaited prince from her fairy-tale book. She felt again the sweet warmth of his mouth on her own. And suffered once more the thrill, shock, and shame of embarrassment of Roe catching her at bath in her all togethers. J. Monroe Farley might not be her prince, but he wasn't going to be Eda's either!

"You don't need my permission to make a fool of yourself, Eda Piggott," she said tartly. "Mr. Farley is a city man, a real honest-to-God city man. He's just here to study us and study our music. He's looking us Ozarkers over like we was some strange breed of critter he's never seen before. He's not nearly about to settle down and marry here."

Meggie shrugged. "If you want to set your cap for him, you'd best be prepared to be taken for a fool. The whole mountain will be laughing at you when he leaves here before the first snow."

Eda's face turned red but she was not about to be cowed so easily. Her bright brown eyes were sparkling with anger and she was primed and ready to give Meggie more than a little piece of her mind.

Her response was interrupted by the ringing of the call to order bell. With their attention distracted, Mavis, Polly, and Alba quickly stepped in between the two angry young women and hurried them up to the area in front of the schoolhouse where the evening's entertainment was about to begin. Deliberately, Meggie forced her thoughts away from Eda Piggott's foolishness. She was not about to let her silly friend ruin the Friday Literary for her.

Buell Phillips, attired in his snowy dress shirt and a pair of fancy-tooled leather suspenders, took his place at the top of the schoolhouse steps. He continued to toll the bell up and down until the group was appropriately hushed and closely assembled on the slope. He set the bell back in its box next to the door and looked across the crowd with paternal approval for one long moment before he spoke.

"It's time, my dear friends and neighbors, for the Marrying Stone Mountain Literary Evening Debate," Phillips announced to the crowd. "Tonight our topic is the following."

Holding a piece of brown paper some distance from his face, he squinted almost painfully as he read, loud and carefully, the words written there.

"Resolved: Fire is a better friend to the farmer than water."

He looked up from the paper and waited with dramatic silence for the crowd to absorb the importance of the subject in question.

Then, as he felt sufficient reverence for the argument had been established, he introduced the speakers.

"The advocate for the resolution tonight is a young farmer that we all know." Phillips's tone lightened slightly as he cleared his throat. "I've always thought him a right smart fellow, but I hear that he's just declared his intent to become a married man, so he cain't be a whole lot smarter than the rest of us."

The crowd chuckled good-naturedly. "Despite that, would you all please indicate your welcome and appreciation for our advocate speaker, the eldest son of Orv and Beulah, Mr. Paisley Winsloe."

A small smattering of applause ensued as Paisley took his place on the first step of the schoolhouse porch and bowed politely to the crowd. He was cleanly shaved and had his hair slicked down. His Sunday-go-to-meeting coat was a little worn and short in the sleeves, but the red polka-dot choke rag done with such care at his throat was store-bought and as fancy as any on the mountain. Meggie's one-time gentleman caller had never looked better.

"Speaking in opposition to the resolution tonight," Buell Phillips continued, "is a farmer that has enlightened and impressed us with his discourse on many occasions from this forum." Again Phillips grinned slightly in preparation for his small attempt at humor. "I asked him once about the development of his ideas and his philosophy and he told me that a man can do a heap of serious thinking when he spends nearly every day of his life staring at the back end of a mule."

The crowd again laughed with admiration at Phillips's wit. Staring at the back end of a mule was what most of the men in the crowd did all day and not a one of them could fail to see the humor in it.

"Allow me to present our opposition speaker for the evening," Phillips said. "The husband of Grace and father of Labin, Tuck, Polly, and Shem. A man who raises the skinniest pigs and the fattest rocks on this mountain, Mr. Labin Trace."

As the crowd chuckled, Trace stepped up to the schoolhouse steps and gave a formal nod to the crowd that was acknowledged with polite applause. The upland farmer was not as prosperous as the Winsloes and Phillipses and others who plowed fields in the hollow, but his shabby overalls were very clean, pressed with neat, hot iron creases.

Meggie glanced over at Polly, who was grinning proudly. She raised her crossed fingers in a gesture of luck.

"As the advocate," Phillips said loudly, hushing the crowd once more with his words, "Mr. Winsloe will go first."

Buell Phillips stepped down from the steps and left the two men alone on the platform to speak.

As Paisley began to make his presentation on the positive qualities of fire for warmth, cooking, and the making of tools, Meggie's attention wandered.

Her glance strayed across the crowd to where Roe Farley stood with her brother. Clearly, Jesse was delighted with his new friend. And Meggie was grateful that Farley's kindness to her brother extended to willingness to still talk and joke with him in public. A lot of the men on the mountain were leery of being seen conversing with Jesse, as if his simplemindedness were catching. It was one of the things she had disliked about Paisley Winsloe. At the cabin Paisley had conversed with Jesse when he had to, but at church gatherings and Literaries, he had acted as if Jesse were a stranger.

Roe Farley apparently had the confidence of a man who didn't have to prove his mental abilities.

Meggie smiled approvingly as once more she allowed her gaze to stray to the two men in her thoughts.

Jesse was listening to the debate with the awed expression of admiration and confusion that was so familiar. Her brother was very aware of his own limitations. She knew that he hated not being as smart as everybody else. But he was warmhearted and generous enough to feel admiration rather than jealousy for those more gifted.

Jesse was clearly entranced by the big words and noble phrasing that emerged from the gap-toothed, tobacco-stained lips of Paisley Winsloe and Labin Trace.

Roe Farley, on the other hand, appeared to be more than a little bit amused at the seriousness with which the speakers and the crowd took the debate on whether the benefits of warmth and water outweighed the disasters of fire and flood.

Meggie's curiosity was sparked. What did a much learned city fellow think of the Ozarkers' attempts to educate themselves and bring culture and civilization to their lives? He might well have found the speakers and her friends and even herself quite comical. Perhaps he did. Somehow the thought didn't bother Meggie. She never had been, nor ever would be, ashamed of who she was and the way she lived. It might not be the way other people lived lives in other places, but it was the way life was lived in the Ozarks and she wouldn't have it any other way. She supposed that in some ways the mountain folk were rather comical. Unaccountably, the memory of the up-and-down plowed cornfield came to her mind and she chuckled out loud.

Apparently it was not only Ozarkers who could provide a

laugh with their foolishness. J. Monroe Farley, a Bay State scholar, was a lot smarter than most of the folks on this mountain. And he might well have cause to chuckle a time or two at their backwoods ways. But he had provided a laugh or two himself.

CHAPTER

NINE

ROE COULDN'T REMEMBER when he'd had a better time. After the "debate" on the beneficial qualities of fire versus water, which Mr. Trace, the opposition speaker, won handily, the Broody twins, Ned and Jed, called a kangaroo court.

At their direction Tom McNees "arrested" Granny Piggott.

"What's the charge?" McNees asked as he escorted the old woman to the front of the crowd.

"Failure to bring any huckleberry pie to the feed," announced young Ned loudly.

The fiesty old woman who was related by either blood or marriage to nearly every soul on the mountain shook a bony finger at the scampish young teens.

"I ain't got no sense of fun about this kindy nonsense," she warned the group testily. The plain clay pipe she held between her teeth was fired up with home-cured tobacco and the scent of it wafted through the crowd.

"If you ain't done nothin', Granny," Jed assured her with a teasing grin, "then you got not a thing to worry about."

Granny was skeptical. "I seen enough of these courts in my time to know that the victim has always got something to worry about."

The twins laughed heartily and the crowd joined in. "You're not the victim, Granny," Ned told her. "You're the criminal."

The old woman's eyes narrowed. "If I ain't 'acquitted' in one dang big hurry, you two scamps won't never taste another pie of mine ever."

Not willing to be intimidated, the twins added bribery and threats to the charges and called their Uncle Pigg up to sit as judge.

Pigg ambled up to the schoolhouse porch with no particular hurry and sat down on the top step gazing down at Granny Piggott, who was actually his aunt rather than his grandmother, as if he'd never seen her before.

"This is a big lot of foolishness," she proclaimed loudly. "I'm an old woman. I can't be expected to stand here at one of these kangaroo courts like I was just another young fool!"

Pigg nodded and spit a big wad of tobacco off to the side, expertly hitting the south pole on the hitching rail. "Bring yer granny a chair, boys," he ordered.

Within minutes Granny Piggott, still fussing like a wet hen, was seated before her accusers and Pigg Broody was calling up a jury.

He picked Pastor Jay to be the jury foreman. The confused cleric couldn't quite grasp what was happening, but went to stand at the left of the steps as the judge directed. He began frantically thumbing through his Bible as if he thought he was being called upon to read.

Also selected for the jury was Sidney Pease, a sleepy toddler who was sucking his thumb. Sidney's mother didn't like the idea at all, but his father thought it a great joke and stood the little boy next to the preacher.

Pigg's cranky mule Job was called next. The hoots and hollers of the crowd were enough to disturb the stubborn old son of a jackass who was very unwilling to take its place among the jury men. With a lot of prodding and pulling the stubborn animal was finally brought up to be tied to a sapling near the judge. Sidney Pease's mother warned the youngster nervously to keep his distance from the ill-tempered beast.

Last, the judge called Jesse Best, who laughed delightedly at being included in the game. He hurried to the jury stand with an eagerness more reminiscent of a child's skip than a farmer's lumberous gait.

Pigg ordered him to stand between the mule and young Sidney. "If that old mule were to go and kick Jesse in the head, it might do him some good," Pigg proclaimed.

The crowd laughed heartily in agreement and Jesse grinned broadly at the joke he didn't quite understand.

The trial, while quite stylized and pseudoserious, didn't last long. The evidence that the Broody boys supplied was to have every man, woman, and child present open his mouth and stick out his tongue. When not one blue-stained tongue could be found, the Broodys rested their case.

Granny huffed and puffed and complained, but didn't even bother to put up a defense. It took the jury only a couple of minutes to find her guilty.

Pigg Broody cleared his throat loudly. "I'd like to thank these jurors," he said. "And commend them for their clear and clever thinking."

The crowd hooted with laughter at the "clear thinking" of poor Pastor Jay, little Sidney, the cranky mule, and Simple Jess.

When the noise subsided, Pigg formally addressed Granny. "Mistress Piggott, you have been found guilty by the kangaroo court. Do you have anything to say before I pronounce sentence upon you?"

Granny huffed grandly. "You just better watch yourself, Piggott Dunderwaulf Broody," she said. "I won't be agreeing to any chicken house cleaning or outhouse liming!"

Pigg flinched slightly at the use of his middle name, but heeded the old woman's warning.

"I believe that the punishment should fit the crime," he proclaimed. "Granny, you are sentenced by this court to bringing *two* pies to next month's Literary. One for these boys here who've taken you to court and one, of course, for the judge."

The crowd cheered loudly at the decision, but Jesse Best interrupted them. "The jury should get pie, too!" he told Pigg.

The judge looked toward Granny and she shrugged. Slapping his hand against his knee, Pigg added that to the sentence. "But that mule of mine ain't getting a bite," he said. "Huckleberries give that creature the runs so bad, I have to tie him in the creek all night long."

Roe laughed with some embarrassment at that story and glanced around at the blushing young girls, many of which were looking his way.

It was unusual that he felt so comfortable and at ease with these people. They were so very different from him. Strangely, they didn't even seem to notice.

His attention was drawn back to the schoolhouse porch when Onery stepped up there. He took only a minute to pat his son on the back proudly and speak a private word with him before turning to the crowd and raising his hands to hush them for his announcement.

"We've got us a stranger here with us tonight," the old man began.

Roe felt a momentary surprise. He felt so comfortable it seemed curious to be considered a stranger. Smiling, what he hoped was companionably, he made his way to the schoolhouse porch. He was met by Jesse who was toting the Ediphone with infinite care. He smiled at Roe as he set the machine on the top step and gently removed the cover.

"Now Farley here," Best began, "is a gentleman and a scholar, folks. He's a-staying up to my place. He says he's taking a liking to my Jesse." Onery grinned slyly. "Or maybe it's my little Meggie that he's taking a liking to."

The crowd chuckled with delight and Roe stood a little straighter. It might be okay for Onery to tease him about his daughter around the cabin, but in front of all these people was more than awkward. Unwillingly Roe's eyes searched the crowd for Meggie; gratefully, he didn't see her.

"Now Roe here," Onery continued. "He's got himself a real yearning for good old music."

Roe watched the eyes of the crowd peruse him with speculation.

"Now I ain't talking about the shaped notes and the do-re-mes we've all heard from them music professors passing through."

A relieved silence settled upon the crowd.

"Roe, he likes the kind of music that we all have sung and played on this mountain since our folks run the Injuns out."

Roe looked hopefully at the group once more.

"They don't have much music up where he's from," Onery explained. "And so they keep it on these little wax spindles so it don't never go away."

As Onery held up one of the blue wax spindles for them to see, everyone laughed heartily. Keeping music on spindles like spun flax was a good joke.

"I'm serious now," Onery insisted. He turned to the young man beside him. "Roe, show these folks how this here Listening Box of yours works. It listens to what you sing or play and it keeps it and plays it back to you."

Roe's hands trembled; he was slightly ill at ease as he attached the horn to the Ediphone. For the very first time since receiving his fellowship, Roe worried whether he would succeed. He counted on his technology to mesmerize his crowd of backwoods Ozark farmers and convince them to help him with his mission. But perhaps the wonders of the modern world might not be enough. These plainspoken people were not easily impressed by the wonders of science or the prospects of progress. They had their own sense of what was important: Food, family, friends. Roe feared that his own rather limited scope of study might hold no appeal against such basics.

He slipped the cylinder that contained Jesse's rendition of "Barbara Allen" onto the roller. With three rhythmic turns of the crank the Ediphone picked up speed and he adjusted the pace. Carefully Roe set the round stylus gently against the grooves in the dark blue wax.

The squeaky noise that came out of the machine was unrecognizable and Roe hastily adjusted the shiny metal lever that controlled the rotating speed. Jesse's perfect-pitched fiddle playing could suddenly be heard floating out from the shiny tin horn.

There was a gasp of shock from the crowd, followed by a hushed, awed silence.

"That's me," Jesse announced proudly. "That's me there playing. I know it sounds like the machine is playing but it's not, it just listens and that there fiddle playing is me. It's me."

Onery quieted his son and the crowd listened in near reverence to the complete performance of the old familiar tune.

When the last note faded away, there was complete stillness on the side of the mountain for one very long moment. Roe felt the sweat trickling down the back of his neck.

Then Beulah Winsloe began to clap. When she did, her brother, Tom McNees, immediately joined in. Her husband and son followed suit and in another moment a rousing round of applause emerged from the crowd.

Roe let out a long breath. He hadn't realized that he'd been holding it. They loved music. He knew it. Now all they had to do was trust him enough to share theirs with him.

"What I'd like to do this summer," he said, "is to visit with each of you for a few evenings and record what songs that you remember how to sing or play. I'll write down the words that you remember to the old songs and the Ediphone

will make recordings of you singing and playing them. I'd
be happy to record any of your old songs, but I'm especially
interested in the oldest. The ones that came across the sea
with your ancestors."

"My ancestors dain't come across the sea," Orv Winsloe
commented. "They come from Tennessee."

"But before that, Mr. Winsloe, they came from the British
Isles," Roe told him.

"And before that they come from the Garden of Eden,"
Granny Piggott observed, initiating a good laugh.

"It is my premise," he explained, "that many of the songs
that you sing here and now have their origin in the
Scotch-Irish tradition of the Middle Ages. All of that music
and its history has been lost through time. But your
ancestors brought that music to the New World and because
of the isolation of your communities it still exists."

The only sound in the audience was one fussing baby.
The expression on their faces was polite boredom. Roe tried
harder.

"Naturally, because of the lapse in time and distance there
will be changes in the way the songs are performed. That is
an accepted phenomenon called communal re-creation. But
I do think that we will be able to recognize them by their
strophic structure and I believe that perhaps I can find in
these hills examples of all seven of the dominant tune
families of Scotland."

"Who is this Tune family?" Roe heard a young wife ask
her husband. "Are they from the Bay State, too?"

Roe laughed and then wanted to strike himself in the
head. The people were all staring at him as if he'd told some
joke that they couldn't understand.

A sinking feeling settled inside him. For all his study, his
practice, his attempts in Cambridge drawing rooms, he was
still more comfortable with books than people. And now
with this crowd of people, a group that was essential to him

for the evidence of his study, he had proved to be as awkward as in his gangly youth.

When Buell Phillips cleared his throat loudly, his words came as no surprise to Roe. "This is all well and good, Farley," he said. "But the summer is a very busy time for most of us, young man," he said. "We just cain't take off time from our work in the middle of the day to sit around singing."

Murmurs of agreement flittered through the crowd as most of those gathered seemed to share Phillips's concern, once he'd voiced it.

"Perhaps I could come to see you in the evenings," Roe said hastily.

Granny Piggott shook her head. "Working folks is tired of an evening," she said.

"Never knew you to be too tired to sing us a tune, Granny," Jesse piped in.

The old woman gave him an evil-eyed squint. "You just keep yourself hushed, Simple Jess. I ain't forgot that foolishness about the pie yet."

The crowd chuckled good-naturedly again.

"Perhaps," Roe interrupted. "Perhaps I could help out at your farms. I could work for you equal to the time you spend recording and reminiscing for me. An extra hand could make up for the time lost."

As the community began to mull that thought over, Onery stepped forward.

"How about I sweeten the pot a little, folks," the gray-bearded man said. "My boy Jesse is thicker than thieves with Farley here. And you all know what a hard worker and a strong back the boy is. Now he'd be pleased to get his own work done early and go along with our young scholar here to show him the way and help him out. You'll get two a-working for the price of one. Ain't that what you call a fine good deal, Buell Phillips? Wish I could buy cartridges for my Winchester at your store that way."

The people laughed at Phillips's expense. Phillips, who was as tight with the penny as if it was blood kin, was not known for having any "fine good deals" in his store. Wisely the storekeeper let the subject go.

"Nope," Granny Piggott announced, speaking for the entire gathering as if she had the right. "It's a whole lot of foolishness this gathering up old songs and we're not having none of it."

"I don't think it's foolishness," Onery said, hands on his hips, primed and ready to dispute the old woman's words.

Granny puffed her pipe and shook her head. "Well, that's 'cause you're a furriner like him. Ye ain't real kin, you're an in-law. You play the fiddle, he plays that contraption."

"Lord Almighty, Granny," Onery complained. "I've lived on this mountain for twenty-five years. When do I get to be part of the family?"

"When you learn to respect yer elders," the old woman answered smartly.

Fearing an unpleasant dispute, Roe interrupted the two. "Mrs. Piggott," he pleaded, "this is my work and I truly need help with it."

"Just call me Granny," the old woman answered, smiling at him with a friendliness that was in direct conflict with her stubborn refusal to help him. "If I ain't your grandma, then I probably should have been. I'm sorry that this is your line of work, son. But it ain't no way to make yourself a living no how. If you cain't stand trapping or trading, you'd best get to farming."

A murmur of agreement went through the crowd. Roe felt Onery clap him on the back.

"Sorry, Roe," he said quietly, "ain't no help for it. Once Granny's spoke on a thing, that about settles it for most folks around here."

Roe shook his head in surprised disbelief. "They won't help me?"

Onery shrugged. "They don't know ye. Get out there

among 'em and make yourself some more friends. You cain't win over the whole world, but they's always some that can be enticed to change their minds."

Roe acknowledged the older man's words. Bravely, he nodded at Granny, politely acknowledging her judgment. He stepped down from the schoolhouse porch and made his way through the crowd greeting and visiting. His heart was heavy, but he kept smiling. He didn't mention his work or the Ediphone again, he merely talked to the people.

Still, he hadn't completely given up. He listened to the people he met, their histories and their knowledge. Mentally he took note of who might be a big help and who could probably offer very little.

Onery was right, he assured himself. People do change their minds and Roe was determined to find a way to change their minds about him. He was going to do this study and suddenly he wanted, more than was understandable, to do it here in Marrying Stone.

A few moments later a cry for music went up. Jesse stirred out a tune on the fiddle. The crowd clapped and stomped appreciatively. Roe watched his friend move through the quick, short, snappy bow movements that increased the tempo of the tune.

"For a boy that ain't right in the head," Orv Winsloe commented, "he can sure jig that fiddle."

Roe agreed.

Jesse played several tunes for the crowd, including a couple that Roe had never heard. He was tempted to stoke up the Ediphone to do some recording, but decided to leave well enough alone for the moment. He began to regret his good sense when Jesse began to play a jumpy little tune that Roe had never heard. Obligingly, Onery danced the jig and sang the tune as Jesse fiddled.

"I stopped at the tavern to stay all night,
  I called for my lodgin', I thought that was right;

The table was drawed an' the tablecloth spread,
There was hoe-cake, an' hominy an' a possum head."

Roe laughed along with the rest of the crowd and made a mental note to ask Onery to repeat the lyrics for him when he had paper to write them down.

After the fiddling, the young people got up to do a play-party. The series of songs and movements was like an intricate dance, but no music was played.

Eda Piggott grabbed his hand and tried to get him to partner her. After a few foolish moments in the square where he proved, without doubt, that he knew nothing of the songs or movements, Eda let him go.

Thinking retreat to be a good idea for the time being, Roe made his way from the crowd.

On the rise toward the church was a rather large, bright outcropping of rock. He moved closer. In the bright moonlight Roe could see that the rock was a huge chunk of brilliant white quartz, nearly four feet square. It jutted out from the ground at a sharp angle. It was unusual and somewhat startling to observe as it seemed to catch the rays of moonlight and reflect them back to earth. Fascinated, Roe climbed onto the rock and seated himself at the top of it. The whole sky and mountains seemed laid out before him like a platter of visual sweetmeats.

With a strange sigh of unexpected contentment, Roe smiled. Although the rock was not at the peak of the mountain and although the darkness of evening made it impossible to actually see anything but the faint darkness of the horizon and the glittering of stars, Roe felt he could see the whole universe from his bright quartz perch.

"This is the Marrying Stone."

Roe heard the voice beside him and was momentarily startled that he'd heard no one approach. Smiling, he turned to find Meggie Best coming up beside the huge rock.

Without really thinking about it, he reached out and took her hand to help her up and she seated herself beside him.

There was a sad look in her eyes and he knew that she was about to apologize for the community's unwillingness to help him. He hoped to keep the conversation away from the unpleasantness.

"The Marrying Stone?" he asked.

Meggie nodded. Her features seemed especially pretty in the moonlight and her voice was slightly hushed as if she were conveying private secrets.

"That's how the mountain got its name," she said. She leaned back slightly and raised her chin as if trying to absorb the beauty of the warm evening.

Roe gazed at her long graceful neck, the neat curves of her sturdy young body, and the long bare feet that set so prettily upon the slick, almost polished-looking surface of the rock.

"I always thought the view from up here was the prettiest thing I ever saw."

"Beautiful," Roe agreed, but he was no longer looking at the view.

Something in his voice must have given him away, as Meggie turned quickly to give him a curious look. Roe immediately focused on the distant horizon.

"Why do they call it the Marrying Stone?" he asked.

"Because it's where folks get married," she answered.

He turned to smile at her. He was curious about the quaint custom that would have couples taking their wedding vows on an outcropping of rock.

"But what does a chunk of stone have to do with marriage?"

Meggie's eyes were upon him. He couldn't see the warm blue-gray of their depths, but his memory knew the color well.

"It goes back to the Indians, folks say," she told him. "The Osage were real superstitious Indians, I guess. They thought the rock had spiritual powers to change the world and they would come here to ask for changes." She smiled warmly at him. "I guess us civilized folks are about as superstitious as the Indians," she admitted with a laugh. "Before there were preachers in these mountains, or churches or even laws, this stone was here." She ran her hand almost reverently along the smooth bright surface. "When a couple wanted to wed, they'd simply come up to the mountain and stand on this stone to declare themselves as husband and wife and jump from the stone to the ground. That was considered marriage in the eyes of God."

Roe raised a skeptical eyebrow. "That was all that was required?"

Meggie nodded. "That's all that marriage is, isn't it? Just making a promise before God."

"I suppose so," he agreed.

"That's all that folks back in those times thought that they needed. The Marrying Stone was so bright and gleamed so in the sunlight, that I suspect the people thought that God couldn't fail to see them."

Roe looked down once more to regard the strange stone that the hill people had entrusted with such power.

"Even after Granny and her man came to live up here and the first church was built on down the mountain, the hill folks just preferred to be married here at the stone," Meggie continued. "So the Piggotts and the McNeeses decided to build the church up here."

"Mohammed goes to the mountain," Roe said quietly, nodding.

She looked over at him curiously. "Who's Mohammed?"

Roe shook his head and smiled at her. "He's not from around here."

Meggie closed her eyes and took a deep breath of the night air. Roe watched her handsome, youthful bosom rise and fall and felt the swift and stinging fire of desire. He turned away from her and forced himself to stare off into the distance. A companionable silence existed between the two for several minutes. It was a wonderful, sweet silence. It was as if they were suddenly in tune with each other and the beauty of the night.

Roe looked down at the bright glint of the moonlight on the quartz Marrying Stone. It was as if the spiritual power of the stone had created an unusual serenity.

Glancing up, he once more observed the natural beauty around him. The night sky glowed with bright stars overhead and the twinkle of lightning bugs closer to earth. High above, the shadow of dark blue clouds skittered across the heavens. In the distance, he could make out the outline of Squaw's Trunk Mountain. And beyond it just the faintest signs of crests and ridges could be seen almost to infinity, as if these mountains went on forever.

From the area near the schoolhouse, the sounds of warm friendly banter among friends and family added to the peacefulness of the place.

A strange thrill of almost longing welled up inside Roe. All his senses were alive and alert now. He could smell the fertile, mossy ground and the faint fragrance of broom grass near bursting to blossom. He could hear the reedy call of tree frogs interspersed with the creaks of lonely crickets and the rasp of cicadas in the cottonwoods.

The smooth strength and solidity of the Marrying Stone beneath his hands gave him a sense of timeless perpetuity. And the warmth of the woman beside him filled him with a sense of peace, a sense of being settled, that he had never experienced in his life. He glanced from the beauty of nature to the beauty of barefooted Meggie Best at his side. There was something right about this place, something befitting. "I think that the folks may be correct," he said.

"About what?"

Roe took one more long, leisurely look at the vista before him.

"I'd swear that God can see most anything that goes on at the top of this mountain."

She turned to smile at him and their gazes locked. Smiles died away as Meggie reached out and touched Roe's arm. Fire sizzled between them. It startled them both. Against all his better judgment, he kissed her. Just a brief touch of his lips upon hers, but it was enough.

Nervously Roe pulled away, clearing his throat. He was stunned by the unwanted feelings that assailed him and uncomfortable now with the nearness of the young woman who only a moment ago felt so right at his side. From the corner of his eye he could see Meggie, her color high in the moonlight, tensely straightening the faded blue homespun material of her dress.

He cautioned himself. It was easy to be lured into the magic of the mountains and the nearness of a pretty woman. But he was only a visitor in these hills. At the end of the summer he'd be returning to the ordered civilization of Cambridge, Massachusetts. He was in the Ozarks to collect interesting music of the Celtic heritage, not to play around with the local girls. Meggie Best might be playing around also, but she was playing for keeps.

If Meggie were another girl, a mill girl or one unrelated to his friends and these hills, Roe thought, he might give her a whirl. She was a pretty, earthy sort of creature, so different from the women in his past or the woman that would be his future. And he remembered the hot sweetness of her kiss. But there was no possibility of playing fast and loose with Meggie Best without tying himself up with strings. And strings were not something he was looking for on this sojourn to the Ozarks. He'd be leaving these mountains in the fall and he'd be leaving alone. And it would not behoove him to leave behind a broken heart.

Besides, Meggie was not at all his type. She was a plain mountain girl with a fanciful nature. One minute she was practical and abrupt; the next she was lost in some dream world with romance and princes. The kind of woman he wanted would fit easily into the world of Cambridge salons and academia. Meggie Best would not. Yes, it definitely was right to keep his distance. Tonight, and for the rest of the days and nights that he was in these mountains.

With that thought firmly in mind, Roe deftly rose to his feet. He turned to Meggie, smiling with unconcern that was very much feigned. He was ready to offer some inane comment that would diffuse the unwelcome aura.

Whatever he'd intended to say was lost forever when he was distracted by the sound of an animal moving in the underbrush behind them.

Both turned toward the noise at the same moment, surprised that any woods creature would venture so close to what was obviously a human gathering. Roe's eyes widened in disbelief and Meggie gave a little cry of shock to see the curious little weasellike creature in handsome fur of black and white coming up behind them.

"Skunk!"

Meggie screamed with as much terror as she would have felt for a rabid bobcat or an angry mama bear.

Quickness and strength flooded through Roe's veins like water over a broken levee. He grabbed Meggie's hand and jerked her to her feet.

"Jump!" he ordered.

And they did.

The crowd came hurrying toward them at the sounds of commotion. Then, almost as one, they stopped and stared at the two young people who stood together, hand in hand, after jumping the Marrying Stone.

CHAPTER

TEN

"THERE WAS A skunk there, I tell you!" Meggie's eyes were narrow with fury and her voice was strident with frustration.

"If you say they was a skunk, Meggie, I believe ye," her father answered. His throaty chuckle, however, belied his words.

She looked across to Roe who was silently leading the mule, Jesse at his side. He'd said nothing, nothing, since the unfortunate incident at the Marrying Stone. But then, nearly everything in the world had already been said.

"Was it a polecat or a civvy cat?" Jesse asked.

Her brother seemed to be the only one on the mountain who had taken their excuse for jumping the Marrying Stone at face value. Unfortunately, what Jesse thought was not held in high esteem in the community.

"I don't know which it was," Meggie answered. "I didn't take that long to look at it."

"Did you get a look at it, Roe?"

"Well, yes, I suppose I did. It *was* a skunk."

"Polecat or civvy cat?"

"What's the difference?" Roe asked.

The young man shrugged. "They's both skunks, I mean they put out a stink just alike," Jesse explained. "But the polecat is all black with a white stripe down the middle. When he goes to spray ye, he arches his back like some cat or something. The civvy cat has lots of stripes or spots, usually one running along each shoulder. And when he takes a notion to spray you, he does a handstand on his front legs."

"You're joking."

Jesse shook his head. "Ain't no joke, Roe, you can ask Pa."

Roe shook his head. "I didn't take time to notice its stripes, but I do know the thing didn't do any handstand."

"It was probably a coon," Onery said.

"I told you it was a skunk!" Meggie's words were nearly screeched.

Onery chuckled again.

Her frustration was understandable.

From the moment she had realized why everyone was staring at them so, Meggie had tried, unsuccessfully, to explain their impromptu jump.

"Skunk?" Orv Winsloe questioned. "If you saw a skunk up there, where did it go?"

Pigg Broody chuckled. "It went right back to fantasy land where it come from." He spit a large jaw of tobacco for emphasis. "Ain't no skunk nor no other varmint gonna come this close to a noisy crowd of folks."

Buell Phillips readily agreed. And if that wasn't bad enough, Tom McNees, who could never be counted upon to agree with the Piggott kin on anything, found the skunk story as incredible as the rest of them.

Meggie, shaking her head in disbelief, tried to reason with the crowd. "Why else would we have jumped like that?" she asked.

Knowing smiles and titters of laughter were her reply. Granny Piggott spoke up with what the others were thinking. "Meggie Best, ever' one of us knows you'd been pining away for years for some stranger to come up the mountain to court ye. Now this fellow is finally come, and I guess you just wanted to make sure you got your mark on him before one of these other gals ketched his eye."

Openmouthed and dumbfounded, Meggie looked over at Roe in horror. His expression was so disconcerted, it was almost as if he agreed with the rest of them.

"Roe!" she exclaimed.

"Hear that," Beulah Winsloe said knowingly. "She's already calling him by his given name."

Farley finally snapped out of his state of shock and offered his defense. "We saw a skunk," he stated unequivocally. "It came right up behind us and we were forced to jump."

"Maybe the Good Lord sent that critter your way?" Pastor Jay offered.

"What?"

"Pastor Jay, Mr. Farley and me are not thinking to marry."

"We certainly are not," Roe agreed with conviction. Meggie was embarrassed at his vehemence and was tempted to give him a swift kick in the shin.

"But you jumped the Marrying Stone," the aging cleric said evenly as if that settled everything.

"The Marrying Stone is no legal wedding," Meggie countered.

"The gal is right about that," Buell Phillips announced with exaggerated self-importance. "As Justice of the Peace, I can tell you certain that this couple ain't wed 'til I fill out the paper."

"We don't want you to fill out the paper!" Meggie said. "We don't want to marry. We were just trying to get away from a skunk." She looked around anxiously at the crowd. There wasn't a face that expressed belief in her words.

"Pa!" she called out finally, seeking the last resort of young women everywhere, Daddy's help.

"Now, Buell, Granny, Pastor Jay," Onery said calmly as he moved up through the crowd, "let's not all go off half cocked here." His limp was more pronounced than earlier, but his eyes were twinkling with sheer delight. "If the younguns say they ain't married, then they ain't."

Granny Piggott huffed loudly. "They jumped the Marrying Stone. That was a weddin' for me, Onery Best, and for you and the gal's mamma, too."

"We jumped the stone 'cause we *wanted* to," Onery answered. "Weren't no skunk a-chasing us."

Pigg Broody spit another loud shot of tobacco. "They wasn't no skunk."

"There was a skunk!" Roe and Meggie answered in unison.

Onery chuckled. "If'n these younguns is seeing skunks, they's seeing skunks. Ye cain't make 'em man and wife because of it."

The people had finally allowed themselves to be talked out of a wedding, but gossips were still whispering when the Best family gathered up their belongings and headed for home. Polly Trace had hurried over to Meggie when she was out of sight of the crowd and hugged her.

"You clever gal," she said, giggling excitedly. "You sure showed that Eda. I swear I thought the gal was going to swaller her teeth when she saw you two had made the jump together."

Meggie didn't even bother to try to defend herself. She knew that Polly didn't believe her any more than anyone else had. It *was* curious for a skunk, or any woods critter for that matter, to walk up on a noisy gathering of folks. But it *had* been a skunk. She had seen it, she knew. Her brow furrowed with concern. If she was beginning to doubt it, what was Roe thinking? He'd said that he'd seen it, but was he believing now that she'd tricked him?

A flush of red-tinted humiliation stained her cheeks. After the way she'd thrown herself at him that first day and then letting him kiss her again tonight, he might just think that she'd tried to trick him into jumping the Stone with her. She shuddered with embarrassment, then, thankfully, sanity prevailed.

Jumping the Stone was an old superstition. Neither of them believed it and it meant nothing. And there *was* a skunk.

When they arrived back at the cabin it was very late. As Roe and Jesse stabled the sloe-eyed mule, Meggie helped her father into the house. His bad leg had stiffened up on the long ride and he could hardly walk.

Once she'd helped him into bed, she unrolled her own tick and blankets and kneeling down she began spreading them on the floor. Her father groaned slightly with his sore muscles as he turned over in the bed and watched her work.

"You'd better be making that pallet a little bigger, Meggie-gal. Now that you're a married woman and all."

"Pa!"

His only reply was a low, hearty chuckle.

It was a private little joke between father and daughter; unfortunately it was at that moment that Roe and Jesse stepped through the door.

Meggie watched Roe's dark-eyed glance take in her disheveled appearance as she knelt in the lamplight. Then his attention strayed to the low, clover tick pallet at her knees. His gaze stayed overlong before it skittered back to Meggie's own. A strange thrill passed through her heart like the dizzy dash of a dozen hungry hummingbirds. She saw desire in his eyes and she felt it in her own throbbing veins.

"Pa was making a joke," she explained unnecessarily.

Roe cleared his throat. "It just isn't very funny anymore, Onery," he answered, addressing the man in the bed. "I suggest that we drop this subject completely and forget that it ever happened."

Onery chuckled again. "I won't be saying another word," he promised. "Course, I cain't control what other folks'll be saying."

Meggie knew that he was right. And as the long sleepless

night progressed and she lay wide-eyed in her lonely pallet, she found that she could not forget that it happened either.

They had been so close there for those few long moments. It had felt so good. The quiet camaraderie of a man who had seen and done things that Meggie couldn't imagine. And sharing with him the realities of her own world. And maybe, maybe for a moment when he kissed her she had pretended that he cared for her, that he was her beau and that they had slipped off to the Marrying Stone to be alone and share little secrets.

She heard the creak of pine planks above her as if someone rolled over in the loft. She knew it was Roe, even if she hadn't been able to hear the familiar rhythmic snore she recognized as Jesse's; she knew that Roe was no more able to sleep this night than was she. Her father's teasing words had seen to that.

The sweet taste of his kiss stayed with her. The short, stiff remains of whiskers on his upper lip made stark contrast to the warm softness of his mouth. He had not just wanted to kiss her. He had wanted her as a husband wants a wife, in that private, naked way that she could hardly imagine. And she had wanted him that way, too.

Even in the privacy of her pallet covers, Meggie still managed to blush. She couldn't think about this anymore. She didn't want to think about it anymore. Determinedly, she sought her normal place of refuge from the realities of the world, the fantasies. Tonight, she decided, she would imagine herself as a mysterious princess, completely veiled and hidden from view. Three strong, handsome lancers would be vying for her hand, loving her, sight unseen, just for the beauty of her melodious cultured voice.

Meggie smiled at the situation. It was a good one, guaranteed to take her mind off the worrisome present. But as the first lancer removed his helmet, her heart stopped. It was J. Monroe Farley in knightly armaments. Determinedly, she shifted her attention to the second soldier in attendance.

But as he bowed before her and revealed his face, he too was J. Monroe Farley.

"I choose him!" she announced loudly, pointing toward the third man, yet unknown to her. He walked toward her and the evening's shadow left his visage. With jet-black hair and spectacles perched upon his nose, he bowed gracefully over her hand.

"I'd swear that God can see most anything that goes on at the top of this mountain," he said.

"Oh!"

With a huff, Meggie sat up in her pile of coverlets and shook her head. She couldn't even escape her thoughts in daydreams anymore. She covered her face with her hands and sighed. She was weary and droop-eyed, but still she couldn't sleep. Morning was coming in a hurry and the problem that she and Roe had inadvertently created last night would still be with them.

Again she heard the creaking of the boards in the loft above her. She could not wish it away if she wanted to. And she was honest enough with herself to know that she didn't really want to.

Meggie was squint-eyed and yawning the next morning. She was the first one to leave the cabin; heading for the upground woods, her mind was gratefully blank in the gray darkness still a half hour before dawn. The sleepless night had left a weariness that was numbing, and in its own way a comfort.

Through the honesty of the long night she had tried to sort out her feelings and make sense of what had happened. Roe Farley was definitely the finest-looking man that she'd ever seen. And he was a kind fellow, too. She was sure of that by the way he befriended her brother and treated him like an equal. He was smart, too. There was no denying that, and Meggie had always thought that a man for her would have to be at least as smart as she was. He was capable of deep feelings and contemplations. She'd recognized that in him as they talked on the Marrying Stone. And despite her attempts to dispel the memory, she couldn't quite forget the hot, sweet taste of his lips on hers.

As she found herself a private place among the sumac bushes, she imagined herself in an intimate embrace with Roe Farley. He would be shy and unsure, she thought. Undoubtedly she would have to coax him into touching her. But it would be gentle and sweet, and being held so close in his arms would be worth the embarrassment of having to pull up her dress and expose her legs.

Meggie headed back to the homestead. Her mind was now completely in the clouds as she imagined herself in a bright blue wedding gown being carried across the threshold of the cabin in the arms of J. Monroe Farley. He was nervously declaring his love for her and begging, as if he were one of the love-stung lancers, for the honor of her touch. She smiled slightly and hummed with pleasure at the thought. His hands would move, slow and hesitant, across her trembling skin. And his kiss would be light and soft against her lips. She shivered sensually. It was a fine fancy, a pleasant diversion. It wasn't meant to come true, of course. Daydreams were simply to be enjoyed, an innocent pastime that hurt no one. The thought of Roe Farley's arms around her was warm and welcome. So much so that a soft sigh escaped her lips as she made her way across the yard.

This sweet spell and unthinking sense of well-being was abruptly shattered, however, as she walked past the clothesline that was strung from the edge of the mule shed to a crosspole at the side of the small clearing that was the cabin yard.

Stunned, she stood staring in frozen amazement for a long moment. Then with a cry of abhorrent dismay, Meggie hurried over to view the horrific sight more closely. A plump, young turkey, already plucked and cleaned, hung by its ugly red feet on the clothesline. Its long gobbler neck was stretched full length and the bird's head nearly touched the ground as it swayed back and forth in the morning breeze. Next to the bird, a brightly colored piece quilt, damp with dew, fluttered slightly. On the ground near the crosspole a barrel of sorghum sat invitingly. A sack of flour leaned against it and a half peck of coffee beans sat on top. In every direction around the pole more items were stacked. There was a big smoked ham, a strip of hand-tooled leather mule harness, jars of egg preserves and pickled pigs' feet, a thin box of store-bought vellum writing paper, and a shiny new cooking riddle. Tears formed in Meggie's eyes. The sight—one that she had dreamed about since she was a little girl—was suddenly so unwelcome.

"What's all this stuff?"

The question came from behind her and Meggie whirled in guilty surprise to see Roe standing in the clearing staring at the housewares and foodstuff with confusion.

Meggie was dumbstruck for one long moment. She didn't know what to answer. These were the first words he had spoken to her since the awful moment that they had jumped the Marrying Stone. Shame, guilt, and embarrassment all vied for prominence in her thoughts.

"What is all of this doing out here?" Roe asked once again.

Tears sprang to Meggie's eyes, but bravely she pushed them back. In a breathy rush of explanation she answered, "We've been pounded!"

"Pounded?"

He looked at her curiously. Meggie opened her mouth to explain, but found the words wouldn't come. With a little squeaky noise of humiliation, she turned and ran into the house.

"Meggie!"

She heard Roe calling out her name, but she neither stopped nor slowed her step.

Finally reaching the sanctuary of the cabin, she found no

safety there. Her father and brother were both up now, scratching and yawning, and looked at her curiously as she came running in through the door.

She stared at them for a moment, her expression one of a frightened rabbit cornered by a pack of dogs.

"Meggie, what's going on?"

She heard Roe's voice again, closer now. He was coming to the cabin. Defeated, Meggie sat heavily in one of the cane-bottom chairs at the table and hid her face in her hands.

She heard, rather than saw, Roe step across the threshold.

"What's a-going on this morning?" her father asked, his voice still cranky with sleep.

"There's a turkey and a bunch of food stacked up next to the clothesline pole," Roe said. "Meggie says we've been 'pounded,' whatever that means."

Jesse's expression was puzzled. Onery grinned broadly and laughed loudly. "Lord Almighy, Roe. You and my Meggie-gal are in it deep now."

"In what deep?"

"In marriage deep. Them is weddin' presents, Farley. The folks on the mountain are a-settin' you up in housekeeping."

Roe stared at Meggie. His look was accusing.

"We are *not* married!" he stated emphatically.

Onery was still laughing. "You're preaching to the converted, Roe. I know you ain't married and you know you ain't married, but these folks, they's thinking that you are. I guess it's up to you and Meggie to make 'em start to thinking differently."

Roe sputtered and cursed under his breath at the necessity, but angry words changed nothing. Not only would these Ozarkers not help him with his work, now they thought that he was married to one of their own.

Onery was right, of course. It was up to the couple in question to make their kinship, or lack of it, understood. And they quickly got that opportunity. Meggie had barely

scraped the remains of undercooked eggs, hard, heavy
biscuits, and scorched bacon from the table before Pastor
Jay came to call.

"I wanted to be the first to come out and congratulate the
young couple," the preacher said as he made himself
comfortable at the table.

Meggie heated up what was left over of the morning's
coffee and Jesse and his father made a hasty exit, leaving
Roe and Meggie to face the man of God alone.

"I'm so glad that you've come, Pastor Jay," Roe said to
the old man. "There seems to be a very mistaken impression
among some members of the community and Miss Best and
I want to correct that impression as quickly as possible."

The preacher smiled at Roe and nodded before taking a
drink of the near boiling liquid that Meggie had set before
him.

"Miss Best and I," Roe continued, "jumped from the
Marrying Stone because we were attempting to escape from
a skunk. There was no intent to anything further."

Again the preacher nodded.

"We don't consider ourselves married. And we don't want
anyone else to think of us that way either."

"I'm very glad to hear that," Pastor Jay answered. He
smiled warmly at Meggie and reached across the table to pat
her hand. "I believe your coffee is improving, Margaret
May. I remember when I'd have to run out of the door to
spit a mouthful out in the grass."

Meggie flushed.

Pastor Jay turned his attention back to Roe. "Yes, I'm
right glad to hear that you don't consider yourselves
married."

Roe sighed audibly with relief and gave Meggie a
confident grin.

"We're going to need your help, Pastor Jay, to convince
the rest of the people in this community."

The pastor chuckled lightly. "It won't take that much

convincing. Why, I've been preaching for twenty years that just jumping off the Stone ain't enough anymore. The world's a-changing and the Lord expects us to keep up with the times. A couple these days has got to make vows in the church and have their wedding prayed over just like folks in the rest of the country do. Just 'cause we've been blessed with the Marrying Stone, don't mean we can take the gift for granted."

Meggie and Roe exchanged a puzzled glance. Meggie cleared her throat and spoke up.

"That's what we think, too, Pastor Jay. We think that for a wedding to be a wedding, it has to be in church. Nothing less than that really counts."

"That's wonderful," the preacher answered. "I'm delighted with you both. And don't worry about the folks here on the mountain. You aren't the first to marry in the church as well as jumping the Stone and I think that it's a tradition that is going to really catch hold. How soon do you think you'll want your church nuptials to occur? I can read the banns tomorrow at the service if you're set."

"What?" Roe and Meggie asked in unison.

"Then again, you can wait until the planting's all done or some which time seems better to ye. I'm not opposed to you taking your time about the churching. Handfasting has been our way on the mountain for years. If I rushed every couple that ain't got around to being churched down the aisle, it'd look like a stampede."

"Pastor Jay, we don't wish to be married," Roe insisted.

The preacher nodded. "Yes, I expect you think it's unnecessary, but in years to come, you'll be glad that you did. I've known you both since you were just little tots hanging upon your mothers' skirts," the preacher said with a wistful remembrance of the past. "And it will be one of the greatest pleasures of my life to formally unite these two fine old mountain families in the bond of your wedlock."

"Pastor Jay—" Meggie began.

The preacher ignored her plea and patted Roe on the arm affectionately. "I know that your father don't hold much with preaching, son," the pastor said. "But I am right sure that he'll want to come to the house of God to see his boy united in matrimony."

"My father?"

"Yes, sir." Pastor Jay took a long, pleasurable swig of his coffee. "I've been trying to get Gid Weston back into the Lord's house for more years than I can count. If it takes a wedding to do it, then so be it."

Roe and Meggie exchanged an appalled expression. Roe shrugged helplessly.

"Pastor Jay," Meggie began. Quietly taking the old man's hand, she looked deep into the preacher's eyes, willing him to understand. "Gid Weston is not Roe's father."

The preacher was startled for a moment and then waved away her words. "That's just an untrue, unkind rumor, Margaret May. And I'm ashamed of you for believing it."

The pastor tutted with disapproval.

"I asked Sarah Weston that question right to her face twenty years ago and she swore on a stack of Bibles that there ain't never been no man for her but Gid."

Dumbfounded by the preacher's reply, Meggie was temporarily at a loss as to what more to say. She rallied as quickly as she could, knowing the importance of making the preacher understand. "I didn't mean that Gid's sons weren't his own, Pastor Jay," she said. "I meant that Roe is not one of Gid's sons."

The old man gave Roe a long look. "He don't much favor, does he?" The preacher shook his head once more. "Don't give it another thought, girlie. The boy bears Gid Weston's name, so it don't matter a whit what folks say or have said. His name's Weston, so he's a Weston. And your own younguns'll be the same, sure as a fiddler'll fetch up fawnch."

"His name is Farley."

"Come again?"

Meggie pointed at Roe and spoke louder. "His name is Farley."

"Is it?" The preacher looked across the table at Roe, momentarily perplexed. He put a trembling, brown-spotted hand to his brow as if deep in thought. Then after only a moment of concentration, the old man shook his head and smiled.

He offered his hand across the table to Roe. And Roe shook it as if the two were just now being introduced.

"I'm sorry, son," the preacher said with genuine warmth and honesty. "I get mixed up from time to time."

"It's all right, Pastor Jay," Roe told him, relief evident in his voice.

"I was thinking you were called Monroe Weston," he said. "But if your name's Farley, it's Farley. I got it now, and I'll remember next time."

"Thank you, Pastor."

Roe glanced over at Meggie and she smiled back. Pleased that at least they'd gotten a start on setting the preacher straight.

"Farley. Farley." He repeated the name as if trying it out on his tongue. "Farley Weston. Yes, I believe I can remember that now."

CHAPTER

ELEVEN

"IF THAT CRAZED old fool is the spiritual guidance of this community, I'd say Marrying Stone is in for a difficult day of reckoning!"

Roe's words were marked with as much self-derisive humor as anger and frustration, having spent the better part of a wasted two hours attempting to give Pastor Buford Jay a mild brush with reality.

"He's not a crazed old fool." Meggie felt obligated to defend the man. "He's just old and a little confused."

Roe carefully locked the wooden case for the Ediphone and carried it to the cabin doorway.

"Yes, I couldn't help but agree, *Mrs. Weston*," he said the name sarcastically. "The old man is a little confused. And I am getting off this mountain before I become as confused as he is."

"Where are you gonna go?" Meggie asked.

Roe shook his head. "I haven't an idea."

"You won't get very far in these hills without a mule."

The fact didn't require an acknowledgment, but Roe did give her a slight nod of agreement.

"Well, the least I can do is pack you some victuals and provisions," she said with a sigh as she headed toward the food safe.

"Please don't. I think I'd rather live on grass and berries than to eat more of your special kind of cooking."

Meggie turned on him in fury. "What a hateful thing to say! It's not my fault that skunk came up to the Marrying Stone. I'm not any happier about this than you are. My family has been nothing but generous to you since you came to this mountain. And now that there's trouble, I'm just letting you walk out and leave me the mess to straighten out. And you can't even be kind enough to keep from complaining about my cooking. I know I'm no cook. And you, J. Monroe Farley, are no prince!"

"And I thank God for that, for if I were, I'd undoubtedly not be able to leave this place alive!"

"You . . . you—"

"Tsk, tsk, children. Not twenty-four hours from your jump and you're already having a spat."

Startled at the interruption, Meggie and Roe turned to the doorway where Granny Piggott stood dressed in her "visitin' gown" and adorned with a new cotton homespun slat bonnet.

"Granny, what a surprise," Meggie said, swallowing her anger and forcing a welcoming smile to her face. She glanced back nervously at Roe, warning him to take a light touch with the old lady. "Won't you have a seat."

The elderly woman looked around the cabin in distaste. "I can't see no sense in sitting inside when the weather is neither cold enough to see yer breath nor hot enough to melt your starch." She glanced over at Roe. "Bring me a chair out here in the yard, young man."

As she turned away she glanced down at the Ediphone on the floor. "And bring along this Listening Box of yourn, I'm thinking to sing ye a tune or two."

Roe and Meggie exchanged puzzled looks behind the old woman's back, but followed her outside.

"You want I should bring you some tea, Granny?" Meggie asked.

"Tea? Lord Almighty, child, I ain't got no use for the stuff in the spring and summertime at all. A cup of cool water will suit me fine."

Following her outside, Roe and Meggie were surprised to find Jesse helping Oather Phillips unload a piece of furniture from the back of a skid cart.

"You no-account boys be careful with that, now," Granny called out to them. Turning, she spoke again to Meggie and Roe. "Brought you two a little weddin' present."

The two glanced at each other, puzzled, as Roe set the cane-bottomed chair in the shade near the house for the old woman.

"It's a bedstead and cording," she said. "I figured Onery weren't about to give you his, and a young couple shouldn't have to get to knowing each other on a floor tick pallet."

Meggie's face flushed fiery red and she couldn't meet Roe's eyes.

"Though my man and me spent more than a few months that way when we was newly wed." The old woman seated herself heavily and moaned slightly as if the relief of taking rest was almost more comfort than she could stand. From the depths of her skirt pocket she drew out her old clay pipe. It was slate-blue with a long, curved stem to cool and sweeten the home-cured tobacco mixings she carried in a little coarsely woven pouch. The old woman carefully packed the pipe bowl and tapped it down with her fingernail.

"Bring me a bit of fire, Meggie," she said casually. As the young woman hurried into the cabin, Granny turned her attention to the new bridegroom who watched her curiously from the porch. She motioned him to sit down and he did.

"My man Piggott," she continued, "he brung me up this way on a flat boat. There weren't no one living up here, just come here for weddings in them days." She smiled. "I was as green as grass back then. But, Piggott, he was, too. Me, I hadn't seen fifteen years yet, and he weren't but a few months older. But he had his own rifle, a muzzle-loader that he'd traded a year's work for, a couple of hunting dogs that he'd trained hisself, and a half-growed sow. So he thought he was old enough to wed. And he thought I was mighty pretty in them days, so I was thinking I was old enough, myself."

She chuckled lightly. Meggie came out of the cabin carrying a half-green hickory twig that was glowing orange with fire on one end. The old woman took it with thanks and held it up to the bowl of the clay pipe. With a strong sucking pull on the stem, the twig flamed up brightly and lit the tobacco in the bowl. Granny made several long pulls that brought great billows of smoke out of the pipe to assure herself that her smoke was well and truly lit. Then she stuck the cold end of the hickory twig into the ground, saving the fire to relight the pipe later if it went out.

After a long, self-satisfied draw of tobacco, Granny continued her story, this time with both the young people as her audience.

"After we jumped the Stone, we built us up a little four-by-four joiner down in the far holler before the bad weather came. That first winter it was him and me, that sow, and them two hunting hounds sharing a cabin." She laughed gleefully as she looked up at the young couple before her. "We was right happy. Suspect we was too ignorant to know no better."

Again the old woman laughed. Her humor was contagious and Roe and Meggie found themselves smiling also. Though when they glanced at each other, the joy faded slightly.

"But, I'm thinking," Granny continued, "that the two of you are older and a good deal smarter than we was. I just hope that you'll be as happy. And I want to do what I can to help you get yourselves a good start in life."

Meggie was silent.

Roe nervously cleared his throat. "That's very kind of you, Mrs. Piggott. Meggie and I—"

"Now, I tole you, son, to call me Granny. 'Specially now that we's kin and all."

Roe swallowed and looked ill at ease.

"Oather!" she called out to her young companion. "You and Jesse treat that piece of cherrywood with some respect, now. Your Uncle Elvy carved them pieces hisself more than twenty year ago."

They watched the two young men clumsily carry the bed fixings up to the porch where they leaned them against the side of the cabin.

"Don't know where you'll have space inside to set it up. Course, sleeping outside ain't no hardship in summertime. If you get busy, young man, you can have another room added to this place afore winter sets in good."

"I don't know, Granny, I—"

"So where's that Listening Box of yourn?" she interrupted. "Now mind you," she said, shaking her finger at him. "I still think this is one fool way for a fellow to be a-trying to make his livin'. But since you are family and all, now, well, I'm going to be willin' to help as I can. And I'll see that my kith and kin sing fer ye, too. But I'm telling ye, son, sure as the world, you'd best get another string fer yer bow. This collecting old songs on spools of wax, it ain't no kind of work to be counting upon. If you can't take to farming or trading, they's still meat aplenty in these woods. The big bears is mostly gone of course, and deer is scarcer than bathwater in the time of drought, but they's good eatin' critters enough that's welcome to the man who's a-willin' to hunt or trap 'em."

Roe accepted the old woman's advice with a silent nod. Oather and Jesse took seats on the edge of the porch, anxious to watch the workings of the Listening Box and to hear Granny sing.

Roe began setting it up out under the tree. He placed it

upon an upended barrel, so that the old woman would have to neither stand nor stoop to be able to sing into it.

"Now what do ye think I oughter sing fer ye?" she asked.

"Whatever you'd like, Granny," Roe answered as he anxiously cranked up the machine and adjusted the speed. He set the sharp cutting stylus against the whirling wax cylinder and adjusted the tin horn conveniently for the old woman.

"Just put your mouth as close to the horn as is comfortable and sing whatever you'd like," he said.

Granny was thoughtful for a long moment. "I remember this one," she said. "It's real sad and sweetlike, for a young couple in love." She leaned forward slightly and with a high-pitched twangy tenor, she began to sing.

> "Her form was like the dove,
>   So slender and so neat,
>   Her long brown chestnut curl
>   Hung to her tiny feet,
>   Her voice it was like music
>   Or the murmur of the breeze
>   And she whispered that she loved me
>   As we strolled among the trees."

As the old woman sang the sweet old love song, Roe's expression was pensive. The song was familiar to him and was not old enough to help with his work, but the old woman who sang it knew it well. And he suspected there were many more that her mother or grandmother had sung to her that could be excellent evidence for his thesis. A thrill of excitement spread through him. Suddenly he was not so eager to leave this mountain.

He glanced over at Meggie. She was listening to the old woman sing. Her eyes had turned dreamy again and he actually had to fight the urge to smile. Meggie Best was not one to allow her worries to concern her long. Even now, as the people of Marrying Stone were saying that they were married and as he was packing his things to leave her sight forever, the explanations to be all hers, still, the sweetness of a romantic ballad could set her thoughts into fancy.

> "But if you e'er see a lass
>   With long, brown chestnut curl
>   Just think of me, Jack Haggerty,
>   And my own Flat River girl."

Roe applauded politely and the others joined in as the old woman finished.

"I ain't much for singing," Granny Piggott declared. "But I do know a song or two."

"I'm sure you do, Granny," Roe answered. "And 'Flat River Girl' is a beautiful song."

"That the kind that yer collectin'?"

"Yes, but I really care for the older ones."

"Older ones?" Granny looked puzzled. "How can ye tell how old they are?"

"By the words they use and the way the song is written. Songs with the same line twice, for instance, are quite an old style. Like 'What will you do with your pretty little babe? Dear son, come tell to me. I'll leave it all alone with you to dandle on your knee, knee, knee. To dandle on your knee."

The old lady's blue eyes brightened. "My mam used to sing me that tune," she said. "Lor-a-Lor, I ain't thought of such in years."

"I'd love to hear some of the songs that your mother sang to you," Roe told her.

Granny smiled thoughtfully for a moment.

"Here is one fer ye," she said finally.

> "Come go with me, my pretty fine miss,
>   Come go with me, my honey,
>   Come go with me, my pretty fine miss,

And ye'll ne'er want for money.
Ye'll ne'er want for money."

As the old woman sang eight complete verses of the tune she called "Gypsy Davy," Roe listened with interest. If Granny Piggott would sing her songs for him, and she would get her friends and family to do the same, his prospects on Marrying Stone Mountain had suddenly greatly improved. He glanced over at Meggie. Personally, it might make good sense to go ahead and leave. But listening, at last, to the nineteenth-century Ozark version of a sixteenth-century English ballad made the idea of leaving no longer greatly appealing.

"Just a few weeks," Roe said to Meggie as they sat alone in the silence after Granny had left. He'd managed to record a half-dozen songs that he'd never heard before, two or three that had all the earmarks of Celtic origin. "If I could have just a few weeks to either confirm or deny." He hesitated slightly and then finally spoke the words that were on his mind. "What if we don't tell folks we aren't married, we just don't say anything at all."

Meggie was silent, thoughtful. In the back of her mind she could still hear Granny's voice as she told the sweet, funny story of her marriage to old Grandpa Piggott. She imagined them, young and in love, and carving out a place of their own, side by side, in this isolated wilderness.

"I know that it is not entirely honest," Roe continued. "But it is such a wonderful opportunity. It's a gold mine here, Meggie. A gold mine of history and music."

Meggie didn't care much for gold mines, historical or otherwise, but the fantasy of pretending herself married to Roe Farley was an enticing one.

"The period in history that we are saving in these bits and pieces is one of the most glowing and important in the history of the English language. It is like the crossroads between an old tribal world of superstition and isolation and the enlightenment of universal Anglo-Christian values. And it can only be saved here, Meggie. Here in these dark, backwoods homesteads, among these special, separate people that you know as family and friends. These families have unknowingly been the preservation of these long-gone days. But now, modern machinery is here to keep safe for all time what you have managed to sustain."

Roe stood to pace the ground before her.

"It would mean so much to my work. And my work is so important. Just think about the gift we'd be giving, you and I, to future generations of English-speaking people. Saving these songs is not bringing our ancestors back from the dead, but it is, in a way, making them live in us again. It's like putting water on the last dying flowers of spring or cutting a swatch of baby hair on a child you are sending off to school."

He sat down beside her, his bright brown eyes were wide with sincerity and anticipation. "If we don't do it now, Meggie, if we don't save it here, while we can, we may never get the opportunity again. It's important that it be done and it's paramount that we do it now. And you, Meggie Best, you can be a part of that."

Meggie wasn't thinking about saving the last flowers of spring, swatches of baby hair, or the music of a time long gone. Meggie's thoughts centered on the clean, masculine smell of the man who sat so warm and close beside her. And the sweet, sweet fantasy of working alongside that man if only for the summer. As Granny had helped carve a homestead in the mountains, Meggie saw herself working alongside Monroe Farley, a scholarly, princely man whose work came out of an Ediphone Listening Box and who needed her help, if not her life, as a helpmate.

His songs were like her fairy tales. They were a way to touch dreams that could never be lived. He touched her dreams. She wanted to touch his.

"All right," Meggie said quietly. "I'll do it."

Roe was momentarily stunned. He'd never expected her to give in so easily. Her quick capitulation made him think more deeply and consider more wisely.

"Maybe we shouldn't," he suggested. "Once we start a lie like this, it will be very hard to get untangled from it."

"No, no. We'll do it. We won't really have to lie at all. We'll just let people think whatever they want. But we'll have to tell Pa the truth," Meggie stated firmly. "I have to insist on that. Pa must know everything."

"Of course he will," Roe agreed.

"Living here and all, he'll see the truth anyway and it would just be best if he were in on this from the start."

Roe nodded in agreement. "We'll tell your family the truth. That is the only thing to do."

Meggie glanced up. "Just Pa. If we tell Jesse he won't understand and he'll be confused."

"Won't he be confused anyway when people talk about us as though we're married and we're not . . . not living as married."

Meggie shook her head. "Jesse doesn't know anything about that," she said with calm assurance. "We just won't say anything at all to him and he'll just think that things are the way they are."

Roe had his doubts about that, but decided Meggie knew her brother much better than he did.

They sat silently together for a long moment. Roe's expression, at first joyous, became slowly more and more concerned.

"I'm not sure you should do this," he said finally.

"Me?"

"Yes, you. If we pretend we're married, what will that do to your future?"

"My future? I don't suspect it will do anything at all to it," she said.

"When the fall comes," Roe asked thoughtfully, "and I

have to leave, can you just say I was a no-account and ran off?"

Meggie thought about that for a long moment. "That's no good," she said. "People are going to know you by then and it'll be hard to believe that a man like you would be so dishonorable."

Raising a surprised eyebrow, Roe gazed across the porch at Meggie. Honorable? Meggie Best thought him honorable.

"No," she continued. "You can't just run off and leave me. 'Cause then I'd still be married to you forever."

"You're right," Roe agreed. "Of course you'll want to *really* marry someday and have a family and all of that." Strangely Roe found the idea of that prospect not at all pleasing.

"I suspect so," Meggie answered. "Though, truth to tell, if things on the mountain stay the way they are, there is not a fellow here that I'd take to husband. Not a one of them interests me a bit."

"Well, maybe your *real* prince will come for you one of these days. I sure wouldn't want you to have to turn him down if he did."

Roe had meant the comment to be light and humorous, but he saw that he'd embarrassed Meggie.

"I guess there's no way you can forget my talking foolishness the other day," she said.

Roe hastily apologized for his teasing. "It's really not that foolish," he said. "I suspect that we all have ideas in our mind about the person we hope someday to marry."

Meggie shook her head. "I bet you don't sit around thinking about some princess dropping into your world from out of the blue."

Roe was thoughtful for a long moment. "No, I guess that I never thought of a princess specifically," he said. "But I have thought about the woman I would want someday to marry."

"Well, everyone gives it a thought, I reckon," Meggie

said. "But most folks don't waste their time on spinning fancy dreams in their mind."

"Actually, I think, Meggie, that most people do. Over the years I've given the idea of marriage a good deal more thought than was strictly necessary," he admitted.

"I don't believe it."

"Well, it's true. I've spend many frivolous moments lolling over the question of what sort of woman I want to someday marry."

"And what kind of wife did you come up with?"

Roe chuckled. "Oh, the usual type, I suppose. I imagine her as being a bit pretty," he said. "No great beauty, mind you, I'm not greedy, but someone nice on the eye." He hesitated. "Bright, she'd have to be bright. Intelligence is very important; I want a marriage where the husband and wife converse easily together. She'd need to be socially skilled, because I'm not particularly. And I want her to have excellent family connections. That would be a boon to me in my work."

Roe glanced at Meggie to find her listening with surprising interest.

"Fortunately, she wouldn't need to have any great wealth or inheritance. My father's business ventures have left me with a comfortable legacy. But I would like her to be well read and interesting. A woman who could step easily into my world."

Meggie nodded gravely, taking his words into serious consideration.

"The future deserves important consideration, Meggie. I don't think you need to be ashamed of spending your leisure time pondering it."

Meggie smiled at him, clearly pleased that for once someone seemed to understand her dreaminess and not put it up to ridicule.

"And that future is just the reason why we can't just let

people think that we are married and expect no consequences from such a lie."

Meggie nodded. "I suppose you are right about that," she said. "It just won't do to leave things up in the air so."

"If there was some way to be married now and then not be married later, I would agree to the deception," Roe said. "But I don't see any way to manage that."

Meggie was thoughtful. "It's just that folks have got to see things work out one way or the other or they just can't never live in peace again."

"I don't think there is any way," Roe said, "to pretend we're married for just a little while and then to gracefully back out of it later with neither of us any worse for the experience."

"I think there is a way," she said.

"There is?" Roe asked, disbelieving.

Meggie sat staring thoughtfully into the nothingness beyond the woods for long moment, a tiny smile just curving at the corner of her mouth.

Roe watched her entranced. She had that expression he'd come to recognize as her dreaming look. Her eyes were glazed and her face serene, but her mind was clicking faster than the crank on his Ediphone. Her dreamer's fancy was scheming up a plan. With a surprisingly complete sense of confidence, Roe waited.

"There is only one answer," she said finally. "You are just going to have to die."

"What?"

"You have to die. Not now," she explained quickly. "At the end of the summer when your work's all done."

Roe stared at her dumbfounded. When she saw the look on his face, she laughed out loud.

"Dad-burn and blast, Farley," she said, elbowing him playfully in the ribs. "You look like you expect me to stick a knife to your gullet any second."

"What do you mean, I have to die?"

"Well, I don't mean that I'm going to plant you six feet under up in the churchyard," she answered.

"Then what exactly do you mean?"

"Well, now just think about it. When you get your work done in the fall, you'll have to take a trip back to the Bay State. Even if you planned on staying with me forever, you'd have to go to turn in those wax rollers of yours, wouldn't you?"

Roe glanced thoughtfully at the Ediphone and nodded. "Well, yes, I suppose so."

"And were you really my husband and had to go away, why I'd be sad and sorry to see you off. But I'd send you just the same."

"You wouldn't have much choice. It's my work and it's important."

Meggie nodded reasonably. "And you'd promise to come back as quick as you could. But sometimes heaven don't let us keep some of our promises."

Roe nodded gravely as he listened. "And?" he asked as the silence lengthened.

"After you're gone a couple of weeks, I'd say I got word that you was killed. In an accident on the Mississippi, maybe, or in New Orleans or something."

Roe raised an eyebrow.

"I'd be torn up and tragic something awful. You can believe that. And I'd wear black for you for a full year. But I'm young and strong and I'd make it through my grief somehow."

Meggie's expression had taken on an overly dreamy look as she dramatically clutched her hands to her chest.

"You see what I'm getting at, Farley?" she asked him. "I'll be a widow and you'll be free and none will be the wiser."

Roe's brow furrowed thoughtfully for a long moment. "Meggie," he said finally, "I think it just might work."

*   *   *

The first appearance of Mr. and Mrs. Monroe Farley at church the next day was an event. After the protests of Friday night and the silly story of the skunk on the Marrying Stone, the community was glad to see the young couple owning up to the truth and generally they were being wished well.

They'd stepped into the churchyard clearing as the bell continued to toll. Most of the same crowd from the Friday Literary was in attendance, with the exception of a few of the wildest young men and some hard-grizzled older ones.

Meggie and Roe had spent much of the walk to the church together. Jesse had hurried ahead of them, nearly skipping with delight. Eager to tell anybody and everybody that his frien', Roe Farley, was now his brother, too.

Roe and Meggie had not spent the time whispering sweet nothings in each other's ears. They were carefully going over the details of their story. Determined to get the most from the situation with the least entanglement. If asked straight out if they were married, it was decided that they would simply answer, "We jumped the Stone." Beyond that, they decided it best to say as little as possible.

Roe stood tall and strong at Meggie's side and she felt somehow bolstered by his presence. Dressed in his patched city clothes, Roe looked very much like a handsome prince and Meggie, in her best homespun, felt dowdy beside him.

She was nervous and unsure. It was one thing to decide to pretend to being married. It was quite another to make the whole congregation believe that it was true.

They were walking together through the dewy grass when Meggie's girlfriends, all dressed in bright colors like a bouquet of wildflowers, hurried up to greet them. Giggly and excited, they obviously wanted to gather Meggie into a hug as they always had, but hesitated as if shy in front of her new husband.

"Meggie, we're so happy for you," tiny Polly Trace told

her with a warm squeeze of her hand. "I think it's all so romantic."

Roe smiled broadly. A little too broadly, Meggie thought. He was so good-looking, she worried that he might turn one of the girls' heads. He'd certainly turned hers.

Mavis Phillips giggled as usual, her laughter tossing her bright red curls. "And that skunk story was the funniest reason given for jumping the Stone that I've ever heard."

Meggie, uneasy, cleared her throat intending to make some sort of reasonable explanation. But Alba Pease spoke up before she could.

"It is the newest way to get yourself married," the teasing young clown told them with a bright smile and a glint in her eye. "We simply need to remember to lure some likely fellow up to the Stone and have him look deep into our eyes. If we're as lucky as Meggie, he'll be seeing skunks for sure." She winked at Roe.

Feeling the blush of embarrassment stain her cheeks, Meggie saw no humor in Alba's joke. But beside her, Roe laughed out loud.

"I think you've got it wrong there, Miss Pease," he said. "When I look into my bride's eyes, the last thing I ever think about is skunks."

Polly sighed, and Mavis and Alba giggled. Eda stood slightly back, observing quietly. A moment later Roe was drawn away into the crowd of men by the jokes and Broody twins. Representatives of both the Piggott and McNees clans wanted to offer well wishes to the lucky groom.

Meggie was left with her friends. And without her husband's protection, Eda Piggott spoke her piece.

"I wish you the best of luck," she said stiffly.

"Thank you, Eda," Meggie said. "I . . . we . . . some things just happen."

"Oh, I know," Eda said. "Sometimes things do happen. But I believe you said it yourself the other day. The whole mountain will be laughing when he leaves you before the first snow."

"Eda!" With a less than ladylike jerk, Alba pulled the jealous young woman away from the group and shot Meggie an apologetic glance.

Anger welled up in Meggie, but she held her head high. She knew she was being baited, and she wasn't about to give Eda the pleasure of seeing her react. However, she couldn't quite get past the truth that, everyone laughing or no, Roe Farley *would* be leaving before the first snow.

That was a long time off, of course. At least it had seemed so yesterday. Right now it appeared to be hurrying toward them.

Roe was laughing a little too loudly when he managed to draw away from the jabbing jokes of good humor offered by the menfolk. He took Meggie's arm at once and with as much haste as they could manage through the friendly, curious crowd, he led her to the church door.

Pastor Jay was waiting, as always, to greet his flock. "Good morning, Farley, Mrs. Weston," the old man said as they entered the doorway. "I had hoped your father would be with you this morning."

"Onery's already in his seat," Roe answered.

"No, not Onery, I meant *your* father. I do a goodly amount of praying for Gid Weston's soul," the preacher admitted.

"Pastor Jay," Meggie began once more, but with a gentle touch on her arm, Roe stilled her words.

"We appreciate that, Pastor Jay," he said simply and moved past the preacher.

"Pastor Jay is beyond our help," he told her as they walked down the smooth pine plank floor toward the front of the church. Only one large, glassless window lightened the building and it was at the far end of the church behind the pulpit. The benches were that, benches. Plain polished oak slats on short legs, no backs, no arms and certainly none

of the padded prayer rails common to churches in
Cambridge. If a man were to fall asleep during one of Pastor
Jay's sermons, he'd likely fall flat on the floor.

As they took their places next to Jesse and Onery,
Meggie's father looked over at her and shook his head with
consternation. "You two are sure causing quite a commotion. I thought ye might."

Meggie looked around to see every eye in the church
upon her. She knew that what her father said was true, but
didn't know quite how to stop what was started.

Buell Phillips, dressed as finely as Roe, but not looking
nearly so comfortable in his clothes, stopped by the pew and
offered his hand.

"Welcome to the family, Farley," he said with a polite nod
to Meggie. "Even though you are an outsider, son, I want
you to feel as much a family member of the Piggotts as yer
new wife."

"Thank you," Roe answered.

"We're a loyal and right-thinking clan and we stick
together for everyone on everything." His manner was
pompous and superior and Meggie wished she could just tell
him to shut up and go sit down.

"Just 'cause you weren't born a Piggott, don't mean that
you aren't as much one of us as if you were. Why ask Onery,
he'll tell you that we always treat him like he's a part of us."

As Buell stepped away, Jesse said with quiet curiosity,
"Pa always says he don't want to be a part of them
hardheaded Piggotts a'tal."

Roe turned his chuckle into a more circumspect cough.
But Meggie didn't feel much like laughing.

The service started with Pastor Jay leading the congregation in singing "How Firm a Foundation." No music
accompanied him, but the preacher waved his hand and
stamped his foot against the floor of the raised pulpit to keep
time.

Meggie still felt all eyes on her and wondered if her dress

looked too shabby and if her hair was neat in the back. Mostly she wondered what Roe Farley thought of her church, her family, and his make-believe marriage to a scatterbrained Ozark mountain woman.

As the last harmonic notes faded, Pastor Jay bowed his head and prayed. Meggie, her heart still pounding from fear of imminent discovery and her mind still skimming over the possibilities of what Roe Farley might be thinking, barely listened to the words until she heard her name mentioned.

Her eyes popped open and she raised her head in genuine horror as the preacher's words permeated her consciousness.

"We ask, Gracious Father," the preacher said, "that you see it your way to bless the newest union in our congregation, our own young Meggie and Farley. That you watch and care for their hearts and bodies and allow that they be fruitful and fulfilling of your plan for them."

Meggie felt cold as stone and trembled. That her lie, their lie, was being made in church seemed momentarily the most wicked evil ever done. Suddenly she felt the touch of Roe's hand.

She glanced over to see him looking at her. His brown eyes wide with sympathy and guilt. But his whisper was soft and warm against her ear, tickling the fine hairs on her neck.

"It's only a small untruth and for a good purpose," he said. He squeezed her hand warmly and his strength gave her courage.

She smiled at him bravely, and found herself settling in more closely beside him. If they were to pretend to be married, it would only seem natural that they act like newlyweds. He was warm and strong and handsome beside her. And it wasn't really so big a lie as that.

FROM THE JOURNAL OF
J. MONROE FARLEY

May 21, 1902
Marrying Stone, Arkansas

Am making progress beyond my wildest dreams. The young woman with whose family I have taken up residence is helping me, with a bit of innocent subterfuge, to win over the people of the mountain. The matriarch of this particular community has given me her blessing, and with her approval, the populace is anxious to offer their knowledge and remembrances. Last Sunday at the church meeting, I received so many offers of help that I had to begin making appointments to see all of the willing participants.

Meetings and recordings are made mostly in the evening as the spring and summer is a very busy time for the mountain people. Young Jesse and I go out on mule back late in the day to homesteads and cabins all up and down both sides of the mountain.

That actually suits me very well as the farmer, Mr. Best, keeps me quite busy earning my keep around his place. Not only am I expected to help his son Jesse with planting and livestock care, I am now involved in adding a small room onto the log house in which the family lives. I have my own bed now. A gift from one of the local people. Jesse and I have set it up in the empty foundation of the soon to be extra room. I find that I don't mind sleeping out under the weather; however, I am not at all looking forward to the rain. I am learning a good deal, as I knew nothing of rail splitting, carpentry, or mud daubing prior to my introduction to it here. It is hard, hot work and I believe my very weary arms are now perhaps twice the circumference they were when I left Cambridge. I have no idea upon what occasion I might find my newfound knowledge and prowess to be needful, but still I am eager to learn the primitive ways and have discovered a certain sense of accomplishment in the product of my more rigorous labors.

Tonight, young Jesse and I will be "chasing meat." His term. We have been so busy with the farm work and building, there has been no opportunity for hunting. So tonight, having no appointments of my own, Jesse has invited me to go with him. As the young man is not allowed to carry a gun without his father present and since we will be hunting at night, I can't imagine what our prey might be. But I will go along as is expected. Perhaps Jesse will bring his fiddle and play. His music is such that I have no doubt that he could coax birds out of the trees if necessary.

CHAPTER

TWELVE

IT WAS FULL dark and Roe was already weary before the night hunting expedition even began. The evening breeze lightly ruffled Roe's hair as he made his way down the well-worn trails.

The sounds of tree frogs and katydids filled the darkness. In the distance an old owl screeched angrily at some unwelcome visitor to his neighborhood. Carrying a gray burlap tow sack, Roe followed the beam of light that glowed from the grease lamp that Jesse carried. The grease lamp was merely a quart-size cast-iron cooking vessel that was filled near to the brim with rancid grease. A thin cotton cord served as its wick and what the homemade lantern lacked in brightness and reliability, it made up for in efficiency and expense.

"It's better than pine knots," Jesse had explained when he'd lit it up. "Got more control of the fire and yer less likely to dump it on the ground and start up a blaze."

Roe didn't question his statement. Nor had he thought to question Jesse about what they were to hunt, but Roe was surprised to see the young man carrying only a small, three-pronged spear tied to a length of cord.

"What is that thing?" Roe asked. "A harpoon?"

Jesse looked puzzled. "What's a harpoon?"

"It's something that you kill whales with. Whales are like very big fish."

The young man nodded a little uncertainly.

"Well, maybe it is a harpoon," Jesse said. "You can catch fish with it, if you're a mind to." He held it up to the light for Roe's closer inspection. "This is a gigger. It's what you use to go giggin'."

"Gigging?"

"Yep."

"Is that what you call hunting at night, gigging?"

Jesse laughed delightedly. "Your thinkin' is downright peculiar, frien'. Hunting at night is hunting at night. Giggin' is giggin'. Course, most giggin' is done at night, but it ain't a rule or nothing."

"What kind of things can you hunt at night?"

"Oh, coons, possums, most anything that you've a hankering for. The light scares the critters and freezes them in their tracks. Mostly I hunt possums at night."

"And you kill them with this gigger?"

Jesse's eyes twinkled with delight. "I don't gig much for possums," he answered with laughter at his good little joke. He held his shoulders straight and proud. Pleased that on the subject of hunting, he was both more knowledgeable and more experienced. "Now, don't you worry, Roe. It ain't hard a'tal. You'll get the hang of it in a jiffy. You just follow my lead and we'll have a plate full of great eating before the night's half gone."

They had reached the widest part of Itchy Creek. Jesse began to slowly, quietly make his way along the edge of the bank.

"Just keep your ears open for the croaking," he whispered. "When you come upon a feller, you just shine the light in the frog's eye and while he's watching it, you stab him with the gigger."

"Frog?"

"Bullfrogs," Jesse answered. "You know, those big green ones. We're a-giggin' for bullfrogs."

"Jesse, what on earth are we going to do with a dead bullfrog?"

"Not one." Jesse pointed to the tow sack Roe still held in his hand. "We'll need a sack full to make a decent mess."

"A decent mess of what?"

"Frog legs."

"Jesse, I don't think—"

"Shhhhhh," Jesse hushed him. The deep-throated croak of the bullfrog was loud along the bank. With the careful, quiet moves of a cat stalking a bird, Jesse moved up the bank toward the sound of the bullfrog's presence.

With the grease lamp in his left hand, Jesse flashed the light before the big green frog. Just as the young man had said, the stunned river dweller was frozen in place just long enough for Jesse to thrust the gigger into the unwary fellow's back.

"Got 'im!" Jesse yelled with delight. "Open that sack, Roe. We got our first catch of the night."

To Roe's disbelief, the big bullfrog was more than a foot long and frantically kicking his heavily muscled hopping legs. Holding the tow sack open, he watched Jesse push the frog off the end of the forked prong.

"You ain't never eat frog legs?" Jesse asked.

"No, not ever."

"My frien', you've a delight coming that even you cannot imagine. Frog legs are so good, even Meggie cain't ruin 'em." Jesse chuckled happily.

"I'll take your word for it," Roe answered, less enthusiastically.

"See how easy giggin' is," Jesse said. "The next croaker we find is all yours."

"I don't know, Jesse."

"Now, Roe, we both know how smart ye are. Yer smarter than me, smarter than folks around here, so you are sure enough smarter than an old green bullfrog. You can't let that dumb ole creature get the best of you."

Roe was quite willing to do just that, but seeing himself through Jesse's eyes made a difference.

"It ain't like you're a-killing some cute hoppy toad," Jesse explained. "Bullfrogs is big and ugly and just sit on the banks all day and eat flies. They don't serve mankind much purpose, except that they is meat. And if a man's a man, he's obliged to fetch up the meat."

Jesse's words were so sincere and so reminiscent of Onery's way of speech that Roe was immediately certain that the young man had been served up that exact lecture upon some long-ago gigging trip when he was as hesitant and uninterested in participating as Roe was now.

Jesse was sharing his knowledge, simple though it might be, and Roe didn't have the heart to scorn it. Smiling, Roe hoped he looked more appreciative than he felt.

"Just lead me to the next croaker, Jesse," he said. "I'm ready to try my hand at this gigging business."

Jesse grinned with pleasure and threw his arms around Roe's shoulders, hugging him with the warmth and love of a brother. Roe managed not to flinch.

"Frien'," Jesse told him. "We're about to fetch up the best mess of Arkansas frog legs a body has ever tasted."

They continued to walk along the edge of the wood near the riverbank. Jesse was slightly stooped and listening. Roe followed behind carrying the big gray tow sack, the contents of which continued to jump and wiggle within the bag. Only a couple of minutes passed before Jesse stopped suddenly. He motioned to Roe, who could then also hear the deep, bass-throated croak along the bank.

"Your turn," Jesse said with a delighted grin as he exchanged the gigger and lamp in his own hands with the sack in Roe's.

Roe tested the weight of the gigger in his right hand a couple of times before determinedly heading off in the direction of the calling bullfrog. He stepped easily, as Jesse had done, placing each foot carefully in the grass before moving up the other. The break of a twig or the snap of underbrush would be enough to warn the noisy croaker on the bank to flee from danger.

When he got as close as he dared, Roe pushed the grease lamp up near the creature's head. As before, the noisy green fellow was stunned stiff into silence. Roe took a deep breath. Raising the gigger high, he plunged it with a goodly amount of force right through the wide, slick, slimy back of the big old frog.

"You got him!"

Roe heard Jesse's cry of congratulations and it distracted him prematurely. The bullfrog jerked strongly at the gigger and dived headlong into the safety of the creek.

"Whoa!"

"Hang on to the cord," Jesse urged.

Roe managed to hang on and a minute later pulled the still fighting and protesting bullfrog back onto the bank. He picked up the gigger and held it high. The angry frog was kicking and twitching on the sharp, pronged metal piece.

"Now all we got to do is get him into the sack without letting the other one out."

It took a good deal of maneuvering, a couple of false starts, and some laughter to get both frogs in the sack at the same time. But by the time the two had managed to spear a couple dozen of the hoppy critters, they'd become experts at slipping one frog off the gigger without allowing any of the others access to the opening in the sack.

They were still walking the rustling length of the river-bank listening for the noisy croak when the rustle of something much bigger was heard in the brush behind them.

Roe started. But Jesse looked back with more curiosity than concern. "Ain't no bear steps that careless," he told Roe. "Over here," he called out. "Is that you, Pa?"

"It ain't your Pa, Simple Jess," the voice answered back.

A moment later a big strapping man in a wide-brimmed felt hat stepped out of the shadows. "It's Gid Weston."

"Oh, it's *my* Pa," Roe answered jokingly.

When the man looked at him curiously, Roe hid his grin at the small private joke and offered his hand. "Pleased to meet you, Mr. Weston. I'm J. Monroe Farley."

The man nodded slightly, his eyes moving over the newcomer as he took Roe's measure. Roe obliged him by doing the same, wondering what there was about himself that the pastor had mistaken for a son of the man before him. He found Weston to be near his own size and frame, although he was a whole generation older and wore his age like a sagging sack of beans around the middle of his waist. He didn't appear to be all that clean and his odor was pungent with sweat and wood smoke, bear grease and stale liquor.

"You're the city man what come and married up Best's daughter," he said.

Roe cleared his throat and nodded.

"He was my frien' afore he was her man," Jesse stated proudly. "I'm teachin' him how to gig and we got near a full poke of the biggest ole bullfrogs on the river."

The man nodded and held out his hand. Jesse handed him the sack of bullfrogs and he weighed it thoughtfully. He made a small approving sound.

"You done caught this many already and the night ain't even half over," he said.

Jesse shook his head proudly. "It's a good night for it and Roe and I, well, we ain't bragging but we ain't missed but two frogs all evening and one of them weren't hardly big enough to worry about."

"That's awful good giggin'," Weston said. "I ain't had no time for such myself lately." He looked thoughtfully from one young man to the other for a moment. "A mess of fried frog legs sure sets well on a man's belly, don't it?"

"It sure do," Jesse agreed easily.

"Suspect I oughter send some of my boys out to fetch me up a mess myself."

"They's plenty on the river," Jesse said.

"Course, those boys of mine don't listen to their daddy worth nothing no more. And they's all about half lazy. Take from their mama's side of the family, I think."

"Pa always said that you was pretty lazy, too," Jesse told the man with innocent honesty.

Weston chuckled lightly, not bothering to take offense. "Well, when it comes to night giggin', I guess your pa maybe is speaking the truth. Tell you what, boys," he said, stepping closer and eyeing the frog sack assessingly. "You got the whole rest of the night to get as many of these bullfrogs as you've a mind to. I'll trade you halves of what you caught already for a gallon jug of donk. It oughter make the hunting of them a sight more pleasant anyhow."

"What's donk?" Roe asked.

"Donk?" Weston said. "You don't know donk?"

"But I do, Mr. Weston," Jesse answered eagerly. "I know donk and it's a trade!"

It was very late and Onery was already snoring loudly in the bed as Meggie stirred the hot kettle next to the fire. She wrinkled up her nose at the smell and grabbed up the already discolored battling stick that she was using to stir and agitate the material. The concoction, known as a blue pot, was a mix of indigo and madder root boiled together in lye. It was not as easy a fotched-on dye as walnut leaves or sassafras bark, but it could make her plain homespun cloth into the color of the prettiest periwinkle-blue on the mountain. And a pretty new dress was just what she needed. Meggie was downright determined to have one for her new life on the mountain.

Being a married lady, even a pretend one, was a good deal more interesting and exhilarating than Meggie had expected. She hadn't thought that folks would treat her differently or that the approach of the world around her would change. But it had, quite suddenly, and Meggie hadn't caught up to it yet.

She put the lid back on the kettle to try to keep the stench of hot lye from escaping out into the room.

She could hear her father's rhythmic snores from the one-poster bed on the far side of the room. Dying cloth was usually done outside. And no one dyed cloth in the middle of the night. But if she was to have a new dress by next Sunday, she needed to get the fabric colored right away. And she had to have a new dress by Sunday. If she didn't, folks might start thinking that her marriage wasn't going so well, or that her new husband was not a good provider. She blushed at the lame excuse. At least she should be honest enough with herself to admit that what she really wanted was to look something special when she walked into church next Sunday with Roe at her side. Not so that other folks would notice them, but so that Roe Farley might notice her.

She was Farley's new bride. At least that's how everybody she knew saw it. Unfortunately, she knew that neither she nor Roe could ever see it that way.

It was amazing how easily the people of Marrying Stone had accepted their little lie. She had thought there might be trouble, questions, curiosity. But her father had warned her to the contrary.

"None of these folks on the mountain is going to be worrying one iota about you and Farley. But, Meggie-gal," he'd said with a concerned furrow in his brow, "I'm a-worrying. And you ought to be, too."

"Pa, there is nothing to worry about." Meggie had spoken with a lightness that she didn't really feel.

Her father shook his head. "Ye can't just pretend you got feelings for a man for the rest of the summer and then jest let him walk out of yer life. Yer gonna get attached to this feller just as sure as the world. I don't want to see ye hurt, Meggie."

"Oh, Pa," she said. "Don't worry about me. I'm not about to get attached to some city feller," she lied, knowing full well that she already was. "I know exactly what I'm doing," Meggie insisted. "I'm helping Monroe get some of his work done and enjoying myself a little."

"What kind of enjoyment do ye get from pretending like you's married? Seems to me it's kind of like pretending ye got a bad head cold."

"It is fun," Meggie said. "Pulling a little joke on everybody on the mountain. Having people think that this city feller is wed up with me. And," she added with deliberate laughter, "it sure makes Eda Piggott turn greener than persimmons in springtime."

Her father tutted in disapproval. "That kinda green jealousy ain't a bit like you, Meggie. You are either changing, girl, or you're pretending with your ole daddy, too."

Meggie had no answer for that and didn't offer one.

Onery gave her a long look, clearly worried. "I cain't see that no good can come of this thing." His tone softened. "You watch yer heart, girlie. I'm afeared that you're likely to get it broken."

Meggie had similar fears. It had seemed easy, right at first. They'd just let people think that they were married. A little harmless lie that would allow Roe to do his work and maybe let her spend some more time with him, smiling at him, pretending with him. It didn't occur to her that being married would change her status in the community and that the opinion of both Roe and herself was now as intertwined as poison ivy in the pussy willows.

"That man of yours is gonna need another string for his bow," Granny Piggott had insisted when she had come to call along with half the married womenfolk of the community. Bearing recipes and helpful counsel, the women crowded the small area within the cabin. They stretched a quilt frame across their knees and chatted openly as they sewed together a wedding ring quilt for the new couple and offered their congratulations.

"You've always been a good worker, Meggie, for all your silly dreaminess. It's yer task to convince this city feller that scaring up a passel of old tunes and saving them on wax ain't going to put victuals on this table come wintertime."

"They pay him cash money for his work," Meggie answered. "It's not like he's doing his collecting just simply for the pleasure of it."

"You'd best get that cash money from him and sew it into a mattress tick," Beulah Winsloe said. "Men ain't got no sense about currency."

"Roe has sense about everything," Meggie said. "Any woman would be real lucky to have him."

"I'd say that you was especially lucky," Beulah Winsloe said as she tacked a curved piece in place. "Everybody knows what a poor cook you ere. If that don't bother him, then he must be a real tolerating and forgiving man."

The women all giggled. But Lessy Phillips scolded Beulah for her unkindness. "Don't you worry none about it, Meggie," she said. "You know you've got you a fine man that'll stay with you, even when you're at your worst. And you always have the comfort of knowing he didn't marry you just to get free victuals and housekeeping."

There were nods of agreement all around on that.

"You'll just get one word of advice from me," Wyla Pease said as she stopped to thread her needle. "It's real tempting once yer wed to let yerself go." The middle-aged woman gave a meaningful glance to her young daughter-in-law, Ruth, who since Sidney's birth four years ago had simply continued to get broader and broader in the backside. "Just because the man knows what you look like at your worst, don't mean he wants to look at you that way all the time."

Young Ruth snappped the thread she was sewing and gave her mother-in-law a stricken look.

"Ruth's built jest like her mama," Granny Piggott defended. "That boy of yourn saw the mother afore he seen the daughter. If he was going to be complaining, he shouldna' ever said the 'I do.'"

"My son would never utter a word of complaint!" Wyla protested.

"Good," Granny answered. "So if it don't bother him none, it shouldn't bother you."

Firmly put in her place, Wyla turned her concentration to the tiny line of stitches she was putting in the quilt. Meggie caught Ruth giving the old woman a grateful look.

Deftly changing the subject, Granny turned to Meggie and asked if she knew how to tell when she was taken to nesting.

Choking slightly on her words, Meggie answered with some embarrassment. "It's when your bleeding don't come."

The women all nodded.

Granny still saw fit to enlighten her. "As soon as you start waking in the morning all dauncy and like to puke, you tell yer husband to start taking swims in the cold creek. When you're carrying a babe, don't you be shaking the ticks out of the mattress more than oncest a week."

Around the quilt from the old woman, young and old giggled with immodest delight.

"Now that's an old rusty," Dorey McNees, a young cousin of Beulah's, said emphatically. "As long as your man can remember to be gentle and caring when you're in the family way," she told Meggie with a reassuring pat on the hand, "you can do all the sweetems and pleasuring you want, right up until yer lying in."

Granny snorted. "Remember to be gentle and caring?" She shook her head in disagreement. "I don't know about these young fellers today. But I never heared of a man what could remember so much as his own name when he's stiff as a poker and into the short rows."

The women laughed heartily.

Flushing a bright pink, still Meggie came quickly to Roe's defense. "Mr. Farley is always gentle and caring," she stated unequivocally.

Granny raised an eyebrow. "Now that surprises me, girl." The old woman scooted back away from the quilt frame and pulled her pipe out of her pocket and made to light it. Although Meggie never allowed smoking inside the house, she wouldn't have even attempted to try to stop Granny Piggott. "That Farley reminds me of my man, Lord rest his soul," she continued. "Both ere quiet and deep thinkin'. Slow to decide, but sure when they've resolved. My Piggott was a gentle feller, like yourn, in the daytime. But, lands-a-mighty, when I blew out the light of an evening, he'd batter the bedclothes 'til they was nothing but rags and lint."

The women around the quilt frame squealed with delight and worthy applause. Meggie, who could remember Granny's husband as a quiet, old gray beard, was shocked.

"Granny Piggott, you oughter be shamed," Beulah told her, laughing. "Look at this little gal. Lord, Meggie, I never dreamed that yer cheeks could get so red. You look like you've been plowing in summer without a hat."

"Well, she's only been married for little more than a week." Wyla chuckled naughtily. "That city feller's probably still telling her that he's got the only pepper pole that does that."

The wild married-women talk nearly embarrassed Meggie past living. Even now, days later with none to see but the blue pot, she still found herself blushing at the memory.

After the men had returned to the cabin, Granny had checked the foundation of the new room to the cabin. With a fine good humor, Meggie thought, Roe had taken up the project of the walls and roof. With Jesse helping and her father giving the direction, the little eight-by-eight room being raised on the back of the cabin would nearly double the space that they already had.

They had barely got the log base down against the ground

before Jesse and Roe had already set up the new bed in the empty space that was to be the room.

"Might as well set it up to make sure that it fits in the room," Roe said. "I believe I'll sleep out there from now on. It's better sleeping outside than in the loft."

Meggie nodded in understanding.

"Jesse can teach me all the names of the stars while I'm snoring in the moonlight," he added, slapping his friend companionably on the back.

"I don't mind sleeping in the loft," Jesse answered. "That new bed is for you and Meggie."

Meggie blushed. Roe choked. And Onery nervously cleared his throat.

Other than that, Jesse's comment was ignored. As was every comment made around the cabin about marriage, weddings, and beds since the day that she and Roe had commenced their foolish deception.

Meggie stirred the blue pot once more. The cloth inside seemed sufficiently colored, so she moved the kettle away from the flames and banked the fire for the evening.

Reluctantly, she went to spread her pallet on the floor. Somehow all the thinking and talking that had been done in the last weeks about men and women had sparked something inside Meggie.

She hated to lie down on her pallet at night and close her eyes, but she couldn't put it off any longer. Daylight would be upon her soon enough and keeping her wits about her was important if she was to keep her thoughts to herself.

Tiredly she lay down and closed her weary blue-gray eyes. And as soon as she did, just as she expected, she started having those feelings about him again. The loving feelings, she'd begun to call them. They were sweet and warm and she both craved and dreaded them. She longed for the strength of Roe's arms around her. And continually she remembered his look when he'd seen her naked in the bath.

Squeezing her eyes shut, Meggie tried to blot out the memory.

She drew a deep breath and rolled over upon her stomach, burying her face in her arms. Willing herself to sleep.

Quietly, she caught herself listening, just listening. Roe and Jesse hadn't come back from gigging, unless they'd avoided the cabin and were lying out in the new bed. Meggie strained her ears trying to make out the sound of Jesse's snore, but heard nothing.

Pa's snore, however, was deafeningly loud and inexplicably, after living with it for more years than Meggie could recall, the sound kept her awake.

Disgusted, she stood up and in the darkness made her way to the door. On the porch the air was cool and still and the bright stars twinkled over the tops of the mountain.

She closed the door behind her and sat down on the step, tucking the skirt of her josie tightly around her legs for warmth.

Actually trying not to, Meggie listened for the sounds of men in the half-raised add-on. There were none. The gigging must be mighty poor for two men to stay out half the night trying to gather up a mess of frog legs.

CHAPTER

THIRTEEN

IT WAS SO late, even the crickets were asleep as two men lay sprawled in the soft grass of a small clearing near the banks of the river. Jesse was still sucking on the remains of the earthen jug of donk. Roe's eyes were closed.

"What are ye doin'?" Jesse asked finally, half sitting to observe the man beside him.

Roe didn't open his eyes. "I'm just holding on to the grass and leaning against the ground."

Jesse chuckled. "That's donk."

"Why do you drink this?" Roe asked with a moan.

"I don't," Jesse answered. "Pa never let me, not even oncest. But I heard fellers talk about it lots and always wanted to find out for myself."

"Well, now we know." Roe did raise up a little then and with one eye glanced over at Jesse. "How come you aren't as drunk as I am?"

Jesse shrugged. "Guess 'cause I done threw up a couple of times."

Roe nodded and then wished that he hadn't. "That must be it."

A long, comfortable silence settled between the two men. Jesse took another long swig on the gallon jug. "They's lots of things in this world that I ain't done, but I'm a-wanting to do," he said.

"We all feel that way," Roe answered.

"But most fellers just ain't got around to doing all the things that they want. Some things, I just ain't never going to get to."

Roe was silent for a long moment. "I guess that's so, Jesse."

"I ain't fussing about it," the young man assured him quickly. "If I cain't never learn no book reading or figure my numbers above three, well, that's jest the way, ain't it?"

"I guess it is, Jesse."

"It does make me mad that I cain't have my own gun, nor earn money to buy me a dog." Jesse tipped the jug up high in the air, allowing the last drops of donk to cross his lips. "But someday," he said with the sincerity of a vow, "I'm gonna have a gun and a dog."

Roe nodded. "That's not a bad ambition, Jesse. I'm sure that as you act responsibly, your father will be more ready to let you have your own gun. And once you have a gun to hunt, well a dog will just make sense."

"Pa ain't gonna get it for me though," Jesse declared. "It's gonna be my gun and my dog and I'm gettin' 'em myself."

"I'm sure we'll all be very proud of you, Jesse."

The young man grinned and then, to Roe's surprise, threw back his head and howled at the moon.

"Lordy, this donk is something," Jesse said as he rose to his feet, took two steps, and then tripped over some hidden something in the high grass and fell head over heels and landed backward with a loud thump.

Both men laughed uproariously at what happened, until Jesse's laughter turned strained. "I've hurt myself," he told Roe, through hiccups. "Think I may have busted my leg."

Roe tried to stand up to go to him, but quickly decided it was much smarter to scoot across the grass. When he reached Jesse's side, the young man was still laughing at his antics, but there were genuine tears of pain in his eyes.

"Where does it hurt?" Roe asked.

Jesse showed Roe his ankle, which was already beginning to swell. Roe sat on the ground and took the other man's foot in his lap. Carefully he began to turn it.

"I don't think that it's broken," Roe told him. "But it's wrenched pretty bad."

Jesse nodded without speaking.

Roe looked around him with dismay. "I don't know how I'll manage to help you back to the house."

"Maybe I'll just stay here," Jesse answered. "It don't hurt much if I just stay still."

A wave of unwelcome nausea swelled in Roe's throat. He wished he could just stay still, too.

"I don't think you can just stay out here in the middle of the woods," he said as he looked around the clearing. His thinking almost as unclear as his eyesight, he tried to decide what was the best course of action. He was not steady enough on his own feet to carry Jesse to the cabin. But he worried that dragging him would surely cause a worse injury.

"You know, frien'," Jesse said, changing the subject. "You tole me that frien's always tell each other the truth."

"That's right, Jesse, they do," Roe answered only half listening.

"Well, I told you some of the truth, but I ain't tole you all."

"All the truth about what?"

"About the things I want, the things I ain't suppose to have but that I'm aiming to get anyway."

"Oh?" Roe asked, thinking that talking might be just the thing to keep Jesse's mind off his injury.

"It ain't just a gun and a dog that I'm a-wanting, Roe," he said quietly. "They's a bigger thing, a better thing, and Pa'd whoop me fer sure if he knowed I was thinking about it."

"What's that?"

"Someday, Roe," Jesse said in a cautious whisper, "I want to get me a woman."

"A woman!"

"Shhhhhh," Jesse quieted him. "Ain't no call for yelling it out."

"Sorry," Roe said. "I guess I was just surprised." Thinking for a moment, Roe shook his head. "No, I guess I'm not surprised. I don't think you'd be a man if you didn't *want* one," he said.

Nodding eagerly, Jesse blushed a little. "For the most they don't pay me no mind," he said. "But I can look and smell 'em just the same."

"Did you ever kiss one?"

His eyes widening in shock, Jesse shook his head negatively. "Pa says I cain't, never."

"Never?"

There was a faint sadness in his bright blue eyes. "Pa says that if'n I be kissing and squeezing on the gals, then they be thinkin' to marry. But there ain't no daddy on the mountain gonna want me for his son-in-law."

The simple truth of his words cut through Roe like a knife and was just as painful.

"A man would be lucky to get you in his family," Roe told him. "You're a hard worker and an honest fellow. A woman could do a lot worse."

Jesse grinned. "You're beginning to sound like Meggie, all right and ready to pitch a fit on my behalf." He shrugged and gave a light chuckle. "Pa says it's fate. Just like me being born simple. It's the way it is and it cain't be changed."

"Is that what you think, Jesse?"

The young man shrugged uncomfortably. "I don't know what to think. Pa is most always right. But still, I want a woman." He sighed wistfully. "Did you ever want a woman, Roe?" Jesse asked. "Truth now, remember we are frien's."

"Yes, of course I've wanted women."

Jesse nodded. "I thought so," he said. "In fact, I think you spend a bit of time wanting my sister Meggie."

"Well, I . . . well, yes I suppose I've had feelings like that about Meggie."

"Yep, I could tell you both got it bad."

Roe's brow furrowed, but he didn't have time to respond before Jesse's next question.

"Have you ever covered a gal?"

"You mean—"

Jesse nodded. "Yep, I mean—"

Roe cleared his throat and gazed momentarily at the heavens before answering honestly. "I have."

"What's it like?"

Roe shrugged self-consciously. "It's nice."

"Nice?"

Laughing, Roe shook his head drunkenly. "Maybe nice isn't exactly the right word. It . . . it feels real good."

Jesse nodded. "Better than doing it with your hand."

Roe hiccuped with surprise and then chuckled. He shook his head slightly in disbelief. "Yes, Jesse. I'd say it's better."

"Did the woman you done it with smell good?"

He was thoughtful for a long moment. "Honestly, Jesse, I don't believe that I remember how any of the women I've been with smelled."

"You've been with more than one?"

"A few, just a few."

Jesse pondered that for a moment. "Pa says that most fellers say they been with a lot of women, even if it ain't so."

Roe nodded. "I suspect some do."

Jesse grinned at Roe with pride. "But you didn't notice how they smelled?" he asked.

"Mostly I guess they smelled sort of sweaty," he answered. "Sometimes they smelled like perfume."

"Perfume." Jesse said the word in an awed whisper.

"I don't particularly care for perfume," Roe admitted. "Too much of it makes me sort of sick."

Jesse nodded solemnly as he sat up straighter. "So what does it feel like when you're inside a woman?"

"Jesse, I don't think we ought to be talking about this."

"You're my frien', Roe. If you ain't gonna tell me, then who is?"

Thoughtful for a long moment, Roe finally nodded in agreement. "Well, it's warm," he said. "It's real warm."

"Yeah," Jesse said, urging him on.

"And it's tight," he continued. "At first you think it's too tight, and then it's as if she opens up like a flower and almost pulls you inside her."

Jesse's eyes widened. "She pulls you inside?"

Roe nodded. "Yes, sort of. Then as you move back and forth, you can feel the draw and give of her muscles against you." Shaking his head, Roe drew a deep breath, looking out into nothing as he remembered and imagined. "The pressure is so good that it almost hurts," he said. "You want to push on to the end, 'cause that will make it feel better. But you don't want to stop either, so you try to hold it off as long as you can. When you can't wait a minute longer, it's like everything inside you, all you think and all you are, just comes pouring out inside her and you're not in you anymore, you're in her."

Jesse was gazing at him in wide-eyed wonder. He appeared so impressed with Roe's carnal knowledge that it was somewhat embarrassing.

Roe laughed drunkenly. "Of course, that only lasts a couple of seconds," he assured Jesse hurriedly. "Just a couple of seconds and you're back to being just a tired, but sated fellow who feels rather guilty and rather grateful to the woman with smeared face paint who let you spend yourself inside her."

Jesse shook his head in disbelief. "You done that lots of times, Roe?"

"Several times, Jesse. Not lots of times."

"Weren't you ever scared?"

"Yes, I was pretty scared the first time," Roe admitted. "And a little scared every time."

"Every time?"

"A man can always make a fool of himself, or hurt the woman, or, worse yet, not please her." Roe's expression slowly broadened to a grin. "But I guess," he admitted, "I always want to do it more than I'm scared to do it. So I go ahead and do it."

Jesse laughed with him at the little joke and they punched each other in the shoulder with camaraderie.

The young man's smile slowly faded and he nodded gravely. "I'm scared, Roe. But I want to do it, too."

Nodding, Roe didn't have any idea what to say.

"I am a man, just like you, just like any other man. And I don't really mind not being smart," Jesse continued. "I'm used to it and it just don't bother me much. Even when folks is teasing me, I jest ignore 'em and say, they's joking around and not meaning to be hurtful. I don't bother about it. But when I'm a-standing near a sweet-smelling gal, I jest get these feelings all over and it ain't like the hurt feelings. I cain't push 'em away."

"There is nothing unusual in that, Jesse," Roe said. "The feelings you have for women are from your body. They have nothing to do with being simple and being simple doesn't stop you from having them."

"But Pa says that I cain't never let 'em go."

Roe's brow furrowed in worry and thoughtful consideration. "I'm sure your father only wants what he thinks is best for you, Jesse," Roe said. "But he's a father, too, and maybe he's not thinking of you as quite a man."

"I don't suspect he ever will."

"But I do, Jesse. I think you are a man."

Roe's quiet words had the power to raise Jesse's drooping chin and bring a warm smile to his face. "Thanks, frien'," he said.

The quiet of the late night was all around them. The

woods were dark and looming with the rustle of leaves and the long grass beneath them was damp with dew. Their eyes were momentarily content with the hazy vision of liquor.

"You know what we need to do, Jesse?" Roe asked with sudden excited determination.

"What?"

"We need to get you a woman."

"What?"

"Like you said, not a lot of women or one forever, but I'm sure that even in this backwoods there are women of, shall we say, uncertain virtue."

Jesse's eyes widened.

"Well there's the Widder Plum down near the blackberry hollow," he said.

"The Widow Plum," Roe repeated.

"That's what she calls herself, but I heard the fellers saying she ain't a widder a'tal, just her man runned off and she entertains fellers of an evening."

Roe nodded. "Well, Jesse. I think that you and I had better pay a call to the widow."

"Tonight! Can we go tonight?"

"Of course we can't go tonight," Roe answered. "You can't even walk. You'll have to get your ankle healed up before you can go pay a call."

"It's feeling better already," Jesse insisted as he lurched to his feet.

Roe wrapped an arm about his waist and encouraged Jesse to lean against him. "We're going to get you back to the house and let you lay up a couple of days and when you're fit, we'll go to see this widow of yours."

Jesse hollered with donk-driven delight. "I cain't wait!"

"Sure you can, you've waited all this time. A few days won't matter."

The two half walked, half dragged themselves across the field, making their way home.

"At the Literary the other night," Jesse admitted in quiet

confession, "I was standing behind Althea McNees. She's the one that's about to wed Paisley Winsloe."

Roe nodded, remembering the young woman.

"Oh, she smells real good, Roe," Jesse told him breathlessly. "She must put sweet spices in her soft soap, I think."

Roe smiled.

"I was jest standing behind her and smelling her and I wanted that so bad, Roe, I was near fit to cry."

Nodding, Roe patted his friend on the shoulder. "I've felt that way myself a time or two, Jesse," he said. "It's normal. It's what every man feels from time to time. We can't be blamed for wanting. Sometimes we're not allowed to act upon what we want, but that doesn't mean we still don't want it."

"Did you ever feel that way about Althea McNees?" Jesse asked.

"No, not about her," Roe admitted.

Jesse nodded. "You feel that way about Meggie," he said with certainty.

"Meggie!" Roe's head spun around so quickly, it made him dizzy and he nearly dropped Jesse on the path.

"Yeah, Meggie. My sister, your woman," Jesse said. "Truth, remember."

"I . . . I sometimes feel that about Meggie," Roe admitted.

Jesse shook his head. "I swear, Roe, I don't understand none of this marriage thing. If you want to and you're not scared and you done it afore," Jesse asked, "why ain't you laying with Meggie?"

The question, to Roe's mind, came out of nowhere.

"Meggie?"

"You're her man, ain't you? Everybody says so and ye ain't denied it much since that first day. You jumped the Marrying Stone together. That gives you the right to be doing it whenever you want."

"We may have the *right* and it still not be right, Jesse."

"It's got to be right. It ain't like me wanting Althea McNees and she wanting to wed up with Paisley Winsloe. You're wanting Meggie and she's a-wanting you. So, if you're both a-wanting why ere ye sleeping in yer new bed alone?"

Roe cleared his throat nervously. "It's complicated," he said. "And what makes you think that Meggie wants me?"

Jesse laughed out loud. "That's a good one, Roe. Lord, Meggie's so stuck on you if you crossed yer eyes that gal'd be looking slant-back for all time."

Meggie heard them long before she saw them. Disturbing the quiet night sounds of crickets and tree frogs was the stamp and crash of grass and broken underbrush and the low-pitched giggling of her brother Jesse.

With more curiosity than concern, Meggie hurried into the woods bordering the clearing. It wasn't until she saw them crossing Itchy Creek, Jesse leaning heavily upon Roe that she gave a little startled cry.

"What happened?"

The two men looked up at her.

"Hey, Meggie," her brother called out. "My frien' Roe and I are jest sharing a bit of hospitality." He giggled loudly. "Or was we sharing a bit of donk?"

"Donk!" Meggie's expression turned furious. "Monroe Farley, have you gone and got my brother drunk?"

Jesse had quit walking midway across the stream. Roe, holding the sack of frogs, the gigger, the grease lamp, and the empty jug in his hands, still managed to drag Jesse to the near shore where the two, together with their gear, fell in a heap at Meggie's feet.

"I didn't get him drunk," Roe answered. "He got me drunk."

"But it's a good thing I'm drunk, Meggie," Jesse piped in. "'Cause I done broke my leg and if it weren't for that fiery donk, I'd probably be hurting real bad."

Roe had laid back against the grass and closed his eyes in the vain hope of stopping the ground from spinning. "Don't worry, Jesse," he said, only half joking. "I got a feeling that there will be plenty of hurting to go around tomorrow."

Meggie dropped down on the grass between Roe and her brother. "Dad-burn and blast, Jesse. Let me see your leg."

"It's not broken," Roe told her as he took in a deep breath that brought the warm, clean smell of her to him. "He's just wrenched it some. I'm sure if we get him to bed and he keeps off of it for a couple of days, he'll be fine."

"That's easy enough for you to say," Meggie snapped.

Roe chuckled. "Believe me, it's not easy for me to say anything. My jaw doesn't seem to be attached right and my tongue is as thick as one of your pasty griddle cakes and tastes almost as bad."

Meggie huffed in indignation and was tempted to hit Roe over the head, but figured in his current state that it wouldn't hurt him nearly enough.

Roe was squinting at her now. "You know, Meggie," he said, "you got the prettiest feet of any woman that I ever saw."

Jesse cackled. "And she smells good, too, Roe. Don't be forgetting that."

"Who could forget with her sitting here right next to me?" Roe took a deep breath and sighed. "You smell wonderful, Meggie."

"Don't be silly," she answered tersely. "I probably smell like old blue pot dye. Now get on your feet and help me get Jesse to bed. If Pa catches him drunk like this, we'll never hear the end of it."

Unsteadily, Roe made it to his feet. Jesse had, for no apparent reason, taken up giggling again. And his laughter made it even harder for him to stand up. Roe and Meggie hoisted the huge young man between them and began to carry him toward the cabin.

"Hush up now, Jesse," Meggie ordered. "The last thing in the world we want is for you to wake up Pa."

"Nope, can't tell him a thing," Jesse whispered. "It's our secret, me and Roe. We're both men and men have got needs."

"Well, the need for two men to get liquored up on donk is a shame on this earth," Meggie complained.

"I ain't talking about drinking needs, Meggie," Jesse protested. "I'm talking about them other needs. The ones that—"

"Jesse, what you *need* is to do less talking and more walking," Roe interrupted him. "I'm not too steady and you are going to break your sister's back for sure."

"No, Meggie's strong," Jesse insisted to Roe. "She ain't no fainting flower. My sister is tough as nails. She's whooped me a time or two when we was younger. Course, I don't expect she'll do that to you." Jesse hooted with laughter at the idea, but his carriers ignored him.

"If we just put him in the outside bed," Meggie said, "then we won't wake Pa and maybe he'll never know."

Roe shook his head. "There isn't a thing in the world that gets past Onery. He'll know for sure."

Meggie's irritation slipped through. "Maybe you don't mind getting my brother in trouble, but I want to help him all I can."

They reached the four-log-high beginnings of the new cabin room and Roe managed to hoist Jesse over and get him onto the bed.

"You'd help your brother a whole lot more if you'd just stay out of his way and let him live his life for good or for ill."

"Oh, you mean just let him get drunk if he's a mind to and break his leg out in the woods."

"His leg isn't broken and yes, if he wants to get drunk or get his own gun and a dog or whatever, you and your father ought to let him do it. It's little enough for a man to ask of life."

"Oh, I see, Mr. Scholar from the Bay State, after a few weeks in the Ozarks you've not only become an expert on cooking and plowing, you're also an expert on my brother."

"I just meant—"

"If you two don't stop yellin'," Jesse interrupted them, "you're going to wake up Pa for sure."

Guiltily the two hushed. In the dim light of the moon, they examined his injured ankle, Meggie concurring with Roe that the wrenched joint would be better with time and required no splint or bandage.

Carefully, Meggie pulled the worn summer coverlet up to her brother's chin and gave him a sisterly kiss on the forehead. He was already snoring.

Meggie turned to speak to Roe, only to find he was staggering back toward the creek. Still angry, she hurried after him.

"Where do you think you're going?" she asked as she made it to his side.

Roe gave her barely more than a glance. "I'm going to get the frogs," he said. "If we leave the sack there by the creek, they will surely manage to escape by morning."

"I'm surprised you even caught any."

"That's what we went out to do," Roe replied. "In fact, we caught so many that we traded half for the donk."

"Whose idea was that?"

"It wasn't mine."

"Oh, I suppose you're going to tell me that Jesse got the idea to get drunk."

Roe reached the stack of discarded gear by the creek and jerked up the tow sack, carefully securing the closure. He didn't even bother to look at her as he spoke. "I'm not telling you anything, except that your brother is a man, just like me, and he gets the same kind of ideas that I get."

Angry, Meggie reached over and grabbed Roe's shirt, forcing him to face her. "Jesse is simple."

"Some things in life are pretty damn simple."

The two stood there in the silvery light of the moon for a long moment, the fine, combed cotton cloth of his shirt clutched in her hand. She meant to pull away, but she gazed up into his eyes and could not. She saw it there, in his eyes. It was that look, that same esurient look she'd seen before, once when he'd held her in his arms and later when he'd caught her at her bath. It was there now in his eyes, glittering imminent and feral.

Meggie felt him tremble for one hesitating minute before his hands went around her waist and he pulled her into his embrace.

"I want you," he declared almost angrily before he closed the distance between their lips.

Meggie was startled by the raw passion of his kiss. The touch of his mouth on hers was neither gentle nor reluctant. His lips parted over hers demandingly and the clutch of the arms around her waist was sure and controlling.

"R-Roe," she stuttered in stunned surprise against his lips. "Roe, I—"

"Meggie," he answered her in a whisper against her flesh. "Meggie, stop me if you must, but do it now, now while I still can."

In answer she melted against him, quivering in awakening awareness of dazzling sensual desire.

Roe pulled her tightly against him and his hand moved across her back from shoulder to waist, pressing her bosom against him, as his lips moved over her own.

Completely unprepared for the sensations that assailed her, Meggie maintained her grasp upon his shirtfront as if it were a lifeline.

The taste of Roe Farley was hot and compelling against her mouth, but when his mouth moved down the tender softness of her throat, gooseflesh raised upon Meggie's skin and shuddering waves of desire flowed through her.

Pull away, pull away from his touch, her reason implored her. But her heart hammered within her loudly, drowning out all warnings.

Eagerly, she wrapped her arms around his neck and crushed her inexplicably aching bosom against his chest. The crowning buds at the tips of her breasts had swelled and bloomed at his touch. She snuggled against him even closer.

She heard a groan from deep inside his throat. One strong sun-browned hand slid up her side to cup her breast. His touch was firm and sure as he teased the hardened nipple between his fingers.

Meggie gasped with pleasure and he pulled gently along her earlobe with his mouth.

She crushed herself to him. "Closer, I need to get closer," she whispered.

"Oh, Meggie," he ground out hoarsely. "I'll get you close. Closer than you've ever been to another human soul."

Roe slipped his arms beneath her knees and carried her only a few yards away before laying her in a bed of sweet-blooming clover.

He followed her body to the ground, his knee gently parting her thighs.

"Meggie, sweet Meggie," he whispered as his mouth moved down her throat to her bosom.

She trembled at the heat of his kiss and the cool of the night breeze upon her dampened breast. The feelings that coursed through her were new and untamed. She felt removed from her body as if it had an existence separate from her own. Yet, never in her life had she felt so aware of her senses and desires as she did now.

Roe pulled up her josie. Not slowly or surreptitiously, but with purpose. The nakedness of her legs chilled Meggie. But she sought warmth, in the heat of his body.

"You're beautiful, beautiful, Meggie," he told her as he

ran his hand up and down the naked flesh he'd uncovered. "I knew the day I saw your pretty bare feet that your legs would be strong and shapely. The kind of legs to wrap around a man's waist."

She didn't need further invitation. Meggie clasped her knees about him and held fast as he rocked in place atop her, stoking the fire that blazed up between them.

"Does it feel good?" he whispered. "There is more, Meggie. Let me give you more."

"Give me everything," she breathed.

Roe sat back on his knees, keeping her thighs spread before him. He smoothed upward the pale, tender skin of her inner thighs.

"What curls, Meggie," he said. "What seductively tempting curls." He coursed through them with his fingers.

She jerked and twitched at the intimate caress. As his hands explored more firmly, she strained and wiggled against him.

She heard him sigh with contented delight as he whispered into her ear. "Perfect."

His words both excited and entranced Meggie as she quavered in his embrace, her head turned against the fresh spring softness of the clover beneath her.

Roe eased one long finger into the honeyed heat of her. Meggie gasped aloud at the intimate touch.

"Oh, my sweet darling," Roe muttered as he slid another finger inside. "You are so ready, you are so wonderful." With one hand he fumbled at his britches. "Damn, I've got to get these trousers off."

They weren't off, but they were down as he moved over her, circling his waist with her legs once more. He set his mark true and as he thrust himself inside her, Meggie cried out. It was not so much from pain, as from wonder.

Fully inside, he lay over her. "Are you all right, Meggie?" he asked her as he kissed her ear.

"Yes, I'm—" Meggie had no other words as tiny,

glistening tears from emotions she didn't understand escaped from the corners of her eyes.

Roe felt the dampness on his cheek and tried to kiss them away. "I can't stop now, Meggie," he pleaded. "Don't make me stop now."

"Don't stop," she answered.

Roe needed no further sanction. With strong, powerful thrusts he drummed a rhythm older than time or music. Meggie's answering fire strained melody to the highest and lowest of fevered pitch. Until, with muscles tense in consummate ecstatic rapture, they cried out together in perfect harmony.

CHAPTER

FOURTEEN

THE SUN WAS near the middle of the sky when Roe Farley squinted his eyes open. The light seemed to stab through his head like a hot knife. Moaning, he rolled over and buried his face in the trampled clover beneath him. The sweet smell of it was welcoming to his aching body and soothing to his tired soul. He'd never before appreciated the gentle grassy scent. But this morning it was a glorious fragrance as dear and as precious to him as his Meggie.

"Meggie?"

The word passed his lips in a quiet whisper. A long second passed and the sound faded before Roe's head popped up from the grass. His eyes opened wide with shock.

"Meggie!"

He ran a hand along the ground beside him as if he didn't trust his own vision. Finding no soft, feminine body at his side, he sat up.

His quick, intemperate move seemed to rock the universe, and he fell back clutching his temples.

"Donk," he groaned and silently cursed the unholy brew. He'd got himself royally drunk, crazed with liquor, and had taken illicit advantage of Meggie Best.

"Mindless drunkard," he cursed himself with anger that stirred him to resolute purpose. He couldn't regret the pleasure, and he had no idea of what he meant to do or say. But he knew only that he must see Meggie, he must talk to her, hold her, comfort her. He began running toward the cabin.

Cold chills and dizziness overcame him and he stopped. Leaning against the long lean trunk of a giant white oak, he waited impatiently for the queasiness to pass. In his mind he felt the smooth, clean touch of her flesh once more. He tasted the salty spiced flavor of her skin and felt the stretch and give of her intimate body as he pressed his own inside her.

He bent forward, willing the unholy spin of the ground to subside. As soon as it did, he hurried on toward the cabin.

On the distant hillside, he could see Onery out working in his fields and as he hurried into the yard, he could hear the moaning complaints of Jesse who still lay in the new bed in the half-walled cabin room. Neither sight drew more than a cursory glance nor one iota of his attention and concern. He was hurrying to Meggie and in that moment, nothing, no one else, mattered at all.

He came around the corner of the cabin, calling out her name. He felt a rush of tenderness. She was there. But the polite nod and casual morning greeting he received was not at all what he expected.

Meggie sat in a straight-backed chair, a huge skinning knife gripped comfortably in her right hand. In the dishpan on her lap were the legs and backs she was preparing for the evening's meal. Beside her, a bucket contained the severed heads and slimy hides of the big green bullfrogs Roe had helped to catch the previous night.

"Meggie—" he began, still not knowing what he was about to say.

She looked over at him as casually as if he'd just strolled up from the barn for a dipper of water. "I don't suppose you're hungry," she said calmly. "But there's pone in the kettle and coffee's still hot on the fire."

She turned back to her frog butchering with such indifference that Roe stood staring in puzzlement until she glanced up to look at him again.

"Last night, Meggie—"

Only the scarlet flush that stained her cheeks revealed that she even understood his words. She cleared her throat a little uncomfortably.

."Get you some coffee and pone, Mr. Farley," she said calmly. "It'll settle your stomach and then we can talk and I'll settle your mind."

There was nothing of the dreamy scatterbrain in the Meggie Best that sat before him. She was quiet, purposeful, and practical. Roe felt as if he had never seen her before. He hesitated only a moment before deciding that perhaps she was thinking more clearly than he. Such a momentous moment as theirs should not be faced on an empty stomach. With a nod of polite excuse, he stepped into the cabin for his breakfast, but was not even tempted to linger.

With a full cup of thick black coffee and a chunk of the half-burnt, half-raw cornbread, he hurried back out to the porch. Meggie didn't look up from her work. Roe watched her. He didn't even pretend to try to eat or drink, but just stood beside her watching with abhorrent fascination as Meggie methodically sliced off the heads of the wiggling frogs, gutted them, and then ripped the skin back from shoulder to feet. The gentle, romantic glow that had wrapped him in a fog dissipated as the everyday reality set in. He'd never imagined himself enamored of a woman who could gut and peel her own foodstuffs. A return of the queasy feeling Roe had suffered earlier prompted him to look away from the sight and clear his throat uneasily.

"I suppose I should speak first," he said. His voice took on a deep, responsible tone that he thought appropriate for the moment.

Meggie looked up at him. "There is no need," she told him quietly.

"What do you mean, there's no need?"

She shrugged with deliberate unconcern and answered with carefree nonchalance. "I already know what you have to say, Mr. Farley."

"Oh?"

"You were liquored up and now you are very sorry. I wasn't liquored up, but I'm sorry, too. We agree on that, Mr. Farley. So there's no need for us to dwell upon it."

Roe found her manner unsettling and became somewhat annoyed at her apparent reluctance to use his given name.

"My dear Miss Best," he said with formality that bordered upon arrogance. "That was not at all what I had intended to say to you."

Meggie turned to look at him. Her hair was unusually neat and tidy this morning and was pulled very tightly away from her face in a fashion severe enough to seem almost a punishment.

"Then what were you going to say, Mr. Farley?" she asked.

The question immediately deflated the smugness in Roe's stance as reality swept upon him in a rush of consequence.

"I was going to say . . . I mean I am saying . . . or rather I'm asking . . ."

Roe nervously took a deep swig of the coffee in his tin cup and scalded his mouth. The pain effectively cleared his muddled thinking and he knew, in that one moment with perfect clarity, the purpose for which he'd hurried toward the cabin and the reason that he stood next to this woman.

He glanced down at the coffee as if the brew itself had somehow brought this moment to fruition. Cursing under his breath, he tossed the remains in the cup out onto the dusty ground, and threw the untouched pone to the yard chickens, who in a noisy cackle scrambled around it eagerly.

Looking down at his clothes, Roe took stock of himself and realized that his shirt and trousers were grass stained and wrinkled, he smelled of corn liquor and was badly in need of a morning shave. But the time was upon him, and like a bitter elixir would not grow more pleasing for putting it off. He took one moment to smooth back his sleep-tousled black hair and then formally went down on one knee.

The new position, bowed down in the dirt before Meggie's bare feet, gave him an even closer and more distasteful view of the frog heads' bucket. Deliberately, he focused his gaze upon the woman, determined to ignore what she was doing.

Gracefully, he looked deeply into the blue-gray eyes of the young woman and said the words that he expected any young woman would long to hear. Words that he himself had not expected to say for several years to come.

"My dear Miss Meggie Best, my love, my heart," he declared poetically.

The stench of the frog bucket momentarily captured his attention and he glanced down at it in dismay. Purposely he raised his gaze once more to the young woman before him, cleared his throat, and continued his discourse. "Miss Best, as a single man of good prospects and respectable character, I would like to ask that you consider my address and declaration. It would bring life to my weary journey and purpose to my days upon this earth if you would but consent to be my helpmate, to share my destiny, bear my children, to be my bride and take my name."

Though he had not prepared, Roe had thought that his proposal had actually come out quite prettily. He patiently awaited the lady's demure acceptance.

Strangely enough, Meggie said nothing. And to Roe's dismay, she immediately returned to her task, as if the chore were of much more importance than the words he'd just spoken.

Roe leaned back on his heels and stared at her. He had never proposed to a woman before, and he felt relatively certain that more reaction than this was usual. "Meggie, I just asked you to marry me," he said softly.

"I know that you did." she answered. "Though with all those fancy words you use, a woman could get a bit confused I suppose."

Roe lingered on his knees in front of her as she skinned the frog and cut it into parts.

"I'm waiting for your answer, Meggie," he said.

Without bothering to even glance in his direction, Meggie gutted another frog over the bucket. "There isn't any need to answer, 'cause there wasn't any need to ask the question," she said.

Roe stared at her for a long moment and then nodded slowly, thoughtful. "Oh," he said quietly, "you mean that last night, although not in words, the question was really already asked and answered."

Meggie did look up at him then and her expression turned downright cross. "No, that's not what I mean at all!"

"Then what?"

"I mean, you don't have to ask me to marry you."

Roe felt a measure of pride swelling up inside him. Of course Meggie would never try to trap a man into marriage. He smiled at her warmly.

"I know I don't *have* to ask you, but—"

"But nothing," Meggie interrupted. "You're only asking because I did that loving thing with you."

"That's not the only reason," he assured her.

"I can't for the life of me think of another," she said. "You had me that way and now you think it's cause to marry."

Roe rubbed his eyes. The pain in his temples was throbbing again and he wished he could wipe it away as easily as he did the sweat from his brow. "Well, that's certainly reason enough," he said.

"For most, it is," Meggie agreed. "But for us there is no cause. There just isn't any need."

Roe was clearly puzzled. He knew that his brain was still foggy, but he couldn't imagine why none of this was making any sense.

"Meggie, I admit that I was quite drunk last night," he said. "But I was not too drunk to realize what we did. Or to realize that it was your first time."

"That makes a difference?"

"No, it doesn't to me, but I'm sure it will to the people here on the mountain."

"But don't you see, it doesn't have to change a thing."

"No, I don't see."

"Folks already think we are married," she said. "When you go off and we say you've been killed, then that's the end of it. If I was to marry later, my man thinking me a widow would expect nothing else."

Roe stared at her in disbelief. Rising to his feet, he shook his head and began to nervously pace back and forth in front of her. Finally, he stopped to look at her again. She'd returned to her task as if there was nothing more to be said. Roe gazed up to heaven for guidance before speaking again.

"I guess I've gone at this all wrong," he said. "What we did last night, Meggie, has more meaning than just what other people think. There's . . . well, there is just more involved."

Meggie looked up and gave him an impatient sigh. "I may be a green hill girl, Mr. Farley," she said. "But I know where babies come from. And I tell you it doesn't matter. If I'm a widow or a widow with a child coming, it's all the same difference."

"Well, it's not all the same difference to me!"

Meggie huffed slightly and shook her head. "You're letting your gallantry take the reins of your good sense," she said. "I'm the one who is supposed to be walking around with my head in the clouds all the time. Well, my feet are on the ground this morning and yours should be, too."

"I think that they are," he snapped. "You're the one who is not making any sense."

"Roe, last night we done something we shouldn't have. But it wouldn't make it right if we married. It would just make it more wrong. At the end of the summer you'll be going back to the Bay State and I'll be a-staying here."

He stared at her in silence.

"Now, I can't go there, I'd never be able to leave Pa and Jesse and the mountain. And you can't stay here, you're a scholar and have no way of making your living out in these woods. If we was to marry, you'd be leaving just the same at the end of the summer. And we'd both be caught in a marriage that would be more millstone than matrimony."

"Meggie, what happened between us last night—"

"Is best forgotten!" Meggie sighed heavily and bit down upon her lips. "You were donked, and I was seeing starlight, but it's morning now and we've both trotted out our better judgment. We just decide not to let such a thing happen again and go on about our business."

"Meggie—"

"There is not a thing left to say, Roe Farley. Now let me get to washing these frog legs. Pa was real pleased at the mess you and Jess caught. He'll be wanting them for nooning. You should get yourself cleaned up and see what you can do for Jesse."

Using the corner of her apron for a pot holder, Meggie lifted the lid off the big cast-iron skillet that sat in the hot coals. The frog legs and backs were bubbling nicely in the grease. Meggie kept them covered. It was said that when the fat got hot the frogs would hop right out of the skillet and head back to the creek bank. She knew that to be not exactly true. But during frying the tendons in the legs of the frogs would contract, causing them to jerk and quiver as they cooked and Meggie didn't want grease splashed on her floor. She could not stop, however, the tiny, sizzling spatter that resulted from one salty tear falling into the pan of frying frog legs.

Covering the skillet once more, she wiped away the glistening tears that stained her cheeks. He had actually asked her to marry him. What a princely thing to do. She had wanted him to, wanted him to so badly. But she hadn't really thought that he would.

Rising to her feet, she checked the bread in the fireplace oven. It was a perfect brown, risen high and just right with a rich yeasty smell. She hefted it out on the board to cool.

Maybe Roe Farley *was* a prince. But she had been right to refuse to wed him. The man should not be punished for what *she* did. Marriage to a backwoods nobody like her would be a punishment. She was nothing at all like the Bay State princess that he had in mind. Roe Farley shouldn't be forced to marry her for something that wasn't his fault.

And there was no question in her mind whose fault it was. Roe had been half dazed and besotted with drink. But Meggie had had no liquor in her veins. She'd merely had stars in her eyes. That was crime enough.

All her life she'd thought her dreaminess to be an innocent pastime. While most folks had left their pretend games in childhood, she'd carried hers with her and relished those moments of make-believe that took her away from the worry and work that was her life. Ignoring the occasional scold, she'd seen no harm in her pleasant flights of fancy. Now she knew that seeing the world as you hoped it might be could be as dangerous as a deliberate lie.

Last night, in the sweet rowdy warmth of Roe's arms, she'd pretended that their marriage was real. She'd pretended that she was truly loved, and that she had a right to accept the worship of his body. A blush stained her cheeks as she recalled the passionate, intimate things that they had done. Things that were meant only for two who are one.

She remembered Granny Piggott's words and her own little lie. The old woman was right. Kind and gentle were not the words that came to mind with her man's lovemaking.

Her man. The designation caught her unawares and jolted her sense of reality. The little quiver of desire that fluttered through her sputtered sadly and fell like ash. She would never do those things again, not with Roe. Never would she feel the intensity of his desire and hear him cry out her name. Another tear stole down her cheek and she pushed it away.

She tried to imagine the touch of another man. It was difficult. No other man she knew seemed worthy to take Roe's place and the thought of having any other man touch her intimately was an idea that sickened her. Deliberately, she attempted to conjure up her dream prince once more. He could love her and share sweet passion with her. But every image that came to her mind was of Roe Farley.

A shadow darkened the cabin door and Meggie looked up to see her father standing there. She was grateful that the dim light of the cabin masked her reddened eyes and tearstained cheeks.

"The meal's almost ready," she told him briskly with what she hoped was a welcoming smile.

He nodded and tossed his hat on the peg beside the door. "Corn's looking good," he said calmly. "The weeds are sure getting to your vegetables though."

Meggie nodded. "Maybe with Jesse laid up for real work he can help me get the garden cleaned out."

Onery grunted his approval. "How is yer brother?" he asked.

"Oh, I think his ankle's going to be fine," Meggie replied. "He just needs to stay off that foot for a few days and he'll be back working in the fields in no time at all."

Onery sat down in one of the chairs and leaned way back to observe his daughter. "I wasn't asking about his leg, I was asking about his head."

Meggie glanced up with surprise.

"That devil-brewed donk won't kill ye, but it will sure make a man wish himself dead."

Meggie was stunned. "He told you?"

The old man shook his head. "He didn't need to, Meggie-gal. My head may be covered in gray hair, but my mind works as well as it ever did."

She nodded slowly. "Are you going to punish him?" she asked in a soft whisper.

"Seems kind of purposeless, don't it? Nothing could make him any sorrier than he is already." Onery chuckled lightly. "Besides, I'm not exactly on the side of the angels here. I've drunk enough of that vile corn liquor to float a bear oil log all the way to New Orleans."

Meggie pulled the frying skillet away from the fire. She knew of her father's past, but respected him for all the things he'd done right in his life. She set the pan on a towel on top of the table and began removing the frog legs from the hot grease.

"Of course, I wouldn't want Jesse to make a habit of this," she said honestly.

Her father waved away her concern. "Jesse's mind ain't a wonder, but the boy's got a good bit of sense about him."

Meggie knew her father was right about that. Using the towel once more, she removed the skillet's cast-iron lid. A cloud of steam and appetizing scent filled the room and her father sighed with pleasure.

"Ooooh, don't they look wonderful?" Onery said, smacking his lips eagerly.

"Thank you," Meggie answered modestly. She looked down at her achievement with some pride. The frog legs were a perfect golden brown, evenly fried on all sides and not a burnt edge or a raw strip in sight. "They do look mighty good," she admitted.

Her father chuckled. "I knew you'd be fixin' the best-tasting frog legs in the country today."

Meggie looked up at him curiously. From a man whose opinion of her cooking was far from high, this was extravagant praise.

"I'm glad you had such faith in me, Pa."

"It was more than faith, Meggie-gal. It was knowing you. Knowing you since you were a little girl and knowing how you are."

Her expression was puzzled. He continued.

"When you are worried, somehow your mind don't wander so much as regular. If your mind don't wander, you don't make such mistakes. Yes, Meggie-gal, I've known you all your life and the more worried you are, the better you cook."

Her face pale, Meggie was deliberately calm. "What in the world would I have to be worried about?"

Onery shrugged and gave his daughter a long knowing look. "Oh, I don't know for sure, darlin'. But I'd suspect you might be a little worried over whatever it was you done alone with that Roe, out in the woods last night 'til dawn."

Meggie's hand trembled as she forked the frog legs out of the grease and onto a platter. She said nothing, but her face was pale and she swallowed nervously.

"So," Onery continued. "Are you and him *really* married now, or are ye still just pretending?"

Meggie glanced nervously toward the cabin door as if looking for help. Roe ought to be coming in for his meal soon. She didn't know whether to wish he would hurry or that he would never come.

She grabbed up a tin plate from the shelf. "I don't know if I should take a plate of this out to Jesse or help him come in to the table."

Onery reached across the table and stilled his daughter's hand with his own.

"Meggie, are you married to that feller now, or are you two still pretending?" he asked again with a quiet intensity that was disconcerting.

Meggie raised her chin. "We're still pretending."

Onery's eyes narrowed. He folded his arms across his chest and stared at her, his expression belligerent. "I ain't liking that, Meggie-gal. I ain't liking it at all."

Ignoring his words, she began dishing up a generous portion of the frog legs into her father's plate.

"I thought that Roe to be a pretty fine feller," Onery

continued. "But it sure don't sit well, him playing fast and loose with my youngun."

"Now don't get ole-outraged-papa on me," Meggie told him. "I'm a grown woman as you well know. I can make my own mistakes and considering the mistakes you and Mama made, well, I reckon that I'm due some."

"Maybe you are, but that doesn't mean I can let some sweet-talking city slicker take advantage of your good nature."

"No, Pa, don't," Meggie said too loudly. She dropped the serving spoon into the skillet and splashed hot grease across the clean oilcloth.

Her father looked at her sharply and she deliberately moderated her tone, but the words still trembled in her throat. "He's already asked me to wed him, Pa, and I wouldn't. So that's the end of it."

"You wouldn't?"

Meggie shook her head. "There was just no sense in it."

Onery raised an eyebrow in displeasure before tucking his napkin into his shirt collar. "It makes a good bit of sense to me."

"Pa, he's from another place and he's going back there," she explained. "I'm from here and I ain't about to leave."

His brow furrowing in puzzlement, Onery eyed her curiously. "I thought that's what you wanted, Meggie," he said. "I thought you wanted some furriner to come and take ye from this mountain."

"That was just a dream, Pa. Just something for me to set and ruminate about." She sighed heavily as if she had just left all her childish fancies behind. "I won't never leave this mountain. I won't leave you or Jesse. Truly, I don't long for far-off places, except just to see them. I love this mountain and the mists in the woodlands and the changes of season. My life is here and my family, too. I won't never be leaving Marrying Stone."

Her father nodded thoughtfully. "Then maybe Roe could take it in his mind to stay."

"I don't want him to," Meggie said adamantly. "He's got his own work in the Bay State. If he was to stay here he'd need another string for his bow. Granny's right about that. There is no call for scholars in the Ozarks."

Onery shook his head in exasperation. "The feller's been doing pretty good work 'round here. I suspect we can afford to keep him. But, Meggie, this is not the thing that ye ought to be a-dwellin' upon. How he makes his living has not a thing to do with his duty to you. Don't you remember, I couldn't make my living as a fiddler on this mountain neither. But it didn't mean I wasn't willing to lend my hand to farming or try something different for the sake of your mama."

"There is just no sense in that, Pa, no sense in it at all."

Onery huffed in disagreement. "Seems to me that you two have done crossed the line of deciding this thing with common sense, Meggie. Now you've got to decide with your hearts. You love this man, don't deny yourself that on the grounds that it ain't good judgment or that he don't owe ye no happily ever afters. Love is rare enough in this life that when you come acrost it, you'd best grab ahold, little gal, and hang on for dear life."

"I didn't say that I love him."

He eyed her skeptically.

Meggie picked up the knife and began sawing away at the light bread with the energy required for butchering a hog. "Pa, I done what I done with him. And I ain't sorry about it. I pure-dee liked it. But I ain't about to marry Roe Farley and you, nor no one else, is going to make me."

"Ye might be carryin' a babe."

"If I am then I am. It makes no difference."

Onery cursed under his breath and looked with dismay at the young woman who was his daughter. "Just like yer mama," he complained.

FROM THE JOURNAL OF
J. MONROE FARLEY

June 16, 1902
Marrying Stone, Arkansas

A more beautiful place to spend the springtime than this mountain, I cannot imagine. Wildflowers bloom everywhere and food is in abundance. The woods and creeks are full of game and fish and even in the hottest part of the day the weather is quite bearable.

Almost unassisted I have finished the cabin room add-on. Yesterday I cut the doorway into the back of the main cabin. I can't express the tremendous sense of satisfaction that I felt when I nailed the last shake shingle to the roof. It must be the same feeling a master has upon completion of a piece of music. This little room is something I created, and unworthy as it may be, it is mine. I am thinking to build something else before I leave at the end of summer. A privy for this homestead would be a fine luxury.

The collecting continues to go very well. Now that I am considered somewhat as a part of the family, everyone is only too eager to be of assistance to me. I am recording so much in fact that I begin to run short of cylinders and may be forced to leave the mountain earlier than anticipated. The diversity of the repertoire I have encountered is startling. A scholar could spend years on this project.

CHAPTER

FIFTEEN

THE RAIN CAME down, not in spurts or drizzles but full drenching all morning long. Roe and Jesse were in the woodshed riving cedar shakes for the roof of the planned privy. The activity was simple, monotonous, and requiring great spurts of pent-up energy. Perfect for Roe's current frame of mind. He set the froeward rending ax carefully at the right width of the cedar block. When he slammed the blade through with a burl maul, he twisted the froe handle to split the board with the grain. It was a skill that had taken more than a couple of days to perfect, but now Roe did it easily as he allowed his mind to wander.

His privy plan called for a four-by-four post and beam shed with diagonal bracing set on skids. The skids could be used to move the outhouse to another site when necessary. Onery Best was not impressed by the idea, considering it an unnecessary luxury. But Meggie had been pleased.

"Oh, wouldn't it be grand," she had whispered in that breathy, dreamy way he'd seen so little of lately.

If Meggie wanted an outhouse, if she thought having it was something grand, then Roe would make certain she got one.

He'd spent the bulk of his waking hours the last few weeks thinking about Meggie Best, what she might want and how he might provide it for her. While his mind should have been filled with excitement at the growing collection of Elizabethan music that was to be the centerpiece of his fellowship presentation, he found his thoughts and his eyes constantly strayed to the barefoot woman who had shared an evening of passion with him in a bed of clover.

"My foot's just as good as new now," Jesse told him.

Roe glanced up a moment from his work and nodded. "I'm glad to hear that, Jesse." He turned his back to his work and his thoughts once again to his fancies. But the young man did not.

"I 'spect I'm about as well as I'm gonna be," he continued a little more loudly than was necessary.

Murmuring agreement, Roe split another shake of cedar as he turned to his own thoughts. Meggie hardly had a word to say to him these days. In fact for the most part she pretended he was not there at all. The days immediately following their illicit night were awkward for both of them.

Clearly, Onery had guessed and was not at all pleased. How Meggie prevented her father from coming for Roe with a shotgun, he didn't know. But he hadn't, and he and Meggie had settled into a quiet, polite coexistence; however, sometimes when neither of them had a guard up, their eyes would meet across the room, and it was there once again. The shattering intimacy they shared had not dimmed with time but had grown into something stronger, sterner, more formidable.

"You forgot, didn't ye?" Jesse said.

Puzzled, Roe hesitated at his task and looked up. He was hardly aware that Jesse was present. "Forgot what?" he asked.

"You forgot about what you tole me the night we went giggin' and drunk the donk."

Roe stared for a long moment, trying to recall what he might have said to Jesse, then he simply smiled and shook his head. "I may have forgot. That donk does take the brains out of a man, doesn't it?"

Jesse didn't return his smile, but bent to his own work. Roe might have returned to his own task, but the aspect of the young man's movements was slow and sad. Something was definitely wrong.

"What is it, Jesse?" Roe asked. "What did I forget?"

He shrugged. "It don't matter."

Roe stopped his work completely, resting the froe against the cedar block, and walked over to Jesse's side. "Tell me, Jesse," he said.

Jesse smoothed his pale blond hair out of his eyes, but he didn't immediately answer.

At his hesitation, Roe continued, "I thought we agreed that friends tell each other the truth."

That caught the young man's attention and his blue eyes looked directly into Roe's brown ones.

"Yep, that's what we said."

"Well, I think that not saying anything at all is a bit like telling a lie."

Jesse considered his words for a long moment. "Yep, I guess ye could say that."

Roe grinned. "So tell me, Jesse my friend, what did I forget?"

Jesse became somewhat flustered. His cheeks turned bright pink and he dropped his head to stare at his own bare feet.

"What is it?" Roe prodded.

When he finally spoke, Jesse's voice was so low Roe had to strain to hear the words.

"You said that maybe we could visit the widder."

"The widow?" Then in a flash of remembrance, he recalled their conversation.

Roe had spent so much of the last weeks thinking about his own problems, he had forgotten about Jesse's.

"The Widder Plum, I tole you about her," Jesse said. "She

ain't really a widder the fellers says and she'll let a feller play fast and loose with her fer some fresh-killed game or a trinket from Mr. Phillips's store. I ain't never seen her, but fellers say she's pretty and kindy young. Course, they said that when I was still shorter than Meggie, so I reckon she cain't be so young no more."

"I remember now," Roe said. "Jesse, I'm sorry that I forgot, but yes, I clearly remember it now."

Jesse looked up at him. "Was it just donk talking or do you think I could maybe . . ."

"Well of course, Jesse," Roe answered. "It's just that—"

"Just what?"

"Just . . . I don't know." Roe was surprised at his own hesitation. "It just doesn't seem like as good an idea as it did that night."

Jesse nodded solemnly. "No, I don't guess that it does," he said, clearly not believing that at all. Stoically he sighed. "It don't matter, Roe."

"Of course it matters," he answered. "You are a man just like any man. You work and worry and die just like the rest of us; you deserve to live your life like any other man would."

"But you don't think I should . . . get to lay with a woman?"

"Jesse, honestly, I don't know," Roe admitted. "I think, yes, I think that you should get to do that if it's what you want. But somehow things seem different to me now than they did that night. Maybe . . . maybe I just need to give the idea some more thought."

The young man appeared satisfied. "It's all right. Yer still my frien' even if I never get to . . . get to do that."

"Now I haven't said no," Roe assured him. "I just . . . well, I think we need to think about it a little more. Women are . . . well, Jesse, women are kind of complicated."

The young man nodded. "Like ciphering?"

"At least as complicated as ciphering," Roe said. "You think, when you're just thinking about them, that you can lie with a woman and have a little pleasure and then it's over."

Jesse nodded enthusiastically. "Yep, that's what I want."

"But it's not simple like that. When it's over, it's not over."

Jesse eyed him curiously. "You mean you still remember it," Jesse said. "That's all right with me, Roe. I *want* to remember it."

"But it's not just remembering," Roe said.

With exasperation he ran his hand through his thick black hair that had grown a bit too long during his sojourn in the mountains. He didn't understand it himself, how could he explain it to Jesse.

"It's more than that. It's like . . . like . . . well, when we took that licking from your father together."

Jesse nodded.

"It doesn't seem that a thing like getting hit with a hickory switch would do much to a couple of big fellows like ourselves."

"It sure hurt like the devil," Jesse said.

"Yes, it did, but more than that, because we did that together, because it was something that we shared, it made us closer. We became better friends that night and long after the sting of that switch is gone, the friendship remains."

Jesse's expression was bewildered. "Do you mean that laying with a woman is kindy like taking a switching?"

"No, Jesse, that's not what I mean at all." Roe sighed in exasperation at his inability to express himself. "I'm not sure what I mean," he admitted. "But I do think that we need to think about it some more."

Jesse nodded and sighed. "I been thinking about it. At night I cain't hardly think of nothin' else."

Reaching out to his friend, Roe wrapped an arm around Jesse's shoulder. It wasn't until he saw the surprised expression on the young man's face that he realized what a new and unexpected gesture it was. Jesse had always hugged Roe. This time Roe hugged Jesse. The two grinned at each other.

"Don't worry about thinking on women all the time, Jesse. That seems to be about all I can think about these days, too. It must be this mountain air."

Jesse answered seriously. "I don't think it's the air, frien'," he said. "For you, I'd bet it was that new door between your sleeping place and where Meggie lays out her pallet."

Roe's mouth opened in shock. Clearly, Jesse saw more of the world than he was given credit for.

The sound of splashing captured their attention and they glanced out the door to see Meggie hurrying across the yard. She held an apron of plain cotton homespun over her head to keep off the worst of the rain. It did not, however, manage to keep her from splashing her skirt hem as she rushed barefoot across the ground.

She was quite damp when she raced through the wood-shed door.

"It's really coming down out there," she said breathlessly.

Her smile was beautiful and so welcome to Roe's eyes. He couldn't remember when he'd seen it before. No, he could remember when he'd seen it and it was part of the memory that haunted his dreams.

"How's your father?" Roe asked, grateful to have reason to speak to her.

"Not much better," she answered. "He's sleeping finally but the rheumatism in his gimp leg is as bad as I've ever seen it."

"He's been working too hard," Roe said.

"It's my fault," Jesse admitted quietly. "With me laid up, there was just more work to do this summer."

"It's nobody's fault, Jesse," Meggie quickly assured him. "Onery does exactly what he pleases. His mind is a bit troubled this summer is all. And he stands on his bad leg too long trying to forget his worries."

Jesse looked puzzled. "What could Pa be worried about?" No one answered him.

"I would think that this rainy weather would have as bad an effect on his rheumatism as anything else," Roe said.

Meggie nodded. "I've been making his bark tea from wild cherry and wahoo to ease him. But I usually put snakeroot in it and I ain't got a bit."

"I could go out and pick some," Jesse volunteered.

"In this rain?" Meggie asked. "You'd catch the pneumonia for sure yarbing in the woods in a frog-strangler like this."

Jesse temporarily acceded to his sister's wisdom, then his eyes brightened. "I could take the mule down to Broody's place. Ma Broody keeps yarbs, don't she?"

"Yes, she does," Meggie admitted.

"It's on the ridge's path near the whole way," Jesse pointed out. "And I could wear Pa's pommel slicker and I wouldn't hardly get wet a'tal."

She hesitated.

"I know the way as well as I do my name," he assured her. "I ain't about to get lost betwixt yeer and thar."

Meggie nodded. "I'd be pleased if you went, Jesse," she told him.

The young man grinned broadly, "I'll be there and back before sunset," Jesse promised. "I'll bring you snakeroot."

"And you could ask Ma Broody if there is anything better I could be giving Pa."

"I'll ask," Jesse told her. "But I know that if there was, you'd already be giving it to him."

He turned to Roe with light apology. "Sorry I cain't stay here and rive shingles with ye, Roe. But I got to get yarbs for my pa."

"It's all right, Jesse. I think I can manage the rest by myself."

The young man nodded. He was clearly delighted, aware of the responsibility that he'd taken upon himself.

"I best get started right now," he said, grabbing his broad-brimmed hat from the peg.

"Don't forget the pommel," Meggie cautioned.

"It's in the barn with the tack," Jesse assured her. "When I ride out the door, I'll be covered and dry as a terrapin in the high grass."

With that he was gone and hurrying to the barn. Roe and Meggie both watched him. When he disappeared into the broad clapboard door of the barn, Roe turned back to his shingles. Meggie hesitated at the doorway.

"I'm sure he'll be all right," she said.

"Of course he will," Roe assured her. "Jesse knows every inch of this mountain and he's a pretty good hand at taking care of himself."

Meggie nodded. "I know that he is, but I guess I still worry."

Roe smiled. "It's good to have a sister to worry about you," he said.

Meggie turned to glance at him. She gave him a long curious look. "You don't have any sisters." It was a statement, not a question. "You don't talk about your family much."

"There isn't anyone to talk about," he said. "My parents died when I was young. I hardly know the other people I'm related to."

"It seems strange, not having any kin."

Meggie's observation was disconcerting and the following silence between them was long and extremely uncomfortable, broken finally by a holler from Jesse as he left the barn. Meggie waved to him and watched until he was out of sight. Roe continued with his work.

"I suppose I should get back to the house," she said.

Roe looked up at her and then glanced out into the yard

beyond. "It doesn't seem likely to let up any," he said. "It's too bad you don't have your own pommel slicker."

Laughing at the idea of a woman having her own slicker, Meggie shook out her apron and placed it around her shoulders. "This works well enough to get me between the house and the yard," she explained.

The smile that Roe had missed was there upon her face. Her cheeks were flushed a pretty pink and her blue-gray eyes seemed darker and deeper than he'd ever noticed before. The sight of her warmed him deep inside and from his heart, and deep within his chest the lines of a song burst forth in a full broad baritone.

> "She had her apron wrapped about her
> And he took her for a swan."

Meggie was astonished at the clear, pure sound of his voice. She realized that she'd never heard him sing before. With a curious sense of camaraderie she offered the next stanza in her slightly nasal soprano.

> "Ah, but alas it was me
> Polly Vaughn."

He smiled at her. She smiled back.

"Is that one of the songs from across the sea that you're collecting?"

Roe nodded. "Yes, it's old English," he answered. "Murder ballads were very popular in olden times. I think it may have been a way of teaching people about the consequences of crime."

Meggie was thoughtful. "Our people still sing them."

"And they have made up their own," Roe said. "Have you heard 'Poor Omy Wise'?"

"Oh, yes," she answered. "It's such a sad story."

"It's not just a story," Roe said. "It's actually based on the murder of Naomi Wise in Deep River, North Carolina, in 1808."

> "He told her to meet him at Adams's spring.
> He said he'd bring money and a weddin' ring.
> So fool-like she met him down at the spring.
> But he'd brought not money, nor a weddin' ring."

Meggie listened to Roe sing the words and joined in with him.

> " 'Have mercy on my baby and spare me my life.
> I'll go home a beggar and never be your wife.'
> He kissed her, he hugged her and turned her around
> And pushed her in deep water, where he knew
> That she would drown."

"You mean it's all true?"

"I don't know if it's *all* true, but she was murdered. And her sweetheart, Jonathan Lewis, was hanged for the crime."

Meggie shook her head sadly. "It's hard to believe a man would kill a woman who was carrying his child. A decent man would want to marry her."

"Of course, he would," Roe agreed. "But maybe she wouldn't marry him."

She almost disagreed with him, as little Omy's desire for marriage was made clear in the song. But when Meggie looked up, she realized that Roe was no longer talking about two long-dead lovers in a far-off place.

She swallowed nervously. "I'm not carrying a child," she said finally.

"Good," Roe said, then realized the minute the word left his mouth that he didn't feel "good." He felt confused and relieved, disappointed and grateful. Truthfully, he didn't know what he felt, but it wasn't good.

He looked into her eyes for a long moment and she turned away.

"I'd best get back to the house," she said.

"Stay." It was whispered, but she heard it.

At first he thought she would leave anyway, but she draped her apron across her arm and turned back to the room.

She wandered aimlessly for a couple of minutes, looking at things that were familiar, not looking at him, before making a seat for herself on the crossbar of a sawbuck.

The silence between them was uncomfortable and Roe had the fleeting wish that he hadn't spoken. But the sight of her lifted his spirits somehow and if she went away the day would get that much grayer.

"I've never heard you sing before," she said.

Roe looked up and shrugged modestly. "There is so much good music around me and I love to hear it."

"You have a wonderful voice."

"Untrained," he answered. "I usually only sing when I'm all alone."

"I guess that's what most of us do," Meggie said.

Roe glanced at her curiously. "Is it?" He moved over to her and took a seat on a nearby planing bench. "I don't actually know very many people well enough to know what they do when they are by themselves. When I was a boy and scared and alone," he admitted with a self-deprecating grin, "I used to sing to myself to keep away the goblins or the bogeyman or whatever."

She smiled back at him, the tension between them lightening. "Lots of bogeymen in the Bay State, are there?"

"More than enough," he assured her.

"Did ye run to your mama's bed to ask her to chase the bad dreams away?"

"No." He shook his head thoughtfully. "I can't even recall my mother's face. I remember being in her room, but I don't remember her."

Roe heard the wistfulness in his own voice and cleared his throat before he continued. "I was only five when my father sent me off to school. I was by far the youngest boy in attendance. Even the most rigid of parents usually kept their boys at home until age eight."

Meggie's brow furrowed. "You must have been awfully smart to need schooling so early."

"It wasn't my need for schooling, it was his need to get me out from underfoot." He glanced over at Meggie, but couldn't bear the look of concern in her eyes, so he dropped his gaze and focused instead on her long, narrow bare feet, damp and muddy from her run across the yard. Suddenly, he wanted to tell her, to tell her everything.

"My mother was sick," he said. "She never truly recovered from my birth. My father wasn't much for children and I was undoubtedly loud and rambunctious." Roe was smiling, but there was no pleasure in it. "Truly, I hardly recall those days. My earliest memories are being at school."

"Where you sang songs to keep away the bogeymen."

"Yes."

"I'm sorry," she said. "You must have been very lonely at the time."

"Oh, I got used to it," he assured her. "I guess I've always been lonely, my whole life until—"

He didn't finish the statement. Somehow he didn't have to. Both of them knew, suddenly, unquestionably, what he was going to say.

Roe stared out the open doorway, then glanced back at Meggie. Her expression was understanding. As if she knew what his confession had cost him. As if she was happy that it was her family and her community that had kept Monroe Farley from being alone again. He smiled at her.

She grinned back.

They sat there, sharing the moment as the rain continued to pour down, running along the edge of the single slope roof and spattering loudly onto the already soaked ground. Once more the silence lay between them, but there was no uneasiness about it.

To Roe's surprise, Meggie took a deep breath and began to sing. Roe listened to her for a couple of moments deciding that her unusual voice was not as bad as he'd first thought, before blending his own with hers.

They discovered that between the two of them they knew nine verses to "Polly Vaughn." It was warm and pleasurable singing together, their very disparate singing tones joined in such unexpected harmony. After "Polly Vaughn" they sang "Silver Dagger." To better combine their voices, Roe sat at her feet in the dirt by the sawbuck. He loved being close to her, and the sheer pleasure of sharing the simple music was like a burst of sunshine on the dark, rainy day.

Song after song they sang together. She taught him "Taney County Bad Companions." He taught her "The Old Man Who Came Over the Moor."

"Do you know this one?" she asked him.

> "Come all you pretty fair maids
>   Who flourish in your prime,
>   Be sure to keep your garden clean,
>   Let no one take your thyme."

Roe's eyes widened in shock, then, grinning, he listened to the sweet sound of her voice.

> "My thyme it is all gone away,
>   I cannot plant anew,
>   And in the place where my thyme stood
>   It's all grown up in rue."

She sang the song sweetly as if it were but a children's tune like "Mary Contrary" or "Cat in the Fiddle." But Roe knew the old English ballad and his thoughts flew from its pretty words to the archaic meaning in its symbols. A meaning obviously unknown to Meggie Best. The sprig of thyme represented virginity, while the bitter leaves of rue construed remorse and sorrow for the unsanctioned pleasures of the flesh. The sweet garden song she sang was a warning to young women in the less sheltered times of the past not to trust the false hearts of men who asked for their bodies before they asked to marry.

> "The pink it is a pretty flower
>   But it will bud too soon,
>   I have a posy of mine own
>   I am sure 'twill wait 'til June."

Roe looked up to the young woman who had given her thyme to him and for whom the plucked flower would never live long enough to see the wedding day. Still, as he watched her face and heard her voice, he couldn't regret the tenderness that she had given so freely and had asked him no price. But he couldn't help but worry that one day she would feel regret.

> "In June comes in the primrose flower
>   But it is not for me,
>   I will pull up my primrose flower
>   And plant a willow tree."

As the last sweet note faded, Roe reached to clasp her hand in his own. Her eyes widened as she stared at him. He rose to his knees and brought her long, work-callused fingers to his lips.

"Marry me, Meggie," he whispered.

"Roe, I told you I—"

"I know what you told me. In my heart I've heard you tell me over and over. But that's not the answer that I want to hear."

He pulled her closer and pressed his fingers to her lips.

"Roe, you can't possibly think that—"

"When you're this close to me, Meggie, I can't possibly think at all."

He reached for her and she knelt beside him. His hands caressed her cheeks, her brow. He traced the line of her jaw, smoothing one damp curling strand of hair out of her face.

"I think of nothing but you, Meggie, nothing at all. I ache for you," he whispered against her ear.

Roe heard the catch in her breath. Gently, he eased apart the long plait of hair that hung down her back. He raked his hands through her hair as if it were a treasure of pure gold. Then he twisted the strands in his fist and used them to pull her closer. Closer. He pulled her closer until her lips were a hairsbreadth from his own. And he trembled.

He fought the desire to pull her against him and kiss her again as he had in the sweet bed of clover they had known before. He had been hurried then, maybe too rough. He wanted to be sweet for his Meggie. He wanted to be tender and patient and husbandly. This time he wanted it to be perfect. This time he would let neither the effects of strong drink nor his passion control him.

Her little nervous breath felt warm against his own skin. He bent forward only slightly, just to touch his lips against hers.

"Marry me, Meggie," he whispered an instant before their mouths met in a gentle kiss, as genteel as it was unsatisfactory.

Roe swallowed determinedly and tried to pull away from her to wait patiently for her answer. But it didn't come in words.

With a tiny cry of desire, Meggie wrapped her arms around his neck and pressed her body against his own.

"Kiss me, kiss me, Roe."

Meggie pressed the sweet soft warmth of her bosom

against him. She had tried so hard not to want him, not to need him. But the invitation of his arms was more than she could refuse. The hard points of her nipples, swelled with eagerness for his touch, and the tender, innocent kiss that they had started quickly became an achy, clenching need to possess.

Roe drew a sharp gasp of breath through his nose; to Meggie it looked like a stallion catching the scent. She felt him clasp her around the waist. With more instinct than calculation, her hands skimmed the long, muscled length of his back to bury themselves in the wild strands of his thick black hair.

She felt the movement of Roe's hands upon her. While his right hand continued to knead and tease her breast, his left slid down the round curve of her buttocks, pressing her body close against him.

It was a wild kiss, hurried and incendiary. His mouth opened over hers and he begged to taste her. Meggie's own lips parted and she was jubilant as she slipped her tongue inside his mouth. He tasted as exotic as cinnamon and as homey as apples. She inhaled the fragrance of him and was lost.

Tighter and tighter she pressed herself against him. She wrapped her legs around him and could feel the stiffness of his erection against her now. They were near enough for joining, but yet unjoined. It was exhilarating. It was enticing. With a sound near pain he moaned against her ear and buried his face into the soft sanctuary of her hair. She felt beautiful and powerful, and she felt on fire.

Desperately she squirmed beneath him, trying to ease the throbbing ache of desire that plagued her. She meant to get closer, she needed to be closer and she spread her legs even wider before him to make that happen.

"Oh, Meggie! I only meant to kiss you," he confessed in her ear with hoarse, hard-won words. She smoothed her hands up and down his back, urging him against her, begging him to make love to her.

"But kissing is not enough," she cried plaintively. "I need you inside me, Roe. I need you now."

He made no protest, but laid her on her back on the damp dirt floor, following her down. In one hasty movement, he jerked the long, cotton homespun skirt that covered her up to her waist. The soft, oft-washed cotton of her flower sack drawers offered the last impediment to her nakedness. With eager, fumbling fingers she undid the ties at her waist and helped him skim them down her legs.

He was staring at her nakedness in the gray light of afternoon, the rain beating now as fierce a tempo as her heart.

"You are so beautiful, Meggie," he whispered.

It was with pride as well as desire that she opened her legs for him and urged him astride her.

Roe wedged his knee high between her thighs. She gasped. He used the thick strong muscles of his thigh to begin a strong seductive rhythm of caress and pleasure.

Meggie's eyes opened with desire and tiny cries of pleasure from the back of her throat. She stared up at him and saw in his face the mixture of control and pleasure that so taunted and enflamed her need.

"Roe, yes, Roe," she called his name as she squirmed beneath him. "Please, I need you. I need all of you. I'm begging," she cried as she fanned the flames that were already nearly out of control.

She heard him moaning, as if the man were in pain, and realized he was voicing his own need to her, Meggie Best, the woman in his arms.

"God help me, Meggie, I can't stop."

"Don't stop!" she pleaded.

To ensure that he didn't, she pulled his galluses from his shoulders and jerked at his shirt.

Any good sense or right thinking that either might have

possessed was blinded by the haze of red-rimmed passion that glittered between them. The need to mate, to join, to unite as man and woman prevailed.

Their movements together were almost rough now and desperate. He had to be inside her. She had to have him inside her now.

She tugged at the buttons on his butternut duckings. He offered the help of his own fingers for only a minute before Meggie managed to unfasten his trousers. There was no gentleness or ease as she dragged them off his hips. He was naked beneath them, and Meggie had to touch his nakedness. She had to touch it now, she had no patience for finesse.

Her hands on the bare flesh and caressing his buttocks nearly sent him over the edge. Roe, too, sought the secrets of her private flesh.

"Meggie, I can't wait. I can't wait."

Her answer was a joyous cry as once more she wrapped her legs around his waist. Shaking with desire and clasping his flesh in her hands, she eased him inside her.

He was hot and hard and filling and her body clinched him with need.

He swore with delight and ground his teeth against the need to spill himself inside her then and there.

"You're so good. You feel so good," he told her.

Meggie's reply was an inarticulate gasp of pleasure.

With labored effort, he held himself rigid and quivering on the brink until he'd revived a semblance of his control. Meggie continued to squirm beneath him, too impatient to wait. When he began a slow, steady thrusting, she rocked and moaned beneath him.

He cried aloud at the pleasure of it.

"I can't be slow," he told her. "I can't be careful."

"Love me, Roe," she begged. "Love me hard, love me now. I can't wait!"

And he didn't. Planting his elbows firmly in the unyielding ground, he began pounding her body with quick, deep strokes, the resulting fire of which startled them both.

Again, again, again, Roe slammed himself full-length inside her, only to retreat and slam again. Meggie tightened her limbs around him tenaciously, still she was not close enough.

"More," she pleaded. "More."

Roe sat back just enough to grab her ankles. Bending her farther upward he wrapped her ankles around his shoulders and began to move inside her once more.

Meggie cried out in momentary alarm at the depth of his newly positioned stroke. But when he hesitated, she grasped his buttocks in her hands and urged him on. Her lips widened in a mask of passion and her eyes closed in breathless wonder.

In less than a half-dozen powerful, pounding thrusts, she reached the pinnacle and careened off as eagerly as if it were the Marrying Stone, screaming his name as he spent his seed inside her.

CHAPTER
SIXTEEN

MEGGIE LAY WITH her head upon Roe's chest. The only sound she could hear was the beating of his heart. She banished all thoughts from her brain. It was too warm and muddled a moment, with the world too far removed to be wasted by thinking. Outside the rain had ceased and the sun peeked through a break in the clouds on the far western horizon, filling the sky with bright colors of pink and mauve and shining into the doorway of the little woodshed where they lay. The scent of earth and cedar and sex mingled with the scent of the man beside Meggie, and the aroma was very dear. She was very satisfied.

Roe gave a deep sigh and lovingly dragged her atop his body.

"You shouldn't be on this cold dirt floor," he told her in a warm whisper.

She stretched languidly above him and rested her head in the crook of his shoulder. It was a wonderful, safe feeling and she wanted to relish it, drag it out as long as she possibly could. Loving Roe Farley was like all of her daydream fancies coming to life at once. But, of course, it wasn't real. Couldn't last. Fanciful imaginations were pleasant and comforting, but they couldn't be confused with the real world. And as Roe began to stir beneath her, she knew the real world was about to intrude once again.

"Are you all right?" he asked her. "I should have found us something to lie upon."

"I don't mind," she murmured into his neck.

He ran his hand up and down her back as if to warm her. "I meant to take my time, Meggie," he said. "But once I . . . I touched you, I just couldn't wait any longer."

"I don't mind."

She could feel him smiling against her throat. "I was too rough."

"I don't mind."

Roe chuckled then and pulled her head up out of its comfortable position so that he could smile up into her eyes. "I've never known a woman so easy to get along with."

His teasing warmed the languor in her heart. "And you probably never will." She lay a sweet kiss upon his lips. It did not evoke the fiery passion of earlier, but still its power was dazzling. When their mouths parted, Roe took her face in his hands. He gazed at her with such intensity that Meggie finally looked away.

Her heart was beating like an Indian tom-tom. Deliberately, she tried to quiet the joy that leapt to her breast when he touched her.

"Oh, Meggie," he said. "I thought that singing with you was wonderful. But no music on earth can compare with this."

Meggie felt her lip begin to tremble and she sank her teeth into it to stiffen it. The pain stung. It was time to get up. It was time to walk away. Purposely she moved to do just that.

When she felt his hand upon her breast, she turned back.

"I love to see you naked," he whispered. "I know that you're beautiful, but I still like to view the evidence."

Suddenly, she wanted him to see her again, too. She wanted that moment between them. She wasn't willing to give it all up yet. Meggie bunched the material of her dress in her hand and looked at him questioningly. "I can just take this off," she said.

"Mmmmmm," he moaned as he stilled her hands. He closed his eyes in pleasure as if he'd just tasted something sweet. "You tempt me, Meggie. Naked with a woman in the woodshed was surely one of my boyhood fantasies. But I think we've spent enough time rolling around in the dirt." Reaching up playfully he tugged at her nose. "What I want to do is to try out our new bed. I'm sure Granny Piggott didn't give it to us just for sleeping."

Meggie wanted to try out that bed, too. She was thoughtful for a moment before a frown began to gather in her brow. "We can't do that, Roe. Pa is there."

"I don't mean now, sweetheart," Roe laughed.

The word *sweetheart* sizzled through Meggie's consciousness and she wanted to grasp it like a straw.

Lovingly, Roe ran his hand along her back, teasing and touching. "But tonight, ah, tonight, Meggie."

Once more she buried her face in his neck and kissed him, anxiously. "I'll try," she answered against his ear. "As soon as I hear Pa snoring, I'll try to sneak in there."

"What?"

"I said as—"

Roe sat up and pulled her up with him upon his lap. "I heard what you said. I just don't know why you've said it."

"We can't just go to bed together. Pa wouldn't like it a bit." Meggie felt the weight of reality growing heavier and heavier.

"I thought perhaps . . . perhaps he would understand."

Meggie shook her head. "Oh, no," she told him. "Folks here are very strict about this kind of thing."

Roe nodded. "I understand. I just thought that since we'd already jumped the Marrying Stone . . . but if we need to stand up before the preacher, then we do. How soon do you think old Pastor Jay can marry us?"

"Marry us?"

"Yes, marry us."

Meggie smoothed the hair away from her face and began to rearrange her clothes. "Roe, I told you that it's not necessary for us to get married."

She kept her words calm and deliberate, hoping to avoid any conflict.

Roe was silent for so long, she finally looked up at him to find him staring in disbelief. "Meggie." His words were quiet. "Didn't you just tell me that you were going to marry me?"

"I didn't say anything like that."

"What was this all about?" he asked, gesturing to the place they had shared on the floor of the woodshed.

"It's not about anything, it's—"

"Damn it!" Roe rushed to his feet, unceremoniously dumping her on the cold damp dirt. "You tricked me."

"Tricked you?"

"I wouldn't have done this again if I'd thought you weren't going to marry me."

Meggie gave him a disbelieving look and shook her head. "You didn't even give a thought to marriage. If you were thinking at all, you were just thinking about loving, just like I was."

"All right," he said. "I admit I let my passion get ahead of my good sense. But I did ask you to marry me, and I'm sure I had your consent."

"I didn't agree to anything. I just didn't answer."

Roe stared at her as if he couldn't believe what he was hearing. He shook his head and tried again. "Meggie, people don't do this without getting married."

She raised a skeptical eyebrow. "People do this without getting married all the time. I may be an ignorant Ozarker, but I know that much about the world. Fornication, the Bible calls it, and it happens all the time. You know that as well as I do. I bet it even happens in the Bay State."

"Well, certainly it happens, but it shouldn't."

Meggie nodded. "That's because people would talk or they could have a baby or something bad. But I told you before, those things are not a problem for us. Nothing has changed. When you finish your work, you can go on back to where you came from. I'll tell folks that you've died and none will be the wiser."

"You think that having a baby or what people might say are the only reasons people don't do this without marriage?"

"Well, no, those aren't the only reasons. I know it's a sin and all that."

"And all that doesn't bother you?"

"Of course it bothers me," she snapped.

"But not enough to make you marry me."

"I think heaven will surely understand. It's not like we're hurting anybody."

"What about a child?"

"I told you there isn't any child."

"There could be now," he said, somewhat louder. "Do you think I would have risked that again if I had thought you weren't going to marry me?"

"If there is a child, he'll be fine."

"No, he won't. He'll be alone. He'll be hurt."

"Everybody on the mountain will be his family," she said. "I can promise you he won't have a day of being alone. He'll just think that his father has died."

"And what will his father think?" Roe asked. "Will his father think that the boy is fine, living on a subsistence farm with a crippled old man, a simple boy, and a woman?"

"Don't worry, I do intend to marry eventually," she assured him. "Then the child would have a father."

Roe's eyes were blazing. "What's wrong with the one he already has? If you're going to marry eventually anyway, why not marry me now?"

"I can't marry you. It would be a permanent mistake."

"It's not right," Roe repeat in angry disbelief, and then

began pacing across the floor as he raked his hair impatiently. "What do you mean a permanent mistake?"

"You know exactly what I mean. You want to marry me because we've . . . we've done this together."

"That's what usually happens. When a couple . . . anticipates their wedding night a bit, then they get married."

"What usually happens is that men do this with women, and if they don't *have* to marry them, they walk away. Don't you listen to these songs you collect? That's what most of them are about. A man doing this and walking away."

"We're talking about real life here, not songs."

"Songs are like the echo of real life. Men lay with women and then just walk away all the time. I don't know why you can't be just like the rest of them."

"Is that what you really want? You want me to be some heartless cad who just leaves you here?"

"That's exactly what I do want. I cannot go where you're going and I won't have you stay here. And I won't be tied to a man that's not around. I want to be free to marry for the right reason."

"And what reason is that? Love? Is that what you're trying to make me say, Meggie? That I love you?" Roe was clearly angry now and had raised his voice loudly. "Well, maybe I do. I've never been in love. I don't know anything about it. Maybe this is it."

"If it was love, you'd know it."

"Would I? How would I know it?"

"You just would."

"Oh, I suppose all *princes* are experts on love and immediately recognize it on sight," he said sarcastically.

"You are no prince," she replied.

"Well, thank you, Meggie Best. At least you are right about one thing. I am not a prince. I'm a man."

He stopped and drew a deep breath. He clenched his hands at his side. The sight of him standing in the small woodshed, holding back his temper, sent a strange little thrill through Meggie's body.

When it seemed he'd gained control of himself once more, he turned to look at her. "All right, Meggie. I understand that you don't want to come with me and that you don't want to be left alone. I think I can understand that. I can even respect it. I realize what a fanciful nature you have and that you probably have dreamed of marrying for some grand passionate love."

Meggie's face flushed. She was the one being practical here. She was the one who figured out the plan so that he wouldn't have to marry her, but she didn't reply.

"Perhaps I don't know enough about love to offer it to you," he continued. "But I can offer you this. I'm willing to give up my home, my career, everything with which I am familiar to stay on this mountain and make you legally my wife."

Meggie's mouth went dry as dust and her heart nearly leapt out of her breast. "Now why would you want to do a fool thing like that?" was all she said.

Roe paled visibly, but he answered quickly enough. "Because it's my obligation to do so."

His words acted like a splash of cold water. "No thank you, sir. You are relieved of your obligation," she said. "I don't need any favors."

"I'm sure you don't," he snarled. "Any day now some real prince is going to come walking over one of those ridges and have all the right reasons. Well, I wish him all the luck in the world, because he's going to need it."

Roe lay in the new room in the new bed and stared at the ceiling above him. His confusion made him unable to sleep. He should be glad, he told himself over and over again. He'd enjoyed himself, found some pleasure with her, and he was still free to return to his life. It would have been a disaster to stay here and marry her. She was not at all the kind of woman that he should marry. She would never understand his work; she could never be a help to him socially. Meggie Best might well be the best speller on Marrying Stone Mountain, but she certainly wouldn't shine at a Cambridge garden party.

Yet, he couldn't quite conquer the nagging thought that he wanted to marry her. With pleasure, he recalled not the passion they'd shared, but those moments they'd spent singing. Her voice mixed with his own. With that kind of sharing, a man could never be lonely again.

In the main room he heard Onery stirring. The old man had been a little bit better at suppertime, but he was still clearly in a lot of pain. Even after drinking two full cups of Meggie's bark and herb brew, his rheumatism was still paining him to distraction.

"Jesse!" the old man called up toward the loft. "Jesse, my leg's a-cramping. Come walk me about."

"I'll do it, Pa."

The voice Roe heard was Meggie's and she sounded wide awake.

"Jesse didn't get back with the snakeroot 'til after dark," she told her father. "And he was so cold and wet I sent him straight to bed. Just let him sleep and I'll help you."

"You ain't got the strength for it, Meggie-gal," her father answered. "I need a big fellow to lean on."

Without another thought, Roe rolled out of bed and pulled on his trousers. He slipped the galluses over his bare shoulders and walked across the wide, slightly raised block that served as the threshold separating the main cabin from the new room.

"Am I big enough?" he asked.

"Did we wake you up, Farley?" Onery answered his question with one of his own.

"I wasn't asleep," Roe said.

He walked across the main room to the fireplace. Taking

a tallow candle from the mantel, he used a stick to stir the ashes in the fireplace just enough to get a light.

He set the glowing candle on the table. Its meager flame revealed just a hint of the room around him.

In the far right corner he saw Meggie sitting up in her pile of bedclothes on the floor. She was sleepworn and tousled. The faint glow of candlelight shimmered on the untidy mess of hair that hung down her back. Roe felt a strange clutch inside him.

"Go back to your pallet, Meggie," he told her quietly. "I'll walk Onery around until his cramp eases."

She didn't answer, but she did scoot farther down into the covers, turned to face the wall, and lay down. She pulled the bedsheet up to her neck.

Purposely, Roe turned away from the sight of her and walked over to Onery's side.

With a good deal of moaning and complaint, the old man had managed to sit up on his bed. He dangled his feet off the edge.

"You about ready to wear a path in the floor?" he asked.

"There isn't much else I could do on a night like this," Roe answered.

He helped the old man to his feet, wrapping Onery's arm around his shoulder. Onery's face was ashen with pain, but he only grunted stubbornly. Roe grasped him around the waist and encouraged him to lean his weight into his arms.

The first steps were hard won and small.

"Is it your hip or your leg?" Roe asked.

The old man gave a vivid curse under his breath. "It's both," he answered. "My dang hip is creaking and aching like a wagon wheel plumb out of grease and my old lame leg is throbbin' like a thumb blackened with a hammer."

"Would it help if we got your boots on?"

"In the house? Lord Almighty!" Onery exclaimed. "It'd just be a pure waste of shoe leather."

Onery moaned aloud in pain as he tried out his weight on

his bad leg. After only a second, he leaned heavily against Roe.

Slowly, they made their way across the room. The old man's leg was stiff and painful to him and dragging it about cost him dearly of his strength.

"Lord, it is a sight getting old," Onery said. "I used these legs to walk as far east as the New River country and as far west as the Nations." He whistled loudly, in lieu of a curse. "Now it near kills me to walk acrost my own cabin."

"It's just the weather," Roe assured him.

He nodded. "Yep, just the weather. It sure is a shame that the dang weather spends so much time being wet or cold."

Roe couldn't argue with that logic.

"Well, at least the rain today is past. In a couple of days things will dry up completely and you'll be back to yourself."

The old man laughed derisively. "That I will. I'll be back to being a crippled old man," he said.

When Roe made no comment, he continued, "I ain't complaining, mind ye. I'm glad to be alive and I'm happy not to be no more worst off than this. I'm no young man these days."

"Age happens to all of us," Roe agreed.

"That it does, son, indeed it does, and to tell the truth I wouldn't never go back. Not to my own youth no how."

"You weren't happy as a young man?"

Onery chuckled. "I was too happy. That was my problem. I wouldn't go back to being that itinerant fiddle player who just came and went as he pleased."

Roe was surprised. He knew how much the old man loved music and also how much he hated farming.

"You don't miss it at all?" he asked.

He shrugged. "I miss being that young and strong and healthy," he answered honestly. "But I don't miss the life even though I could tell you some stories that would scare the ghost outta good people."

"A sinful life was it?"

Onery hooted with laughter. "More than I'm willing to tell. Truth to say, son," he said in a quiet whisper and with a wary eye toward Meggie's pallet. "They's a pretty gal in near ever' town from here to Georgia that knows my name. And more than one youngun that's got my face."

"You must have been quite a swain with the ladies," Roe smiled, grateful that the talk was diverting his attention from his pain.

Onery snorted. "I weren't nothing a'tal. I was fair enough to look at, I suppose, but I didn't have a mil in my pocket or a serious thought in my head."

"But the women liked you anyway."

"Ain't nothing gals is more interested in than some stranger that they mamas are busy warnin' them against."

Roe's brow furrowed. "Yes, I suppose that's true," he answered, casting his own glance toward the pallet across the room.

"It is for some, even for my Posie, Lord rest her soul, she was as stuck on me as a tick on a hound. But there was a difference, of course."

"Of course."

Onery stopped in the middle of the room and looked Roe straight in the eye. "The difference was that I was stuck on her, too."

The old man's eyes glazed slightly as he spoke of his long-dead wife.

"It were the strangest thing," he said. "When I was with her, I felt like I just belonged there. Right queer, ain't it?"

"Yes, I suppose so."

"She were a pretty thing, my Posie," he continued. "She had that cornsilk hair like Jesse's and those big blue eyes." He sighed. "Mind you, I'd seen better. But there was something about her. I never did truly understand it. It was almost as if we was meant for each other from the day that we met."

"Perhaps you were."

"Not according to her," Onery said. "She weren't gonna have me. Do you know that story?"

"Jesse has told me some of it."

"She thought I wouldn't make her a good husband," he said. "And I suspect she was right. At least she was then."

"But you changed," Roe said.

"Yep, I sure did. But I wouldn't have, not if I hadn't had to."

They stopped to turn once more. Onery took a deep breath as if he were readying himself for a dive in deep water and then he began to walk again.

"The truth is, if she'd married up with me easy, I probably wouldn't have changed at all," he said. "Oh, I would have still loved her, that's for certain. But I would have grown tired of all this hard work and before long I would have begun wishing I was back on the road."

Roe listened thoughtfully.

"But she didn't marry me easy. She didn't marry me a'tal. I come back here and she's got that little baby that don't seem quite right and all the folks treating her like she was the whore of the county. I offered to marry her like I was doing her a good deed." The old man chuckled at the memory. "That Posie, she looked at me like I was lower than the dirt."

Onery turned slightly to look at Roe as he spoke. "She made me work to get her. It wasn't enough that we was spooning silly for each other and had a baby besides, I had to prove that I could be her man."

Roe nodded thoughtfully.

"It just made sense, I guess," Onery said. "Anything that's worth having is worth working for."

Once more Roe glanced over toward Meggie. He wanted to ask Onery if maybe she was doing the same thing as her mother. But he wasn't ready to talk about Meggie yet. And certainly not to Meggie's father.

Deliberately, he changed the subject.

"I bet you learned a lot of songs while you were traveling."

"Oh, that I did. I did indeed. I ain't sung you near nothing that I know."

Roe smiled. "I'm going to have to get you to give me your English ballads for my collection."

"I suspect I got a few ye ain't heard," Onery told him. "Course I have to bring 'em to memory. That ain't always easy. It takes a bit of time."

Onery stopped near the end of the bed. "I think that's about enough, son. If I was to walk any farther, I'd be too tired to get into the bed."

Roe helped him, gently easing his bad leg onto the feather tick without bending the knee. The old man's face was as white as a sheet by the time he got situated, but his words were still lighthearted.

"I thank you, Roe Farley," Onery said. "You ain't a half bad feller for a Yankee son of a lawyer."

Roe laughed at the old man's joke. It was easy to understand how Jesse was mostly such a happy, easygoing fellow. Roe thought he might have been less serious himself if he'd had a father like Onery Best.

"Wish you was staying the winter here," Onery said. "Cabin gets close in the winter and we do a lot of singing and playing."

"I bet you do."

"It's mighty pretty up here in the wintertime. Snow covering the trees like sugar candy and tracking meat is easy as falling off a log," he said. "On the real cold days when we got no call to go outside, that Jesse he plays that fiddle from sunup to evening and Meggie and I bellow out tunes 'til our throats is sore."

In his mind Roe could almost see the cold winter day that Onery described. The feeling it evoked in him was near envy. "I'm sure it must be nice."

"Nice? It's downright terrible," the old man laughed. "Ain't nothing so bad as being holed up in a cabin with two younguns who's as ticklish about confined places as I am. And that gal of mine cooking up something she's like to burn and smellin' up the place something awful with scorched beans or taters."

Laughing along with him, Roe shook his head. "You don't paint a very pretty picture of it."

"Oh, it ain't much of a picture, for sure," Onery agreed.

"But it does sound awfully good," Roe admitted.

"You stay this winter, son, and you'd get yer ears and yer Listening Box full for sure."

Roe was thoughtful for a long moment. It was amazing how tempting the invitation was. "Perhaps I could stay," he said.

Onery nodded. "It's an idea. You could collect yourself a slew of songs and it'd give you a bit more time."

"More time for what?"

The old man grinned wisely. "Oh, I guess it'd give ye more time to see my Meggie."

FROM THE JOURNAL OF
J. MONROE FARLEY

July 14, 1902
Marrying Stone, Arkansas

The weather has become quite warm and somewhat uncomfortable. Completed the work on the new privy and I must admit it has turned out to be a better idea than even I had first thought. Mr. Best's leg continues to pain him considerably and on some days he just sits in his chair and stares out across the distant hills. This has left the entire work of the farm to Jesse and myself. Meggie helps when she can, although her work at the house and taking care of her father keeps her busy. Her garden has suffered some from bugs, but we continue to enjoy fresh vegetables now in addition to the usual pork, chicken, and occasional wild game.

My collection of old English ballads and communal re-creations continues to grow and I have been forced to shave the wax on several less valuable cylinders in order to make room for the new songs that turn up on this doorstep nearly every day. Just last week Mr. Piggott Broody, an older and rather eccentric member of the community, sat in the yard and sang "The Lass of Roch Royal." The original story was in many senses changed, but still maintains Georgie Jeems, the Fair Annie, and the false lady.

I am considering staying on here through the winter. It is possible that I might send for more wax cylinders through the drummers that serve Mr. Phillips's store. Winter seems an especially good time for singing and playing. And I am loath to leave with Mr. Best ailing.

CHAPTER

SEVENTEEN

THE BRIGHT DAWN and cloudless sky suggested that it would be a perfect day for a wedding. Dressed in Sunday best and carrying a new willow basket with the freshest and most perfect of the garden produce, the Best family, with Roe Farley along, headed for the Marrying Stone wedding of Paisley Winsloe and Althea McNees.

Roe and Meggie were both concerned about Onery's health as his leg continued to bother him, and the trip was a long one and not wholly necessary to make. A drawn-out argument ensued over whether any or all of them should go. However, the old man declared that he was fine and neither of them had the audacity to dispute his word. Donning a fancy long-tailed frock coat, somewhat worse for wear and very much out-of-date, Onery insisted that he would go.

With Jesse's help they got him situated upon the old mule in a way that seemed unlikely to further pain his bad leg. The mule halter in his hand, Jesse led the way down the narrow path to the church. They were getting a late start, but Jesse kept a brisk pace through the ridge rows.

Roe and Meggie walked together lingering some distance behind the mule. The pathway through the trees was narrow, but patches of sun shone through and dappled the shade. And the air was fragrant with new growth and withering forest duff.

Meggie kept her eyes straight ahead and Roe tried to follow her lead, but he kept stealing glances at her. And the temptation to talk to her overwhelmed his better judgment. He missed the sound of her voice, laughing with pleasure or strident with complaint. More than once he'd been tempted to plant a worm beneath her coffee cup just to shake her out of her calm, quiet control.

"That's a pretty dress." It was not merely a polite compliment, but a sincere comment. She looked especially lovely in the vibrant blue.

"I've worn it several times before," Meggie answered evenly, still not deigning to look his way.

"I know you have," Roe said. "But I've never told you how nice you look in it. That color is perfect with your eyes."

Meggie shrugged. "Just luck about the color. I was dying it the night that—" She hesitated as a blush stained her cheeks. She cast him a quick glance and then answered in haste. "The night you and Jesse got drunk."

Roe gave her a long look as they both remembered that night. "Then, it's even more beautiful than I thought."

Meggie did look at him then, her eyes widening. It was there between them once more; the emotion, the desire, the knowledge. They had shared a secret, special rite of passage and forever the link forged between them would bind.

He saw Meggie's lip tremble uncertainly, then deliberately she lengthened her stride to outpace him. Roe allowed her to go. He no longer knew what to wish for or what to hope. He didn't want to leave his life's work behind him to become a poor Arkansas farmer. Yet, he was loath to leave this woman and her family.

Though darker thoughts plagued him he merely allowed himself to feel content as he watched the rhythmic sway of her from behind.

Since the day in the woodshed, Meggie had spent a good deal of her time trying to avoid him. When she wasn't doing that, she merely pretended that nothing had happened between them. The only time she'd allowed anything else to peek through was when she and her father took their first tour of the new privy. Roe smiled as he recalled the memorable afternoon.

It was a simple square building, with a less than grandiose purpose. Yet, Meggie had made him feel like he had erected a palace. Gazing in awe at the structure, she praised his carpentry work and marveled at the convenience. Her enthusiasm was highly contagious and even Onery grudgingly admitted that an outhouse might be a fair idea after all.

When the old man returned to the house, Roe hadn't been able to resist reaching out to grab her arm.

"I'm glad you like the privy," he said. He tried to keep his expression light and conversational, incapable of dredging up the deep feelings between them.

She smiled at him, but there was a sense of poignant sadness behind it. "It's very fancy. We'd never have got one if you hadn't come here." She glanced back at the little building with near reverence in her eyes. "It will give me something to remember you by when you're gone."

Meggie walked away then, leaving Roe to stare puzzled at the little square building that he'd created. He didn't want her memories of him to be only a privy.

Now as he watched her walk in front of him, the wide skirt of the blue homespun dress swishing back and forth in an enticingly feminine fashion, he once more warred with himself.

He would return to Massachusetts when the summer was over and forget that Miss Meggie Best had ever existed. She didn't want to marry him. She didn't want to go back east with him. And she would definitely be a liability among the better class of people in Cambridge. Marriage to her would mean a life in the wilds of these mountains, at least part of the time. A thing he was sure was contrary to his nature. Still, what he shared with her was more than just a

memorable passing fancy. He wanted to leave her with
something. He wanted to leave her his name.

That *was* what he wanted, he realized. He couldn't bear
the thought of her marriage to some other man and of her
forgetting the moments that they had shared together. He
wanted her to be his, and his alone, forever. She'd spurned
his proposal of marriage as if he were no one of any
consequence in her life. Perhaps she didn't want to live with
him. But he was going to marry her. If it took staying here
all winter to convince her of that, he was ready for it.

They were still a mile from the church when they began
to hear the tolling for the wedding. The huge bell had a
deep, beautiful, full-bodied sound that echoed through the
mountains in a way that made it seem a part of the sounds
of nature. It was a wonderful noise, and, Roe thought, that
forced to take a side, he'd have to agree with the McNeeses
that the bell should stay and the bell tower made bigger. Roe
smiled at the thought. Fortunately, he wasn't really family
here, so he wouldn't have to make a choice.

As they came within sight of the church, it was clear that
virtually everyone on the mountain had turned out for the
wedding. The hillside around the church was filled with
young girls in their Sunday best homespun giggling behind
their hands and flirting with red-faced swains, shaved and
slicked up for the occasion. Women labored over plank
tables that groaned with the weight of the food upon them
and gossiped among themselves, hesitating in their conversation only occasionally to scold a rowdy child. Men
gathered in small groups to chew half-green tobacco,
complain about their crops, and brag about their fishing.

Granny Piggott sat in a cane-bottom chair under a shade
tree and smoked her pipe. They stopped for only a moment
to greet the old woman. She held the pipe between her teeth
and patted Roe playfully upon the stomach.

"I believe you are putting on some weight, boy," she said

with a cheery cackle. "Is marriage making this gal a better cook?"

"I believe it is, Granny," Roe answered, glancing over at Meggie who stood somewhat unwillingly at his side. "She hasn't ruined a thing in the kitchen in a very long time."

The old woman raised a curious eyebrow as she glanced over at Meggie. "It ain't the husband that's supposed to get fat, it's the wife," she said.

"Meggie don't never eat much," Jesse piped in.

"I ain't talking about eating," Granny answered with a pointed look toward Roe. "It's the other kind of belly growing a young couple oughter be workin' upon."

Roe cleared his throat nervously. Fortunately he was saved from making any reply by the opportune interruption of Buell Phillips.

"The wedding is about to start," he announced. "You'd better find yourself a good view. Nearly everyone on the mountain is here."

Roe nodded and Phillips hurried away, circulating through the crowd as if he were permanently a candidate for some political office.

"I'll just stay here by Granny," Onery told them. "I can lean against this tree and take the weight off my leg. You younguns go on and find you a place."

Meggie looked as if she might protest, but Roe preempted her argument with a quick agreement.

"You just rest here with Granny," he said. "Jesse and I will watch out for Meggie."

Onery chuckled. "You do that, son," he answered.

Nodding a rushed good-bye, the three left Onery and their family's pounding gift at the base of the tree where Granny sat, keeping watch over the plunder. They hurried into the crowd to find a likely site to watch the proceedings. As they moved across the clearing, again and again their attention was drawn by one acquaintance or another.

They watched the Broody twins as the two gleefully stole

Ada Trace's pink hair ribbon. This forced the young lady, in her first appearance in long skirts, to jerk her hem to her knees and chase the two scamps across the clearing, squalling with unladylike fury.

Beulah Winsloe, standing within a circle of like-minded matrons, took her role as mother of the groom quite seriously. "Of course she's a perfectly fine young woman," Beulah told them. "But unfortunately she has no graces and hardly any raising at all."

Althea McNees stood alone near the Marrying Stone, her brown eyes wide with nervousness and her cheeks pale. Her long, thin body seemed almost to tremble from the nonexistent chill of the afternoon. She looked very young and very frightened.

Her closest male relative, her Great-uncle Nez Beath, cheerfully laughed and joked and swapped stories with Pigg Broody, clearly grateful to have Althea, who was well into her teens and an extra mouth to feed at his place, finally become the responsibility of somebody else.

That somebody else, Paisley Winsloe, showed up at the very last moment on the edge of the crowd with his cousin Eben Baxley. The two, laughing heartily and stumbling together, were both a little worse for drink, but given the fact that a man didn't marry every day, folks graciously overlooked the social misstep.

Jesse stopped slightly up and to the left of the Marrying Stone and gestured the others to join him. The spot afforded a great view of the entire area. Roe urged Meggie in front of him so that she could see, then turned his attention to the festivities.

Pastor Jay captured all eyes as he stepped out onto the church steps and waited. A polite silence slowly settled across the crowd. The preacher's expression was disapproving and he gave a stern admonishment to the two young men as Paisley half stumbled his way to the front.

When the young man was in place, his coat straight and

his hair slicked back, the bride came forward. Althea, on her uncle's arm, was dressed in a pale pink calico gown that emphasized her slenderness. As she stood at Paisley's side, she was slightly taller than he was. Her very natural grace, along with his still obvious inebriation, made the two appear rather mismatched. But the quiet solemnity of their words belied the impression.

"Who giveth this woman's hand in wedlock?" Pastor Jay bellowed out to the crowd.

"I do, Pastor," Nez Beath answered.

The preacher nodded and Althea's uncle retreated into the crowd. There was a moment of conferring within the group and then Paisley took Althea's arm and with Eben in their wake they followed Pastor Jay to the top of the Marrying Stone. They took their places above the crowd where everyone could see them and they could see the heavens above.

The sun shone down like an angel glow upon the young couple as Pastor Jay read the wedding vows and they repeated them. There was no wedding ring, such a costly display among mountain folk was thought unnecessary. But a prayer for the couple and all those present was offered. Then the preacher, with a broad smile of satisfaction at a job well done, declared the couple wed.

Paisley didn't kiss his bride, but smiled at her before he turned to nod at his cousin Eben who placed a small silver coin in the pastor's palm. His part of the ceremony now completed and paid for, Pastor Jay offered a handshake to the groom and a fatherly kiss on the bride's forehead, before he and Eben walked down the hill at the side of the Marrying Stone.

Smiling, Paisley and Althea turned to face the crowd who waited in silence. As the couple surveyed the gathering of family and friends, the moment of quiet lingered in the midday sun. Finally, Paisley grasped Althea's hand. She gave him a nervous grin and then a nod of approval. In an instant the two made the short jump from the crown of the Marrying Stone and became, in the eyes of God and man, husband and wife.

A roar of approval broke from the crowd, punctuated by applause and whistles. The most exuberant of the folks surged forward to compliment the bride, tease the groom, and congratulate both.

"I think weddings are pretty nice," Jesse declared with a deep, heartfelt sigh. "I suspect it's almost as good as being married."

Roe's glance strayed to Meggie and was caught by her own look. Raw, exposed, and vulnerable, they stared at each other for long tense moments remembering their own leap into a new life and what had happened since. In his memory Roe could feel the soft give of her body beneath him. Simultaneously he could hear her telling him to go on his way. She didn't need or want him. She'd find someone else after he was gone. A primal hurt seemed to stab him in his heart. He couldn't understand it, but it was real and it was painful. And somehow he knew only this woman could heal it.

"Meggie—"

Bringing a hand up to her mouth, she stopped the words that she might have, in that moment, uttered, and hurriedly turned away.

Eager to put distance between herself and Roe Farley, Meggie hurried through the crowd of people, her heart pounding. How could Roe Farley always ensnare her like that? How could he always catch her unaware, with her feelings exposed? Like Jesse, she'd always thought weddings to be pretty nice. And she always thought that her marriage would be a dream come true. But dreams were only pleasant for a very short time, and reality went on forever. Meggie Best had fallen in love with a prince in a dream and that prince didn't exist.

She made her way to the gaggle of young girls who were her friends. They hugged her excitedly, each a little teary-eyed and awed by having witnessed the wedding ceremony. Polly could hardly keep her emotions in check. Mavis rhapsodized over Althea's lovely homemade gown. Alba giggled about the gentlemen's obvious inebriation. And Eda tried to pretend that she was totally bored by the entire occasion.

The bride and groom made their way through the crowd to the shade tree where Granny Piggott waited for them. As if the two distant young relatives were her very own children, the old woman got to her feet and cried for joy as she hugged them both happily. Watching the sight, Meggie felt a strange hurtful tugging in her heart and turned back to her girlfriends as if they were sturdy flotsam in a stormy sea.

"We were almost late," she said. "Did I miss anything?"

"Only half the fun," Eda Piggott answered quickly. "We were all watching the bride wait to see if the groom was going to show up."

"Oh, Eda!" Polly complained. "Everybody knew that Paisley would show up."

"Althea didn't appear concerned at all. Although I certainly would have been if my future husband had been out all night with that no-good Eben Baxley."

"They are first cousins," Mavis said. "Paisley couldn't be expected to ignore him."

"Well, if you ask me," Eda replied snidely, "Paisley seems to enjoy Eben's company a good deal more than he does Althea's."

"Oh, for heaven's sake, Eda." Polly was losing patience with her friend. "As quickly as that courtship went, they must be in love."

Eda sniffed. "Love? Paisley was calling on Meggie just last winter. He certainly got over her in a hurry."

Meggie flushed bright pink at the implication. "Sometimes that's just the way. People do fall in love overnight," she said.

"I suppose, I wouldn't know about that," Eda said, looking with abject disdain at Meggie. "Of course the new Mrs. Farley could explain it to us."

"What do you mean?"

"I mean you didn't have any courtship at all, does that mean love or just that you were desperate to grab hold onto the man?"

The blush fled Meggie's cheeks as quickly as it had come, leaving her chalky pale.

"Eda, now you stop that!" Polly snapped. "Meggie's business is her own. And her marriage to Mr. Farley is definitely her business. If she wanted us to know about it, she'd tell us."

"It's not that I don't want to tell you about it," Meggie assured them quickly. "It's—"

Meggie hated the lie that she'd gotten herself into and she detested having to sustain it among her friends. She would tell them the truth, she decided, but only as much as she could stand.

"I do love him," she whispered softly. "And I'm glad that we jumped the Marrying Stone. I don't regret it for a moment."

She had carefully avoided any comment about Roe's feelings and she was grateful that no one thought to question.

She looked up into the eyes of her friends and saw only happiness. Except for Eda, whose nose was still in the air, her friends were glad for her. Her joy was theirs and they were thrilled to share it. Sadly, Meggie knew they wouldn't be if they learned the whole truth.

"I need to speak to Althea," she said.

Hurriedly, she clasped one hand after another in a gesture of friendship before she stepped away from the group.

Eda sniffed. "Married talk, I suppose. Too important to be shared with the likes of us."

Alba shook her head and rolled her eyes dramatically before smiling at Meggie. "Go ahead and give Althea your good wishes," she said. "We'll keep Eda here. She's so green, she should be growing in a garden."

Meggie barely heard the young woman's huff of complaint and the giggles of the other girls as she made her way through the crowd toward the bride and groom. The mood of the people she passed was cheerful and welcoming. Time and again she was greeted with her own congratulations and polite inquiries about her father's health and her new husband. It was only when she reached the newly wedded couple that she realized that Jesse and Roe were already there.

Meggie hesitated for a moment; she thought to redirect her steps elsewhere, but quickly concluded that with Eda and the other girls watching and the whole mountain in attendance, she could hardly let on that she was avoiding either her husband or her brother.

Casually, as if it were planned, she stepped up beside the two men. Jesse, red-faced and stammering a little, was holding his fiddle out for Althea to examine.

"I can make real pretty music for your wedding, Miss Althea," he said. "I don't mind that you didn't ask me, I brung my fiddle anyways."

Paisley Winsloe's expression was sour and he made a point of not looking directly at Jesse. But the new bride smiled broadly.

"That would be wonderful, Simple Jess," she said. "Having music will make it seem like a real wedding."

"What do you mean 'a real weddin'?" Paisley asked, with more than a hint of belligerence in his tone.

Althea blushed and glanced at him uneasily. "I mean like . . . like a big family wedding or something of that sort."

"Lord, woman, ever' soul that the both of us knows is here," he replied impatiently.

"Oh, I didn't mean—" She hesitated nervously. "It was a lovely wedding and your mother has been very kind. What I meant was . . ." She turned to Jesse once more. "I mean . . . thank you for bringing your fiddle to play for us. It is a wonderful wedding gift."

"Wedding gift?" Jesse repeated her words and then smiled with pleasure. "Yep, it's my gift, my own, to you all from me and not no one else," he said.

As Meggie watched her brother wander away, a satisfied grin upon his face, she heard Roe offering best wishes.

"You're a lucky man, Winsloe," Roe said, good-naturedly mimicking the words that had been said by the other men present on several occasions already.

Paisley chose to take exception to his words. His speech was still slurred slightly with drunkenness. "Indeed, I am," he said a little too loudly. "I got the prettiest gal on the mountain." He gave Althea only a momentary glance before giving Meggie a pointed look. "And she's got herself the most promising young farmer in Arkansas."

His boastful words not being quite enough, Paisley's eyes narrowed as he glared at the two of them. "I got the best acres of corn bottom for miles," he declared. "And I own the finest pack of hunting dogs on this mountain. The woman that weds me gets her own milk cow, that just come fresh this summer."

Meggie actually flinched at his bragging words, but reminded herself that liquor-speaking was not to be taken seriously whether it was sweet or raging. To her surprise she felt the touch of Roe's hand as he reached for her. Familiarly, he pulled her up next to his chest and wrapped his arm possessively around her waist. Meggie hardly had time to catch her breath before he spoke.

"I can only hope, Mrs. Winsloe, that you and Paisley are as happy together as my bride and myself."

As if to emphasize his words, Roe leaned down and kissed Meggie full on the mouth. Shocked, Meggie had no time to think, consider, or resist. She opened her mouth to the sweet familiar warmth of his and slid her arms lovingly around his neck.

A hoot of laughter exploded behind them. With Meggie's gasp of surprise, they broke apart just in time to see Pigg Broody plant a wad of tobacco on the ground near their feet.

"Good Lord, city feller," the old man declared loudly. "It's the other man's weddin'. Yer s'pose te be kissing his werman, not yer own."

All the crowd nearby joined in Pigg's laughter.

"Newlyweds," someone said by way of explanation.

"Our hill gals are sure good for kissin', ain't they," Pigg commented.

Roe grinned. "I couldn't agree with you more, Mr. Broody."

"Don't let the city feller show ye up, Paisley," Pigg continued, pointing a bony finger at the other man. "Ain't ye gwonna give yer werman a buss?"

With a good deal more force than was necessary, Paisley pulled Althea into his arms and planted a sloppy kiss upon her lips. She squealed a bit unhappily, but the sound only brought more laughter to the crowd around them.

Meggie didn't wait for more. Shaking, she hurried through the crowd to the safety of the trees. It was only when she'd left the clearing and was running down the lonely wooded path that she heard the sound of Roe running behind her.

"Meggie, wait!"

She heard his call, but she ignored it. Inexplicably, tears were running down her cheeks. She wouldn't stop for him. She couldn't. She had to get away.

The grip on her arm that brought her up short was surprising and she cried out. She hadn't thought him that close.

"Meggie, what the devil?"

"Let go of me!"

He released her, but she didn't attempt to run anymore. She stared up into his face, angrily wiping the tears of frustration from her cheeks.

"Why on earth did you say that?"

"Say what?"

"That you wished them as much happiness as us. What are you trying to do, put a hex charm on their marriage?"

Roe stared down at her as if she'd lost her mind, then he shook his head. "Meggie, don't be foolish. I was just trying to take Paisley down a peg."

"Oh, well," Meggie answered with feigned understanding. "After all he's just an ignorant mountain boy, that shouldn't be much trouble for a city scholar like yourself."

Roe's brow furrowed. "It has nothing to do with mountain and city," he said. "Paisley was trying to make you regret turning him down."

"He was just drunk."

"He was full of liquor all right and full of himself. But if he had something to say to me about you, he should say it right out and not wait for a jug of donk to give him courage."

"I can't imagine what anyone would have to say about me to you." Meggie's voice was raised in anger. "And as for the donk, well, you should know about liquor for courage. It was the reason that you reached out to me that night, wasn't it?"

"Perhaps it was, Meggie," he answered honestly. "But I don't regret it."

"Well, maybe I *do* regret turning Paisley Winsloe down."

"What?"

"I wish I'd married Paisley Winsloe."

"I don't believe that for a moment."

"Just because you don't want to marry me doesn't mean that he didn't."

"Damn it, Meggie. I've asked you to marry me. I've asked and I've asked. I can't believe you'd marry Winsloe when you turned me down."

"You should believe it. Paisley Winsloe can offer a woman a lot more than you can."

Roe snorted unkindly. "Yes, I heard. A pack of hunting dogs and a milk cow."

"I don't mean that."

"Then what? The corn bottom?"

"He can offer love."

"Love?"

"Yes, love," Meggie shot back. "He obviously is in love with his wife, and I think he would have loved me." She turned away from him, frustrated once more at the tears that gathered in the corners of her eyes. "You can't offer that, can you, Mr. J. Monroe Farley? Oh, you are willing to do your *duty* to me and pay for the crime of taking my innocence but you aren't willing to offer me love. You don't know a thing about love."

Roe was silent, staring at her stiff, unyielding back. She couldn't read the expression on his face, nor could she see the sudden pallor of his skin.

"Nobody has ever loved me," he told her quietly. "How could I know anything about love."

"You couldn't," she answered, her voice as sad as it was certain. Still, she couldn't turn around to face him. "I don't blame you, Roe," she said. "I can't. But I won't accept a marriage based on anything less."

His silence answered her unasked question.

"I don't want you to stay here any longer," she continued. "I want to be married to a man who can love me and the longer you stay here, the more unlikely that is to ever be." The desolate sigh she uttered cut him to the quick. "Go back to the Bay State, Roe Farley. Go back there and maybe someday I can be as happy as Althea and Paisley."

CHAPTER

EIGHTEEN

ROE FARLEY HAD returned to the wedding celebration, or *infare* as it was called, with a heavy heart. Meggie had made her choice and it was very clear that even if he decided to stay through the winter it wouldn't work. His presence made her unhappy, and there was no longer a reason to delay. As he joined the noisy celebration he found that he no longer moved among the people of the community as if he were one of them. He was an observer now, an outsider. He wasn't really Meggie's husband and he never had been. He was leaving.

As the evening wore on he listened to Jesse play his fiddle. He watched the exuberance of the people dancing— some square dancing and others doing a sprightly jig that he was sure came over from Scotland and Ireland along with the music he'd collected. He watched with a half-conceived idea of involving the dancing in his study, but his heart just wasn't in it. Dutifully he checked on Onery to see that he was not overdoing things. He allowed Granny Piggott to tease him again. Pastor Jay stopped to speak to him and asked once again about Roe's father, Gid Weston.

Oather Phillips attempted a serious but stumbling conversation with him about politics. Labin Trace talked philosophically about the blending of the Christian wedding and the Marrying Stone superstition. And Roe made polite conversation with other folks on the sidelines of the dancing.

People liked him. He was accepted. But it no longer mattered. He was leaving.

Later that night he lay alone in the snug little bed that Granny Piggott had given to him and his bride and tried to make sense of his life, his future: A skunk in the wrong place, a need to gain the trust of the wary mountain folk, and a too close acquaintance with kill-devil donk had led him to this turning point in his life. And there was no way back, just one direction or the other.

It was before the first light of dawn that he heard Meggie rouse to stoke the fire. There was no reason to wait longer. He got up and slipped on his duckins and went into the main room to join her.

Kneeling upon the hearth, Meggie's honey-blond hair fell long and free down her back and glowed in the bright orange reflection of the new morning fire. The thin cotton josie that she wore hugged the contours of the body that he knew so well and that still enticed him. But this morning when she looked up at him, her blue-gray eyes weary from sleeplessness and slightly swollen from tears, his heart lurched. It was pain. It was sadness. It was disappointment. He was leaving. He was leaving Meggie Best behind.

She stared at him in silence, and then as if she could feel the emotions in his gaze, she turned her attention once more to the fire.

"I'll have some coffee ready in a bit," she said.

He nodded. "Coffee would be nice."

He glanced around the cabin. The austere, primitive room that had appeared so foreign and exotically unfamiliar only a few months ago now felt like home. A home he would never see again.

Roe hesitated only a moment before speaking the words

he had come to say. "I met a drummer at the celebration last night who is staying at Phillips's store," he said. "The man is going to head out for Calico Rock this morning. I'm going with him."

Meggie looked up at him quickly. For a moment he hoped that she would beg him to stay. She needn't even beg. If she would merely ask him to or suggest that he might, then he wouldn't leave her. He would stay if she only asked.

But she didn't.

"I'll pack you some victuals in a tote," she said.

Roe waited. "So I suppose this is good-bye."

"I wish you Godspeed," she answered quietly and turned her attention to the coffeepot.

Roe waited silently beside the table as long as he could, but there was to be no reprieve. He handed her a small scrap of paper he'd torn from his notes.

"This is where you can send for me," he said. "If I'm not there, someone will know how to find me. If you need me, Meggie, I will come back."

She raised her eyes to his and nodded slowly. "I won't be sending for you, Roe."

"If there's a—" Roe glanced over at Onery's still-sleeping form upon the bed in the corner. He then whispered his next words. "If there's a baby I—"

"There isn't," she answered emphatically.

Roe nodded gratefully, but what he felt was disappointment.

Meggie measured the coffee into the water and spoke conversationally. "I'll wait a fortnight or two after you leave," she said. "And then I'll just announce to folks that I've had word that you were killed on the journey. No one will question it."

She sounded so unconcerned that it seemed almost as if she spoke of somebody else, some other man, another couple who were planning their future as if it were the plot of some romantic tragedy.

"I'll dress in black for the rest of the winter," she said. "And that will be the end of it."

The casual finality of her words was like a dousing of cold water on Roe's aching heart. He nodded at her gravely. "All right then."

She looked up at him, her face a mask, revealing nothing. "Good-bye."

It was all that she said.

Jesse, however, was not so easily placated. A quarter of an hour later he wandered into Roe's room to find him packing.

"Why are you puttin' your oddments in a poke?" he asked Roe.

Still sleep-tousled and yawning, the young man's question was mere curiosity.

"I'm leaving," Roe answered simply.

Jesse immediately was wide awake. "What do you mean, you're leaving? Where are you going?"

Roe steeled himself against the sting of shame at his own selfishness. Neither he nor Meggie had given a thought to Jesse, his grief, his loss of a friend.

Jesse couldn't be let in on the scheme he and Meggie had designed. He could never know that it was all a lie. Jesse was simple, and for him their marriage had been the truth and so would be the loss of his friend.

"You knew that I would have to return to Massachusetts at the end of the summer," Roe said uncomfortably.

The young man's expression was puzzled. "But it ain't the end of the summer. We've still got the hottest month ahead of us."

"Well, I'm sure you can manage August on your own. You know that I must present my collection of music to the fellowship committee. It's completed now, and I can be back in Cambridge in two weeks and present my material within a couple more."

Jesse nodded but still looked worried. "So you're going back to the Bay State to take your Listening Box."

"Yes, I'm going to the Bay State, but I'm leaving the Ediphone here. I'll just take the cylinders that I need. I'm not even sure what's on some of the rest of these. I'll leave these for you to play on the box for when you need to hear music, but don't feel like making your own."

Jesse sighed with relief. "If you're leaving the Listening Box, then you're for sure coming back."

"Did you think that I wouldn't?"

"Oh, no, I just seen you acting strange of late."

Roe, hating to lie, turned his attention to the gunnysack he was packing and mumbled a mildly positive sound.

Accepting his friend's word, Jesse smiled with satisfaction and plopped down comfortably on the bed. "You've been acting so peculiar lately, I was beginning to get kindy scared. I guess if you go on now you can be back for harvest," he said.

"Yes, there is certainly time enough for that," Roe answered vaguely. Guilt ate at him. His simpleminded friend was honest and open, and Roe had told him friends never lie to each other.

"Don't worry about nothing here," Jesse said. "I can take care of things 'til you get back and Pa's for sure gonna be back on his feet anyday now."

"I hope so, Jesse."

Jesse's mood had greatly improved, and he was unable to feel any worries or concern.

"You going fishing in that ocean when you get back?"

"I doubt that."

"But you will get to ride a train."

"Yes. I will be riding a lot of trains I'm sure."

"That'll be something, won't it?"

"Yes, Jesse. I guess it will," he answered with feigned excitement.

The young man was quietly thoughtful for a few moments as he apparently tried to imagine the wonders that his friend would be seeing.

"When you get back the foxes'll have their winter pelts on," he said.

"I guess they will."

"I can teach you to go hunting. Last winter Paisley let me borrow one of his dogs. I don't 'magine we can do that this year, especially after you two nearly had a fawnch last night." Jesse laughed as he recalled it.

"Paisley was in his liquor last night. I'm sure he doesn't even remember what happened," Roe assured him.

"Sometimes Pigg Broody lets me run one of his old hounds," Jesse said hopefully. "It'll be a real good time, you'll see."

"It sounds very nice, Jesse."

Roe saw in his own mind the sharp cool months of autumn with Jesse hunting foxes in the brightly colored woodlands with a borrowed dog. But Jesse wouldn't be filled with joy as he was now, he'd be grieving for a friend who would be dead by then, at least dead to him.

"And then in the winter maybe we can go to see the Widder Plum." Jesse's eyes sparkled with mischief and excitement. "Remember about me and the widder. You was thinking about it."

Roe looked up at the simple young man lounging at the end of the bed. He realized suddenly that although he had called many men his friends, he had never known friendship until he met Jesse Best.

"I have thought about that widow, Jesse," he said. "And I don't think that you should go to see her."

Jesse's smile immediately dimmed. "You changed your mind about me getting to be with a woman?"

"No, no, not really," Roe answered, only realizing the words himself as he spoke them. "I hope you do get to be with a woman one day. But lying with just any woman, just coupling with her to get some pleasure, some release; that is not what I'd want for you, Jesse." Roe hesitated, hoping the other man would understand. "When the woman is special," he told Jesse, "being with her is special also. That's what I want for you. I want you to have a woman that you can feel deeply about, a woman who feels deeply about you."

His handsome young brow furrowing in confusion, Jesse asked, "Do you mean love?"

Love. The word continued to haunt him. Jesse wanted it. Meggie wanted it. Roe wanted it, too, but he had no idea what it was or how to get it.

He shrugged. "Maybe love. I don't know much about the subject myself."

Jesse was thoughtful. "Do you think a feller that ain't smart can be in love?"

Thoughtful for only a moment, Roe answered him. "If there is anyone in this world who is capable of loving or being loved, Jesse Best, it has to be you."

Roe seated himself beside Jesse and with a gesture of camaraderie that felt as natural as it was, he slung an arm around his friend's shoulder.

"I don't want to see you waste that love on some quick, sinful coupling with a well-practiced but unfeeling female," he said. "You deserve much more. You may not be equal to other men in the quickness of your mind, but there is no one, Jesse, more human than you. Don't ever allow yourself to accept less than any other man."

Jesse studied his friend's face for a long time, not truly comprehending his words but appreciating them nonetheless.

Finally he nodded his blond head solemnly. "I suspect I understand your meaning, Roe. I shouldn't settle for eating up the chicken feed when I could wring a young pullet's neck and fry her up for supper."

Roe smiled for the first time that morning. "Yes, Jesse. I guess that is exactly what I mean."

The young man grinned back at him, his handsome,

innocent face guileless and believing. "You're my frien',
Roe, and friends always tell each other the truth. I won't be
feasting on no chicken feed while you're gone," he promised. "When you come back, well, maybe you could help me
find a woman of my own. Maybe you could look the gals
over and tell me which one might take to me."

Roe didn't answer, but Jesse failed to notice as he grinned
wickedly. "Is there a trick to figuring out which pullets fry
up the most tender?"

Forcing a smile to his face Roe hugged his young friend
tightly and then stood up to resume his packing.

Jesse hadn't noticed the cloud of unwilling deceit that
covered Roe's eyes. It was from ignorance and honesty that
he spoke. "If I could have whatever I want," Jesse confessed, "I'd want to be married like you and Meggie."

"Onery, I'm leaving," Roe said as he approached the old
man seated on the porch.

Looking stronger and healthier than Roe had seen him in
weeks, Best nodded. "That's what I heard." Onery gave Roe
a long assessing look. "Don't suspect we'll be seeing you
again."

"No, sir."

Rubbing his long gray beard, he sighed heavily. "It's a
shame," he said. "I've been thinking about this for some
time, son. Trying to figure a way for you and my Meggie to
quit chewing on the middlin's and go straight for the ham
butt."

"Mr. Best, I . . . I never intended for things between
Meggie and myself to go as far as they did. And I've asked
her to marry me more than once."

"I know that, son." Onery nodded, understanding.

"Meggie has made it quite clear that she doesn't want me
here, and if I am going to have to leave her, I should do it
soon."

"Makes sense." The old man nodded sadly. "I've always

been so proud of that girl of mine. A lot has been put upon her; her mama's death, me crippled, and of course, her brother. But Meggie, she's always been the strong one and I've always been grateful that she grew up being so much like her mother."

He looked up at Roe and smiled wanly. "But at times like this I wish she'd gotten herself some of the selfishness that comes from my side of the family."

Roe didn't understand what selfishness would have to do with it, but he offered the old man what comfort he could.

"After I'm gone and she claims me as dead, she says she'll marry someone else," he said. "A woman like Meggie could pretty much get any man she decided that she wanted."

Onery snorted. "That she could. Course she never wanted none before you showed up."

Roe had no answer for that. He waited as the old man rocked thoughtfully in his chair gazing off in the distance at old Squaw's Trunk Mountain.

"Did I ever tell you about my wife?" Onery asked. Somewhat surprised at the change of subject, Roe permitted the old man to continue his rumination.

"You've mentioned her a time or two, and I think I've heard about her from other folks on the mountain."

"Heard tales about us, did ye?" Onery chuckled ruefully. "We was a scandal indeed on this mountain. Having a child without a wedding. Folks at the church was spitting their eye teeth and her own folks done throwed her out of the house." He shook his head disdainfully at the memory. "I was a rambling fiddle player, bone idle most of the time and with a wild streak as long as the White River rapids. Ah, but she was sweet and soft and passionate." The old man sighed in pleasure at the memory. "I swear I think she let me lay with her the first time just 'cause she knew how bad I wanted to. It was something different, son. She was something different. Something that I ain't never had the like of before nor since."

He turned to look at Roe again, studying him. "I knew it was pure sugar bread, but I didn't pay no mind. When it came time for me to move on, she sent me on my way. I didn't want to go. At least that's what I said. I argued with her from daylight 'til dark about it for a week or more. I knew she was no cull list squirmy. But, son, truth to tell, I didn't really want to marry her."

Onery sighed heavily and gazed again at the mountains in the distance. "I had had a good life a-ramblin' around and I was loath to give it up. I thought it would be good again. It'd be having a fancy choke rag around my neck, batch of bald face whiskey, and a pretty new gal in ever' town."

Onery hesitated for a long moment. "But it weren't." He peered closely at Roe. "How is it, oncest you've seen love, son, oncest you've felt it and tasted it, ain't no use trying to go back to the nigglin' life. It ain't there no more fer ye."

Roe's brow furrowed, trying to understand.

"And I tried, son. Lord knows I put a lot of miles between me and this mountain. I drank hard, played hard, run hard. But what I couldn't outrun was how much I needed that woman. And what I couldn't stand was the fact that she didn't seem to need me a'tal!"

Roe agreed. "I guess she *was* like Meggie."

"She was. That she was. But this talk she gave me about not needing me, it was a lie, you know."

"A lie?"

Onery nodded. "She said she didn't need me and she said she didn't want me. She said she could raise our boy on her own or find another man to take him on. But she was fooling herself as much about that as I was about wanting my ramblin' ways back."

Onery stared once more at the distant mountain, lost in thought. "I guess it's a bit like our Jesse."

"Like Jesse?"

"Yes. Ye see there ain't nothing really *wrong* with the boy's mind. He can think and figure and remember just like all the rest of us. But it's as if his head is kindy sluggishlike. It don't learn quick and it don't always recall what it sorted out the day before. That's the way she and I were. We couldn't see that we was in love with each other and that if we didn't live together, well, then there weren't much sense in living at all."

"But you did convince her to marry you."

"I did indeed." The old man chuckled and shook his head. "I just said to her, 'Woman, I'm here to stay and you can love me or loathe me but I ain't never leaving no more.'"

Roe glanced back at the door to the cabin behind him and then turned to contemplate the wooded path beyond the homestead. "I'm happy for you, Onery. But when she sent you away, she left the door open. She didn't plan to announce your death. I can never return here. I'll never see this place again."

Onery nodded solemnly. "Yep, that's the way things look." He looked as if he wanted to say more, but he just kept staring at the mountain in the distance.

FROM THE JOURNAL OF
J. MONROE FARLEY

September 23, 1902
Cambridge, Massachusetts

This P.M. I presented the final segment of my first drafting of the results of the Ozarks music study to the fellowship committee. Although I am confident that my evidence was sufficient, there were members of the committee who failed to believe that the presence of previously undiscovered Spenserian and Elizabethan music among native Ozark hill people was anything but curious coincidence. I argued very well, I believe, but the disfavor I faced was overwhelming.

Somehow the truths presented were in conflict with the peculiar bias of the majority of committee members. It appears to me that they generally refuse to believe that the unlettered, isolated people of the Ozark Mountains could have managed to preserve a heritage that the academic circles of this country and the British Isles have irrevocably lost.

While I played cylinder after cylinder of near ancient song, the gentlemen continued to ask me to tell once more the stories of the bear grease on the bread, the privy I had to build, or the young women who never wore shoes.

My work was taken seriously on no point and it was even suggested by one pompous theorist that I had frittered away the fellowship funds on no account. Ultimately, I was strongly encouraged to desist in this vein of inquiry. I announced that I was preparing a paper for the Journal of

Theoretic Musicology *and I was sternly warned that my finding would be considered frivolous and could possibly hurt the reputation of my work and of the fellowship committee. It was strongly suggested that after a reasonable period of time to take care of personal business and to clear my notes, the fellowship committee would hear a request for further expeditions in the remote areas of Scotland or Ireland to get my pursuit into a circumspect direction. I suppose that is what I will do. I am confident that I am not wrong, however I may be, unfortunately, the only one.*

I went to the seaside near Boston last week. I watched an old man and his grandson fishing from the pier. It reminded me that I had never fished from the ocean. As I gazed off across the water I thought about Jesse and Onery and worried for them. The days must be getting shorter and colder there now. I wonder if Pigg Broody was willing to loan Jesse a dog for hunting.

Of Meggie, I try not to think at all.

CHAPTER
NINETEEN

THE COLD BLUSTERY wind of early October sneaked beneath the cabin door and chilled the room. Meggie wrapped a worn shawl around her shoulders, snuggling beneath it. She had already thrown another log onto the fire but it was a sog, turning black and smoldering, and wouldn't burn properly.

The first snowfall of the year had blown in overnight. It was way early and looked as if it wouldn't stick, but it blanketed the homestead clearing, making it appear clean and bright and new. It only made Meggie feel colder and she didn't need snow or ice to feel cold these days. Cold had become a way of life for her.

"Whew-eee!" Onery called as he came barging through the door and across the threshold, stamping the snow that lingered on his boots onto the dirt floor. "It's sure enough biscuit weather out there this morning."

Meggie made a murmur of agreement as her father took off his damp wool coat and hung it on a peg near the door. His color was good beneath the gray of his beard and he seemed strong and young once more.

On the day that Roe Farley had left Marrying Stone, her father had risen from his chair on the porch and declared himself completely well. He'd still been as weak as a newborn

colt at the time, but he had pushed himself from one task to
another until he had his strength back and was able to do
most of the work he'd been accustomed to.

"I've been half-work brickle all my life," he told Meggie.
"I malingered as long as I dared. Truth to tell, I thought it
might make your feller stay."

"He couldn't stay," Meggie answered.

It was the only conversation that the two of them had
shared concerning J. Monroe Farley, but not a day went by
when his name wasn't mentioned in the cabin.

"Wait 'til Roe gets back. Wish Roe could see this possum
I kilt," and "If Roe were here I could get this done in half
the time" were among the near constant utterances from
Jesse's mouth.

Meggie knew that he missed his friend and was com-
forted by talk of him. But its frequency was a nagging
heartbreak for her.

If other people wondered about the growing length of
Farley's absence, Jesse did not. Roe had said that he would
return and for Jesse that was enough.

For Meggie the delay had been a wrenching battle with
procrastination. Going ahead with her plan always seemed
like something that she should do tomorrow. The lies were
to be monumental, the effects permanent, and the pain
unbearable. Jesse had become a part of that reason. Meggie
thought her plot had been designed so that everyone could
get what they wanted. Roe could have his work in the Bay
State and some woman more suited to the life he wanted.
Her father would be spared the shame of his daughter's
sinful communion. And the people of Marrying Stone could
have a logical resolution to what had quickly become a very
sticky problem.

But Jesse would not be getting what he wanted. And of
course, neither would she.

"Something smells real good this morning, Meggie-gal,"
her father said. "What you got cookin' in that pot?"

"Conohany," she answered, referring to the mixture of hominy, wild herbs, meat, and nuts that was said to be an old Cherokee recipe.

"Mmmmmm. Jesse'll be glad to hear that."

"Where is Jesse?" she asked.

"I got him fixin' the dog-leg fence next to the pigsty. Why?"

Meggie took a deep, soul-searching breath before turning to her father. "I have news from afar," she lied. "My husband was killed on his journey to the Bay State."

Her father's brow furrowed and he cursed under his breath.

"Today! Land sakes, Meggie, it's snowing out there. How could you get a missive today?"

"Pa, I have to," she answered. "I just can't wait any longer. I . . . got it today."

Onery sighed heavily and sat down in a chair. "I was hoping that you'd changed your mind."

Meggie wiped her hands nervously upon her apron. "It has to be this way, Pa. We was never meant."

He snorted in disapproval. "You was 'as meant' as any other young couple getting themselves married up."

"We had different lives. We come from different places."

"Surely ye do. And you got different bodies, too. That's what marriage is about, Meggie-gal, making differences intertwine into something whole and new."

Meggie didn't want to argue. "He didn't love me, Pa," she said.

"I'll believe that when I see coons a-taking up farming," the old man answered. He raked his hair with his hands helplessly. "What do ye think love is, Meggie. Do you think it's heart pounding and breath stealing and verse reciting?" he asked. "Yes, ma'am, there is some of that involved, but mostly love is quiet and caring and friendlylike. It's wanting to tell that person something afore you whisper it to another soul. It's not being alone."

He pointed a finger at her accusingly. "Meggie-gal, you loved that feller the minute you laid eyes upon him. I know you thought he was one of those princes in your storybooks, and I worried that you'd be disappointed when you realized that he was real and no daydream. But you ain't stopped dreaming yet, have ye? You're still thinking your life is one of them fairy tales, only this is one of those that come to a bad end."

His voice softened to pleading. "Meggie, I'm askin' you, beggin' with you, send word to Roe that you want him back. I think it's the only way I'll ever see ye happy and laughing again."

"Oh, Pa." Tears welled in Meggie's eyes and she reached out to her father. He pulled her as if she were a little girl once more and held her tight in his embrace as she sobbed her pain and pleaded with him for understanding. He held her and rocked her and wiped her tears with his handkerchief.

"It's done, Pa," she said. "I threw away the address he left. The harvest is in and I own the corn. It's too late for me to wish it weren't so."

The door burst open and Jesse rushed in shaking the snow from his hat and grinning broadly. When he saw Meggie in his father's arms and the tears streaming down her cheeks he stopped short.

"What's wrong?"

"Roe is dead," she answered quickly before she could change her mind. "I've just got word. Roe died on his journey."

Meggie tried not to listen to the sobs coming from the cabin loft. Jesse was up there, trying valiantly to bury his grief in a goose-down pillow, but he could still be heard.

Onery had taken the mule out to notify the neighbors of his son-in-law's demise. By sunset Meggie knew there would be friends and family come to sit with the new widow. Meggie dreaded their arrival. However, it wouldn't be difficult for her to feign grief. Since she'd broken down that afternoon, it was like a floodgate of tears had been opened and she couldn't seem to stop its flow.

Adeptly she assessed the caldron of water, walnut hulls, and red oak bark that boiled over the fire. Meggie was dying her funeral costume. When she had collected her clothes, she'd meant to stain only things that were old and worn. The stockings and bonnet she'd selected were much used and near threadbare, but when she reached for a near tattered work dress hanging on her peg, the bright blue homespun gown that she continued to wear to church on Sundays had caught her eye. She had tinted it on that long-ago night. The night she'd lain with Roe in the deep clover by the creek. On the way to Althea's wedding he had said it was a pretty dress. He had said that the color was a perfect match for her eyes. Somehow it was that dress that she had reached for. And it was that dress that now simmered in the hot mixture bubbling on the fire.

Picking up the battling stick she used for laundry, she stirred the brew thoughtfully and raised some of the fabric out of the dye to test the color. It was black. Dull, lifeless black. It was the color of her life, the color of her heart.

She hadn't meant to hurt her father. She hadn't meant to hurt Jesse. She knew that both were hurting now, but it was for the best.

Maybe love was more like her father said than it was in fairy tales, but Roe Farley had claimed no love for her at all. And he shouldn't—it would have ruined his life. Perhaps her dramatic ending to their ill-fated marriage was a plot contrived from a fanciful imagination. But it was a plot he had gone along with. Roe had been, in his way, as romantic as she was. He also knew what kind of woman he wanted to marry and plain, mountain-reared Meggie Best could never be that woman.

A teardrop dribbled off her cheek and splashed in the dye vat.

"Meggie."

She heard the plaintive voice from the loft entry and looked up. "I'm here, Jesse."

"I'm so sad, Meggie," he said through hiccuped tears. "I can't seem to stop it."

"I'm sad, too, Jesse."

There was nothing else to say. The moments passed between them with only the crackling of the fire and the swash of the clothing in the caldron breaking the silence.

"Meggie?"

"Yes, Jesse."

"Would you play the Listening Box?"

"What?"

"The Listening Box. Roe left it for me for when I needed to hear music, but didn't feel like making my own."

She didn't want music, silence was preferable to the sounds he had captured on his spools of wax, but she had hurt Jesse and she couldn't deny him this request.

With some reluctance she set the battling stick up against the wall and, wiping her hands, walked to the place of honor next to her father's bed where the Ediphone was kept. She picked it up carefully by its carrying handle and brought it to the table. She opened the lid and assembled the horn in the way Roe had shown her. She picked a cylinder at random and slipped it onto the spindle. She turned the crank, adjusted the speed, and set the curved stylus against the grain of the wax.

The sound of Ebner Pease singing a very nasal tenor filled the room. Pease sang, "Oh, the taters they grow small in Arkansas."

The lively, bantering lyrics were meant for frolicking evenings and laughing among friends. In her mind's eye she could see Roe grinning as he scrambled to write the words on a piece of the fine bond paper he always carried.

Inexplicably the pleasant thought brought tears to Meggie's eyes.

"Oh, they eat them tops and all in Arkansas."

It was Granny Piggott herself who arrived with Onery just a little before dark. The old woman was already dressed in black and her expression furrowed with concern.

"I told the rest to stay away tonight," she said with businesslike efficiency. "I think that was the thing to do."

"Yes, it's fine, Granny. I don't really need anyone here."

"Lord knows, a widow always needs someone on the first night," she replied. "But someone ain't everyone." She tutted meaningfully. "When I lost my man I needed a bit of time to accept it without half the mountain standing around watching me for signs of breaking down."

"I'm not going to break down."

"Suit yourself, child, I don't mind if you do. I think you got a right." She sighed and shook her head. "You looked for happiness for so long and when it finally shows up at your door, fate snatches it away before you've hardly got time to get used to it."

It was Granny who fixed the supper that night, bustling around the kitchen and taking over as if the cabin were her very own. And it was Granny who washed up the dishes and swept the hearth. Being needed added new life to the old woman and she was a powerhouse of work and a tower of strength for the family to lean upon.

"You'd best stop that sniveling now, Jesse Best," she said as she handed the young man her handkerchief. "I ain't a-telling you not to grieve, but it would pain your friend Roe to see you carrying on like this."

"I'm sorry," Jesse whispered, trying to dry up his tears.

"We're all sorry," Granny said, smoothing the young man's hair lovingly. "A good feller has gone to his grave and we'll miss him too much. But we just got to hold on to how glad we were to have had him with us. And how lucky we were to get to know him at all."

"He was my frien'," Jesse said.

"Yes, he was," she answered. "And he always will be."

After supper was done, Jesse was sent up to bed as soon as was reasonable and the young man quietly cried himself to sleep in the relative privacy of the cabin loft.

At Granny's insistence, Onery took the bed in the new room.

"She won't be wanting to sleep in there tonight if she sleeps at all. You go ahead and rest yourself, Onery Best. She's gonna need you to lean on come the morrow."

Reluctantly her father had retreated and within moments the rhythmic pattern of his deep snore was added to the nocturnal sounds of the night.

Granny helped Meggie to wring out the newly dyed mourning dress and hang it by the fire.

"It must be hard for you to believe that this is true," the old woman commented.

"What do you mean?"

"He was so young and healthy and full of life when he left," she said. "Without ever seeing him sick or hurt it's difficult to really accept the truth."

Meggie said nothing, hating the lie that she passed for truth, but feeling grief in her heart near to the real thing.

"I couldn't believe that my Piggott had died," Granny continued. "I kept thinking that any minute he'd be coming around the corner of the house with something to show me." Her voice quieted with emotion. "It was only the laying out of his body that made it real to me. Without his body, I think I would have been glad to fool myself into thinking that he wasn't really dead."

"Oh, no. I don't have that problem," Meggie said. "I'm very sure that Roe Farley is dead. There is no question about it in my mind."

Granny raised an eyebrow in surprise but took her words

at face value and didn't bring the subject up again. Together they cleaned up the dying vat and swept the dirt floor. With a small stick of green wood Granny drew rug pattern designs into the packed dirt and readied the cabin for company.

Meggie gathered the scraps of black crepe kept in the bottom of the sweetwood chest and pressed the wrinkles from them with a hot fireplace stone. Once the crepe was hung and the house decorated for mourning, the two women settled in chairs by the fire to await the dawn.

Her thoughts in a whirl of guilt and confusion, Meggie was disinclined to conversation. And the old woman didn't force her into foolish chatting for the sake of making noise. The silence lingered, broken only by the scrape of the chairs upon the floor.

Granny pulled the clay pipe out of her pocket and packed the bowl with sweet-smelling tobacco. The piece of green hickory she'd used for "rugging" the house now served as her pipe lighter. It took several vigorous puffs to get the tobacco to catch fire, but once it was burning to her liking the old woman took a long drag and let the smoke out slowly into the chill air of the room.

"Do you want a draw?" she asked Meggie, holding out the pipe to her in offering.

"Oh, no."

Granny nodded, a hint of a smile curling at the corner of her lips. "Don't care for tobacco, do ye? I didn't when I was your age neither. But I like this pipe," she said. "It offers me comfort."

As Meggie watched, the old woman held the pipe out at a distance before her where she could more clearly see it and examined the long curving piece of blue fired clay as if she hadn't seen it for a while.

"It was my man's pipe, ye know."

Meggie's eyes widened in surprise. "No, I didn't know."

Granny nodded. "I'd never smoked a day in my life,

never cared for the scent of tobacco and fussed about it smelling up my house." She took a long draw on the pipe. "That was the way I was 'til the day I buried that man." She leaned far back in her chair and stared into the fire as if she could see her past written there. "It was such a commotion and people crying and moaning and hugging me." She chuckled without humor. "And me, I was as numb as if I'd been standing bare naked in a snowstorm for half a day."

She shook her head and smiled sadly.

"That night after the funeral was done and I'd put him to the ground I come back to the place. It was so empty and I felt so alone. And, of course, I weren't alone at all. I had two of my younguns still at home. And they was weeping and mourning their lost daddy. I had to be strong and solid for them. And I did it, because I had to."

She stopped her story to tap the pipe and put the fire to the tobacco once more.

"That night, after I'd got them all tucked into their shakedowns, I went to sit by the fire. I knew I wouldn't be a-sleeping. But I didn't want to start crying again neither."

The old woman glanced over at Meggie. "I seen his pipe there, this pipe, and his little poke of tobacco. Suddenly it was like there was nothing in the world that I wanted more than to smell that man's pipe tobacco once more."

The old woman gazed into the fire and shook her head. "So I did the only thing I could. I lit up his pipe. I've been smoking it ever since, more than twenty years."

Granny sighed heavily. "I've been a widow longer than I was a girl. But I still miss my man and smoking this pipe makes me feel close to him."

Meggie's eyes welled with tears. She reached across to grasp the old woman's thin bony hand in her own. "Granny, I want you to know that you can smoke that pipe in my house anytime that you want."

The old woman raised an eyebrow and chuckled lightly.

"I always have," she said honestly. "I never let other folks' disapproval stop me from anything that I wanted to do."

It was the truth and they both knew it. Meggie found herself smiling, too.

"You and your mama were always kindy that way," Granny continued. "Just a-doing whatever you've a mind to and the devil take the hind part." She gave Meggie a conspiratory grin. "I always figured you two took it from me."

Meggie laughed lightly through her tears.

"Now I'd be willing to bet," Granny continued. "That there is something around here that you could find that'd make you feel close to that man of yours when you're a-needing some comfort."

Meggie's smile immediately disappeared. "Oh, no."

"Yes, yes, there is bound to be something."

Nervously, Meggie started twisting the fabric of her apron. "Roe never smoked a pipe. He didn't smoke at all."

"He probably knew you didn't like tobacco in the house," Granny replied. "Now there's got to be something around here that brings you close to him again."

"There's the room he added to the cabin."

The old woman glanced back to the doorway where Onery's snores could still be heard. "Yes," she said. "Your bed will always bring you close to him, Meggie. But truth to tell, it won't always offer you comfort."

Meggie said nothing, knowing that it never had and never would.

"He built the privy, too," she said.

Granny grinned mischievously. "Well, I guess you could go sit a spell when you are missing him. But folks would start thinking that you got the gilflits."

To her surprise, Meggie actually laughed at that.

Granny let the sound grow to its crescendo and then recede into the quiet of the firelight before she spoke again.

"I think that thing may be it," she said.

"What thing?"

Granny Piggott pointed to the Ediphone still sitting on the table where Meggie had left it. "That Listening Box. It was his. His machine. His work. I bet if you played one of those recordin's he was so fond of you'd feel close to him again."

Meggie looked at the Ediphone for a long moment. The last thing she wanted was to feel close to Roe. She thought the pain of it would surely kill her.

"I played one of the cylinders earlier this evening," she said. "Jesse asked me to."

"How did it make you feel?"

She shook her head. "I can't really say. It was Ebner Pease singing 'Arkansas Taters.' It was kind of funny, but it made me kind of sad."

Granny nodded. "Pick another one of them cylinders and let's hear it."

Meggie hesitated. She didn't want to. "It's really late," she said. "And it might disturb Pa and Jesse."

"Go on, girl," Granny insisted. "We need to see if that's the thing or no."

Reluctantly Meggie got up from her chair and went to the table. There was a scattering of cylinders, each properly stowed in its own round strawpaper container. At random she picked up one of the cylinders and set it onto the play spindle. Once more that evening she cranked the machine and set the stylus to the wax. She stood there watching the wax roll turn round and round, blanking out her thoughts, deadening her soul. Then the song began.

Almost immediately Meggie could hear the sweet sound of Jesse's fiddle in the background, but the familiar voice that filled the room was one she had heard raised in song only once before on a rainy afternoon out in the woodshed.

"Well met, well met, my own true love,
    Well met, well met, said he.

I have just returned from a journey long
And 'twas all for the love of thee."

The sound of his voice, as if he were there in the room, ripped through Meggie's heart like a knife. She cried out loud as if in pain, covered her face, and dropped to her knees.

"What have I done!" she exclaimed.

In an instant Granny was there beside her, holding her, comforting her.

"There, child, there, I knew you needed a good cry. I know it hurts, but life hurts. It has to hurt sometimes, else we'd never be able to appreciate when we was happy."

They knelt there together on the floor until the cylinder finished. Then wiping her eyes and with a grateful kiss to Granny's cheek, Meggie managed to make it back to her feet.

"It's not like you think," she told the old woman guiltily. "I'm not worthy of your concern."

"Piddle," was Granny's response as she led Meggie back to her chair.

After they had taken up their positions by the fire once more, Meggie managed to get control of her emotions. She hated the lie she perpetrated, but she wanted to talk now, she wanted to grieve for the loss of the man she loved. It was far too late to even bother with the whole truth. So Meggie spoke only of her feelings, not of the facts.

"I don't know why I miss him so much," she said.

"Now that's as foolish a statement as I ever heard," Granny replied. "You miss him because you loved him."

Meggie nodded sadly. "Yes, I did love him. I suppose it is time that I admit that." She stared sadly into the fire. "But it wasn't like we married for love. There really was a skunk up on the Marrying Stone that night."

Granny nodded. "Yes, I imagine that there was. The Lord works in mysterious ways."

Meggie felt uncomfortable about blaming heaven for the debacle.

"We were just going to ignore it, let you folks think what you want and go on our way," she confessed. "But when you came by and were suddenly so eager to help him with his work, well, I suspect he decided that it might not be such a bad thing to be married to me."

"And it wasn't a bad thing at all."

"No, I guess it wasn't bad. But I wasn't at all the kind of woman that he wanted."

The old woman shrugged. "It's not likely that a wife ever could be."

"What do you mean by that?"

"Women don't always want the right things in a man. And men don't have even an idea of what they want," she said. "Why, one minute their bodies tell them they want a wild woman that makes their blood rush. The next minute their good sense reminds them that they need a hard worker who is sturdy enough to help plow the field and birth the babies. They want a woman who'll mind their word and not be giving no jawing. But they also want a gal they can complain to when they are scared and unsure and who's smart enough to talk clear about the things goin' on."

"So the wife has to be all those things?"

"No, the wife is none of them," the old woman answered. "The wife is a wife and no further definition is necessary." Granny leaned forward in her chair to look more closely at Meggie. "Roe Farley married you and you were his wife. Nothing further even need to be said."

Her face flushing with embarrassment, she glanced away. "But he doesn't . . . he didn't love me."

"And did you think he would?"

Momentarily Meggie was taken aback. "Well, yes."

"Lord Almighty, child," Granny said. "Love ain't something that heaven hands out like good teeth or keen eyesight. Love is something two people make together."

Shaking her head, the old woman leaned back in her chair once more and tapped on her pipe. "Love, oh, my, it starts out simple and scary with all that heavy breathing and in the bed sharing," she said. "You a-trembling when he runs his hands acrost your skin, him screaming out your name when he gets in the short rows. That's the easy part, Meggie. Every day thereafter it gets harder. The more you know him, the more he knows you, the longer you are a part of each other, the stronger the love is and the tougher it is to have it."

Meggie's brow furrowed in puzzlement. "Pa says it's the differences in two people intertwining."

Granny nodded. "And he's right about that. Your life becomes a part of someone else's and that can be hard, very hard. But, Meggie, it is so much worth the effort."

Silently Meggie acknowledged that it was, but love couldn't be built by only one person.

"If a man didn't really want to marry you, but he just feels like he ought to . . ." Meggie shrugged as if the conclusion was self-explanatory. "Well, that's no way to start out a marriage."

"I've seen worse ways to start them out," Granny said. After a long moment the old woman offered a small sigh and chuckled. "I loved my man and he loved me, Meggie. So, I suspect you must think he come a-courting me with ribbons, geegaws, and pretty words."

"Well, didn't he?"

Granny took a long draw on her pipe before she answered. "Meggie, that man didn't come a-courting me a'tal. He come for my sister Asmine."

"What?"

"Asmine, my sister Asmine, she was a year younger than me and the prettiest gal in our part of the Caintuck," she said. "My Piggott was mighty keen on marrying her and come to set with her twiced a week without fail all that winter long."

Granny tapped her pipe and took another long draw of tobacco. "I wanted that man from the first moment I saw him. Asmine always got whatever feller she wanted, but I was determined that she weren't gonna get this one."

The old woman shook her head. "I was so green jealous of my sister I could taste the bitterness of it ever' time I swallowed. And that Asmine, she played Piggott like he was a fish on her line. Teasing him, then pouting up, starting spats, and flirting with other fellers."

Granny looked down at the blue clay pipe and then glanced up at Meggie. "One night we was at a kitchen sweat dance across the river," she confessed. "Asmine was paying Piggott no mind that night and he started tipping some bald face field whiskey. After the dance I snuck away from the house and went to his place. Just like I figured, he was passed out cold on his shakedown cot. I crawled right in there beside that man."

After a moment Granny laughed out loud. "Lord, when he waked up the next morning, he liked to have a conniption fit a-thinkin' he'd peeled a red onion without recalling it."

The old woman shook her head as she remembered. "And my Pappy squalled near loud enough to raise the roost. He was fit to kill Piggott, had the Springfield loaded and pointed right at his gullet. He was sure the feller had been riding and tying with his own two girls."

Granny hesitated in her speech for a moment as she allowed the memories to flow over her like warm molasses.

"We was married up quick enough to smell the powder," she said. "That's why we come to this country in the first place. Piggott was sorrowing so about not getting Asmine that he couldn't even live in the same mountains with her. I felt pretty bad about it myself, her moaning all the time like a sick hog about me stealing her chub. I begun to think that I'd done a real bad thing and made an awful mistake."

She reared back in her chair. "That's when I took to calling him Piggott, rather than Mr. Piggott like he told me.

I wasn't about to let him start a-running me like Asmine done him. I figured that he ought to shoulder some of the blame for the thing, him being stupid enough in the first place to fall for my silly sister instead of myself."

Granny looked over at Meggie, the young woman was stunned to silence.

"I figured we weren't never going to be happy," she said. "But the truth is, Meggie, that we was. And I believe he and Asmine coulda' never been that happy. We was meant to be together and that's why things happened like they did."

Meggie nodded politely, still reeling slightly from the unexpected confession. "I'm so glad that it worked out for you, but for most people the love comes first not later."

Granny disagreed. "I think you'd be surprised about that, child. Even those that think they are in love when they say 'I do' find out later that they didn't have one inkling of what it's all about."

"They must have some inkling or they wouldn't look so happy at their wedding," Meggie said. "Think about Althea and Paisley."

"Althea and Paisley?" Granny looked at her in stunned disbelief for a long moment and then cackled with laughter. "You think those two married for love?"

"Well, didn't they?"

Granny tutted with disbelief. "Althea needed a place to go. Her Uncle Nez was plumb sick of keeping her. He'd been after her for a year or more to marry someone and get out of his house. And poor Paisley, he was more desperate to wed than she was. His mama's been running him like a clock since he was in knee britches. The only way that poor feller seen out of it was to get a woman of his own." Granny chuckled. "Then the fool wasted half a year trying to cozen you into it."

Meggie's eyes widened in surprise.

"Lord Almighty, Meggie," Granny continued. "The only love match we've had on this mountain for three harvests or more is you and your Mr. Farley."

CHAPTER
TWENTY

"GID! GID WESTON!"

The man stringing for craw-dad turned to see who had called his name. With shock his eyes widened, he clutched his chest and dropped to his knees.

"Farley! Roe Farley. Lord Almighty, I ain't even had one little drink this morning, and I'm still seeing ghosts."

His fine cloth coat splattered with mud and a fancy leather satchel clutched in his hand, the young man hurried over to him.

"I'm not a ghost, Gid," Roe said. "Ghosts don't get their boots muddy in this mush. I'm as alive as you are, but I am lost. I've been wandering about this swampy bottom for half a day. I can't find the path up the mountain."

"It's really you and ye ain't dead?" Gid asked, looking him over closely.

Roe grinned and shook his head. "As far as I know I'm as alive as you are."

Gid reached out to touch his shoulder and when he felt the flesh and bone his expression eased and he laughed out loud. "Roe Farley, you ain't dead at all. You want a drink?"

Roe chuckled and shook his head. "No thanks. The last time I tried that donk of yours, it nearly killed me. I just need to find the path. I want to get to the cabin. My wi—my Meggie hasn't seen me for too long a time."

Weston nodded vaguely. "And she's gonna be surprised," he said. "But she ain't at the cabin."

"Oh?"

"No, she's at the church, like the rest of the folks on this mountain, 'cepting me."

"At the church? On Tuesday?"

"For the funeral."

"Funeral?" Roe's eyes darkened with concern. "Onery?"

"Oh, Onery's there, too. It ain't his funeral. It's yourn."

"Mine. Today. She waited this long?"

"Waited?"

Roe glanced up at the mountain hopefully and then back down at Weston. "I've got to get to the church right away, Gid. Which way is it?"

"I'll take ye," he answered. "We can run over that near ridge and be there in two looks and a jump."

Meggie sat on the front row of the church garbed in her black dress and bonnet. Her eyes were dry, but her heart was weeping copiously. To her right sat her father, his arms folded tightly across his chest, his anger and disappointment barely beneath the surface. Jesse was on her other side. His eyes still red-rimmed, he was biting his lip to keep from shedding tears in public.

The congregation of the Marrying Stone church mournfully sang "Rock of Ages, cleft for me" and Meggie fought the chill that had settled in her soul.

All the night long and through the morning she'd thought upon the things Granny Piggott had said. And upon her father's words, too. She thought about Roe. In her mind, she could see him smiling with Jesse, staring down at her from the hole in the roof, crying out her name. She could see his face as he pleaded with her to marry him. And it broke her heart.

She'd set him free to go back to the Bay State to a life that had never made him happy and to a woman that he wasn't sure even existed. She'd told herself that it was a selfless thing that she did, something that was best for him. But in truth, it was her own childish stubbornness that had refused his offer. She had wanted a prince. A prince that was besotted with his feelings for her. A prince that would dote on her eternally. One to sweep her from her feet like in a fairy tale, and marry her for love.

Roe Farley was no prince. He was a man.

She had expected him to love her and he hadn't. But he'd hardly had time to know her. She'd thrown herself at his feet and then complained when he hadn't been grateful. Roe Farley, having never loved or been loved, had been supposed to take to it like tadpoles to pond scum, because Meggie Best wanted it that way.

Silently she berated herself for her foolishness as she stared at the empty altar before her. Life had offered her a real man and a real chance for happiness and she'd deliberately thrown it away to nurture a fancy.

Now that tale had ended, with no happily ever after, but the finality of death. And it was a story she'd plotted herself.

She'd insisted, at least, that the funeral service be simple. And she refused a headstone in the boneyard. Roe Farley was dead to her, dead to these people, but forever more in her heart he would live. Not as a conquering prince or dashing lover, but as a good and gentle man who had held her close and had wanted to marry her.

Meggie felt Jesse tremble beside her and she reached over to clasp his hand in her own. He looked strong and handsome in his Sunday suit with his hair slicked back. But since the bell had begun tolling at dawn that morning, his emotions had been raw and his tears close to the surface.

"You go ahead and cry if you want," Meggie had told him at breakfast. But he'd shaken his head.

"Pa ain't crying," he'd said. "And Roe wouldn't neither. I ain't no baby boy, Meggie. I'm a man just like them. Roe said so and he's my frien'. He never lies to me."

The last strains of the old hymn faded and Pastor Jay stepped up to the pulpit. Meggie swallowed her trepidation and wadded her hankie in her hand.

The old man looked ready and purposeful as he stepped before them. His white hair gleamed in the sunlight that streamed in from the window behind him. He was still very tall and straight for a man of his age. And his voice was still powerful enough to speak with the authority of heaven. His eyes scanned the crowd meaningfully, obviously noting who was there and who was not. He opened his mouth to speak, but he didn't. Faster than a turkey takes a worm, the old preacher's expression changed and he seemed puzzled, confused.

"Is it Sunday already?" he asked his congregation.

Several churchgoers cleared their throats and a couple of children giggled behind their hands. The preacher continued to look at them questioningly until Deacon Buell Phillips stepped up to the pulpit. Leaning closely he whispered into the old man's ear.

"Funeral?" Pastor Jay asked loudly. "We're having a funeral? Where's the body?"

Again the deacon conferred with the pastor and the old man nodded his head. He looked over to the family mourners' bench and smiled sadly at Meggie.

"I'm so sorry about your loss, sister," he said.

Buell Phillips sighed with relief.

The pastor continued, "I'm afraid I didn't know your late husband."

"Of course you did," Phillips snapped impatiently under his breath.

Again the pastor looked confused. "Oh, well maybe I did," he said lamely, scratching his head. "But I can't seem to bring the feller to mind right now."

He looked over at Phillips who appeared momentarily nonplussed.

"Maybe you ought to eulogize the feller, Buell," the pastor said. "You seemed to know him."

"Me!" Phillips was aghast. "I don't know a thing about giving a funeral."

"Ain't nothing to it," Pastor Jay told him. "You simply tell what you know about the man. And right now, I don't know a thing about him. Sorry about that, sister," he said to Meggie.

"But I can't—" Phillips began.

"I can."

The words came from the family mourners' bench and Meggie and her father turned to stare at Jesse in disbelief.

"Oh, for heaven's sake, this is ridiculous," Phillips said, turning to the other men on the deacons' bench for guidance and agreement.

Murmurs among the crowd were loud and spirited. Jesse gave no time for them to ponder; he rose to his feet and stepped in front of the congregation.

He was clearly nervous. His blue eyes seemed big as plates and his upper lip trembled as if he might burst into tears any minute. But he didn't.

He looked at his father and Meggie. Then he looked out over the congregation.

"I don't speak in front of folks much," he said. "Mostly 'cause I'm kindy simple and folks don't never listen to me no how."

He glanced back at Pastor Jay who was still standing at his place behind the pulpit. "But if the preacher don't remember Roe Farley, well . . . I do."

Jesse cleared his throat and raised his chin bravely. "Roe Farley was my frien'," he announced. "He didn't have to be. Some folks probably wondered why he was. He was right smart, smarter than most of you here. He knew that when he come to this place, but he never let on like it."

The young man cleared his throat. The slight trembling in

his voice had ceased and he was gaining confidence with every word that he spoke.

"At first he didn't let on about how smart he was 'cause he wanted folks to like him. And folks don't like people who are different much. Later it was because he knew he weren't no better than you because of it."

Jesse tugged unthinkingly on the sleeves of his suit coat. "Ye see," he said, "Roe Farley figured out that having a smart mind was a gift from God. Just a gift, like something yer pa hands ye at Christmastime. It wasn't something that you earned or something that ye deserved. It was nothing a feller could really take any pride in having 'cause he didn't have nothing to do with it. God did. If a feller got his nose in the air about being smarter than some other folks, why, it was as silly as thinking he was something 'cause his eyes were blue or he had a wart on his lip."

Jesse hesitated as he looked across the crowd hoping that they would understand.

"And Roe Farley, he taught me that not having a smart mind was not something I need to be 'shamed of. Like the smart feller, I didn't have nothing to do with it either."

Jesse smiled proudly. "Roe knew that what ye do with what ye got is what really is worth countin' in this world. He admired us here on the mountain. He comes from a real fancy place with an ocean and trains and more folks than we seen in our lifetimes. Now us, we didn't have nothing like them folks. We didn't have nothing at all. But we had our tunes and songs. Roe said that was brung from acrost the sea a long time ago. They was ours and we kept 'em. That was a good thing and he was grateful to us for it. That's what Roe's Listening Box was all about."

Jesse's quiet voice had mesmerized the congregation who sat thoughtfully, reverently silent.

"Now Roe Farley weren't perfect," Jesse continued. "He made mistakes. I make a lot of mistakes myself. I feel bad about mine. And he felt bad about his. But he didn't try to hide 'em or pretend they didn't happen or blame them on somebody else. He just owned up to what he done and he tried to do better next time."

Hesitating for a moment, Jesse caught his sister's eye and she smiled encouragingly. "Now some people thought that Roe Farley a-marrying my sister was a mistake. My sister, Meggie, was one of the folks that thought that way. But it weren't no mistake as I can see it. Roe, he loved Meggie. He told me . . . well, we talked sometime about personal things and he told me that the way he felt about love and life and people, it changed because of my sister Meggie. She cared about him and no one had never cared about him afore."

Tears gathered in Meggie's eyes and she dabbed them with the black hankie.

"Now some of you folks probably think that Roe was just talking and that he didn't mean all the things he told me about it being all right that I got a simple mind and about how he cared for my sister Meggie. But I know he weren't just making up lies. Roe Farley was my frien' and frien's tell each other the truth."

"That's right, Jesse."

The unexpected voice came from the doorway of the church. The entire congregation turned to see. Several people screamed. Beulah Winsloe fainted dead away.

"I told you that I was coming back, Jesse," Roe said as he took a step up the aisle. "And I just couldn't lie to my friend."

"Roe!" Meggie stood up, her eyes staring wide as the man she loved began walking toward her.

"I heard what you said about making mistakes, Jesse," he continued. "This little mistake is one that your sister made. I'm not dead. And I don't plan to be for a very long time."

He was at the front of the church now, within arm's length of the woman whom he loved.

"You're home," Meggie whispered.

"I'm home," he said.

The crowd came to life then. Women began shouting "hallelujah" and babbling to each other in joyous disbelief. Children began scampering around as if the church service had suddenly become a community picnic. The menfolk slapped Roe on the back companionably and welcomed him home.

Onery clapped his hand and pumped it with delighted vigor. "I knew you'd come back, son," he hollered over the noisy crowd. "Somehow I just knew it."

Granny Piggott was laughing and crying at the same time. She reached over and grabbed her nephew Pigg Broody around the neck and gave him a big buss on the cheek. The old fellow shook his head and spit a wad of tobacco into the can that he carried and commented to anyone who could hear him that "It's the dangest thang I ever seen in my life."

Jesse was jumping up and down like a youngster at the candy counter waiting for his turn to hug his friend. When his opportunity came he threw his arms around Roe like a big blond bear.

"It's so good to see you, my friend," Roe told him.

"I tried not to cry," Jesse confessed. "But I missed you real bad and there is so much I want to tell you and show you."

"I hope we have a lot of time together for telling and showing," Roe answered. "And someday, when I really do die, I want you to say all those things about me all over again."

Jesse nodded, but then admitted honestly, "I don't know if I can remember all them things that long."

Meggie still just stood there, stunned. Her heart was beating. She was breathing. But a sense of unreality gripped her.

As Roe came to stand in front of her a silence slowly fell upon the crowd. "Hello, Meggie," he said quietly.

Her voice trembled as she answered. "Hello, Roe."

Roe allowed his eyes to wander her face, her eyes, her hair half hidden beneath the plain black bonnet, the long length of her body, the tips of her toes peeking out beneath her gown.

"You're wearing shoes," he said with amazement.

"It's nearly winter," she told him.

They continued to gaze at each other, lost to the people around them. Meggie's hand trembled as she reached out, so gingerly, just to touch his coat.

He gathered her fingers into his own and brought them to his lips. A strange sound like the breaking of ice on the river on a spring morning resounded in Meggie's heart.

"There is something that I've got to tell you," he said.

She waited, wide-eyed and speechless for his words. There were things she had to tell him, too.

Roe cast a momentary glance in Onery's direction and gave him a hint of a smile. "Woman," he began gruffly, "I'm here on this mountain to stay. You can love me or loathe me but I'm not leaving you ever again."

Meggie felt her throat tighten as she stared at him.

"And there's something else I've got to tell you, too," he continued more gently. "I love you, Meggie. I've never loved anyone or had anyone love me. So I suppose I didn't recognize it for what it was at first. But I know now, Meggie. I know that it is love."

"I love you, too," she whispered.

"Praise God and hallelujah!" Pastor Jay shouted loudly from the pulpit.

The congregation turned their attention to the old preacher. They were surprised to find that rather than a comment on the young couple's reunion, the pastor was paying no attention to the people in front of him at all. With an expression of dazed thanksgiving and his hands raised to the heavens, he was staring toward the doorway at the back of the church.

As one, the people turned to see what he was looking at.

Gid Weston stood, just inside the threshold, looking as surprised at the preacher's outburst as everyone else.

"Gid Weston, you are the answer to my prayers," Pastor Jay proclaimed. "I promised God that I'd give up my pulpit when I got Gid Weston to darken this church's door. I'm an old man, my friends. I'm tired and ready to step down from this lofty service God has placed upon me. And now heaven has given me leave to do just that."

The congregation was stunned into silence and Gid Weston's eyes were as wide as a mama mink caught in the glow of a grease lamp.

"Not so fast, Pastor Jay," Roe said quickly. "I won't have you retiring from your pulpit before you marry me officially."

The preacher was momentarily startled and looked at Roe questioningly. "Who is it that you want to marry, son?"

"Why, Meggie," he answered.

The pastor's jaw dropped open and he looked plainly scandalized. "Young widows usually do marry quickly, but during the funeral is highly unusual."

It took several minutes of explanations to convince Pastor Jay of the rightness of Roe's request.

Roe wanted Onery or Jesse to stand up with him, but the preacher insisted that Gid Weston was a better choice. Wanting to get married more than he wanted to argue, Roe acceded to the old man's wishes.

The bride, dressed forlornly in black, and the groom, travel-dusty and with two days' growth of beard, followed Pastor Jay out the church door, up the small incline in the clearing to the summit of the Marrying Stone.

The sun shone down on the remaining traces of the first snow of the year causing it to glimmer brightly against the clear blue sky. The air was clean and fresh and new as if time itself were just beginning. And the young couple who stood together on the ancient stone that had seen so many lives eternally joined together was very much in love.

"Do you take this woman to be yourn, for better or worse, rich or poor, for this life ever, forsaking all?" the preacher asked.

"I do," Roe answered.

"And do you take this man as husband, obeying and keeping, for this life ever, forsaking all?"

"I do," Meggie said.

They turned to look at each other, eyes dazed with loving disbelief. They were together. They were here. And heaven itself was watching.

"Before God and this company," Pastor Jay bellowed out, "I declare ye according to the Word to be Mister and Missus . . ." The old man hesitated. "What was your name again, son?" he asked.

"Monroe Farley."

Pastor Jay nodded and began again. "Mister and Missus Monroefarley Weston."

Meggie opened her mouth to protest, but she didn't get the chance. Roe accepted the pronouncement given for its intent and laughed.

Possessively he grabbed her hand.

"There is not a skunk in sight this morning, Mrs. Farley," he told her.

Meggie smiled. They didn't need one. In an instant, before God and the good people of the mountain, Meggie and Roe Farley jumped the Marrying Stone.

The sun had barely disappeared behind the mountain when Meggie and Roe made their way through the doorway to the new cabin room. The wedding infare had been set up makeshift and haphazard, but it had worked. The company had eaten the funeral fare, Jesse had played his fiddle for the dancers, and Gid Weston had even hung around to provide a little imbibement for the less saintly of the congregation.

Roe and Meggie were tired and weary, but they were happy. Happier than either of them had ever before hoped to be. Together they hung a patchwork quilt across the opening to the main room to afford them some privacy.

"I think I'll make us a door tomorrow," Roe said.

"That might be a good idea," Meggie agreed.

He turned to the woman who was his bride and ran his hand around her waist, pulling her body up close to his.

"Are you glad that I came back?" he asked.

She feigned coyness for only a minute and then replied, "How can you doubt it?"

Roe grinned. "I don't, but it's good to hear you say it all the same."

She grinned back at him and he placed a tiny kiss on the end of her nose. They embraced warmly, both sighing with the warm, welcome fulfillment of holding the other half of their life so close. He breathed in her scent deeply. And his strength held her fast.

"I'm so glad that you love me," she whispered.

He pulled away to look at her. "Not as glad as I am that you love me."

They stood silently together grinning like a couple of well-fed whistle pigs for long moments.

"You ready to go to bed?" Roe asked.

Meggie blushed. "Yes, well, of course."

The two waited a little uncomfortably in the middle of the room for one of them to make the first move.

"Why don't you take your hair down?" Roe asked.

Immediately Meggie's hands flew to her head and she released the braided coronet that adorned her head with such undue haste she spilled hairpins to the floor.

"I'll get them," Roe said, but when he squatted down, she was right beside him.

They were close, very close, and he brought his mouth to hers, reveling in the sweet taste of her, so well remembered and so much desired.

As the kiss lingered they rose to their feet, the pins completely forgotten.

They finally parted but continued to stand very close, both of them breathing with exaggerated effort.

"You want to help me get down to my josie?" Meggie asked.

Roe swallowed any apprehension he might have felt and nodded. He turned her back to him and dutifully worked the buttons of her jet-black gown as she held her hair up and out of the way.

Meggie closed her eyes in near rapture at the gentle touch of his hands upon her. Determinedly she found her voice and tried to speak offhand.

"I've been sleeping in this room since you've been gone," she said.

Roe pressed his lips to the pale nape of her neck that he had exposed. "I was hoping that you had," he said. "I dreamed about it, you know. In my lonely nights in Cambridge I imagined you asleep on these quilt coverlets."

Meggie felt the warmth of his breath on her skin. It raised gooseflesh all up and down her back and a fluttering in the depths of her chest.

"I imagined you in these quilt coverlets, too," she confessed. "I imagined you here with me. But not sleeping."

He ignored his own shaking hands as he undid the final button at her waist and chuckled. "Meggie, Meggie, Meggie," he said with deliberate teasing. "You talk with the brazenness of a woman who would lay in the grass with a drunken frog gigger."

Not to be outdone by his teasing, Meggie gazed back at him over her shoulder, raising an eyebrow speculatively. "It depends, Mr. Farley, upon just who that frog gigger might be."

He gave her a nod of appreciation and then pulled the bodice of her gown away from her body. Eagerly he helped her lift it over her head and then allowed himself the pleasure once more of viewing his woman in a thin covering of homespun cotton.

"You are beautiful, Meggie," he whispered. After a moment he looked down at the crow-black dress that he still held in his hand.

"But this thing isn't. I think you should burn it," he said. "I'm not overly fond of the color black."

"It's my best dress," Meggie protested. "I'll have to wear it until it's a rag of threads."

"Oh? You're going to be a very practical wife, are you?"

"I have no choice," she answered. "I just got married, you see, and my new husband has given up his job as a scholar to be an Ozarker at leisure. He doesn't have his own farm. We don't have a corn bottom, a pack of dogs, a milk cow, or a hog to our name."

"Guess we'll have to live on love," he said.

"That makes pretty poor eating," she declared.

"Oh, I don't know," Roe said, moving in close. "I'm actually quite fond of nibbling on it from time to time."

He proved the truth of his statement by catching the lobe of her ear between his teeth.

The sensation made Meggie gasp a meaningful "Oh!" as the heat of desire sizzled through her. The new sensation was more than a little frightening. This was no girlish fantasy of love. What happened now between them was real and would have meaning and would be a part of the fabric woven of their lives. Meggie Best was really married to a man whom she really loved and this was really their bedroom where they would really conceive their own children. It scared her. Nervously, she pulled away from him.

"Meggie?" It was a whispered question.

"Let's get into the bed under the covers," she said, hurrying to climb up onto the rope-supported tick. "And douse that light."

He watched her scamper under the quilts and he smiled. "Marriage is all new to me, too, Meggie," he said quietly.

"It's not something that I know anything about. It's not something that I can learn in books."

She nodded in agreement. "We will just have to catch on about it together," she said.

It was obvious that she was trying to be very brave. Still she bit her lip with concern. "Do put out the light, Roe. I think we ought to start out in the dark."

Roe looked at her a long moment and then grinned. "In a minute," he said. "First I've brought something for you."

"For me?"

Roe handed her a parcel wrapped in soft brown flannel. "Open it," he said.

Nervously Meggie unfolded the cloth. Inside it was a shiny silver spoon tooled with a design very similar to the one of wood she'd given him all those months ago.

"It's beautiful!" she exclaimed.

He pulled the wood one out of his pocket. "I've carried this one with me since the day that I left here."

"I thought you just forgot to return it when you left."

"I couldn't leave it behind. Just like I couldn't leave you behind either," he said. "When I knew I must return to your arms, I asked the jeweler to make this one especially for you. So that you would carry it always and never leave me either."

"Never," she said with solemn sincerity. "I love you, Roe Farley. I could be unselfish once and send you away, but I'll never have the courage to make that mistake again."

He kissed her then, long, lovingly, passionately. When their lips parted, she smoothed the cool metal of the spoon along the softness of her cheek.

"You like it," he said.

"It's a wonderful present. The kind of gift that a prince would bring."

Roe smiled. "You like *princely* gifts. I brought you one of those, too."

"Another gift?"

He nodded. "Do you want it now?"

"Oh, yes," she answered with the excitement of a child.

"I'll get it for you."

Meggie sat up in the bed bright-eyed.

From the inside of his satchel Roe retrieved a fancy blue silk jewel case. The sides were beaded with delicate freshwater pearls and the tiny gold latch at the front was heart-shaped and locked with a delicate filigree key.

When he handed it to Meggie, she gasped.

"For me?"

"The box was my mother's," he said. "My father gave it to her on their wedding day. It's one of the few things of hers that I have."

"It's beautiful," she whispered in awe.

"I always intended it for my bride on her wedding night. Even before I had any idea who that bride might be."

Meggie nodded and swallowed a little self-consciously as she gazed at the beautiful piece of jeweled art so out of place in the primitive Ozark cabin. "It's something that even a very fancy city woman could appreciate as a gift," she said.

"Yes," Roe answered. "I guess that it is. That's why my father bought it for Mother, I suppose. I could have given that box to nearly any woman." Slowly a grin spread across his face. "But what I've put inside the box is something that I would only give to my Meggie."

Her eyes widening, Meggie's heart soared with joy at his words.

"May I open it?"

"Oh, yes, Meggie. I want you to."

Eagerly, but with great care she turned the tiny key in the lock and raised the delicate little latch.

She opened the lid with joyous expectation. Then she hollered like bloody murder. A small green tree frog, at least as surprised as Meggie herself, hopped out of the satin box and onto the quilt coverlet.

"Varmint!" she screamed, scrambling out from beneath the covers of the bed.

Her new husband hooted with laughter.

"Roe Farley! You promised!"

"I didn't promise. Jesse promised."

She jumped to her knees in the middle of the bed and delivered a blow, worthy of a pugilist, to his midsection.

"You . . . you . . . you . . ." she sputtered, unable to think of things bad enough to call him. "You—"

"Husband." He provided the word for her.

With a cry of fury, she began pounding him in angry earnestness. Roe only managed to stop the rain of blows by wrapping his arms around her and falling back upon her on the bed.

The new position offered more pleasurable pursuits and as the fight went out of her, he grinned down into her face.

"I love you, Meggie," he said simply.

"I should beat you senseless," she replied. "But I love you, too."

She wrapped her arms around his neck and slid the galluses off his shoulder and showed him that she meant every word that she said.

As the footboard began to rock and the bedcord whined with strain, the confused little tree frog used his long hind legs to lower himself off the end of the bed. He waited nervously on the floor, sure that at any moment a new calamity might overtake him. After several minutes, when no one tried to catch him or step on him, he began hopping toward the doorway searching for the exit. It wouldn't do to spend the night with two people who had no more sense than to go to bed with the light on.

FROM THE JOURNAL OF
J. MONROE FARLEY

January 5, 1907
Marrying Stone, Arkansas

Have just this morning heard from a gentleman at the Library of Congress in the Columbia District concerning my collection of Ozark songs and tunes. The institution is actively seeking to preserve American folkways and has already contracted with at least two other music collectors in other parts of the country. He was quite interested in my premise of the perpetuation of Middle English in an isolated zone and assured me that a similar finding has been made concurrently in the Appalachians. Although he apologizes for the low sum of money he is offering (he obviously does not understand the value of actual currency in the Ozarks), he is interested in acquiring my recordings to keep for posterity. He tells me that by making gold impressions of the wax cylinders the actual sounds themselves can be saved for time in memoriam. That offers me great comfort and encourages me to continue in my efforts.

The snows have not been too bad yet this winter, but I fear the worst of the weather may be ahead of us. Fortunately with the good crops we got last year, we have more than enough to sustain us 'til June if need be.

Onery continues to have bouts with his bad leg, but appears in fine fettle otherwise. Our little Edith watches over him like a guardian angel. Which is, of course, not at all true to her rather devilish nature.

Meggie has "stumped her toe" again as they say here in the mountains and professes to be grateful to be carrying this child in the winter months when she can lounge around a bit and the whole population of Marrying Stone knows nothing about it.

Jesse was married on Christmas Day and we are all delighted for him. He and his new bride will be coming to take supper with us one day this week. Meggie has suggested rather strongly that I take Onery's Winchester and try to get her a wild turkey to roast. I see no reason to go to the trouble since she can just as easily burn a chicken or a possum head and it will taste exactly the same. Perhaps she can serve it with some of her special piccalilli.

Come take a walk down Harmony's Main Street in 1874, and meet a different resident of this colorful Kansas town each month.

A TOWN CALLED
✤ HARMONY ✤

__**KEEPING FAITH by Kathleen Kane**
0-7865-0016-6/$4.99

From the boardinghouse to the schoolhouse, love grows in the heart of Harmony. And for pretty, young schoolteacher Faith Lind, a lesson in love is about to begin.

__**TAKING CHANCES by Rebecca Hagan Lee**
0-7865-0022-2/$4.99

All of Harmony is buzzing when they hear the blacksmith, Jake Sutherland, is smitten. And no one is more surprised than Jake himself, who doesn't know the first thing about courting a woman.

__**CHASING RAINBOWS by Linda Shertzer**
0-7865-0041-7/$4.99 *(coming in September)*

Fashionable, Boston-educated Samantha Evans is the outspoken columnist for her father's newspaper. But her biggest story yet may be her own exclusive–with a most unlikely man.